ONLY EAGLES FLY

Graham Guy

Also By
GRAHAM GUY

Eleven Days

Savage Skies

ONLY EAGLES FLY

Graham Guy

First published 2001.

Second Publication 2014 by DoctorZed Publishing

DoctorZed Publishing books may be ordered through booksellers or by contacting:

DoctorZed Publishing
IDAHO
10 Vista Ave
Skye, South Australia 5072
www.doctorzed.com
61-(0)8 8431-4965

ISBN: 978-0-9942084-2-2 (sc)
ISBN: 978-0-9942084-3-9 (e)

A CIP number for this book is available at the National Library of Australia.

This is a work of fiction. Names, characters, places, events, and dialogues are creations of the author or are used fictitiously. Any resemblance to any individuals, alive or dead, is purely coincidental. The views expressed in this work are solely those of the author and do not necessarily reflect the views of the publisher, and the publisher hereby disclaims any responsibility for them.

Cover image © Kevron2001 | Dreamstime.com - Man Walking At Sunset Photo
Cover design: Scott Zarcinas

Printed in Australia
DoctorZed Publishing rev. date: 01/12/2014

Special thanks to:

Mr Bill Peacock QAM
Mr Geoff Brown, Jeppesen Australasia
Mr Rob Paradis, Adelaide Gun Shop
Mr Paul Salamon, Fullbore Queen's Medallist 2000
Mr David Covino, Payneham Home Furnishings

"Nothing gives one person so much advantage over another as to remain always cool and unruffled under all circumstances."

Thomas Jefferson

Prologue

The eagle was high on the wing as the gunman nestled his body into the undergrowth, pulling the stock of the .50-calibre sniper's rifle hard into his shoulder. In full camouflage he was near-impossible to spot, even from a distance of only a few metres. The cover he'd chosen in a disused landing strip just north of the Durack River, north-west of Kununurra in Western Australia, shielded the direct sunlight, but it was still hot.

Got to expect it in this part of the world, he thought.

He began to wonder what twenty million dollars would smell like, how much room it would actually take up in a small plane. He cocked his ear to the sky, straining to hear. Nothing. He checked his watch.

Shouldn't be long now, he told himself. *Twenty mill. Bloody hell! Twenty million bucks. That's gotta be twenty overnight bags. Jam-packed. Even if it's in thousand-dollar bills. Maybe there'll be gold bars.*

He wanted to pee, such was the rush of blood at the thought of such a massive haul. He pretended for a moment he was thrusting his face into a mountain of brand new thousand-dollar bills, and allowed himself the tiniest smile of gratification. This was the moment he'd waited for all his life. And it could all so easily have been lost if it wasn't for a passing comment in a casual conversation.

"They reckon they can grab twenty mill," the woman had said.

"How the hell would you launder twenty million bucks in this town?"

The gunman put his eye up to the Leupold Sniper scope which he'd pre-zeroed at twelve hundred and fifty metres three days earlier—the distance from where he lay prone to where he'd calculated the twin-engined aircraft with its passengers and their on-board booty would come to a standstill. He glanced again at the settings on the Leupold. It was an 8.5 x 25 variable slotted onto the top of the Barrett .50 calibre. He felt comfortable with his choice of weapon, after learning such combinations were used by snipers during the Gulf War. A squeeze on the trigger would send a 500-grain spitzer soft-point towards its target at close on 3000 feet per second, striking with an almost inconceivable destructive force. Again he cast his eyes to the sky. The eagle had disappeared from view. He strained his ears for the slightest sound. Still nothing.

He checked his watch. The urgency to pee was becoming intense, but he knew that the feeling would quickly pass at the slightest sound of an approaching aircraft. Determined to keep his cool, the gunman sucked in some deep breaths. He dragged up the tip of his neckerchief to wipe his brow, wiped his palms on his sleeves, and braced himself. It wouldn't be long now. Nothing to do now but wait.

He unclicked and rechecked the magazine of the Barrett. Seven rounds. One up the spout. Six should do it. As he homed the magazine the sound of the click took his mind back to just a few days earlier.

* * *

In the dead of night he made a silent exit from his rented flat in the Sydney suburb of Ryde. He lifted the garage door and climbed in behind the wheel of his vehicle. As he did so, the passenger door was reefed open and a lone figure brandishing a handgun leapt into the front passenger seat.

Fear turned his gut as he heard the sound of the hammer being drawn back on what he thought was a .38 snub-nose. There was just enough light for him to see his attacker was wearing a balaclava.

"I've been watching you, arsehole. Watching you for bloody months in fact. Why don't we take a little drive and uncover a few of those stolen dollars you've got hidden away in some god-forsaken place?"

He never spoke. As he reached down to turn on the ignition, he hooked his little finger into a key-ring attached to the lower part of the steering column and gave it a sudden jerk. Two distinct, but muffled, shots rang out and his attacker slumped lifeless into a crumpled heap in the passenger seat.

He quickly switched on the interior light of his vehicle. Blood was streaming from a wound in his attacker's neck and another in his chest, the result of two bullets delivered by a pair of pen-guns rigged into the airconditioning vents. Small they might be, but these beauties were deadly at around two metres. He cursed at the mess.

With a fingertip he lifted the balaclava. He shook his head slightly. "Dunno who the fuck you are, bastard, but right now, I gotta get the hell out of here," he muttered.

He hit the start button and roared away from the garage. He quickly gazed around. He was reasonably confident he hadn't been seen by anyone and that his attacker had been acting solo. As his mind raced with what to do with the body, he checked his watch. He had set up a meeting and right now he didn't need this distraction. He had to make the meeting on time and time was running out.

Making a snap decision, he wheeled in off the main road to a dimly lit side street. There was no traffic coming from either way. A solitary street light off in the distance. No late night joggers.

"Perfect," he mumbled.

He spotted a driveway to a vacant lot, pulled in and cut his headlights. He leaned over, opened the passenger door and pushed the body of his attacker from the vehicle.

As he roared away, he again cursed at the hideous mess inside his vehicle. He pressed down harder on the accelerator, turning his wrist to check his watch. "Jesus, I can't be late for this bastard."

He strained his eyes to look ahead. Soon the side street he was searching for came into view. Slowly he made his approach. Up ahead he could make out a dark-coloured sedan parked in the street.

That's got to be him.

He switched off his headlights and idled very slowly to within about twenty metres of the stationary vehicle. Cautiously, the gunman climbed from his car.

From the shadows of a head-high brush fence came a voice barely above a whisper. "You bring the money?"

"Ten grand, right?"

Quicker than a heartbeat, the man the gunman had arranged to meet was standing a metre in front of him.

"Don't fuck with me, arsehole!"

Instantly, he felt the barrel of a handgun pressed against his neck from behind. Then came the terrifying click of the hammer being drawn back. The gunman froze.

Twice in one night to hear that fucking sound is twice too often.

"You're dead, arsehole."

"Jesus, you bastards, I'm only jokin'."

"You want to joke, join the fucking circus. Twenty-five G's, right?"

"Tell this imbecile to lose the gun and I'll give it to you."

The man in front nodded. The gun barrel fell away. But the gunman could still feel his presence close behind.

He began to reach inside his jacket for the money when he paused. "You got the artillery and those two gee-whiz mobile phones?"

The man in front turned on his heel and went to the boot of his car. When he returned he was holding onto a Barrett .50 calibre centrefire rifle and two mobiles.

The gunman's face lit up. "Holy shit, what will that do to a bloke at a thousand metres?"

The seller grinned and held up a .50-calibre round. "One of these?"

The gunman nodded.

"Hit a bloke in the chest with this little baby and all you'll have left will be his fingerprints." The seller gave him an inquiring glance. "You ever fired one?"

The gunman shook his head.

"Then go somewhere the hell away from civilisation and let a few go. The deal includes a hundred rounds. Go out bush and squeeze a few off. Don't shoulder-hold it. Use the pod. And wear your ear plugs. But get a long way from anyone or anywhere because when these mothers go bang it's like a clap of bloody thunder and you'll frighten the shit out of anything within pissing distance."

The gunman was impressed. "Put it all in the boot," he said, handing over his car keys. "When you've done that, you'll get your money."

Without hesitation the seller quickly transferred the rifle, mobiles and all the accompanying accessories from one vehicle to the other. So hasty was the transfer, the gunman was forced into action sooner than he realised. His mind was racing. He was about to hand over $25,000 for a weapon he dearly wanted. But more than that, he still wanted to keep his money.

"You guys want to deal?"

Again the seller was upon him, his eyes flashing anger.

Again the gun barrel from behind jerked into his neck.

"Bloody Christ, you mongrels made me piss my pants. Why all the fucking theatrics?"

"Listen, bastard, and listen good," the seller began. "You've just got hold of the hottest centrefire in the business. They target shoot with these mothers over a mile in the States. Don't even think about asking where this one came from. It's brand fucking new. Still in the greaseproof. I don't know what you want it for. Don't want to know. But what I do know is that if I get sprung with this little lot, I'm in for about seven to ten."

"So no deals, huh?"

"Stop the crap. You got the fucking dough?"

Just a little closer you guys, just a little closer, the gunman urged under his breath. He took one last punt.

"They tell me they're worth around 12 grand in a gun shop!"

"Fuck you," sneered the seller. "Do you want it or don't you?"

The gunman felt the gunbarrel pressed even harder into his neck, but it was all over in an instant. The gunman dropped his hands to his belt indicating he was about to withdraw the cash. Instantly, he pulled hard on two keyrings. Two muffled shots rang out from two pen-guns fitted into his specially constructed leather waistband. One was aimed chest high for someone standing less than a metre behind him, and the other the same for someone standing the same distance away in front. Death was instant for the seller and his accomplice. The two bodies slumped to the ground.

Still with his money in his pockets, the gunman leaned down, picked up the pistol which had been jammed into his neck and plucked his car keys from the street. "Fucking amateurs," he sneered.

He stepped over the bodies, got into his car and sped off into the night.

* * *

The gunman again glanced at the sky. The eagle had returned, only this time it looked to be higher up. His memory shot back to school days when a teacher had said, "Other birds may take to the wing, but remember, only eagles fly."

See what you mean, he thought, watching the bird on the thermals.

Still, there was no wind to speak of. He'd figured the twin-engined aeroplane would land to the right of where he'd positioned himself. If the opposite were true, then it was only a quick body turn and a rapid re-alignment to fix the Leupold's cross-hairs to the other end. He reached down to his trouser leg pocket and withdrew his water bottle. He swallowed a couple of mouthfuls and spat the last lot out.

"Doesn't stay cold for long in this bloody weather does it?" he grumbled. Suddenly, he thrust his ear to the sky. "What the hell's that?" A few seconds later, it became clear the sound was a vehicle approaching, but from a long way off. He looked around. Nothing. Again he unclicked the magazine.

Seven rounds. One up the spout. "Six should do it." Again he smiled reassuredly to himself. He was trying to smell the money. "Cool it man, we're not there yet. Just bloody cool it!"

The approaching vehicle was obviously the passport out of there for those on board the aircraft. It was getting closer.

Now the gunman's heartbeat was beginning to echo in his eardrums. He wriggled his body further into the undergrowth. Then something caught his eye. Way over to his left, a flock of birds burst into the air above a cluster of trees as though they'd been spooked. He studied them for a moment then raised his binoculars.

"Looks like it's getting a little crowded out here." Anger cut into his tone. "Jesus bloody Christ, how did those bastards know where to find me?"

Panic tore into his gut. Everything he'd planned was about to go down the toilet. He had to do something and do it now. But there was no time. The plane was due, by his reckoning in 15 minutes. He raised his binoculars again. There were two men.

Probably about a thousand metres to his left. Although a long way off, he knew immediately who one of them was. And this was certainly one man he didn't want breathing down his neck.

"They bloody followed me! How come I didn't spot that? They bloody followed me all the way from Sydney. Christ! I don't believe it!"

He decided to act. He looked again at the two men. "I reckon they'll stay put. They not only want me, but I reckon they'd be pretty bloody interested in the aeroplane—*and* its passengers." The approaching motor vehicle came into view.

It was as he suspected. It was the greeter vehicle and it made its way to the right-hand end of the airstrip. The gunman decided to gamble.

"Those mongrels didn't walk here. I wonder if I can find their car?" He slunk away from his position. "Gonna have to be damn quick about it." He ran back to where he had parked his own vehicle and covered it with a camouflage car-cover.

He reckoned the vehicle belonging to the other two wouldn't be far away. He was right. About fifty metres away, he saw another vehicle, the sort used by the army, a troop carrier. It was also covered by a camouflage cover. The gunman, in a crouched position, moved swiftly towards it. He scampered under the cover, pulled his Puma Bowie knife from its sheath, and pierced the walls of all four tyres. The spare on the rear door was next.

He peered in through the window. A mobile phone was on the front seat. Bolted to the dashboard was a high-powered radio. The gunman smashed the window with the handle of the Bowie knife and opened a door. He thrust the knife blade into the heart of the mobile phone, then reached down and reefed all the wiring from the high-powered radio. Not satisfied that he'd done enough, he used an available jack handle to smash the steering wheel and then popped the bonnet, reefed out the distributor leads and ran the knife blade through the battery leads. As he was about to leave he noticed tyre tracks leading from the rear of the vehicle.

"So the bastards aren't on foot. Looks like one of those four-wheel motor bikes." Two light-weight loading ramps lay nearby. "Thought so," he murmured. He checked his watch. "Jesus, eight minutes!"

By the time he found himself back behind the stock of the Barrett .50 calibre, the gunman figured he had about three minutes to catch his breath before the plane came into view.

He was wrong. It was more like two. He had just finished drinking what remained of the water in his canteen when he heard the distant drone of a twin-engined aeroplane. He swung his binoculars round to check that his pursuers hadn't moved position. They hadn't. He then focussed on the driver of the greeter vehicle. He was standing by the driver's-side door.

"Bloody hell, is that bastard edgy? Don't worry, baby, it'll all be over pretty soon and I promise you won't feel a thing," the gunman grinned. The sound of the engines was becoming louder. But the sound wasn't coming in from any great height. "More like ground level."

Seconds later the aircraft came skimming into view. It swooped low over the greeter vehicle. The man standing beside it waved as it went over. The aircraft banked and made a low-level pass. Then it took in a wide sweep to make sure there was no danger. The camouflage car-covers had obviously done their jobs well as the aircraft headed way out to the left, banked, dropped its undercarriage and prepared to land. The gunman released the safety catch of the Barrett and put the cross hairs of the Leupold on the first of the two men to his left.

"Twenty million dollars."

He was still saying the words when he squeezed the trigger.

Chapter 1

Will someone get that bloody phone?

The directive came from Inspector John Purseley from within the walls of his glassed-in office at the Mildura CIB.

Purseley enjoyed his job as head of detectives in the Victorian rural city, but the one thing that got up his nose more than anything were phones that rang more than once without being answered.

"Jesus Christ, there's sixteen people in this department."

Someone pick up that bloody phone!

McLoughlin approached his desk and looked in on Purseley, chuckling as he picked up the phone. "Hello, CIB."

"Would Senior Sergeant Ken McLoughlin be available please?"

"This is he."

"Hold please. Commissioner Rowland would like a word with you."

McLoughlin caught his boss's inquiring look. "It's the bloody Commissioner!"

"Shit!"

"Senior Sergeant McLoughlin?"

"Commissioner... sir."

"Don't worry about that so much. I don't mean to bother you..."

"No bother at all, sir."

"There's a matter of some urgency which has arisen. Can you be on a plane first thing in the morning and be in my office by eleven?"

"Well, er, yes I can, but..."

"Don't worry about Purseley. I'll clear it with him. So I'll see you in the morning then?"

"Yes sir, you will. Er, something old or something new?"

"Nothing you're currently involved with."

McLoughlin hung up the phone.

"What did he want?" Purseley demanded.

"I have to be in his office at eleven in the morning."

"Yeah, pig's arse. You got bloody things to do here."

"You want to tell him that?"

"I'll bloody tell him all right. What's he want you for?"

"Wouldn't say. Just said he'd clear it with you himself."

"Yeah, well he'll get bloody told he just can't pluck my bloody blokes willy-nilly to suit his own ends."

McLoughlin heard the phone ring on his boss's desk. "Tell him yourself. That's probably him now," he said with a grin.

Purseley lifted the receiver with a scowl.

"John. Jack Rowland."

"Commissioner. Good morning, sir."

"John, I'm going to need Ken McLoughlin on a special assignment for a while. He's obviously the best this state has to offer. Don't know why the bugger won't come to Melbourne, but he seems to like it out there with you. Do you have any problems with that?"

"None I can think of, sir. He's working on a few things at the moment, but I'll spread them out a bit. Any idea how long you want him for?"

"Indeterminate. But it could be a while. It's a big job. Even for the best in the business. But I do need for him to be here tomorrow."

"Of course."

"Thanks for that."

McLoughlin saw his boss put the phone down. "Well you really told him didn't you?" he laughed.

"I could hardly sit here and say you're not going could I? He'd have my balls in a sling. Now—you'd better get Gwen to organise your flights."

* * *

"Come in, come in, Ken," greeted Police Commissioner Jack Rowland, extending his hand to the senior sergeant.

McLoughlin quickly took in his surroundings. A large office overlooking parklands. A plush-pile carpeted floor. Nice landscape prints on the walls. A few framed photographs on a sideboard, obviously taken at the high points of the Commissioner's career. A massive office desk loaded with a bank of technology.

At a glance, McLoughlin could tell that the Police Commissioner had his entire force on call at the push of a button. And it appeared there was a button for everything and everyone. The air-wing, the dog squad, homicide, the breakers, the drug squad. There seemed to be no end to the buttons. Push one and you went straight through to the very person at the top of the tree.

As it bloody should be, he said to himself.

Jack Rowland now introduced him to the other guests in the room. "The New South Wales Police Commissioner, Colin Johnson. The Victorian Minister for Police, David English and the New South Wales Minister for Police, Andrew Weeks."

McLoughlin was momentarily intimidated by the prestigious company. He exchanged pleasantries with all three men. The door to the Commissioner's office opened briefly and a trolley containing brewed coffee and sandwiches appeared. Jack Rowland walked to it and cast an eye over his guests.

"Please sit down, sergeant, sit down," motioned the Commissioner. "I think for the purpose of this meeting we'll dispense with the titles, if that's all right with everyone."

No-one disagreed.

The Commissioner took a sip from his coffee cup and his expression turned to one of drawn anxiety. "Ken, we've got a problem, which is why I've called for you." He leaned over and placed a foolscap-sized folder in front of him. He flicked open the cover and asked, "Do you know this son-of-a-bitch?"

McLoughlin glanced at the photograph and offered a halfway grin. "John James McGregor-McWeasely."

The Commissioner appeared most taken-aback. But McLoughlin wasn't fooled. He knew Rowland would be most aware of a previous association. This was just a front for his guests.

"I'll be buggered. You know this prick? Excuse the French sir, gentlemen," he began, offering a glance to those seated around him, "but even from his school days, this bastard has only ever been known as the fucking Weasel."

"And you know him?"

"Don't tell me he's still on the scene?"

"Which is why we're all here for this happy little get-together."

"I'm lost," McLoughlin said.

"OK," said the Commissioner. "You first. Where do you know him from?"

McLoughlin thought for a moment, knowing full well the commissioner was only playing ducks and drakes. The explanation would be for the benefit of the other men present.

"I reckon it would be about fifteen or sixteen years ago. There was a fairly major payroll robbery at Frankston. Hundred and fifty grand from memory. I was with armed robbery at the time. We turned the joint inside out, but in the end came up with a big fat zero. But there was one lead. A woman in a bar. She ended up dead. But not before she spilled her guts on this odious little prick.

"Seems he used to fix her up on the odd occasion, but because he was such an ugly little mongrel, she charged him big time for the privilege. She just came forward out of the blue and from what she said, it appeared John James McGregor-McWeasely was our man. Five hours later, she was dead. A .22 to the head. "

McLoughlin picked up the photograph, glanced at it and dropped it back on the desk.

"By Jesus, he was good. We staked out the guy's place for three weeks, but nothing. We had nowhere to go. No known accomplices. Not on any electoral roll. Nothing on hire purchase. No credit cards. No driver's license. No car. No bank accounts. Didn't own anything. And that was back then.

"The prick began to haunt us. We knew he had more form than a dozen derby winners, but everything about him led to a dead end."

Again McLoughlin glanced at the photograph.

"Ugly little prick isn't he? And you're telling me he's still around?"

"We believe so," the Commissioner answered.

"And that's what this meeting's about?"

"It is indeed."

"So what's he done now... or are you still on that case from a decade and a half ago?"

"Let me put it to you this way," the Commissioner said, easing himself out from behind his desk. "Both the New South Wales Police and the Victorian Police believe this man has been creating havoc for at least fifteen years. But he only strikes every now and again. No real pattern, but when he hits, he hits big. There's also three unsolved murders. Wealthy men. All robbed. No enemies. No clues. A point two -two to the head. His calling card. Has to be him."

"Why not just pick him up?"

"Your story about the coffee and hamburgers. He's still pulling the same stunts. He just seems to disappear, but it's got to the point where he has to be stopped because of what's going on."

"Like what?"

"Like about a couple of million in cash at the last count. Chuck in the killings. Plus priceless bloody artworks, gold bars. Christ, you name it. He's into some of this country's richest and most influential people. Colin and Andrew are getting it in the neck in Sydney. David along with myself are wearing it down here. Insurance companies are screaming. The bereaved want justice. There's nothing from ballistics. He's got us by the tit. Quite frankly, we don't have a single thing to go on. In fact, we don't even *know* that it *is* him. But we all agree it has to be. But one thing we do know: Somehow, he just simply disappears off the face of the earth... and always after a major heist or murder."

"And you want me to nail his arse?"

"In a word, yes."

"So what makes you think I can do what the two biggest police outfits in the country can't?"

Jack Rowland placed clenched fists onto the top of his desk. "Because there's a fair amount of opinion going round that you're the best in the business. But you won't be expected to do this on your own. I'll have my deputies pick out three top men and Colin will do the same in Sydney..."

"Hold it right there," McLoughlin interrupted.

Jack Rowland gave him a perplexed look.

"If you want me to nab this prick, then I insist we do it my way."

"Which is?"

"No team of six guys. Just one. And I'll pick him myself."

"Who?"

"Dave Bourke, my partner in Mildura."

"Oh come on, Ken!" the Commissioner scoffed. "Dave's a boy. Jesus! You're gonna need six hard-nosed bloody veterans..."

"No I'm not. I'm not working with six guys I don't know. If I do this thing, then I just want one man who would be prepared to die for me—and me for him. That's how it works. I need to know everything about a colleague in this situation. I need to know what food he likes. When he likes to piss. When he likes to sleep. His favourite colour. His everybloodything. You can't assign blokes to do that. Bourke knows everything about me. I know everything about him. He's smart. He farts when he sleeps and when he gets a skin full of piss he gets pretty brave in chasing arse. But you could put a Bunsen burner under him and he'd never sell you out. He's a shit-shot with a .38. Prefers the .45 Glock 20 semi-auto with a 15-shot mag..."

"They're not on issue," the Commissioner cut in.

"Matter of fact, so do I; so we'll need two, sir," McLoughlin continued, ignoring the Commissioner's comment. "And apart from that, he's a mean son-of-a-bitch when he gets behind the barrel of a four-one-six Remington Magnum..."

"They're not on issue either," the Commissioner again said.

"No sir, they're not. But I think Oakdale proved they should be."

McLoughlin's crack about the four-one-six was lost on the other three men. It wasn't lost on Jack Rowland.

"Just give me Dave Bourke, sir. I don't want six blokes. Six blokes will get me dead."

Commissioner Jack Rowland could tell McLoughlin was deadly serious. He stared hard into his eyes. Then he glanced at the other three men. Individually, each gave a nod of approval.

"So what's the big bloody deal with these damn Glocks?"

"Unbreakable sir. You can freeze them in ice for 60 days, take them out, let them thaw and they won't malfunction. Bury them in dirt, or mud, they still work. Drop one fully loaded into a metre of water for an hour. Haul it out. No problems. You can even run over them and it won't hurt them. They're practically indestructible."

"Tell SWAS what you want. It'll be approved by the time you call them. What else?"

"How secret is this operation?"

"There are five people in this room. That's it. And your Mr Bourke, of course."

"Credentials?"

Jack Rowland opened a folder to the left of the one already sitting in front of McLoughlin. "The mobile phone has been programmed with four twenty-four-hour numbers. Those numbers belong to each of us in this room. You are to call any of them at any time. I want to hear from you once a week. The credit card will get you any motor vehicle, any ticket on any aeroplane, any hotel room... in fact, whatever it is you need, the card will cover it."

McLoughlin smiled. "Bloody hell, a week in Vegas is looking good."

Jack Rowland ignored the comment, but McLoughlin did notice the sly grins offered by the other three men.

"Now all this will be duplicated for Mr Bourke. There is also a special credit card-sized police badge signed by all four of us. That will get you into anywhere you want to go. If you have a problem, use that phone. One of us will always be available."

The Commissioner moved across to the pot of brewed coffee. "Just nail this bastard will you Ken? Take as much time as you need. I thought we'd kick it off in ten days. That'll give you time to tie up any loose ends in Mildura. Inform your Mr Bourke and maybe take a few days off. Go fishing or something. I'd like the two of you back in this office Monday week. We'll call it *Operation Magpie*. Good old Collingwood forever, eh!"

* * *

When McLoughlin left the Commissioner's office he walked outside to the most beautiful day. He looked across the street to the park which he saw from the office. It was a temptation too hard to resist. He checked for traffic and made his way into the highly grassed and tree-covered city sanctuary. A park bench beckoned. He propped for a few minutes, endeavouring to take in the contents of the meeting.

He couldn't work out if he'd just been given a promotion, a sideways move, or a job nobody else would touch with a forty-foot pole. One thing he was certain of. It certainly wasn't his lucky day. He knew full well that John James McGregor-McWeasely would prove a handful.

McGregor-McWeasely was too good for the coppers all those years ago. And, right now, the combined efforts of police in two states still came up with zip.

There's no doubt the prick's a master-thief. And by all accounts, a master bloody killer, too. What the hell have I let myself in for?

As he reached into his pocket for the mobile phone he'd just been given, he contemplated his own personal situation. The other side of fifty. Single. Preferred to have never married. Had figured it wasn't the job for a married man. But he knew he was in the minority as pretty well all his colleagues had been to the altar, the divorce court, and back to the altar again for another go.

McLoughlin had to admit his life was his job, with maybe a spot of fishing here and there and a couple of good videos. There seemed little doubt that when he walked inside his house after a day on the job he was quite happy to close the door, cook a steak and watch a movie. For the next little while, the real world would be far, far away.

He called Bourke to tell him the good news.

Chapter 2

John James McGregor-McWeasely never knew his parents. There were various stories: they divorced; they died in a car accident; he was given up for adoption at birth. It appeared there were as many stories about his birth parents as there were foster parents in his young life. His earliest memories as a boy were of cruelty, neglect, drunken, violent men and abused women. Being shuffled from one foster home to another. And severe headaches. No doubt the result of being belted across the face and head for daring to speak at meal times or wetting the bed.

To a young John James, violence was just a part of normal family life. He was surrounded by it. Every day. And in every foster home he was sent to.

Then there was the ridicule. He could never understand why he was the target of so much ridicule. And the cruelest of all was the nickname school bullies had given him. John James was seldom referred to by his given names. Someone called out to him one day, referring to him as "The fucking Weasel." It stuck and he hated it. And the girls would say, "Geez, he looks just like one doesn't he?" It was to stay with him all his life.

He never experienced kindness, a gentle hand, a birthday celebration, or Santa dropping by for Christmas. Where other kids had new clothes, a new bike, or even a new pair of shoes, John James McGregor-McWeasely only ever received what others threw away. He found it difficult to make friends to the point that, even as he entered his teenage years, having a friend was something that only happened to someone else.

He would dearly have loved to have had a girlfriend. But he couldn't even recall having a conversation with a girl. All girls ever did was poke fun at him. The bigger boys bullied him, school teachers victimised him and parents made sure their children went nowhere near him.

In the case of John James McGregor-McWeasely, so much abuse, violence and ridicule in his early years was to set him on a path of robbery, violence and murder. By the time he was fifteen, he had learned the hard way that he was a social misfit. Slightly built. Skinny legs. Concave chest. Pock-marked skin. Pointy, narrow nose and beady eyes that were too close together even for his liking. Jug ears, thin lips, sallow, drawn beaky face, sunken temples, and a gait that would segregate him all his life. He had been hurled against a wall as a baby, the force of which fractured and dislocated his hip. Not receiving proper medical care, the hip self-mended, which left him unable to walk normally. Consequently, he stood out like a thorn amongst roses with his short, hopping-style steps and rapid pace.

He possessed no musical ability or aptitude for a trade, but despite all his failings he began to realise that he had a brain. John James was quick to pick up on things and was soon to turn ridicule into reward. By the time he was seventeen he was stealing the hub caps off expensive cars then selling them back to their owners. He got a job in the local railway yards. But being small and not physically strong he found the going tough. Even so, he stuck to it, mainly because he was given his chores first thing in the morning and was permitted to work all day unsupervised. Which meant he didn't have to mix with anyone or talk to anyone, but mostly it freed him from the ridicule which plagued his very existence.

The job was boring, repetitive and menial. Pulling weeds, moving freight from one shed to another, loading and unloading railway trucks. He hated it. But he knew that at the the end of the fortnight there'd be a pay packet. Slowly he began to question what he wanted in his life. All his young years he had known nothing but hurt, bullying, violence and rejection. Gradually, he started seeing people as no more than objects to further his own ends.

Try to get close to them and they'll hurt you, he'd say to himself. He discovered that he liked to read. So much of his wages went on books and magazines. And as he buried himself in the written word, he found stories on cops and crime and murder to have a bizarre, if not morbid, fascination.

But what he couldn't understand was, if the crooks thought they were so smart, why did they always end up in jail?

Other things began to take his fancy as well. Like clothes and jewellery and cars. And guns. He would look at the price tags, look at his wage packet, then close the book or magazine.

A turning point in his young life came as he scanned the social pages of a national newspaper. Before him was a photograph of a middle-aged man with a very pretty young wife on his arm. John James looked at the picture for a long time. Underneath, the caption read, 'Wealthy furniture design manufacturer, Cyril Beadmore... '

"That bugger's as ugly as me, and yet look at him! How does someone like *him,* grab onto something like *that*?"

Again he read the caption. Then it hit him like a tonne of bricks. The key word was 'wealthy'. At that moment, John James McGregor-McWeasely made up his mind: he was going to acquire money. And as much of it as he could get his hands on. He went back to the photograph. The caption went on to say how Cyril Beadmore would be entertaining a hundred guests at his Toorak mansion as a second wedding anniversary present to his wife. He closed the newspaper.

"Cyril Beadmore. It looks like you're my man."

Having already acquired his first rifle, the books and magazines he purchased all-too-readily explained how to cut a rifle down—making it more accessible and easy to carry.

He underwent the task with great gusto. Because he was employed in the railyards he was thoroughly versed in the timetables of the passenger and goods trains. He worked out he could jump the midnight goods train to Melbourne, then nineteen hours later jump back on it and be home again in time to start work on Monday morning.

* * *

John James couldn't believe his luck. It was just 7.30 in the morning on the Monday, an hour before he was due at work.

And sitting on his bed in front of him was eleven grand in cold, hard notes. "Thank you Mr Beadmore," he laughed.

John James McGregor-McWeasely was on his way. By now he had just turned twenty. He had also read enough to learn the smartest thing to do after pulling a heist was to go to ground. See no-one. Socialise with no-one, keep your mouth shut and don't spend the money. He socked it away inside shoe boxes, which he stashed beneath the floor-boards of his ground-floor flat. But there wasn't a day that went by when he didn't retrieve the money for no other reason than to sit and hold it—and smell it. For some reason, the smell of money turned him on. Everytime he buried his face in the stuff, he got a erection. Then he'd fossick around for a girlie magazine and fill his mind with dreams and masturbate.

Subconsciously, he always waited for the knock on the front door. But it never came. As each day went by he became more confident that pulling a heist such as the one in Melbourne was a cinch. He con-tinued to scan the social pages of the national newspapers, but finding another Cyril Beadmore wasn't easy. He was also faced with the prospect of maybe having to kill to save his own neck.

Not a problem, he told himself. *People don't mean more than shit to me!*

For the next seven years, John James remained in his job at the rail yards. And during that time he pulled another four jobs. Always the same routine: the midnight goods train to Melbourne and back in time to start work Monday.

He was careful how he chose his victims. He was careful about the time he decided to strike. John James always mounted his attack on the sleeping wealthy at ten to four in the morning. The streets were deserted. More so than at three a.m. At ten to four the night was dead. He was also to learn very quickly that a sawn-off rifle jammed into the mouth of a pretty young wife made a middle-aged man of wealth open his safe in double-quick time.

Yet John James began to get restless. He hated the town where he lived. He hated the people in it and he despised his job. By now he had $93,000 crammed into shoe boxes. He also felt that after seven years it would be safe to start spending the original $11,000 he stole from Cyril Beadmore. But to be on the safe side, he boarded a bus to Sydney and systematically cashed the larger notes for smaller ones at a myriad of outlets.

As he made his way around the harbour city, something about the place grabbed his imagination. He crossed the harbour bridge several times. He paid several cab drivers to show him the sights. He paid others to take him to the best night spots.

On the day he was due to return to his home he stood in Martin Place, cast his eyes to the sky and said out loud, "Just one more job in Melbourne then I reckon I might call Sydney home."

After meticulously creating a false identity, John James paid three months' rent in advance for a flat in the Melbourne suburb of Elsternwick. It was a ground-floor, fully furnished one-bedroom unit of solid brick in a cul de sac.

Perfect, he thought. *That will restrict traffic no end and I'll be able to see who comes and goes.*

Shops close-by. Half a block to a cab rank. Only three other flats in the complex. All rented by young folk with day jobs. He couldn't believe his good fortune.

Upon settling himself in, he carefully rolled up the carpet in the bedroom and laid out a plastic sheet on the floor. On top of the sheet, he placed plain-coloured butchers' paper. On top of that he laid out all the stolen money. Another layer of butchers' paper and he then replaced the carpet. He checked and double-checked that there was no evidence the carpet had been lifted. Even to the point of crawling on his hands and knees and inspecting the three-quarter round on the edging for any giveaway signs of carpet strands.

After three days of staring at the walls and preparing himself for the next heist, John James began seeing images in his mind of previous hold-up victims. He'd just drop off to sleep then find himself sitting bolt upright, bathed in perspiration, a terrified face before his eyes. Try as he might to shake it loose it wouldn't go away. Then he'd begin to shake as he heard the pleading, the sobs, the hysteria and the terror-filled muffled screams of his victims.

This particular night it was most vivid. It was the young woman who was the victim of his first robbery. The wife of Cyril Beadmore. He had forced a rear door of their Toorak mansion and made his way upstairs to where the middle-aged man and his young wife slept. Wearing a balaclava and a hat with a miner's lamp attached, he walked round the side of the bed, grabbed the young woman by the hair, shone the light directly into her eyes and jammed the barrel of his sawn-off rifle into her mouth. The woman woke with a start, terrified.

The whites of her eyes were those of a crazy person. Her attempt to scream was muffled by the rifle barrel plunged deep in her mouth. Instantly her husband was awake. His sleepiness turned to terror as he attempted to go for the bedside light.

"Don't touch the light," John James commanded.

"What the bloody hell... ?"

"You shut your mouth, old man!"

But Cyril wasn't convinced. John James withdrew the barrel from the woman's mouth and smacked him on the head with it. Hard. Immediately the barrel went back into the woman's mouth.

"The safe, old man. Open the safe."

Trying to wipe the sleep from his eyes, Cyril fought to work out the situation. John James knew the bright glare from the miner's lamp and the balaclava destroyed any hope the old man had of seeing who the attacker was. Blood began to run down his face from a deep gash under his eye. His wife was still blurting muffled screams. He told her calmly, "Keep that up lady, and I'll blow your bloody brains out."

Suddenly the woman was still. The whites of her eyes becoming even larger.

"The safe, old man. You've got five seconds to decide. If you want to be a smart arse, the bitch is dead. And so will you be. Three seconds!"

Cyril was frozen to the spot. Somehow he began to move. "Jesus Christ, I haven't got a safe!"

By now the woman was beginning to gag from the rifle barrel.

"Two seconds."

"All right! All right! Jesus Christ!"

Cyril Beadmore found his feet and was quickly inside the walk-in wardrobe. He thrust aside a rack of clothes, stumbled back to the bedside cupboard and reefed open a drawer. Finally his fingers found a key. Moments later, he flung open the door to a wall safe and collapsed in a heap on the floor.

John James pulled the rifle barrel from the woman's mouth then landed a vicious blow to her head with the butt. Her eyes rolled back and he heard her gurgle. Pulling a cotton bag from a pocket, he entered the wardrobe and shone the lamp inside the safe. It was jammed full of notes, mainly of large denominations. He emptied the contents into his bag, checked that Cyril Beadmore had really passed out and made his escape.

News reports on the radio later that morning told of the robbery and of Cyril Beadmore suffering a heart attack. He was expected to survive along with his wife, who was in a serious but stable condition after being bashed.

Upon returning home, John James gave the couple little further thought. He was much too excited at having just pulled off a successful heist. The welfare and healing of his victims were the least of his concerns.

No-one ever cared a bugger about me. To hell with them. This is payback time.

But as the years went on it was the terror-stricken face of the young woman which began to haunt him. For some reason he kept seeing the whites of her eyes, large and stricken with fear. On this particular night her image was particularly vivid. He decided to go out. It was late, but he didn't care. He needed to get out and, for the first time in his life, was desperate to be in the company of a woman. He walked up the block to the cab rank.

"Something that's open, mate. A wine bar, a club. Some place where there might be a nice piece of arse," he told the driver. A few minutes later the cab pulled up outside the Pussy Galore Wine Bar in St Kilda.

The driver turned to John James. "There you go, mate. Bit of a mixture in there, but you'll probably find what you're looking for."

There were about thirty people in the wine bar. Some at the bar. Some sitting alone at tables. Others sharing private moments as couples. He pulled up a stool and ordered a beer.

As John James sat quietly, trying to shake the image of the terrified woman from his mind, a voice came over his shoulder. It was low-pitched, husky and female.

"A mineral water's fine."

He looked at the woman. He figured her for maybe late thirties.

Hair that looked to be red, but almost certainly out of a bottle. Too much makeup covering a rounded and formerly attractive face. Heavy eyeliner, bright red lipstick. The long, red fingernails and decorative rings adorning most fingers put him off a little. But it was the odour she exuded which he found most offensive, cheap perfume and cigarettes. But there was something about the woman which he liked. He decided he'd try to ignore her aroma.

"Why would you want to drink with me?"

"I'm a hostess. I get paid to mix with the customers."

"What else?"

"What do you mean, what else? There's no what else. You wanna get your dick wet, then tell me and I'll arrange it. But that's not me. I just talk to people."

John James seemed happy with the explanation.

"I'm Julie," she said, holding out her hand. John James accepted it.

"Peter," he lied. "And I'm not here to get me dick wet."

"Well, nice to meet you, Peter. Does your wife know you're out?"

"Yeah, that's a good line," he scoffed. "But it might surprise you somewhat if I told you I not only don't have a wife, I don't even know any women."

"Likely story; but you know, somehow I believe you."

"Do you think I'm ugly?" he blurted.

He could tell she was taken aback by the question and was trying to formulate an appropriate response.

"Good god, Peter, I've only just met you!" she exclaimed in a low voice. "Why would you ask me something like that?"

"Do you think I'm ugly?" he asked her again.

"No," she lied. "I don't think you're ugly. Is that the reason why you say you don't know any women? Because you think they would all think you're ugly?"

"Oh, forget it," he replied, regaining his composure and turning on his stool to stare into space.

"You live around here?" Julie asked, attempting to lighten the mood.

John James continued to stare straight ahead and shrugged. "Sort of."

Julie continued to make small talk, but her words were falling on deaf ears. Then, for some strange impulse, John James turned to her, reached into his pocket and pulled out a wad of notes. With a tear in his eye, he pressed the notes into her hand.

"Believe this, or don't believe this. You are the first woman I have ever had a conversation with in my life. All women ever do is ridicule me and call me a fucking Weasel. The money's yours if you'll just sit and talk to me for an hour."

Julie looked at the wad of notes, then flashed a glance over to a young woman sitting alone at the end of the bar. "You'd get a couple of all-nighters with Angie with that sort of dough," she told him.

"Cheaper to have a wank. Besides, I told you, I'm not here for that. Do you just want to talk?"

Julie put the money back into John James hand. "I don't want your money."

"There's five hundred bucks there... "

But the woman interrupted his protest. "I'm only too happy to sit and talk to you," she told him.

John James couldn't believe Julie had given him back the money, but he pocketed it anyway.

* * *

Three hours later, the wine bar had emptied to a handful of people. He and Julie had made their way to a corner table, and all during that time, he just drank and drank... and talked.

At around 3 a.m., Julie helped him into a cab after giving him her phone number and address and inviting him round for dinner at her house in two days' time. As she watched the cab drive off, her knees began to tremble. Something in her instincts prodded her intuition, sort of warning that all wasn't right.

What the hell could it be? All I did was talk to him. Maybe it's what he told me.

Julie convinced herself that it was the information he'd passed on that scared her. She tried to dismiss her anxieties. Then she wondered why she had been so generous with her invitation.

Christ, I never do things like that. I don't even know him. Feel sorry for the poor bastard, I guess. Doesn't know anyone. All people do is take the piss out of him. Besides, I reckon the coppers will have him in custody by then. It's probably all bullshit what he told me, but how the hell would you know?

He hadn't told her a great deal, but enough to raise her suspicions to the point where she felt she had to pass the information on to police. Then she felt fear overtake her body. Suddenly he frightened the hell out of her. Suddenly Julie had become very much a target. Her gut instincts told her so.

However, in a decision which would ultimately be to her detriment, she chose to ignore them.

* * *

John James barely made it to the toilet before he threw up.

He was as sick as a dog and had never known himself to vomit like it. His head was spinning. He peed his pants and excrement ran down his legs. He just wanted to die.

"Fuck the booze!" he groaned, moments before collapsing onto the bathroom floor and passing out.

He awoke six hours later to find himself lying in vomit, excrement and urine. The stench was unbearable. He cursed and swore as he found his feet. His head was splitting from the pounding and throbbing going on inside his brain. He staggered his way to the laundry, tore off his clothes, jammed them into a plastic bag, opened the back door, and threw the bag as far as he could. He slammed the door. He filled a bucket with hot water and detergent and grabbed a mop on his way back to the bathroom.

"Jesus, I don't believe I did this!"

Having cleaned up his mess, he turned on the shower and stood under it for what seemed an eternity. Slowly he regained his senses and the headache began to fade. Then, with a start, it hit him.

"Jesus, what did I tell that woman?"

He panicked. Stepping out of the shower, he rushed out the back door and ripped open the plastic bag containing his clothes. He fumbled through the pockets of his pants.

"Thank Christ for that!" he groaned, locating the piece of paper with Julie's name, address and phone number on it.

As he made his way inside, he suddenly came to the full realisation that he may have told the woman too much. But he couldn't remember. 'What the hell did I tell her?'

What the hell did I tell her?

But nothing would come. But he did recall mentioning something about robbing rich people. "Jesus, now I've got a loose end!"

You stupid dumb-arsed bastard. Now you've got a loose end!

All the stories he'd read over the years about crimes and cops always carried the one distinctive message: Never leave loose ends. It's the loose ends that do the damage.

John James thought of the dinner in two days' time.

Too far away. Can't wait that long.'

He had to move quickly and he knew it. He cleaned himself up and left the flat. On the way to the cab rank, he called in to a shop and bought a box of chocolates. "Gift wrapped please."

He hurried up the street to the cab rank and was more than a little relieved to see a vacant car at the stand. He told the cab driver Julie's address, and as the vehicle turned into her street, up ahead, he saw her leave her front gate in the company of two men and get into a vehicle. He told the cabbie to pull over.

"That's the woman I was going to see. The bitch owes me a month's rent on her house and I haven't been able to track her down. Who's that she's with, do you reckon?"

The cabbie grinned. "They're the coppers, mate. Looks like she owes more than just a month's rent, eh?"

"What do you mean?"

"I can tell you for sure that car she got into is an unmarked police car. Cabbies learn these things. The big giveaway is the hat on the rear parcel shelf. It covers up the radio aerial."

"I'll be buggered. Can you follow them?"

"I can. But it's not going to do you any good. If she owes you a month's rent, what the hell else has she been up to? They were D's, mate, so it's not a parking fine."

"Where do you reckon they're going again?"

John James kept his gazes firmly fixed on the vehicle.

"Russell Street. Police headquarters. Nothing surer."

About fifteen minutes later the unmarked police car pulled into the kerb opposite police headquarters and the three people walked across the street to enter the building.

"Stop here, mate," John James told the cabbie. "I think I might cool my heels for a while and wait for her to come out."

"Suit yourself."

John James paid the driver and made his way through the front entrance of the police building. A young woman on reception, already speaking on the phone, put her hand over the mouthpiece and looked at him inquiringly.

"The three people who just came in. One of them was my wife. Can you tell me where they went?"

"That's Bourke and McLoughlin from armed robbery... just a moment please," she said into the phone. "That was your wife with them?"

John James nodded.

"Do you wish to speak with her?"

"Yes, please."

"Take a seat, sir, I'll call them in a moment."

John James' gut hit the floor. *Jesus, I'm too late! I'm too bloody late!*

He pretended to take a seat and, when the woman was distracted, he quickly left the building. He noticed he was still holding onto the gift-wrapped box of chocolates. They would be the ticket to getting inside the woman's house.

John James then caught another cab and returned to his flat. He waited a couple of hours and dialled her number. There was no answer. He waited another two hours and called again. As soon as he heard the receiver lift off the cradle, he hung up.

"She's home! Thank Christ for that. She's bloody home!"

* * *

Half an hour, later John James knocked on her door.

Julie had been getting ready for work and was applying her make-up when she answered the knock. "Peter! You're two days early," she exclaimed, surprised and scared out of her wits at seeing him standing at the door. Especially after what she'd just told McLoughlin and Bourke from armed robbery.

"Hi Julie," he responded. "Sorry to barge in."

"Not at all," she replied, fighting hard to prevent him from seeing her lips tremble.

"Seems I made a bit of a fool of myself last night and I just wanted to thank you for pouring me into a cab and seeing to it that I got home. I just thought you might like something nice."

Julie noticed he was holding something behind his back.

"Oh, you shouldn't have!" she protested meekly, unlatching the door. "Come in. I'm just getting ready for work. Come through. Would you like a coffee? I do have a little time."

"That'd be nice. Thank you."

She turned her back on him and went to put the kettle on.

"Close your eyes," he told her.

She smiled. "Oh, Peter."

As she did so, it was all over in a microsecond.

John James whipped a pen-gun from his pocket, pressed the end of it to the back of the woman's head and released the firing pin. Julie died instantly. The bullet passed right through her skull and embedded itself into a wall in the kitchen. John James reached for his pocket knife and dug the lead out of the the plaster. Blood poured from the woman's head wound and John James had to be careful not to step in it. He glanced at her momentarily.

"Bloody bitch!" he scoffed. "You're all the same!"

He looked around himself. Satisfied he hadn't touched anything, he checked out the front, then the rear, and bolted.

He had only been back at his flat for twenty minutes when there was knock a on the door. He was still coming down from his hit. His hands were trembling. His gut was still tied in a knot from having killed. Cautiously he went to the door and spoke through it.

"Who is it?"

"Senior Constable Bourke and Senior Sergeant McLoughlin from the CIB. Mind if we have a word?"

John James opened the door. He was petrified.

"Are you Peter?"

John James knew immediately. Julie had talked. So had the cabbie.

"Yes."

"May we come in?"

"Of course," he replied, unlatching the door. "What the hell have I done?"

"Just routine sir. A few questions, if you don't mind."

"Sure... have a seat."

McLoughlin and Bourke cast their eyes around the sparsely furnished flat.

"Lived here long?"

"A few weeks."

"Where are you from?"

"Melbourne now. Left school at fifteen. Got a job. Saved me dough. Thought I'd like to live over here."

"What sort of work did you do?"

"Just labourin'."

McLoughlin's eyes flashed to John James' hands. He could tell they weren't the hands of an office worker.

"Mind if I have a look around?" McLoughlin asked.

"Not much to see."

"Got a job?" asked McLoughlin .

"Not yet. I'm just being a tourist for a while. But I'll start looking soon."

"Got any money?"

"A bit?"

"What's a bit?"

John James went to a kitchen drawer and took out a passbook. He handed it to Bourke.

"Peter Lewis Heatherington. That's you?"

John James nodded.

"Two grand. Not gonna last long is it? Got a car?"

"No."

"How do you get around?"

"Cabs... trams."

"The rent will soon swallow that up," Bourke said, handing John James back his passbook.

"But I've paid three months up front on this place. I'll get a job."

"Been home all night?"

"Yes."

"Ever been to Melbourne before?"

"No."

"Not even overnight?"

John James knew exactly what the cop meant. *How bloody much did I tell that woman?* he bemoaned to himself. "No."

"There's been a few robberies over a period, Mr Heatherington. We're just trying to clear them up. Sorry to take up your time."

With those words, the two police officers left John James' flat.

John James watched the two detectives drive away then raced in to the toilet and vomited until all he could do was dry retch. He had never been so scared. He wondered what the two policemen thought of him. Whether they believed his story. He felt himself begin to shake uncontrollably. When he walked into the kitchen, perspiration drenched his entire body. It got even worse when he came to the realisation of just how close he had come to being caught. Within a hair's breadth of where Bourke had sat were the sawn-off rifle, pen-gun, miner's lamp and balaclava. He had actually hollowed out the leg of the table Bourke had rested his arms on and used it as a hiding place for his 'tools of trade'.

Still trying to come to terms with how much he'd told the woman, he vowed to never ever indulge in a repeat performance of too much booze and loose lips.

* * *

Three hours later there came another knock to John James' door. It was Bourke and McLoughlin again.

John James froze. 'Shit!'

It was Bourke who spoke. "Just a few more questions, Mr Heatherington?"

John James opened the door to let them in.

Bourke produced a photograph. "You know this woman?"

It was Julie. "Uh-huh."

"How well?"

"I was with her last night at the Pussy Galore Wine Bar in St Kilda."

"And?"

"And... er... nothing. What do you mean 'and'?

"When was the last time you saw her?"

"I think about 3 a.m. She helped me into a cab. I was more pissed than I'd ever been in my life. Got home here and chucked me guts up. Flaked out. Woke up about six hours later. Why? She reckon I raped her or something?"

"Did you?"

"Shit man! We just sat and talked and I got very drunk. That's it."

"We have a cab driver who'll place you in her street today."

"So?"

"So what were you doing there?"

"Why all the questions? Why don't you ask her?"

"We feel you can probably answer that one," Bourke shot back.

"Whaddaya mean?"

"We mean she's fucking dead, arsehole!" Bourke cut in.

John James knew that he was required to look stunned. Shocked. He played the part. "When?" he asked.

"Earlier today."

"How?"

"You tell us, arsehole?" Bourke barked.

"How the hell would I know?"

"Why did you go to her street, then follow us into town?"

John James feigned embarrassment. "Because I had something for her."

"Like what?"

He went to a cupboard and opened the door. "Like this."

McLoughlin tore off the gift wrapping.

"Chocolates! You wanted to give her chocolates?"

John James nodded.

"Why?"

"'Cause I fucked up last night."

"How?"

"I dunno," he said. "I just thought I might have. So I wanted to apologise. Is there anything wrong with that? And you say she's dead?"

Bourke and McLoughlin didn't answer. Instead they fixed their gaze upon him to try and stare him down. But John James didn't flinch. Inside, his gut was in turmoil. But he gave nothing away.

Whn the cops left, John James sat glued to the gap in the curtains at his front window. He couldn't stop himself from shaking. As he peered through the smallest of slits, he saw a car swing into the cul de sac, cut its lights and park next to the kerb.

Got to be a cop car. Got to be! Shit! They didn't believe me. They didn't bloody believe me!

His mind was racing. He went to a drawer and took out a pair of binoculars. He moved the curtain back a fraction, enough to put one lens up to the window. As the image was drawn closer, John James could make out two figures in the front seat.

The bastards are staking me out. Shit! Now what? He paced the floor. *Nothing. The bastards have got nothing. OKyou guys! Two can play your game. I'll just stay put. I'll wait you out. I have enough tucker in this joint for a week. We'll see who gets sick of it first.*

John James hardly left his seat by the window for the first week. He ate there. He slept there. The only times he moved were to get food or go to the toilet. The shifts on the stakeout changed every six to eight hours. John James had read enough over the years to know that would be the ploy. To 'smoke him out'. It was a shakedown. It was intimidation. It was the stand-off harassment. He also knew it was a tactic employed by the police when they had nothing to go on except suspicion. But he knew they knew he did the woman. It would become a war of nerves. He also had an inkling that his flat would be bugged or targeted with a directional microphone. All engaged with the one purpose of intimidating him. Making him cave in to the pressure. Having him make a phone call to a friend or associate and confiding his guilt. Evidence not admissible in court, but enough for the police to go on to pursue a line of questioning and investigation.

At the beginning of the second week his food supplies were getting low. So he took to ordering takeaway by phone.

He continued to sit at the window and peer out. Sometimes he'd see a pair of binoculars focussed on his flat. But mostly, two police officers sat watch twenty-four hours a day. He felt himself getting to breaking point, so he took cold showers to harden his resolve.

Into the third week and the situation hadn't changed. The garbage was mounting up inside his flat, but he refused to give up.

I'll see you bastards off if it's the last thing I do!

* * *

On the last day of the third week, John James noticed the stakeout car was in a slightly different position. It had moved up the road just far enough that a street light showed a touch more clearly the two men in the front seat. At around 3 a.m. he was watching them through his binoculars and he could've sworn they were both starting to nod off. He dialled a takeaway and instructed them to make the delivery at the beginning of the cul de sac. He would be waiting for them.

John James checked the car's occupants again. He felt sure they had nodded off. He quickly and quietly left his flat via the back door and scooted down the street. He hid until the takeaway van came into view. He hurriedly paid the driver and waited for him to disappear. He then walked over to the stakeout car and banged on the roof. Its two occupants woke with a start. The one behind the wheel wound down the window.

"Mornin' boys," John James said, smiling. "It's now been three weeks. Thought you might be getting a little peckish. I'll just leave this here for you," he told them, placing a small plastic tray carrying burgers and coffee on the bonnet of their vehicle.

The two police on stakeout were too stunned to speak.

John James knew he'd made a fool of them. A victory for him right now, but most likely a defeat the police would never forget. John James would be a marked man and he knew it.

The stakeout was abandoned within the hour.

* * *

"I see that was a big success," Bourke said to McLoughlin when he arrived for work on the Monday morning.

McLoughlin knew immediately what he was referring to.

"I still say he did it," Dave offered.

"Yeah, well we just put in three weeks to smoke him out and he never gave an inch. Either he's a whole lot smarter than we give him credit for or he's clean. My hunch is he's clean."

"Come on boss, he never left the joint. He never made any phone calls except for takeaway. He just bloody sat there."

"He never left the joint?" McLoughlin asked.

"Never left the joint," Bourke reiterated.

"So who brought the boys the hamburgers and coffee?"

"Yeah, well, shit, hang on... !"

"No, you hang on. If he slipped out then, what's to say he didn't at other times as well?"

"He didn't."

"We don't know that. Just continue a normal line of inquiry on the woman. We've wasted enough time on the little prick. Blokes like him don't stop at one. Once they get a taste they keep going. We'll have our day. Might take a while, but he'll make a mistake. They *always* make a mistake," McLoughlin said.

Bourke offered a wry grin. "Yes, they do, don't they?"

* * *

John James McGregor-McWeasely was so terrified by the police shakedown that it was another week before he even dared to venture outside his flat. He ordered in what food he needed and stayed put. But with two weeks to go on the lease of his flat, he decided on one more job before making a permanent move to Sydney.

The social pages described Ernst and Barbra Cohen as a wealthy retired Jewish couple who lived in suburban Elwood. He had an idea that being wealthy, retired and Jewish, they probably had an inkling for gold.

John James struck at ten to four in the morning. The old man struggled until being struck down with the rifle butt. It was only when

John James threatened to shoot his wife that he opened his safe. A small amount of cash, and as he'd suspected, a large quantity of gold ingots in various weights. He decided it would be smart to grab only the smaller ones for easier disposal and stuffed three handfuls into each of two bags.

Twenty hours later he'd jumped a goods train and was on his way to Sydney.

News of the attack on Ernst and Barbra Cohen spread through the media like wildfire. Mr Cohen was something of a philanthropist and a well-regarded member of the community.

The first person who came to mind to Ken McLoughlin was Peter Lewis Heatherington. He banged on the door of his flat, but soon realised the place was deserted.

"Just as I bloody thought," he cursed.

Later that day he came upon Dave Bourke. "You remember that little fucking prick, Heatherington?"

"You mean ugly features?" Dave asked.

"Yeah, the prick with the funny walk. No such person."

"Bullshit!"

"I've had records do a search. Peter Lewis Heatherington drowned in the Murray River at Renmark two years ago."

"So what are you saying?"

"I'm saying this is the prick that knocked the woman off. This is the prick that's pulled all those robberies, and this is the prick that knocked over the Cohens as well."

Bourke got up to grab his gun and vest.

"Forget it son. He's already invisible. I've just been around to his joint."

Chapter 3

Franco, Luigi and Enrico were the three sons of Giuseppe and Rosetta Mogliotti. With their parents they toiled day and night, along with their three sisters to scrape a living growing vegetables from a minuscule landholding on the western outskirts of Sydney.

From an early age the three boys decided that they hated market gardening; there had to be a better way. For their parents, this was 'the better way'. For their sisters, the better way was to grow up, get married and move away. Which they did. Not more than an hour's drive, but nonetheless away from chipped and broken fingernails and washing the dirt from freshly pulled carrots at midnight.

Only two years separated each of Franco, Luigi and Enrico.

As brothers went, they were particularly close. They loved their mother, were loving and protective of their sisters and condoned their father. None of them could wait to grow up.

School was a waste of time. They spent their teenage years absconding as often as they could and concocting 'get-rich-quick schemes' which would see them into big houses, flash cars and trips to the Riviera. Not one of the three was a scholar. Their interests lay in motor cars. The bigger the engines, the lower the suspensions and the wider the wheels, the more they liked them. And if they could watch their mates get a zero to 100 kilometres per hour on the backstreets of Blacktown in six or seven seconds, then all the better.

As each one left school, he gained employment as an apprentice panel beater in a Blacktown crash-repair business.

During this period their education increased ten-fold. At first they watched in dismay as the owner of the business brought in the wreckage of two vehicles. Two cars of the same make. One would be written off from the front, the other from the rear. And they knew the vehicles had been purchased for only a few hundred dollars from insurance companies.

Immediately, the vehicles were set upon by workers with oxyacetylene torches. Within two weeks, one good car had been created from the wrecks and, after it had passed through the paint shop, only a keen eye could spot the compilation.

The next thing they'd see the vehicle take pride of place on the used-car lot next door. And it sold for thousands of dollars to some poor unsuspecting sod who believed the bit about it only being driven to church on Sundays by a little old lady. It took them a while to learn that the car yard next door was also owned by the man who owned the crash repair business.

Another of their boss's good money-spinners, they discovered, was vehicle sabotage. But he chose his victims carefully.

Invariably they would be young or elderly women who drove the latest models. The vehicle would be dropped off for a spot of panel beating, but when that person came to pick it up, unbeknown to her, parts like the exhaust system, battery, alternator, radiator, hoses, belts (and, in some cases, even the tyres) had been replaced with cheaper or used, generic alternatives.

Franco, Luigi and Enrico used to gawk at the boss's bright-red Ferrari. Often they'd discuss amongst themselves how the owner of a relatively small business could afford such a fine piece of machinery. As obvious as the answer was, the answer to the question of why he kept it hidden from public view was now just as obvious.

After a while, Franco, Luigi and Enrico began to get restless. Apprentice wages weren't high, so they decided what was good enough for the boss was good for enough for them. Pooling their resources, they leased an old shed at the back of a neighbour's market-garden and bought their first two wrecks. After working all day at the crash-repair shop, they continued to toil into the early hours of the morning making one good car from the remains of two. Within a short space of time they saw their first completed vehicle driven away. They'd managed to turn $700 into $7000 in just six weeks.

Over the next five years, one shed grew to two much bigger sheds.

The turn-around time was down to four weeks and the $7000 had grown into amounts of up to $16,000. They stayed clear of the stolen-parts racket, seemingly happy to go with the fast money from wrecked vehicles.

By the time Franco, Luigi and Enrico had turned twenty-four, twenty-two and twenty respectively, the fast buck had encompassed their lives. All three had matching Monaros, and when one went out on a date the other two would tag along. Sometimes it would be six for dinner and a show, other times four or five.

But it was the seedy side of town which attracted them most. The petty crime. The loose, foul-mouthed women. The booze, the deals. As greed became an increasing factor in their lives, they began to search for bigger fish to fry. All three gave up their jobs and concentrated entirely on creating one good car from two wrecks. Turnaround time came back to two weeks and dollar amounts moved up into the $20,000 category.

In line with their parents' wishes, all three boys, like their sisters, went on to marry within their ethnic nationality. But it was the weddings of the three sons which had their mother gravely concerned. At various times she would ask each of them, "What are you doing with your life?" The only reply she ever received was, "Mamma, you worry too much. I make a good living."

At each wedding, Rosetta Mogliotti noticed a group of young men and women who were not part of the family circle.

"Franco, who are these people?" she'd ask.

"Friends, Mamma, just friends."

But Rosetta knew differently. She knew that the area in which she lived had a grimy underbelly. Her instincts told her these people were part of it.

"Oh Mother of God, what are my boys doing?" she'd pray.

She would try to raise the subject with Giuseppe, but he chose only to turn a blind eye.

"Let them be, Mamma. They have been taught right from wrong."

All three marriages went smoothly enough, although for three nights a week, none of the women knew their husbands were drinking and womanising at the Lay Lady Lay nightclub in King's Cross. They just accepted the fact that brothers were brothers and liked to spend time together. Apart from birthdays and family celebrations, the brothers' wives had little or no contact with their husbands' sisters.

But in the murky little world in which Franco, Luigi and Enrico now moved, things were beginning to get tougher. The government and insurance companies were clamping down on backyard car dealers, spare parts rorts, and turning out a clean vehicle from two wrecks. Legislation was introduced to prevent insurance companies selling off wrecked vehicles willy-nilly, and buyers had to have rock-solid reasons for buying them. At times, the three would sit idle in their sheds due to the lack of product.

"Diversify," Franco told his brothers. "We need to diversify."

"Like what?"

"It's obvious the government has screwed our business. Maybe we should look at doing a couple of hits. We all need money and what we've got isn't gonna last forever."

Luigi became alarmed at such a suggestion. Enrico jumped at the chance.

"You mean we knock some bastard off?" he said.

"Do that and we'll all end up in jail," Luigi said.

"No, no, listen to me," Franco went on. "Just think about who lives and does business around here. Lots of people with lots of money. But we stay away from the Italians, OK. We just go for the locals. Blokes we know who are as shaky as a shithouse rat."

Franco insisted that under no circumstance were guns to be used, and that they rely entirely upon the three-P policy: Preparation, Patience and Professionalism. Nothing would be rushed. When a target was settled on, be it a private home or a business, certain criteria needed to be adhered to.

"OK, we do safe jobs and only safe jobs. When we decide on where to hit, first we cut the power off a week beforehand then sit near the place and watch what happens. That will tell us if there's a back-up or silent alarms. If there's no back-up, we go ahead. But not before a week has passed. That should allay any suspicions about the electricity dropping out. Luigi, it will be your job to know at all times where the victim is. If he leaves and starts heading for home and we're still in there, get on the bloody phone. We wear very large, very heavily padded oversized jackets and balaclavas. If we do get seen, the descriptions will be for blokes a hell of a lot bigger than us.

"We go for lone targets. Rich blokes with not a lot of ties. That means there won't be a lot of congestion in their lives and we won't have to worry about a whole lot of people."

* * *

One day at work, a couple of months earlier, Enrico had noticed Fritz, the German, improvise in a way he'd never seen before. It was late on a Friday afternoon when Fritz, half-way through a job, ran out of acetylene. It was too late in the day to order more in, and the job had to be completed. Enrico watched, totally enthralled, as Fritz grabbed a small length of half-inch pipe, quickly threaded one end and attached a connection to a oxygen bottle. He then filled the small length of pipe with welding rods, turned on the oxygen and lit the other end. After adjusting the oxygen bottle's valve to bring the flame to a manageable level, Fritz applied his newly-constructed blowtorch to the steel he'd been working on. Enrico's eyes nearly popped as he saw the ease with which the pure flame of oxygen mixed with welding rods cut through such a hardened metal.

"Where the hell did you learn how to do that?" he asked.

Fritz grinned. "Bloody good trick, eh? My father told me a long time ago, yes. Apparently in the war, some fellas were stuck on the Russian front in a tank that needed repairs to a track. They couldn't get a pin out of somewhere, so this bloke suddenly appears on the scene with his magic stick. Jesus Christ! Magic bloody stick all right! My father. He piss himself laughing when he tell me. After a couple of minutes, this bloody pin... it just melt away. My father, he say he never forget. And he tell me."

"You reckon it might work with a longer rod, more gas and more welding rods?" Enrico urged, his mind racing.

"Maybe! Maybe bloody not, too! You should be ask my father, but he bloody dead now. You probably blow your bloody self up. Whoooosh! Nothing left, eh! This pure bloody oxygen, mate."

Enrico went back to what he had been working on, shaking his head in disbelief. But the idea stuck.

And the more he thought about it the more he wanted to try it out for himself. For several days he found excuses to remain behind after his brothers had left to go home.

Enrico equipped himself with several lengths of pipe of varying diameters and began to experiment. After working out the perfect com-bination to extract maximum heat, he smiled contentedly to himself and put the matter to rest in the back of his mind.

Now, when Franco said, "Let's diversify," Enrico grabbed his opportunity.

Franco noticed an excited urgency overtake Enrico. "The three P's little brother... settle down."

Enrico couldn't contain himself any longer. "Let me show you something," he offered.

The two elder brothers watched Enrico walk to the rear of the shed and draw the covers from a strange piece of apparatus.

They looked at each other and shrugged. Moments later, after Enrico wheeled a large, very thick, and very heavy piece of steel into an open area, they watched him assemble a strange-looking object. His brothers were about to interrupt with a whole barrage of questions when Enrico raised his hand. "Just watch," he told them.

Within moments a hole appeared through the centre of the massive piece of heavy-gauge steel.

"Seeing is believing isn't it?" he smiled.

"What the fuck is that?" Franco gushed.

"Should make pretty quick work of any bloody safe, eh?"

Franco and Luigi stood in stunned amazement.

"Where the hell did you pick up on that?"

"Fritz used a smaller version on a job at work one day. He called it a magic stick, so I got him to tell me about it. Beats the shit out of having to carry oxyacetylene doesn't it? The pipe is about four metres long and I reckon it works best with a diameter of one-and-a-half centimetres. Very portable and very bloody effective. I reckon this little bastard will cut through any-thing. When do we start?"

Over the next two years, the brothers pulled off five safe breakings.

Their targets were always people they knew who were dishonest, and in the case of three of the robberies, no reports were made to police.

Gradually the heat began to lift on the sale of insurance write-offs, and the three brothers were able to return to some degree of normality. The money wasn't like it was previously but, nonetheless, each was provided for handsomely. Even so, the taste of easy money, and the high provided when a hit was on, made them yearn for more. They would speak about it amongst themselves and be consoled by the fact that they'd done five safe breakings and got away totally undetected. But the itch was now going three ways and getting harder and harder to scratch. Their hearts were no longer in turning two wrecked cars into one good one. And each knew the other had only one thing on his mind. Finally it was Franco, the unelected leader of the trio, who conceded.

"OK, we go again."

It was a decision met with broad grins and a loud "*Yeeeesss!*" by his brothers.

The next two years the brothers only pulled two jobs. But they were big jobs. With big rewards. Police were at their wits' end in tracking down who was responsible. Shakedowns on known offenders were increasing. Hardened detectives were coming down hard on their snitches, but nowhere was there a leak. The brothers adhered rigidly to the three Ps, but most of all, there were no big spend-ups. They would still turn out enough cars from wrecks to allay any questions about supplementary incomes. For the three brothers Mogliotti, life was good.

"Be nice though to get one really big bastard wouldn't it?" Franco would surmise to his brothers. "Just one really big one. You know, maybe a couple of mill and we could piss off all this shit and go away and sit under a bloody tree."

* * *

During these years, the brothers adhered to a thrice weekly ritual of visiting their favourite Sydney night club, deep in the heart of the King's Cross no-go zone, where they enjoyed the company of the locals—transvestites, lesbians, homosexuals, drug dealers, drug addicts, prostitutes, thieves, paedophiles, small-time crooks, con-men, and a general mishmash of society's misfits and drop-outs.

Each had their women at Lay Lady Lay. Women who knew better than to ask questions, knew when to smile and when to disappear. Their reward was money and lots of it. Their duties were purely sexual. And whenever their lovers demanded it. Failure to 'come across' would ensure a beating. In the case of Enrico, a particularly brutal beating.

One such woman who dared to refuse Enrico and talk to another man suffered miserably. Enrico followed her home and beat her so severely she became a brain-damaged vegetable. No witnesses. No evidence. Even his brothers never knew. When they asked whatever happened to her, he would shrug his reply and change the subject. But word spread amongst the women that Enrico was the likely assailant, and whilst they were 'nice' to him, many kept their distance.

Franco's woman, a fiery, thirty-year-old Sicilian redhead called Gina was as protective of her man as he was of her. Any woman new to the club who flashed an eye towards Franco was given the 'treatment'. Years earlier, Gina had seen it carried out in her home country on a young woman who dared to be unfaithful to her lover. Her lover's friends grabbed her and sewed the lips of her vagina together with fishing line then smothered their handiwork with super glue. Apart from the humiliation and agony suffered at the time, the victim invariably required several days in hospital and several weeks at home for recuperation. Gina had seen two women off from Lay Lady Lay in this way.

Such brutality turned Franco on, and very rough sex between the two would follow. After the first few times with Gina, Franco came to the full realisation of why men took lovers.

Imagine doing this sort of shit with your wife?

Yet unbeknown to Franco, Gina also liked to play on the other side of the tracks. He didn't know that by day she held a highly respectable job as a consultant in a travel agency in Sydney's central business district. It was only when the sun went down did her dark side emerge... and only on the three days a week she met with him. The other sides to her social life were trade fairs, functions, cocktail parties and travel nights.

It was at a travel agency's cocktail party she was to catch the eye of the guest speaker for the evening, Federal Government Minister Sebastian McAlister.

McAlister, a Presbyterian lay preacher and married man with three young daughters, was highly-credentialed in government circles. The ear of the Prime Minister, a top-gun whenever a peacemaker was needed between warring parties, he was also a hard-nosed negotiator between the factions. He was also a wonderfully gifted public speaker, a snappy dresser, and a man who people felt they could warm to.

As he spoke from the rostrum to the cocktail party guests, his gaze fixed momentarily on Gina's. It was a powerplant of electricity and each of them knew it. Gina turned away quickly, but just as quickly glanced back. Sebastian McAlister faltered in his delivery, but ever so slightly. No-one picked it up. Except Gina. She felt her stomach knot, her throat go dry. She reached for another glass of champagne from a passing waiter.

At the end of his speech, the applause was polite, but enthusiastic, and many gathered by his side to speak with him as he stepped down. She was standing with her profile to him on the other side of the room, sensing him slowly working his way towards her, paying lip-service to those who followed. But as he approached she moved away.

He turned discreetly to his minder and whispered in his ear. The minder then inconspicuously made his way to the back of the room toward her. On hearing the message from the minder, again Gina's and Sebastian's eyes met. She gave the faintest of smiles. She reached into her handbag and scribbled a phone number on a business card.

"Tell him to call me in two hours," she said, and was gone.

Chapter 4

Gina heard a faint knock on her door. She looked up to the clock on her wall. 11:45 p.m. *They've got a nerve at this hour*, she told herself angrily. *Normally I'd be in bed.*

She went to her door and looked through the security eye. "Oh shit!" she gasped, grabbing at her dressing-gown and throwing a hand to her face.

He's never seen me like this!

She panicked, wanting to pretend she wasn't home.

That's no damned good, he can see the light under the door.

She took a deep breath, undid the chain, turned the latch on three deadlocks and opened the door. She was about to protest at the hour and not being prepared when a half-whispered voice cut her short.

"Happy anniversary, gorgeous girl," Sebastian McAlister smiled, holding out a massive arrangement of roses. "Two years to the day since we first set eyes upon each other."

"Oh, Sebby!" she gushed, "you've never seen me like this... Come in... come in," she urged, trying to take hold of two dozen blooms. Sebastian McAlister stepped inside and Gina closed the door after him. "I thought you were in Rome until Sunday?"

"Supposed to have been, but three ministers from various countries got called away so they wound up early. Anyway, bugger that," he said, taking hold of the flowers and placing them on a chair. "How are you?" he asked, seizing Gina in his arms. "God, I've missed you."

Before she had time to answer, his mouth was upon hers and he'd swept her off her feet. Soon the two were in her bedroom. They fell together onto Gina's king-sized bed and within moments he had entered her. It had been two weeks since they were last together. The intensity of their love-making made it seem like two years. Gina was always one for a great deal of foreplay. But this time she seemed happy to forgo the preliminaries. She rolled him over.

"Too much of that and I'm gone," he groaned.

As the moment exploded, each ended up completely drained. Slowly he raised himself up on his arms and kissed her mouth.

"Do you know how many times I relive these moments?"

"The Prime Minister would never believe it would he?" Gina sniggered.

"Not only the Prime Minister! Try a wife and kids, an electorate and a congregation. I'm Sebastian McAlister. Straight-laced. Conservative. Lay preacher. Minister of the Crown. Jesus, tell me if I'm not a walking contradiction!"

"So why do you do it? Not all that work and family stuff. I mean *me*? Am I worth the risk? Christ, Sebby, one word about this and you are totally and absolutely fucked!"

He grimaced at her words, not wanting to face them. She was right. He knew she was right. But he also knew she was one woman he couldn't stay away from. No matter what the cost. No matter how many lies. No matter how much deceit.

Silence fell between them with Sebastian rolling his arm under Gina and dragging her close in to him. She could hear his heartbeat begin to slow and, for several minutes, there was no need for words. Wrapped in each other's arms, they drifted aimlessly, off to places both knew could never be.

Finally it was Gina. "So tell me about Rome?"

"I'll have a quick shower first."

Sebastian moved into the en-suite. A few minutes later as he turned the water off, Gina was standing by the recess.

"Do you want me to dry you?" she asked him.

"No," he told her firmly, feeling his face go red. "You're insatiable!"

"You made me like it," she replied, moving away to lie on the bed. "So tell me?" she repeated, placing a cup of coffee for him on a small table in the lounge room.

"This one was about the cartels. You know, the big drug cartels across the globe and how governments can combat them."

"Many there?"

"Sixteen nations, including the United States and Great Britain."

"So did you have to speak, or just take notes?"

"We all had our alloted time, but the frightening thing is that I don't believe anyone, and I mean *anyone,* can really conceive just how big this damn drugs thing is."

"Really?"

"Massive, Gina. Just bloody massive. And there's no real way of knowing what the bottom-line figures are, because how are you going to get a look at the books of the drug barons? That's if they even keep any."

"Can it be overcome?"

"In a word, no. Too big. Too much money. Too much corruption. At first the dollar amounts were in the millions. Then it was billions. Now for god's sakes, they are talking in the trillions. How the hell do you combat that?"

"So what's the answer?"

"I don't think there is one. Law enforcement agencies can do their best, but for every kilogram of heroin or cocaine seized, there's another hundred, maybe even a thousand, to take its place.

"And when you listen to all these guys get up and speak, it's not so much the drug barons you have to worry about, it's the blokes who the rest of world believes are legit. I mean, the cops know who the barons are. That's just a matter of catching them. What they don't know is who are the barons disguised as legitimate businessmen? And it's not only drugs. Money laundering is a *massive* problem. So much money. And mostly dirty money. It's got to be cleaned up. That's when the haves and the have-nots get sorted out really smartly."

"How do you mean?"

"Well, if you can afford to buy ten mill and only pay five for it, you have to be able to sit on it... maybe even for years. One thing's for sure, the hotter it is, the longer you have to sit on it."

"Good lord! How many real drug barons are out there masquerading as legitimate businessmen?" Gina queried.

"Bloody hell, Gina, there's a truckload of them. No, rephrase that, truckloads of them," he answered.

"So do you think anything is achieved from such a conference?"

Sebastian thought for a moment before answering.

"Probably, if only to create an awareness in world governments of just how big the drugs and money-laundering problems are and that they're not going to go away."

"So if the Prime Minister said to you, 'fix it', what would you do?"

Sebastian McAlister looked at Gina and offered a slight chortle.

"Some of the facts and figures are mind-boggling. Here's a couple off the top of my head. The United States Drug Enforcement Administration, otherwise known as the DEA, and the United States Customs put in a massive effort trying to stop the drugs from entering the US from Mexico. And Mexico is the front line in the world's drug war. Just on that note. They talk about a drugs war. What war? There's no damned war! No-one from this side has even fired a shot. But back to Mexico. Huge x-ray machines peer into giant eighteen-wheeled trucks and there are stringent anti-corruption measures to cope with the $7 billion the drug barons budget for bribes. You get that? Seven bloody billion for bribes. Fifty grand is the going rate for each drug-carrying truck a US customs officer is prepared to wave through.

"But here's the real rub! The narcotics business in Mexico is worth up to $32 billion a year, and if the Mexican government was to lose that from its gross domestic product, the country's economy would hit the fan. That then would be felt on Wall Street, because it has deep connections with, and investments in, Mexico. So the drugs pour across the border day and night. As I say, that's just Mexico."

Sebastian sipped his coffee and went on.

"You know," he continued, "eighty-five million Americans spend $38 billion a year on cocaine alone! British police say nightclubbers spend $1 billion pounds a year on ecstasy. On a world scale, drugs are so big that they take more in dollar terms than the international trade in iron and steel and motor vehicles. That's about eight per cent of international trade.

"And you ask me how would I fix it?" He paused, took a another sip of coffee and grimaced slightly. "I'd mount the biggest task force the world has ever seen, made up of all the services and police I could find and rout the industry. But bear in mind that, just on the Mexican border, a customs officer can make a year's salary by looking the other way for ten seconds. So you would find a lot of resistance to such a campaign. Interestingly enough," he went on, lifting his tone a little, "if the world is suddenly struck down by some new disease, then heaven and earth is moved to find a cure. Unbelievable! But with drugs it's different. It's too big. And there are too many people getting rich."

"So why are the barons masquerading as legitimate businessmen so hard to uncover?" Gina asked.

"Because they're too well protected. You couldn't follow the money trail with a team of lawyers. Going from what I heard in Rome, there's obviously plenty of blind eyes being turned in this country too. But that's about as far as you get. No names. All that stuff. But there's one particular bloke over there that's got them all bluffed. One of the ministers in the Italian Government, Vincenzo Torricelli, was telling me at length about him, over dinner one night. His name is Bruno Formicella. Married. Kids. The whole bit. Something of a fashion guru."

"You don't mean The House of Bruno in Milan?"

"That's it. You know him?"

"I don't know him. But certainly The House of Bruno is up there with Chanel, Christian Dior, Estée Lauder."

"Bruno Formicella. Yep, that's him all right. Lives in Portofino on the Italian Riviera. One of those big bloody villas overlooking the bay."

"And he's a drug baron?"

"Both! Drugs and money-laundering. But no-one can catch him. He's probably more of a middle-man. God knows who he must pay and how much he must pay them, but this guy from the government was telling me that at any one time, little old Bruno would have up to $20 million US on hand in a safe in his house."

"Good god! Why so much?"

Sebastian smiled. "I think it's called buying and selling. He's likely to be one of these blokes I was telling you about. Probably buys ten mill for five, then is actually able to sit on it for years. This little Bruno is apparently so well connected, and so well protected, he doesn't even have security on his villa. No-one's game to touch him. Even the bad guys stay away. Touch Bruno and you're dead meat. I had heard of people like that. Vincenzo says, word is, all he has is a very large safe."

"How large?"

"Very large," Sebastian grinned.

"Very large?" Gina queried, now vitally interested.

"Like a door that weighs a tonne! Talk about a sacred cow! Obviously a very crooked little sacred cow at that. He went on to say that in six months' time, Bruno and his family will be absent from the villa for two days. The only two days of the year when everyone's away."

"Some world fashion spectacular in Milan and he wouldn't miss it for anything. Don't suppose you would, seeing the damn thing is named after you. But this guy says he's been on bended knee to several heads of governments for permission to raid the place during that weekend to see what they can find. And each time he draws a big fat zip. No-one is prepared to go out on a limb to try and nail him. As I say, *everyone* is protecting *someone*. Anyway, enough of all that, tell me about you."

Gina moved over and sat on his lap.

"I miss you so much. Are you sure about this? I mean I really worry that some damn newspaper photographer is going to pop out of the woodwork and there we'll be on the front bloody page!"

"Do you want to call it off?"

"No! God no! I live for these moments. I don't know how long they'll last, but while they're there, I'll just grab them. I don't think I could stand anyone else touching me," she lied, crossing her fingers as her thoughts went to Franco. Jesus, that bastard would kill me if he knew.

"But I can't always see you," Sebastian protested meekly.

"Sometimes, like tonight, it's only at the last moment I realise I have a couple of hours."

"Then it's a couple of hours. I understand. But please. Don't trade them in," she pleaded. "I just seem to come alive when I'm with you."

Sebastian was totally convinced. And Gina could be very convincing.

Even lying in his arms, she thought of Franco. She knew she couldn't have either man, but it was Franco who had her heart. The attraction to Sebastian she knew was the position he held and the power.

Who said power wasn't an aphrodisiac?

She found herself aching for the charge she got from bedding a man where the stakes were very, very high. But now she could sense a more compelling reason to keep seeing him: the man called Bruno Formicella and twenty million bucks. She had to find out more, but that would have to be on another day.

Slowly, slowly, she told herself. *Slowly, slowly.*

* * *

In her office the next morning Gina hooked up to the internet and set up a search for The House of Bruno. Almost immediately she was inundated with hundreds of pages of information.

Christ, I knew our little Bruno was big, but not this big. Bloody hell! Get a load of this!

She read:

> *In September. The House of Bruno World Fashion Spectacular. Come September this year. Milan will come alive as industry leaders and supermodels converge on the fashion capital of the world for what's being regarded as the 'Spectacular To Die For'. Bruno Formicella, who lends his name to this extravaganza of enormous proportions, has poured millions into the event to attract the biggest stars and the biggest names the industry has to offer...*

The publicity blurb went on and on. Then Gina clicked 'disconnect' and made a mental note of where to find it again and got out, not wanting to raise unnecessary attention from workmates about The House of Bruno.

Within twenty-four hours she had purchased a computer and internet connection for her own home. All the while she scanned the pages of The House of Bruno site, she kept hearing Sebastian's words, 'twenty million dollars'. As she went from one page to another, she was stunned at the diversity of the information divulged. But what really took her by surprise was the page: Bruno Formicella. Up Close and Personal.

"Sounds like a good title for a movie doesn't it?" she scoffed.

No detail was spared on the man. Back four generations into the family history. Where he went to school. Even pictures of the schools he attended. Family photographs. His hobbies. Pictures of him racing cars, riding horses, draping his arms around supermodels. Other pictures of being photographed with the famous. His history in business. How he created The House of Bruno. His wife. His children. His garage full of cars... and his Villa. Room by room. Wall by wall. Picture by picture. More out of curiosity than out of interest, Gina decided to take a tour of the Villa.

"How could anyone's ego be that damned big they'd put their bloody bed linen on the net?"

The blurb began:

> *This magnificent Villa, the home of Mr Bruno Formicella and his family, was built around 1790. Although it has been refurbished and rebuilt a number of times, it is interesting to note that today's structure still in fact sits on the original foundations. The Villa is three stories high and boasts some twenty-seven rooms. Mr Formicella, assisted by his highly talented and beautiful wife Antonietta-Serafina, has spent literally millions of dollars turning this magnificent Villa into one of Italy's most prized mansions. Come with us now as we take you on a room by room tour of White Doves, the name chosen by Mr and Mrs Formicella for their magnificent home.*

Gina wanted to laugh and click 'disconnect' but found herself compelled to continue.

Just as the first pictures appeared before her of the sitting room/reception/lounge, her eyes nearly rolled from their sockets. Never before had she ever seen anything so outrageously opulent. She began to giggle in disbelief at the sheer extravagance of super-luxury.

My god! I don't believe this. This is little bloody Bruno's sitting room!

"Shit! *Shit*! You mean there are people who actually *live* like this! Oh, for god's sake! The very graphic images lying before her showed the

Villa nestled among bushland in the hills behind Portofino, its main rooms capturing the view of the port with its moorings of yachts of the world's wealthy.

The blurb continued:

Furniture and accessories of the Villa are selected from the world's finest antiques in Louis XVI, Renaissance and Baroque periods; ornate and elegant. The furniture, accessories and paintings by Australian artists Russell Drysdale (1912--1981) Sidney Nolan (1917–1992) and Emily Kame Kngwarreye (1910–1996) plus those of international artists in Henri Matisse (1852–1919) and nudes of Marthe, wife of Pierre Bonnard (1867–1947), blend so well, they mingle with the antiques without detection. The flora and desert as depicted by Kngwarreye are a particular family favourite. Stay with us now as we take you to the Sitting room/Reception/ Lounge area.

Louis XVI-style gold-lacquered, ornately carved wood surrounds plus salmon-coloured one and two-seater chairs joined to form an arch. The chair backs, for comfort, have circular panels of plush blue and gold velvet studded with gold. The room, which has sand velvet covered walls. is divided into two sections: the formal area and the conversation area. Three gold-lacquered marble-topped coffee tables are scattered around the room. A number of serving trolleys of intricately carved wood with gold inlays create an atmosphere of warmth and friendliness. They sit closely by four gold-lacquered glass cabinets displaying the finest in crystal. The room is lit by a series of twenty-four-piece crystal chandeliers complemented by wall lights of the same design.

The top end of the room is fitted with eight baroque traditional armchairs in lacquered cracquele. The chairs are gold-inlaid wood with hand-painted floral upholstery, hand-woven in blue and beige with gold-threaded worsted wool. They are centred around a marble-topped crystal rectangular table inlaid with gold. The floor is treated with wool carpet — the family emblem etched in gold in the centre of the room

Gina sat shaking her head.

How over-the-top is this?

The screen then took her to the master bedroom. A nine by seven feet wooden bed, canopied in white and pink lacquer inlaid carved lattice and decorated with hand-painted flowers. The canopy, draped in silk...

"This is unbelievable."

Gina went to the next room.

> *The office, as you can see, has two desks and twelve guest chairs of inlaid white lacquer with studded, hand-beaten Italian leather in charcoal grey...*

The descriptions went on and on. Finally she closed her computer down, her head still reeling from what her eyes had witnessed. As she climbed into bed, her mind was racing. All her life she'd dreamed of having a lot of money. Never before had such an opportunity presented itself. Twenty million dollars. She kept hearing the amount over and over. Twenty million dollars. All she had to do was convince someone she knew very well to rip open Bruno's one tonne safe door. Of all the times she and Franco had been together, she never knew what he did. She didn't know how he'd react to a suggestion that he and his brothers carry out a raid on a safe a half a world away.

Twenty million, four ways? That's five each. Yeah! Bet the greedy bastard would want more. But if I came out of it with two... even three, that'd be OK, she consoled herself.

* * *

Gina met with Sebastian McAlister three times over the next four weeks. Each time, she cleverly broached the subject of Bruno Formicella. "Yes, the Italian minister Vincenzo Torricelli had been back in touch."

"Yes, there's no doubt he's into drugs and money-laundering up to his short little neck."

"Yes, police informers say there is no doubt he keeps millions in a safe in his villa."

"Yes, he will be in Milan for two days in September."

Sebastian never suspected a thing. He just took it as Gina being intrigued, if not a little infatuated, by such a larger-than-life character. That was until the last time they met.

They were lying back in each other's arms and Gina was drawing circles around his nipple with her fingernail when rather nonchalantly she asked, "How important is money to you, Sebby?"

"Don't suppose I've ever really thought about it," he told her in an inquisitive tone. "Why the question?"

"Just wondered."

"But you must have had a reason?"

"Sort of. I just imagined everybody thought about money to some degree."

"Well, in that respect, I suppose I do think about it. Like everybody else, I'd be in a fine pickle if I didn't have any."

"Would you like to be rich? Or for that matter, maybe you are already?"

Sebastian laughed. "No I'm certainly not rich. I have a very good income. The house is paid for. I have a few shares here and there. But rich? Good God no! I certainly need that fortnightly ministerial cheque if that's what you mean."

"Let's say for a moment you were rich. I mean seriously rich. What would you do?"

Again Sebastian laughed and spun Gina on top of himself. "I'd whisk you away to the nearest desert island and make love to you ten times a day..." He stopped short when he noticed Gina's mood change. "Will you get to the point," he said sternly.

She levered herself from Sebastian and looked him square in the eye. "Is there anything you wouldn't do for me... for us?"

The question took him by surprise. "I didn't think you'd feel the need to ask that," he told her in a disappointed tone.

Gina didn't flinch, instead she held her gaze. She felt she had Sebastian just where she wanted him. "You know this Formicella character... ?"

Sebastian rolled his eyes. "You mean our little Bruno? Quite fascinated by him, aren't you?"

"Not in the way you think."

"Oh?"

"What I am about to say may totally floor you, offend you or even have you thinking such words are not coming out of my mouth. If they do, say so and I'll drop the subject and never mention it again. That I promise you. But all my life I've wanted to be rich. When you told me about his safe, twenty million dollars and no security, my mind started racing..."

Sebastian sat bolt upright on the bed. "Oh for god's sakes Gina, you're not seriously suggesting... ?"

"Yes I am!" she told him. "By the very breath in me, I am."

"But you're not part of the underworld... at least I don't think you are." Suddenly Sebastian realised just how little he did know about this Sicilian redhead. "You're not, are you?"

Gina chuckled. "Not the last time I looked."

"You're not seriously suggesting a raid on Bruno's safe?"

"That's exactly what I'm suggesting."

"So what are you going to do? Knock on his bloody door and say good morning sir, my name's Gina and I'm here to relieve you of twenty million dollars?"

"Not me specifically, but I do have some people in mind."

"You're crazy! You know that? You're out of your bloody mind!" he told her, making his way into the en-suite and opening the shower.

"So you think I should forget it?"

"I don't believe you should even think along those lines."

"OK... it's forgotten."

But when he turned the shower off this time, Gina wasn't standing by with a towel. After he'd dressed, he walked over to her as she sat gazing out the window. "Come on babe! Don't be angry. What did you expect me to say?"

She turned to him. "Why are we here? Why the fuck are we here? You work 70 hours a week for what you get. You're at the beck and call of every bastard. You'll be old before you know it, and your life will have passed you by pleasing everybody else but yourself.

"You'll collect your super cheque then probably bloody die before you get time to spend it. Do you ever stop to think what you want,

Sebby? What *you* want? Do you? Of course you don't! You just ring when you can, drop by, fill me up, then leave." Gina was in full flight. "I just see an opportunity to make a quick killing. If it's done right, quickly and efficiently, we could walk away with a couple of mill each."

Sebastian looked at her. "I've never seen this side of you before," he told her, almost glumly.

"Does it scare you?"

"Yes, I think it does."

"So we drop it."

Sebastian ignored her comment and began to pace the floor. "Let's say you did decide to do it. Where the hell would you start? Besides, there's no guarantee the money would be there anyway."

"But didn't that Italian minister tell you it would be?"

"Well, over dinner and in other conversations since. But I haven't pressed him on the matter."

"Press him."

"OK. Let's say the money is there..."

"On that weekend in September of the Milan fashion show..."

"OK, in September. How are you going to break into a safe with a door that weighs a tonne... quietly and unnoticed. Steal the so-called twenty million and get away... quietly and again unnoticed?"

"It's possible."

"You don't know that!"

"For twenty million, it's worth the risk of finding out."

Sebastian was getting frustrated. "Gina, for god's sakes, you're looking at Portofino. Hell, I don't even know where Portofino is without looking at a map..."

"Turn left at the top of the leg," she cut in.

"OK, whatever that means. It's eight, maybe ten, thousand kilometres away. You have to get in, do the job and get out. How are you going to do that?"

"Fly"

"Oh, bullshit! What? Just front up to the airline check-in counter and say Please, Mr Qantas man, a return ticket for... how many are going... ?"

"Me and three others."

"Oh, shit! This gets worse! So you want to go too?"

"Yes, in a private plane."

"Oh for fuck's sake, Gina, a private plane?" he said raising his voice and throwing his hands in the air. "You've got it all worked out, haven't you? Did it not occur to you there might be a slight hitch with things like flight plans and reasons for going? How you are going to fund it? Where will you get fuel on the way over and on the way back? Who will fly the plane and where the hell are you going to land it in this country with a pay-load like that?

"And just one other minor detail. Where the hell are you going to get a plane from anyway? Especially one to travel all that way? You'd have to go undetected and that means flying under the bloody radar."

Almost exasperated, Sebastian knelt down beside her. "Forget it babe, just forget it. No good can possibly come of it," he told her. "Besides, that sort of money wouldn't make you happy. You'd be looking over your shoulder all the time. Will you forget it?"

"Will you help me get it?" she replied, her tone determined.

Sebastian sprang to his feet. "I don't believe you. After everything I've said."

"Will you help me, or won't you?"

Gina knew he couldn't refuse her. She also knew that simply by being with her, his entire career and life was down the toilet.

"And if I don't?"

"Then go... and don't come back."

"You don't mean that?"

"See if I don't," she answered bitterly.

He went to her. "Gina, for god's sakes, it's only money..."

"And I don't have any. I just reckon I can pull it off."

"So you're telling me to help you rob a guy of twenty mill or don't come back? Is that all I mean to you?" his tone dropping away as he slumped into an armchair. "I can't do it."

Gina could see she was losing him. She had one last card to play.

"I don't know what your plans are, but mine are to have my own place with two keys. I have one. You have the other. I have a mobile phone and you are the only one with the number. Sebby, I want to grow old with you, even if it's part-time. You are my life. My skin withers and dies without your touch. I only come to life when your heart pounds against my breast. Sebby I only want this for us."

She closed her eyes as guilt raced through her body. She had never known herself to tell such outrageous lies, but this was a situation that called for desperate measures.

Sebastian held her at arm's length. "Tell me you love me!"

"With every breath in my body," she answered.

"Gina, if this leaks, I'm dead. You do realise that, don't you?"

"It will never get out," she promised.

"OK. I will help you, but I don't want any money, all right? No pay-off. The only pay-off I want is you and for those words you just spoke to be the truth, the whole truth and nothing but the truth."

Gina threw her arms around his neck.

"Oh Sebby, thank you. Thank you, my darling, darling man," she gushed.

"So what do you want me to do?" he asked, uneasily.

"Just confirm for me as best you can that Bruno and his family will in fact be in Milan for two days in September. And that safe. Confirm the existence of the safe and that there's always a shitload of money in it."

"But I've already done that," he protested mildly.

"Vincenzo is it?"

"The minister?"

"Yes. Vincenzo... ?"

"Vincenzo Torricelli."

"Talk to him again. Find an excuse. But I just need to know what we already know is full-on." She turned to him with a smile he was never able to resist and breathed, "You want to make me a happy lady again?"

* * *

When Sebastian returned to his own home later that night, he paced the floor, searching his brain for a scenario which he felt the Italian minister would accept. Slowly the bits and pieces came together.

Stepping from the lift the following morning he checked his watch as he made his way to his ministerial office.

Rome is eight hours behind. If I ring Vincenzo at five today, it should be nine o'clock this morning over there. I'll do that.

A full book of ministerial appointments lay ahead for Sebastian McAlister. Before he realised he'd even skipped lunch, he flashed his eyes to the clock on the wall.

Good lord! What happened to today?

He reached for his phone and dialled international. It had hardly rung.

"Pronto."

"Vincenzo? Sebastian McAlister in Sydney."

"Oh, Sebastian, my good friend, how are you?"

The two made small talk for a couple of minutes, then it was the Italian who said, "I could talk to you all day about the soccer my friend, but somehow I don't think that is why you are calling."

"Bruno Formicella," he replied.

"Ah yes, our little friend."

"I might be able to help you nail the little bastard."

"That I find most interesting. Do go on."

"When we last spoke, you mentioned how well connected he was. Do you feel those connections would stretch to Australia?"

"Most certainly. That and other reasons is why I would love to get a look inside his safe. That would tell me exactly what I want to know. But not much chance of that I'm afraid," he said, his voice dropping away to a dejected tone.

"Maybe I can do something from this end."

"Oh?" Vincenzo replied, sparking up.

"What if I approached the Prime Minister for permission to set up a top secret task force, say about six SAS troops and hit that bloody safe when he's away in September?"

"Mama Mia! You can do that?"

"I can try. I feel the hook to get it off the ground is if you firmly believe Bruno has money-laundering and drug connections in this country."

"That is my firm belief, Sebastian. How can I help?"

"I need the best and most accurate information your government can give me on Bruno's whereabouts on that weekend in September, if there'll be any security at the villa and if there will in fact be a stash of dollars if we bust in."

"When do you need to know this?"

"I will see the Prime Minister tomorrow. So if you could call me in a week, then every three weeks leading up to September. We keep in touch daily in the week leading up to the fashion show in Milan."

"Of course, Sebastian," the Italian cried gleefully. "You think we might finally get to nail this little... bastard."

Sebastian laughed. "Keep this to yourself will you. Don't speak to any other minister here about it and be damn careful about any leaks."

"Of course, of course. We'll talk again soon."

Sebastian put the phone down and began to pace the floor of his ministerial office. He convinced himself there was no other way to obtain the information Gina wanted. He began to tremble at the prospect of being found out. His entire life. His entire career. His entire standing in the community. Not to mention his wife and children. The thought of going to prison flashed through his mind. He couldn't stand it.

My god! What have I done? What the hell have I done?

He reached for the phone and was about to push re-dial and call the whole thing off when suddenly he heard Gina's words all over again. 'Oh Sebby, my skin withers and dies without your touch.'

He replaced the phone.

* * *

Gina was over the moon. She had been able to convince Sebastian to provide what information she needed. All she had to do now was sell the story to Franco.

Then suddenly. "Oh, shit! How come I know so much about it?"

You'll think of something, she told herself, wondering already what it would really be like to actually hold a million dollars in her hands.

Chapter 5

Senior Sergeant Ken McLoughlin was travelling slowly down a dirt road when he braked suddenly and swung his vehicle hard to the left, coming to a standstill.

"That's it back there I reckon," he said quietly to himself, craning his neck to see over his shoulder. Then he saw a sign on a gate next to a ramp which read: Katie's Place.

He checked his mirrors, swung his vehicle round and drove across a ramp made from railway tracks. The property was bordered by white fenceposts. A long driveway led down to the house and, as he proceeded, he tried to take in his surrounds. McLoughlin focussed on what appeared to be a myriad of sheds, implements, stables and various other paraphernalia associated with farmyard activities, but it was the house that stopped him. He drove forward a little.

"That's not a home. That's a bloody show-home."

First he took in the white gravel and paved driveway. "That's about half a hectare," he observed. Strategically placed every few metres were Victorian-style street lamps. In the middle was a highly manicured garden featuring Australian natives and a large Italian marble fountain bird bath featuring two exotic fish, mouths wide open, offering an endless stream of water. The massive homestead was built of rust-coloured brick and bluestone, each side of which was shaded with an open verandah. Off to the left was a triple garage and attached to that, what looked like a smaller self-contained home.

He parked in front of a small yard and stable and got out. Over the wooden fence he could see a large chestnut Clydesdale and a newish looking and very big shed. Off to its left, very, very elaborate horse stables. Still trying to come to terms with what he was looking at, a young girl rode towards him on a magnificent white stallion.

"Hello," the girl called from atop the stallion.

"Hi... er, I'm probably lost... but is this where I can find Gabe and Katie Caplin?" McLoughlin asked.

"Sure! That's mum and dad. I'll get mum for you. Come on down."

The young girl turned the stallion's head and cantered off. Moments later, a woman appeared wearing an apron and with her hair tied in a scarf. She was carrying a mixing bowl.

McLoughlin grinned. "Katie?"

"Yes."

"Ken McLoughlin, Ma'am... from the police."

"Oh god, Ken! Yes, *Yes*... oh, I'm sorry... how are you?"

Quickly she knelt down and placed the mixing bowl on the verandah and went to him, her arms outstretched. After they momentarily hugged each other, she said, "Oh Ken, it's wonderful to see you. But look at me! I feel like a wreck. You should have phoned." She turned to the girl. "Emma, ride down the paddock and get your father. Tell him we have a very special visitor."

McLoughlin started to follow Katie inside and stopped. He looked around himself and cast his arm in an outward gesture. "All this, Katie? This is all you two?"

"It's been a lot of work," she answered.

"It's absolutely stunning." Then, "The girl on the horse... your daughter?"

"She was Lorry's little girl. You remember the young woman who worked for me at the club? She was shot by that animal, Slick, or Scarfe, or whatever his name was. Gabe and I decided to adopt her. Actually, there's someone else here you may remember too. Kazumi, our chef. One second." Katie hurried inside the front door. "Kazumi... *Kazumi*," she called.

Moments later the woman from Hong Kong appeared at Katie's side.

"Of course," McLoughlin answered.

"Do you remember Sergeant McLoughlin, Kazumi?"

The woman's face lit up.

"Yes, yes," she gushed. "Sergeant Ken, yes?"

"Close enough," McLoughlin chortled.

"Our Sergeant Ken will be having tea with us tonight Kazumi. Will that be all right?"

Kazumi looked at Katie with the eyes of a child hero-worshipping its idol. "Oh yes, Miss Katie, yes, yes. You Sergeant Ken. You like something special, yes?"

McLoughlin glanced at Katie.

"Don't look at me," she laughed.

McLoughlin felt a little embarrassed. He turned his hands out. "Hell, I'm just happy with a cup of tea and a biscuit," he replied.

Kazumi smiled. "Then you get very special cup of tea and biscuit, yes? Sergeant Ken, Miss Katie. He very special man. He save us all, yes?"

"Now hang on a minute... !" McLoughlin interrupted.

"That's the truth," Katie said. "Without you, none of us would be here."

McLoughlin was most grateful for the sound of an approaching motor vehicle. He turned to see a tractor making good speed towards the homestead. As it approached, Emma was only metres away on her horse when suddenly McLoughlin heard a booming voice over the top of the engine.

"McLoughlin... Jesus Christ! Is that really you? Bloody McLoughlin!"

Gabe bounced off the tractor and raced over to McLoughlin, grabbing him in a massive bear-hug. The vigour of the greeting took McLoughlin completely by surprise. Letting him go, he thrust out his hand. "Oh mate, Jesus, what a bloody thrill it is to see you."

"G'day Gabe," McLoughlin answered. "Been a while hasn't it? Who's this bloke?" he asked, referring to the dog standing by Gabe's side.

"Maaate. Me pride and joy. Say g'day to Ken, old son," he said, stroking his head. "This is Joker. Bit long in the tooth now, but he's still a good dog. Hey, but what about you? It's been seven years, mate... and we've got you to thank for every single one of them, haven't we boy?" he said, still stroking Joker's head.

"No, Gabe come on..."

"No, you come on! If you hadn't fired that shot... !"

"Yes, but it was you who got the both of you out of there," McLoughlin protested.

"Mate, he was about to blow me brains out. Then he'd have got Katie as well. As it was, he bloody near did anyway." He looked squarely into McLoughlin's eyes. "Not a day goes by, I kid you not, without you crossing my mind."

McLoughlin shook his head in disbelief.

"Might have been another day at the office for someone like you, but not for us." Gabe felt into his pocket and threw an object at McLoughlin. "Remember this?"

McLoughlin caught the object and looked at it. It was the shell of the round he had fired which had taken out the shoulder and gun arm of Slick Bennedict. It was the .416 Remington Magnum. The elephant gun.

"Well I'll be buggered!"

"Carry it in me pocket every day," Gabe told him. "Don't I, Katie?"

She nodded in agreement. "That he does, Ken, that he does."

"Anyway, enough of that. How the hell are you?" Gabe went on.

"Oh, you know. The good guys we let go. The bad guys? Some we catch. Some we don't. But what about you two? Hell, I don't believe all this. Take me through the last seven years."

"You staying for tea?"

"Kazumi's already seen to that," Katie smiled.

"Fantastic. Come in mate, come in and have a... what do you want?... a beer? a coke?... cup of tea, coffee?"

"I'm easy."

"Bugger it, we'll have a beer. Don't normally drink in the middle of the day, but I reckon now you're here, might call it a day. Emma, put the tractor in the shed for dad will you please, then come back here and sit with us." He turned back to McLoughlin. "Jesus, it's good to see you. You ever get married? I seem to recall you were single back then."

"Gabe!" Katie scolded.

"Well a man's gotta know these things."

McLoughlin shook his head. "Not for me I guess, Gabe. And you two?"

"Coming up six and a half years next month and just look at her, Ken. Jesus, I get all choked up just watching her..."

"Oh Gabe, stop it," Katie blushed.

Gabe held out one big arm and Katie went to him. As she sat on his lap, a tear rolled down his cheek. "Mate, what this woman has done for me and other folks round here, you couldn't put a value on. She built this place. Took in Emma and Kazumi. Mrs Cropp. You met her yet?" his voice lifting.

McLoughlin shook his head.

"Oh Christ, you gotta meet Aunty Betsy..."

"I'll go and get her," Katie said, already halfway to the door.

"She's still absolutely stunning, Gabe," McLoughlin said of Katie as she left the room.

"Mate, I get a lump in me throat just looking at her."

"You're a very lucky man."

Gabe turned as he heard a door open. "Hello, baby girl," he said softly, "Look who's come to see us."

McLoughlin looked curiously at the little girl in the doorway wiping sleep from her eyes.

Gabe noticed McLoughlin's inquiring look. "You don't know about her?"

He shook his head.

"Come here, baby... this is Natasha Jane... you tell the man you'll be five next month, won't you sweetheart?"

"I don't think I've ever seen a prettier child," McLoughlin said, as he watched the little girl climb onto her father's lap.

"Yeah, well she's our pride and joy. I never thought I would ever have a child. Katie said, 'Let's go for it', so we did. Hell of an imposition to put on a man wasn't it?" he announced, gleaming with pride.

Both men looked towards the kitchen door as they heard the sound of approaching voices. Gabe stood Natasha up and rose to his feet. "Aunty Betsy, have we got someone special for you to meet!"

McLoughlin lifted himself out of his chair and watched a very aged woman enter the kitchen. *She'd have to be pushing ninety*, he thought.

Katie, with her arm through the old lady's to lend her support, took over.

"Aunty Betsy, this is Mr McLoughlin, the policeman who saved our lives at the club that time... Ken, this is Mrs Cropp."

He stepped forward and held out his hand.

Mrs Cropp never took her eyes off him. She grasped his hand firmly and put the other up to his face. "Thank you," she said gently. "Thank you for saving the two most precious things I have in my life."

"I'm just ever so pleased it's all worked out for them," he answered.

"Have you got the man a drink, Gabe?" Mrs Cropp added firmly.

"Oh shit!" he exclaimed. "Bloody forgot all about it," he answered, hurrying off to the refrigerator.

"You'll have noticed that my boy hasn't cleaned his language up, Mr McLoughlin..."

"Ken, ma'am."

"Oh, all right, Ken it is."

Gabe put some cans of beer on the table and sat down. When he looked up, Mrs Cropp was glaring at him. "What the hell have I done now?" he squawked.

"Nothing for the girls?" she asked.

"Oh Jesus! Grab the cordial for Aunty and your mother, will you Emma!"

"I don't want *cordial...* and neither does your wife! Emma! The sherry darling, It's on the sideboard in the lounge."

Katie poured the drinks and a great deal of small talk followed. Finally Katie, seeing McLoughlin might be a little confused with the chopping and changing of subjects, looked at Gabe. "Darling, I think we should go back to the last time we saw Ken and give him the sequence of events."

"Yeah, fair enough," Gabe chuckled. "OK. After Oakdale, it took a while for Katie to get better. While she was recuperating, I asked her to marry me and, god bless her little cotton socks, she said yes. The wedding was in Naracoorte six months later. For a wedding present, Aunty Betsy gave us her farm. Aunty Betsy in effect brought me up. My mother died when I was young. A bit later, the old man. So it was pretty much Aunty Betsy I turned to. I never went off the place for years. Then, of course, Katie went arse-up near where you turned in. I pulled her out of the wreck. She survived OK... and all that came about after she tragically lost the man in her life in a plane smash. His name was Paul Redman. He owned the Oakdale Country Club in Mildura. He left it to her in his will. Then came that stalking crap with that mongrel and Lorry Downs. After the showdown, Katie and I decided to adopt Emma plus still keep a home for Kazumi. Then, out of the blue, Natasha came along, and here we are.

"At first Katie wanted to rebuild the club but, as time went on, her heart went out of it so, despite great protests from me, she decided to put a lot of the insurance money into this place. The little complex on the end of the triple garage is where Aunty Betsy lives. That great big chestnut-coloured bag of bones in her stable is her pet Clydesdale. She calls him Stanley and I reckon by now he'd be pushing twenty-four or 25. Poor old bastard. I've got the glue makers coming out to have a look at him next week."

"Dad, you have *not*!" Emma protested loudly.

"Gabe!" Katie scolded.

"It's all right dear. God will get him for that," the old lady smiled.

With a big grin on his face, Gabe went on. "Kazumi has her own unit at the rear. Emma took a bit of shine to Andalusians, so Katie took her off to Austria last year and came home with two stallions and four mares. She seems to think she wants to make them her life, so we'll see. She bloody better! After writing out the cheque for that little lot, we nearly all had a haemorrhage. So there you go. Katie asked me one day, in an off-handed sort of way, what sort of house I would like, so I said one of those great big rambling homesteads. Christ, I was only jokin'! That little joint next door is where I lived all my life. I was quite happy to stay there. Next thing I know, in roll the semis and up goes this place." He raised his glass. "But without you, mate, none of this would have been possible. So from all of us... thank you. Thank you very much."

Everyone raised their glass and more chatter took place.

Gabe then eased himself out of his chair. "Come on Ken, Katie and I will show you round the place. You want to come Aunty Betsy?"

"Oh, I think I've seen it all before. I might just make my exit if that's all right with everyone..."

The three of them headed outside and watched as Emma cantered off on her stallion. "Any problems?" McLoughlin asked of the girl.

"By gee, at first," Katie began, "we didn't know what we were in for. She'd been brutalised beyond human comprehension..."

"Her hands wasn't it?" McLoughlin put in.

"Yeah! That bastard Bennedict pressed them onto a hot plate," Gabe told him, his face and neck flushing in anger at the thought.

"But we've been very lucky in that regard," continued Katie. "We found a very clever plastic surgeon and over a period of years, he was able to restore them almost to what they were. She's come through it OK. At first we were fearful she may not be able to control the reins of a horse, but she manages just fine. When we first got her home with us... goodness me, we copped the lot. She had nightmares over what that guy did to her mother. But slowly, slowly, we both gave her more love than she knew what to do with. So did Kazumi. And Aunty Betsy. By gee, that grand old lady is a rock." She sighed. "Don't know what this place will be like when she goes. But she really took to Emma... and Emma to her. But the big thing was in getting her to call us mum and dad."

Gabe continued. "We went to this professional, that professional. All had their own text-book ideas until, finally, Katie said, why don't we just ask the child? Leave it up to her to decide."

Katie took over. "So we all sat round the kitchen table. She would have been about six then and we simply asked the question. She never hesitated. Well you could've knocked us over with a feather. And it's been mum and dad ever since. Simple as that."

"Incredible," McLoughlin commented.

As they continued to walk, McLoughlin was revelling in the country air and the laid-back approach to things. He enjoyed seeing all the farm machinery, the sheds, the chooks, the sheep, the cattle, the cats, the dogs, the prized Andalusians.

"And this is Stanley," Katie said, reaching through the railing of the Clydesdale's fence to stroke his nose.

"Bit of a toss up who'll go first," Gabe said. "Somehow I don't reckon one will be far behind the other."

McLoughlin laughed lightly. "What's that?" he asked, aiming his eyeline at the massive structure he recalled on the drive in.

"That's the shearing shed. Put the bugger up last year. Four stand. Ever been in one?"

McLoughlin shook his head.

"Then it's about bloody time you were given an education."

For the next few minutes McLoughlin was taken through the basics in combs and cutters, catching pens, wool tables, wool packs, the wool press, grinders, the hand piece, branding stencils and holding yards.

"It's certainly a long way from murders, kidnaps and sieges," he commented.

"Just on that," Gabe went on, "what brings you down this way?"

"Oh, just on my way to Robe for a bit of fishing for a few days, then I have to collect my partner in Mildura and head off to Sydney."

"Big job?" Katie asked.

McLoughlin nodded. "Real big."

"What... a gang, a murder... or can't you say?" Gabe asked.

"Yes I can say... sort of. It's really the pursuit of one man."

"Sort of like a Bennedict?"

"Different scenario. But a bad bugger, nonetheless."

"Why do you do it?" Katie asked him.

"Someone has to, I guess," he told her.

"Are we to take it you've been summoned?" asked Gabe.

McLoughlin just smiled his reply.

"You are obviously very good at what you do, Sergeant McLoughlin," Katie added.

"We both know the answer to that don't we sweetheart? And I'd say on that note, that's about all the good Sergeant has to say on the matter... am I right Sergeant?"

McLoughlin just shrugged.

"Can you come and see us again?" Katie urged.

He stopped in his stride. "You two will never know what a thrill it's been for me to be here today. Your graciousness. Your hospitality. Hell, you don't know me and yet you've taken me in as one of the family..."

"Don't you understand, Ken," Katie pleaded, "you saved our lives. Of course we're going to take you in as family. You didn't know us either when you fired that shot..."

"That was the job..."

"Bullshit!" Gabe said. "That was beyond the job. You didn't have to call for the elephant gun! And I'll just bet the shit hit the fan over that little lot. You probably won't tell us. Well that's fine. But we want you to know that as far as we're concerned, we are forever indebted to you..."

* * *

Unbeknown to McLoughlin, Katie had Kazumi make up one of the guest rooms that evening.

"Sergeant Ken. He staying tonight. Yes?"

Katie told her he would be, then took a second glance at this woman from Hong Kong. She noticed a particular glint in her eye. "Oh, really, Kazumi? He's single, too!"

"I not know what you mean," she giggled.

"You know what I mean, all right."

Kazumi was about to walk away when Katie called her back. "There'll also be an extra guest at dinner tonight," she told her.

"Yes, yes, Mrs Cropp. She come. I know. OK. OK."

"No. Other than Mrs Cropp."

"Oh?"

"You, Kazumi. You will join us at dinner tonight. I think I might just put you right next to Sergeant Ken... yes?"

"Oh no, Miss Katie... who get dinner then?"

"I think you'll be able to manage," she told her.

"You bad girl, Miss Katie."

"Now remember. No men in your room after midnight."

"Oh, Miss Katie!"

Katie walked away laughing to herself. She found the two men sharing another cold beer and found an excuse to call her husband aside. "I'll tell Ken in a minute that we'd like him to stay tonigh. Is that all right?"

"Yeah, Jesus Christ, the bugger can live here for all I care."

Gabe and Katie went back to join Ken McLoughlin.

"We've just taken a vote. You're staying the night," Gabe said.

"No, no, I can't do that..." McLoughlin began to protest.

"Where were you going to stay?"

"Hell, I don't know. A motel in town. I didn't come here to impose. I just dropped in for a cup of tea..."

"Too late," Katie said. "I've already told Kazumi to make up one of the guest rooms. Now please excuse me while I go and clean up a little. You coming Gabe?"

Ken McLoughlin wandered outside and over to the stables where Emma was grooming one of the Andalusians. He put a foot up on a rail. "Has he got a name?"

"This one's Samson because he's the stronger of the two. The other one is Prince because I reckon he looks a bit royal. And the mares are Queeny, Gypsy. She's funny because she likes to just wander off. Mum's favourite is that one over there," she added, pointing to a particular Andalusian. "So we call her Katie. And the last one is Betsy, after Aunty Betsy. Aunty Betsy's father used to have a team of Clydesdales, and two were called Queen and Gypsy. Aren't they beautiful?"

He nodded. "Do you have a favourite?"

"I love them all, but I do have a soft spot for this one. You watch." Emma turned to face the stallion. "Come on now, go down for me... down... down... down... come on... down."

McLoughlin's jaw dropped as the magnificent stallion dropped to its knees and Emma climbed onto his back. He clapped. "Fantastic... I love it."

"Aunty Betsy said she used to get Stanley to do that for her, so she taught me to do it."

"You're a very lucky girl, aren't you?"

"Would you like to get on?"

McLoughlin laughed. "Hell Emma, I'd fall straight off the other side."

"No you won't. Come on."

She slid off the horse's back. "Up boy... come on... up now."

Immediately Samson stood up.

McLoughlin climbed through the railing. Emma turned again to face her horse. She gently rubbed his nose.

"OK... can we do it again? Will you let this man climb onto your back? Of course you will. Good boy! Come on boy... down... down... down... come on... down. And again Samson dropped to his knees.

Very tentatively, McLoughlin approached the two. Even more tentatively, he put a leg across the animal's back then sat down.

"Up boy... come on... up boy."

McLoughlin grabbed a handful of mane as he felt the horse get back to a standing position.

"Isn't he wonderful?"

"Hell, I could get used to this," he said, patting Samson's neck.

"Do you like him?"

"Takes your breath away, doesn't he?"

"Oh, I just love them to death. Can't wait to get some foals."

The chit-chat between the two continued until they finally made their way back to the house together. As he walked inside, Kazumi walked over to him. "Miss Katie, she say for me to join you for dinner. You not mind, yes?"

"I will be absolutely delighted," he told her.

"Thank you, Sergeant Ken. Dinner be in thirty minutes. I see you then. I also make up your bed in guest room. Miss Katie, she say you stay tonight."

McLoughlin smiled as he watched her walk away. *By hell she's a stunner. Bit hard to tell how old she'd be. Probably round the 30 mark. Maybe 32. Yes*, he told himself, *dinner could be interesting.*

* * *

McLoughlin had his head in a newspaper when he heard Katie's voice.

"If you'd care to take a seat, sir," she jested.

He looked up and actually fell back into his chair.

Katie stood before him, her long, blonde hair falling casually around her neckline, slightly touching her evening gown and partly obscuring her necklace; a twisted rope of Baroque pearls. McLoughlin was fairly impressed with the necklace and matching bracelet, but it was the gown Katie wore that totally blew him away. It was a full length, body-hugging Dolce & Gabbana crocheted dress with slip. He had never been to a fashion parade, but he knew that nothing he could ever witness anywhere else in the world could possibly top the way this woman looked at this moment.

Next instant, Gabe came bounding into the loungeroom wearing a dinner suit and stopped dead in his tracks.

"Lift your chin off your chest, dear," Katie told him. "Do you like it?" she asked as she spun around in front of him.

"What did I tell you, Ken? Puts a bloody lump in your throat doesn't she?"

"Hold the bus, folks!" McLoughlin piped up. "I can hardly sit round here looking like a bushranger with you lot dressed like you were going to the Ritz. Let me change my shirt."

Moments later he returned, just as Mrs Cropp walked into the room. The old lady, like the two men, was visually swept away at Katie's beauty.

Moments later, Kazumi made her entrance in a near-full-length Perri Cutten red chantilly lace dress, complete with Cosgrove Beasley evening bag, a Joyce velvet flower in her hair, Bettina Liano velvet mules with a Peter Lang choker.

"Kazumi, that is simply gorgeous," Katie gushed. "Where did you get it?"

"I got mail order Miss Katie. Save up for long time. But when I see, I had to have. You like, yes?"

"Didn't know I had such a house full of glamorous women," Gabe said proudly.

Kazumi wanted to look at McLoughlin, but shyness overcame her.

He took the initiative, walking over to the dining table and pouring champagne from an already uncorked bottle into six flutes. He filled five, pouring just a little into the sixth.

"Emma," he called."Emma, your presence is required."

As she approached, McLoughlin handed her a flute.

Immediately she flashed her eyes to her mother.

"Just a taste, all right?"

Emma smiled with glee.

After handing out the other four flutes, he raised his own and said, "To the two... no the four," he corrected himself, glancing at Emma and Mrs Cropp, "most beautiful women in the world."

"Jesus, I'll drink to that," barked Gabe. "Now let's eat. I'm bloody starving."

"First course, yes? You come, Yes? Now. Yes?" Kazumi said to them all, then placed her hand through Katie's arm and led her to the dining table.

"Now, it seems to me there's one spare seat. That's the seat next to Sergeant Ken, yes? Kazumi, it looks like that's where you're sitting."

McLoughlin drew back Kazumi's chair.

"Thank you Mr... er... Sergeant Ken... thank you."

Talk throughout the evening was brisk and lively. Kazumi was up and down all the time serving the meal and clearing the plates, despite Katie's protests. But there was no doubting both Kazumi and McLoughlin enjoyed the match-making efforts of Katie Caplin. Their eyes met on various occasions and both felt the magnetism. It was after two a.m. before the last of the wine was drunk. Mrs Cropp had long departed, as had Emma. Over a delightful Penfolds Grandfather Port, Kazumi, now a little more brave, asked Ken McLoughlin, "When you finish current assignment, you come back again, yes?"

"He'd bloody better," Gabe chipped in.

"I think that would be very nice... but on one condition."

"One condition?"

"You let me cook dinner for you."

"Oh no, Sergeant Ken, you not use my kitchen."

"Why not?"

"You mess up."

"I won't make a mess. If I do, I'll clean it up."

Kazumi looked at Katie.

"Don't look at me. You fight your own battles."

"You want to cook for me, yes?"

"That's fair. You cooked for me."

"If I say no, you not come back then, no?"

"That's right."

"Then I say you can cook for me," she replied as she burst out laughing.

"Well thank Christ that's settled," said Gabe. "Bedtime, I reckon."

Katie rose from the table with Gabe. "We'll see you two in the morning," she said.

Then it was just Kazumi and Ken McLoughlin.

Neither spoke for a few moments. But the attraction each felt for the other was mutual. McLoughlin leaned over and ran his index finger down her forearm. When she didn't pull away, he gently took hold of the middle finger on her left hand. She turned her head towards him, but didn't raise her eyes.

"You look positively beautiful tonight," he half-whispered.

A slight smile fell across her face. McLoughlin stood up from his chair and enticed her into his arms. For a few moments they stood together, Kazumi resting her head against his chest. He couldn't believe how wonderful it felt to hold her.

Kazumi felt her heartbeat quicken. She knew she should probably pull away. But she couldn't. McLoughlin raised his hand under her chin and tilted her head back then leaned down and gently kissed her lips.

Again she didn't pull away. But he could tell Kazumi was no push-over. And it pleased him. He withdrew from her, softly touching her cheek. "Thank you for a wonderful meal and an even more wonderful evening. I'll see you in the morning."

* * *

It wasn't until in late morning the day after he'd arrived that Ken McLoughlin was finally able to continue his journey to Robe. He said goodbye to everyone with a hug and a thank you, but when he began to drive off Kazumi could contain herself no longer. Quickly she ran to him. McLoughlin braked.

"You special man, Sergeant Ken. You come back and see me... and everyone? Cook for me maybe, yes?"

"I promise. Keep the fires burning," he told her, cupping her delicate face in the palm of his hand.

"Oh they burn, Sergeant Ken. They burn already and you not gone yet."

Emma rode Samson alongside McLoughlin all the way to the ramp.

He pulled up and looked at her. "You look after everybody now, OK?" he told her.

But Emma couldn't hold back. "You just promise you'll be back, all right?"

Chapter 6

George Hanks was the News Director of RTN ELEVEN, Sydney's only free-to-air, twenty-four-hour, All-News television station.

A veteran of 30 years on the job, cutting his teeth as a cadet reporter in newspapers before moving to radio, then to television. As a journalist, George had pretty much done it all. The war zones, the tears, the tragedy, the heartbreak. The burning buildings, the sieges, the murders, the kidnaps, the rapes, the homeless, the underprivileged, and the celebrities.

He had also covered politics at length, consumer affairs and environment. During his career he had been shocked, reduced to tears and subjected to the back-stabbing environment of the media. He also prided himself in being his own man. He didn't take crap from anyone and was very quick to see through the façade of reporters who were only in the job to satisfy their own egos. And he knew a truckload of them. On his staff were 72 reporters, cameramen, sound technicians, writers, producers, and directors. And he knew only too well that balancing so many egos across a day was pretty much a fulltime job in itself.

When it came to hiring and firing, he almost had carte blanche. Almost. Even RTN ELEVEN had its sacred cows.

His close friend, associate and Chief of Staff was Jack Rider, a man of roughly the same age and experience. Both had been married and divorced twice. Each had been the other's best man. Both had children from both marriages. Both lived de facto. Both also had mistresses. The two were hocked up to the hilt. Both were paying maintenance, mortgages on houses they no longer lived in and school fees. And both wished they had rich uncles who would die and leave them a fortune.

"No bloody fun pushing 50 is it, George?" Jack would say in jest.

"Yeah, well we're not there yet, are we?" he'd answer.

This particular day the two decided to slip away quietly for a catch-up lunch. Something they always liked to do in their almost parallel careers, although in previous years it had been much easier to accomplish.

With the pressure of constant deadlines and no letup from a twenty-four-hour operation, stealing an hour or two became increasingly difficult. They chose their usual quiet, out-of-the-way Chinese restaurant in the suburb of Glebe. Both liked king prawns and fried rice, sweet and sour, and honey chicken washed down with a couple of cold beers.

"So," Jack began, "no bloody picnic is it?" He was referring to the grind of turning out a product every hour of every day.

George knew it. "Got its use-by date, I reckon," he replied, opening the first of two beers to arrive.

"Any shit from upstairs?"

Again, George knew Jack was referring to the pressures applied by management. "Mate, you get 'em a 15-share and they want 18. Get 'em a 10, they want a 12. You know how it works."

"So what's this, the fifth year?"

"Next month."

"You get renewed?"

"Yeah, we both did. Yesterday. Another two years. Sorry, I meant to ring you last night. You got five per cent. I got eight. Bloody big of 'em isn't it?" he said, almost apologetically.

"That's crap, George! Christ those presenters are on a shitload. Not to mention some of those useless dickhead reporters you've hired."

George Hanks laughed. "Yeah, but Jack, they don't have two-year contracts!" he chirped as though achieving such was a major victory.

The truth being that to achieve any sort of media contract was indeed a very major victory. And anything over one year was a bonus. Media owners hate the thought of having to pay out contracts.

"The presenters are on a week," he went on. "The journos are on four weeks. There's no bloody awards in there, Jack. If the readers drop the numbers, they're out on their ear, there and then. The journos get a bit more latitude. They get the 'three strikes and you're out' bit."

An attractive young woman approached the two.

"Same as usual, love," George told her. "Can you remember? It's been a while?"

She smiled graciously. "I remember, sir. Are you both well?"

"Yeah, good, love," George told her.

"Got a question for you," Jack said, sipping his beer.

"Yeah, righto... who?" he smirked knowingly.

"Georgette fucking McKinley!"

He laughed. "What about her?"

"What's the go?"

"You fancy her?"

"Piss off! Not even with yours."

"Every other bastard does."

"Mate, she's so far up herself, she can't even breathe. How come you hired her? Christ, she invented solipsism!"

"Some things I can change. Some things I can't. She's one I can't. But you have to admit, she gets results. Jesus, I don't know how she does it. Must have a bloody good snitch. But she's sacred territory."

"Bullshit!"

"True story."

"How come?"

"Mahogany Avenue."

"Oh shit! Who's fixing her up?"

"Buggered if I know, but she's an untouchable. No weekend rosters. No early shifts. No overnight shifts. No late shifts. A straight deal. Office hours. Monday to Friday, daytime. Unbelievable isn't it?"

"You're kidding!"

"I've got a couple of sacred cows. You know who they are. But she's the most sacred of all."

"But she's a total bitch!"

"Tell me about it!"

"So who picks her stories?"

"You're the Chief of Staff. That's your job."

Jack laughed. "Mate, I'll put her name on the board next to a story I want her to do and she just walks in and says, 'I'm not doing that. Swap me with Jamie or Christine or whoever.'

"And do you?"

"I do now."

"How come?"

"Got a bloody phone call didn't I!"

George looked at Jack with a inquiring look. "Really?"

"Shit!... ages ago. The old man's two-I-C. Ricketts."

'The old man' Jack was referring to was the owner of the station, Sylvester Monkhouse.

"What did he say?"

"You don't know?"

George laughed. "How the hell would I know?" he answered, leaning back in his chair.

"Too long ago... er, Ricketts came on the line. 'Oh Jack, Tom Ricketts. Bit of a problem with Georgette?' The prick totally threw me. 'Not that I know of,' I said and he goes on to say management saw her as special, and when she was hired it was on the condition she could choose her own stories. Obviously George hasn't mentioned that to you? I said you hadn't and then he says, 'I don't see this as a problem Jack, do you?', then he hung up. Well, fuck me! What's the line? If you've got that special thing, then you're flying without wings. Well, she's bloody flying all right... right over the top of every bastard."

George sat there smiling. "Great business this, isn't it?"

Jack threw his hands in the air in despair. "So who's slipping her a length?"

George pondered the question for a moment before answering. "Actually, I don't reckon anyone is."

"Crap!... has to be. Barry's been trying to give her a quick shot for months. Greg's just waiting for her to bend over. But I suppose the only place they're saying, 'while you're down there... ' is around the corner."

"I reckon you're wrong."

"No way!"

"She's had a pretty tragic life you know?"

"In what way?"

"Lost her entire family in a house fire when she was a kid. Raised in foster homes. Doesn't really have anyone in the world. Apart from a rich uncle who only in later years acknowledged her existence. He's her mother's brother. Those two hated each other's guts. To the extent that even when the kid was orphaned, he didn't want to know. So she pretty much had to bring herself up. But like you say, she's a bitch of a thing."

"Who's the uncle?"

"Ever hear of a horse Rogan Star?"

"I don't follow the races, you know that."

"Rogan Star won the third at Rosehill last Saturday."

"So?"

"If you have a look at the fine print, you'll see it's owned by McKinley and Monkhouse. I checked it out. McKinley is McKinley Rubber and Monkhouse is the old man. Georgette is McKinley's niece and both McKinley and Monkhouse have been in bed together for years. They own twelve racehorses between them. The old man owns a bit of McKinley Rubber. McKinley owns a bit of RTN.

"Between them they've got time-share apartments on the Gold Coast, big dollars in a cinema chain in Melbourne, and on and on. I reckon you'll find that McKinley put the word on the old man, and it was just a case of one corporate mate doing another corporate mate a favour. Apparently one of them saved the other's life during the war. Don't know who saved who, but they've been fairly inseparable since. So I've been told."

Jack was quite taken aback. "Shit! That explains a few things doesn't it?"

"Don't let it worry you. Happens all the time. It used to really get up my nose. How do you reckon Kimberly got her job?"

Jack's eyes opened wider.

"She went down on bloody Ricketts!"

Jack really cracked up. He had to suppress his belly-laugh to avoid the looks of other patrons in the restaurant. "I always said she didn't get lips like that sucking ice blocks."

"So you just let it ride over you. Georgette is typical, mate. Too damn pretty for her own good and totally cynical. Maybe that's what happens to you if you've never experienced parental love. But everything to her is a lot of shit. Everything is just passé. Nothing surprises. Been there, done that. Jesus, I don't think you'd warm her up if you put her in the oven. She's cold, calculating and totally materialistic. Dresses in

Armani and swears more than anyone I've ever met. And I've met a few."

Jack chipped in. "Mate... every second word is fuck. Fuck this. Fuck that. Get a fucking life. Jesus, she should've been a bloke!"

"Yeah. But she's typical of female journos in newsrooms. Not all, but most of 'em try and mix it in a man's world. Fuck is just the language of currency. They reckon the more they say it, the better they're accepted. They get off on head jobs, wet dicks and who's screwing who. And the more vulgar the subject, the better they like it. Sometimes when I'm in the office and they don't know I'm there, you should hear three or four of them together over the coffee machine.

"Forget the stories of the day. It's just fuck this, fuck that, fuck everything. My God, if only a very naïve public knew what some of them were really like." George laughed as he drank from his beer glass. "Amazing little word isn't it? Seems to fit every occasion. Blokes use it a lot, but I find a lot of women live by it. But don't sell our little Georgette short. I've seen her out and butter wouldn't melt in her mouth. Mate, when she dresses, you could take her to Buckingham Palace..."

"As long as she kept her mouth shut."

"Too right, but she's off limits. Just let her go. Upset her and you'll upset the old man. He'll get into Ricketts and then he'll ring you. If push comes to shove, you won't win. You know that."

The meals arrived and silence fell between them as Jack attempted to absorb what George had told him. The two men enjoyed their meal, which they interrupted from time to time with various industry gossip. But George could see that his good mate was still bothered.

"Forget about Georgette, Jack."

"It's not that. She came to me today and asked for a film crew to go to Port Macquarie on the weekend."

"What's on up there?"

"Say she wants to try and grab an interview with Bill Murphy."

"Jesus, we used to work together. Bloody good journo, Bill. But of course he's moved on. Big star now. She won't get him. He's almost a recluse. Be good if she could, though. You read his books?"

Jack shook his head.

"Actually, I don't think he's spoken to anyone in the media since the readers of the world started to beat a path to his door. Let her go, Jack. Just remember when you put in the expenses sheet, put her name next to the trip. You won't hear anymore about it."

* * *

Georgette McKinley slipped out of her imported silk dressing-gown, flicked the switch at her bedside and climbed in between the satin sheets of her king-size bed. She felt good. It had been a tough day. Deadlines to meet in the cut and thrust of a big city television newsroom with an ever-present awareness to watch your back and guard your territory. And Georgette's territory had been hard won. She knew only too well the price she had had to pay to achieve her status.

Her uncle may have made the phone call, but there was no way she wanted to start at the bottom. She only hoped gravity wouldn't prematurely take effect and destroy what it was men wanted. And what men wanted was her. Twenty-five years of age, shoulder-length blonde hair, hazel eyes, full lips and a face which offered the qualities of mystery with alluring beauty. She had learned to carry herself with confidence.

In order to keep her figure, she attended fitness classes five days a week and pounded herself to near exhaustion on treadmills, pushbikes and rowing machines. She kept workmates at a distance. Her private life was very private. For most, what she did away from the television newsroom was very much a no-go zone. Georgette wanted another ten years on the big salary.

She felt if she played her cards right, this would enable her to be freehold and provide a nest egg, (*I'm probably not even in my uncle's will*), and give her the freedom to pursue an alternative career.

"Women don't last long on prime time TV past 36, unless you're Barbara Walters, and there's not many of them," she'd tell herself.

And she knew that in maintaining a key role in a newsroom with 71 other over-ambitious egos, she'd have to play the power game... and she'd have to play it better than anybody else. Especially when it came to breaking the big stories.

If you get the scoops, you get the power and you stay in the big league.

It's what drove her constantly. Georgette McKinley knew her colleagues would shake their heads in dismay at her revelations. There'd be office jealousies, especially when she continually came up with the big stories. She knew there'd be the gossip and innuendo. She was also aware of the price she paid for her place at RTN ELEVEN. But she put it out of her mind. She had the body. She had the looks.

So what the hell? It was all over in a few seconds.

Momentarily, 'the price' flashed through her mind...

Tom Ricketts was the all-powerful program manager at RTN ELEVEN. Hand picked for the job by Sylvester Monkhouse because of his astute brain in picking talent and for his years of absolute and total loyalty. Tom Ricketts was every media owner's dream. The company came first, last and everything in between. Long live the company. He was a balding, plump man with stubby fingers and a ruddy complexion. In his late forties, he smoked two packs of cigarettes a day and revelled in the almost daily routines of three-hour lunches with industry colleagues. Secretly, he feared the rapidly advancing revolution of change and rumoured takeovers. But he considered he had about five years before the advent of youth, technology and 'suits' began to call the shots. Time enough to collate the zeroes on his annual salary and prepare to be out-sourced. But, right now, he was king in his domain and he protected his patch through thick and thin. Any executive who looked like getting too smart or too close was quickly removed. And one thing you didn't do to Tom Ricketts was walk in to his office, unannounced. Especially if you were 'unknown'. Georgette McKinley took a gamble. She knocked and simply walked in.

Tom Ricketts looked up. "Can I help you?" he asked, rather bemused that someone would have the gall to do just that.

"Oh, er, hello. I'm Georgette McKinley... are you Mr Ricketts?"

"Yes. Do you have an appointment?"

"No..."

"Where the hell's my secretary?" he bellowed. "Did you check with my secretary?"

"There wasn't anyone there."

Georgette knew there wouldn't be. She had waited in the corridor until the coast was clear so she could make her move.

"Oh, Christ! What is it, young lady?' annoyed that his space had been invaded.

"I thought you may have been expecting me?"

"What's your name again?"

"Georgette McKinley. Mr Monkhouse should've spoken to you about me."

Suddenly it dawned on him. Immediately his demeanour changed. "Oh, shit! Sorry, ma'am." Ricketts rose quickly from his desk and held out his hand to the young woman. As he looked at the stunning young woman he was suddenly aroused. Beads of perspiration formed on his forehead. "So you want to work in our newsroom?"

"Yes, I do."

"Well the role of hiring and firing in that area really falls within the domain of George Hanks, the News Director. But in your case, I gave Mr Monkhouse my assurance that I'd take care of you personally."

"Thank you."

"How badly do you want the job?" he asked leeringly.

Georgette was quick to spot his intentions and played along with him, not thinking it would lead to anything. "Bad enough to do whatever it is I have to do to avoid going in as a shit-kicker, but rather as a senior reporter," she told him.

"I'm told you've only had five years' experience. You mightn't cut it in the big league..."

"Let me worry about that!"

"You're very confident aren't you?"

"I know I can be damn good, Mr Ricketts. I just need the chance."

Ricketts sensed her vulnerability. He moved in closely to her and ran his hand down her cheek. She wanted to cringe as just the sight of him revolted her. But she smiled wantonly.

His hand moved to her breast. Georgette froze, but tried to disguise it. Again, she smiled. Coldly. "Mr Ricketts!..."

"Call me Tom."

"What if someone walks in?"

He walked over and turned the key in his door. "They won't," he told her.

Shit! the bastard's serious. Now what?

Georgette knew she was past the point of no return.

An excited leer fell across the program manager's face. "So you really want to work here?"

"Wh... what do you want me to do?" she asked, almost rigid with fear.

Tom Ricketts took hold of her hand and placed it on his very hard penis. "Put it in your mouth."

"Oh, shit! I've... I've never done that before," she protested.

"Drop onto your knees," he told her.

Georgette did so. Almost immediately Ricketts had undone his fly and thrust his penis into the young woman's mouth. She nearly gagged as he put his hand behind her head and pushed. What followed was a total disaster. As he let go his hot fluid, she was forced to half-swallow and half-gag. He cursed her for screwing up. Georgette was now on all-fours, dry retching.

"The bathroom's through there," he told her, in a tone of disgust.

A few moments later she emerged. "Jesus, Tom! What the hell did you do to me? How am I supposed to cope with that? I told you I'd never done it before."

"You fucked up, lady!" he told her.

"Well, bully for you! What now?"

Ricketts looked at her. A thousand things were running through his mind. But most of all he knew that if she talked to Monkhouse, he was gone. "Start Monday or as soon as you can leave the other place. You'll get a two-year contract and sixty grand to start. Reviewed in a year," he told her. "I'll tell Mr Monkhouse we've met. That's all I'll tell him. I do trust you'll also be discreet."

"Thank you, Tom," she said, still trying to regain her composure.

"Oh, from now on, it'll be Mr Ricketts," he told her.

"So this whole thing is just another day at the office for you?" she asked.

"You want to work in big-time television? Welcome to big-time television. I'll call George Hanks and tell him to expect you. Close the door on your way out."

Georgette glared at him. Suddenly she was enraged at his attitude and behaviour. She leaned over the desk towards him. "I will *never* call you *Mr Ricketts*! If you have a problem with that, then you know who to ring. Shall I tell him to expect your call, *Tom*?"

"Fuck you!"

"Nice man," she said sarcastically, as she turned to unlock the door and leave his office.

* * *

Georgette had only been on the job a short time when she began to get frustrated at not getting a shot at the big stories. So much so that she persuaded her uncle to make another phone call which would allow her to choose her own stories.

He made the call.

But Georgette wanted more. She recalled the words of one of her first bosses. Spotting her ambition, he told her, "If you want to run with the big boys, you better learn to piss in the tall glass," adding, "And it's amazing in this business how many people burn out before they've even caught fire."

She never forgot the advice and applied her thinking accordingly.

She also knew that once she had set the precedent of breaking big stories, there was no going back. She knew she needed three big ones a year to keep her up there. As a result, she worked the social writers and her contacts.

And she was smart enough to know that you don't say yes to everything. She knew she had to choose carefully the opening nights she went to. The VIP functions. The cocktail circuit. And, by working her contacts, she was always able to preview the guest list. If she felt she could enhance her career by being present, she'd attend. She always sought the power-brokers. The cheque books. The decision makers. The movers and the shakers. She saw no value in making small talk with young hot-shot executives who were only interested in satisfying the lump in their pants. Her body was her bargaining chip to be spent wisely and sparingly. She also knew the dangers involved in being regarded as 'easy'.

Georgette McKinley certainly wasn't easy. When she felt the time was right to play her hand, she gave of herself, and invariably her lover would see his pillow talk revealed on the six o'clock news a few days later. She never blew a source or named names. Mostly, her one-night-stands were simply that. High-powered executives with wives, mortgages and children with much to lose if it ever became known that they were seduced by Georgette McKinley. And viewers came to trust her predictions. They knew full well if she stood in the middle of a mud flat and said an announcement by the government was imminent that the land was to be reclaimed for housing trust highrise, it would be.

If she stood in the middle of the international airport and said the north-south runway was to be extended by a thousand metres, it would be. Her information was always spot-on.

She didn't always pay the ultimate price, but she was prepared to. She saw no harm in the giving of herself for another zero in her pay packet. Often she made her quarry play the waiting game. The quick, ten-minute social meeting over a cup of coffee. The discreet phone call. When she felt the time was right, the five-star suite with room service. The hotel room was always the grand finale. If the information was good, Georgette paid the price. Failure to deliver would see her quarry left to play solitaire in a very expensive hotel suite with the departing words, "And don't call me. If you do, I'll send your wife the hotel booking slip."

Her technique was always the same. The warm embrace. A spa together. Just as her target was preparing to enter her, she'd pull away and reach for the towel. As she walked into the bedroom, her power-broker would be following along like a dog at its master's heels. She knew she had the power at that very precise moment. She'd discard the towel, drop to her knees, and place him inside her mouth. Briefly. Then she'd withdraw and move to the bed, thus ensuring her man was at the very height of arousal. As he would seek out her mouth, she would then bluntly ask the question.

"What is your company doing about such and such?"

Often the reply would be a remark in jest. But she would stick to her game plan. She always got her story. In making sure it was true and not some made-up piece of nonsense, she would promise the source of her information would remain anonymous. If he was feeding her a line, she would name him to cover herself. Middle-aged men, privy to boardroom secrets with the most to lose, were always the most gullible.

And the most silent. Georgette knew it and the ploy worked every time. Especially as the targets she chose she knew to be mostly weak men. Men who wouldn't become threatening or dangerous. Men she could string along, exploit and then discard. She was also smart enough not to exploit the practice.

She set her sights on just two a year. But each two was cultivated until she was one hundred percent sure of a result.

The steaming hot bath had eased her muscles, which made the back of her neck feel like it was on fire. But it was a good feeling. She wiggled her toes into the smoothness of the satin, content in the knowledge she was in full control of her life.

Through a gap in the curtain, she spied a solitary star in the universe. She wondered which one it was.

Doesn't matter, I guess, she smiled inwardly. *I wonder if that's me?*

Then she berated herself for being so vain. As she focussed upon the star, her mind went back to what seemed so long ago. She wondered if offering herself for scoops was credible, then realised that also, long ago, she made the choice. No weddings. No kids. The choice was money. With money she could make her own choices. Without it, there wouldn't be any. She didn't want to depend on a man for the things she wanted in life. She'd seen too much divorce, too many people ending up with nothing after spending half their lives together.

No, no. None of that stuff for me.

She'd certainly had her opportunities. If ever she felt her guard beginning to drop, she'd recall her choices and cancel out of everything. She remembered how unsympathetically she was told as a five-year-old how her parents, sister and brother had died in a house fire. She remembered her years of being shuffled from one foster home to another. Of never having a place to call her own. She recalled the struggles of big-hearted, compassionate families who took her in and struggled for every cent they earned. The schools. The second-hand clothes. Her first job stacking shelves at the supermarket.

She remembered staring at the television, totally captivated. "That's me," she'd say. "Somehow, some day, that's where I want to be."

Through sheer persistence, Georgette got her first job in a television station just after she'd turned 17. Because she was such a breath of fresh air and filled with youthful enthusiasm, she became very popular, very quickly. Some of the women who had been in the business for many years were quick to spot her naïveté and her intelligence. They were also quick to pick up on the fact that every bloke in the building, young or old, was trying their hardest to bed the young woman. So several of the women got their heads together and decided on a course of action. Straws were drawn. Three times married, chain-smoking, peroxided Jill McKenzie drew the short one.

She waited her opportunity and pulled up a chair next to Georgette in the tea room. "Well, you've been here two months, kid. You gonna stay in this dump or move ahead?"

Georgette was a little thrown by the question. "Hi, Jill... er... I... I don't know. I've really only just started."

"Listen kid, if you don't want to spend the rest of your life working in a joint like this, then you gotta pick your mark and go down on him."

Georgette's eyes popped open. Jill knew she wasn't tuned in.

"OK, I'll spell it out for you. Work out where you want to go and work on the guy who will be employing you. I haven't had three husbands not to know what I'm talking about here. If you want something bad enough in this world, then you gotta remember, you're gonna have to snitch it from a bloke in the first place. It'll be a bloke who says you can or can't have it. It'll be a bloke who calls the shots. Forget all this glass ceiling crap. It's a man's world. Always was. Always will be. It'll be a bloke who decides how much you're gonna get paid. It'll be a bloke who decides if you stay or go. Now the big thing we as women have got going for us is that what they're often thinking about is what they think with. You ever had a man?"

Georgette dropped her eyes and self-consciously shook her head.

"Yeah, well that's fine, but you can't keep it intact forever. But if you want a bit of advice, use it as a bargaining chip. What you've got, blokes for the next 30 years are gonna be falling over themselves to get to. You ambitious?"

Georgette's eyes lit up. "Oh, yes," she gushed.

"Thought so. You want to get married?"

"No way!"

"You like money?"

"Never had any... but yes, money excites me."

"Then don't get married. You want to work on big-time television and be a star?"

"Oh god, yes!"

"OK. Then you gotta learn how to use the blokes. As I've told you, I'm on my third one, plus a few others in between. I'm telling you, if you want to achieve, you have to ride over the top of the blokes. That means you're gonna have to be three times as smart as they are to get past 'em."

"So what do I do?"

"You reckon you could handle going to bed with a bloke to get a job?"

"Oh, yuk! That's disgusting. I could never do that."

"You want to work on big-time TV or don't you?"

"Of course I do, but not like that."

"Now, you listen to me. If you want to get there on your own merits, it might take you ten years. Maybe more. That's crap! So you take the initiative. *You* get into *his* pants."

The suggestion shocked Georgette, but Jill continued, even though she could see she was embarrassing her. "You'll thank me for this one day, kid. And always remember, when someone looks like you do, every hot-arsed young bastard in town will sniff the breeze and seek you out. So don't go throwing it about. But you've gotta face it sometime. If you seek out the guy at big-time TV, it'll probably be fucking Ricketts... Jesus, what a sweaty-arsed little creep he is... and you do it with him, never let him come near you again. Get the job. Always be polite, but keep your distance. Once you've paid the price, it's paid in full, first time round. None of this lay-by shit! OK?"

* * *

Georgette rolled over in her king-size bed, smiling at her naïveté, and how she had tried to follow Jill McKenzie's instructions at the times she needed to. As the wind blew gently through the slits of an open shade in her third-floor apartment, it moved the curtain to obscure her view of the star. She fell asleep, but at 1.50 a.m. the phone at her bedside rang.

"Oh, shit!" she exclaimed, grappling for the receiver, forcing herself to wake up quickly. "H... hello."

"Hi, you awake?"

"I was sound asleep. Where are you?"

"In town. Will you meet me?"

"Same place?"

"Same place"

"Soon as I can."

"I've missed you."

"Oh god," Georgette gushed. "And I've missed you."

"Don't wear any panties."

Georgette sprung out of bed. Instinctively, she went to her underwear drawer, smiled, and closed it again. She quickly showered and dried herself. She then took a very expensive 'Ranier' she'd bought for such an occasion from her wardrobe and ran a brush through her hair, careful to check her face was free of make-up. She collected her car keys, locked her front door and made for the lift. Moments later, she was on the ground floor, opening the door to her BMW convertible. She pressed another button and the security gate to the car park opened. Soon Georgette McKinley was speeding off into the night.

Fergusson Lane was at the end of an industrial estate on the fringes of the city, deserted, dark and lonely. Georgette felt the pangs of nervousness. Perhaps even a little fear. No street lights. Just a big open and vacant paddock. Even the grass was dead from the fall-out of nearby chimney stacks. Up ahead she caught a glimpse of something shining in the dark.

She flicked her headlights to high beam. As she drew closer, the shining object became familiar, a stretched limousine parked a long way in off the road. Georgette's palms began to get clammy. Adrenaline raced through her body as she felt her heartbeat quicken. Her dry mouth made it difficult to swallow. She brought her car to a standstill a few metres from the limousine. As she cut the motor, she saw the back door of the vehicle swing open. She climbed from her convertible and walked to the opened door. As she stepped into the back seat, she reached out to take hold of the hand that was held out to greet her.

"Good evening, Prime Minister," she half-whispered, "you're up late tonight."

"Take a hike, John," Prime Minister John Talbot said to his driver. "And the others too. I need a bit of space here."

The Prime Minister's driver and his two federal police bodyguards, used to the late-night meanderings of their boss, did as they were asked and moved a discreet distance away from the limousine.

Georgette McKinley first met Prime Minister John Talbot when she came to interview him two years previously. She could tell he was instantly smitten with her, quick to spot his vulnerability. She knew if she played her cards right, John Talbot would be a wonderful source of information. The best, in fact. But would he respond?

She sent out the signals, indicating she could easily be seduced by the trappings of power. Although Talbot was a man in his fifties, he wasn't too bad to look at, she told herself.

Within minutes of her returning to the studio, she received the subtle but inquiring phone call. Two hours later, Georgette McKinley was learning just how insatiable Australia's Prime Minister could be. For the two years that followed, she was always available on his demand. That's when the big stories began to fall into her lap and she began to make a name for herself. With what she got from John Talbot and what she cultivated corporately, Georgette McKinley was able to keep coming up with the goods. And because her liaisons with John Talbot were strictly top secret, no-one, but no-one, ever suspected. As long as he remained Prime Minister and desired her totally, her information pipeline would continue.

She knew he hated doing it, that he wondered if the cost was becoming too high, but he hated even more the thought of not being able to lay between her legs and that whatever the price, he simply had to have Georgette McKinley. What he didn't know was that the moment his information dried up, he would discover she had an unlisted phone number

He handed her an envelope. "Read it and burn it. Don't tear it up. Burn it," he told her.

"When can I use it?"

"The Leader of the Opposition, Stan Philmont, gets rolled next Wednesday."

"Bullshit!"

"Sit on it till Tuesday night." Talbot smiled. "Lead with it. Looks like you get another fifteen minutes of fame, eh?"

"Oh, John, thank you."

"Don't thank me... show me."

Georgette took hold of his hand and pushed it between her legs.

Talbot groaned in a total outpouring of lust, which became all-consuming. "Oh, good girl, you remembered."

.

Chapter 7

Bill Murphy leaned across the kitchen table, picked up a box of matches and lit a solitary candle he'd pushed into a chocolate-coated donut. He watched the flickering flame for a few moments, the melting wax, then sang 'happy birthday' to himself. Still focussed on the flame, his thoughts went back over his other birthdays. Then with a quick puff, he blew it out. He wondered if anyone else would remember the anniversary of his birth. He doubted it. His father had been gone for more years than he could recall. Until his forty-fifth year, his mother never missed one. But now, she too had gone. His ex-wife?

Hardly, he thought, *haven't seen or heard of her for fifteen years.*

His sister, Constance, had long been estranged so he doubted if there would even be a card. He smiled philosophically to himself.

Not a living soul knows that today I turned 52.

He took a cigarette from his soft Camel pack, lit it and drew back heavily. He looked at his surroundings and conceded, *Yes, some people may be of the opinion I live as a bit of a recluse.*

Yet it was no mistake that he lived in rural isolation. For many years he'd planned to slip quietly away, but it was only the best-selling success of his third novel, *The Fires of Midnight*, that allowed him to do so.

Bill Murphy had spent his life in the electronic media, swapping between radio and television, all with the dream of writing a best-seller and living on a clifftop overlooking the sea. Thirty-seven publishers rejected his first work. Forty-two said no to his second, so he concentrated his efforts within the boundaries of the media and cast aside any thoughts of topping the best-seller list. Then, out of the blue, he received a call from a publisher. One who had previously rejected his work. He was encouraged to try again; so two years later, Bill Murphy sent off 645 pages to the London headquarters of Lysaught Publishers.

Three days after his fiftieth birthday, Lysaughts phoned to say that *The Fires of Midnight* was on its third print run and a sizeable cheque was in the mail. To celebrate, Bill Murphy phoned London back, received a projection on sales, then walked into the showroom of the local car dealer. A short time later he drove a brand new Holden Commodore utility to a trailer yard, wrote out a cheque for a new ten by six and made his way back to his rented flat. He phoned his land agent, then various media outlets where he'd been freelancing a living, packed his trailer, closed the door, put the key in the letterbox and drove north out of Sydney.

He wasn't a great hoarder of personal effects. Until his forty-fifth birthday, he'd kept everything. Boxes of newspaper clippings, taped interviews, copies of stories he'd written, plus a heap of memorabilia. After his mother's funeral, and left with the task of cleaning out and selling her unit, he thought he'd have a 'spring clean' himself. So practically everything went. He had even found some old love letters from a teenage romance. He didn't toss them into the rubbish bins with everything else. Instead, he went to the furthest point on the cliff face overlooking the Sydney Heads. When the wind changed and blew out to sea, he ceremoniously tore them up and watched the remnants of a long-lost love disappear into the whitecaps way below.

His ruthless attitude that 'everything goes' meant that what he had left packed easily into his newly acquired trailer. As he drove through the toll gates out from Hornsby onto the Gosford freeway, he still wasn't sure of his exact destination.

He felt it may be up towards Newcastle. Maybe even further. He saw a vacancy sign for overnight cabins at a caravan park on the outskirts of Newcastle, pulled in off the freeway and paid for three nights.

So where the hell am I going to live? he asked himself, settling back into a cabin chair and dragging on a Camel. He knew he wanted to slip quietly into obscurity, but not so far that he left civilisation a three-day drive away. He knew the north coast reasonably well, having travelled it many times over the years, stopping off at various beachside resorts.

As he casually flicked through a road atlas, South West Rocks leapt out at him. He wondered why. As he cast his memory back three decdes, he remembered seeing the place as a young man in the services. It was only an overnight stay and hardly conducive to a holiday, but its beauty, tranquillity and picturesque surroundings had stayed with him, forming an indelible impression in his subconscious mind. Then suddenly, after all these years... back it came. He rose to his feet, stubbed out his cigarette and smiled.

"Looks like it's going to be South West Rocks," he said out loud, almost as though that was the plan all along. The little coastal resort with a population of only a few thousand was about another three hours drive north of Newcastle. "Yeah, bugger it, that'll do. Wonder if I can find a place off the beaten track a bit?"

On the morning of the fourth day, Bill Murphy was loading his trailer and had momentarily left the driver's door to his new utility open. When he returned to the vehicle after locking up the cabin, there was a little black-and-white kelpie dog sitting in the driver's seat. Barely off its mother, the little puppy was sitting on its haunches, its ears pricked and focusing its big bright eyes right at him.

"Well, look at you!" Bill Murphy smiled. He leaned in and picked up the small animal, imediately taken with it. He tipped it over and took a quick peek. "A little boy, eh! So who do you belong to?"

Bill scanned the area. There was no-one about. Being mid-week and off-season, the place was nearly deserted. He put the little kelpie back on the front seat of the utility, closed the door and walked over to the kiosk.

"Anyone missing a dog?" he asked the attendant.

"Nope! No-one's said anything to me," came a casual and uninterested reply.

Bill smiled inwardly. The answer pleased him because for some reason which he couldn't even explain to himself, he liked the idea of keeping the little animal. He returned to the vehicle and, as he opened the door, the puppy was standing on the passenger side seat, wagging its tail. He leaned against the vehicle and lit a smoke. He was in two minds as to what to do. The puppy was obviously well bred. It was also very obviously someone's pet. He thought if he waited a while he'd see someone frantically searching for him. But no-one came.

He checked his watch. "Christ, I can't stay here all day!"

Finally he climbed in behind the wheel. "Righto buggerlugs, it looks like it's just you and me," he said glancing over at his newly acquired passenger. "You want to come and live at South West Rocks? because that's where we're going."

Bill Murphy started the engine and drove out onto the highway. He checked his mirror a few times. Maybe someone would be coming after him, realizing they'd lost their dog. But no-one did.

"So what are we going to call you? You sure as hell looked to me to be a lost and lonely little bugger," he said, giving him a quick glance as he drove on up the road. He tossed around a few names, but none seemed to fit. Bill looked again at the puppy. Then it hit him. Lonely seemed to be the word that stuck. "That's it," he told the pup. "I'll call you Lonely."

* * *

After a couple of hours, South West Rocks loomed ahead.

He drove around the place for a while then took a cabin for a week at a local caravan park. The next morning, with Lonely resting on one arm, Bill Murphy decided to try and find his little piece of paradise. He saw a sign: Real Estate Agent. He parked the utility and walked in.

"Is a dog allowed in here?" he called, as he stepped inside the door.

The woman behind the desk looked up. "Where is he?"

Bill Murphy pointed to a solitary head poking out of his jacket pocket. Instantly, the personality of the woman was transformed. She immediately left her desk to walk over to Bill.

"Oh, look at him! Isn't he gorgeous?" She looked up at Bill. "What's his name?"

"Lonely."

The woman laughed lightly. "I suppose it would be in a pocket that big. How can I help you?"

Bill Murphy explained what he was looking for and was introduced to a salesman.

"It doesn't have to be flash," he told him, "just as long as it sits up high, overlooks the sea, and it's in reasonable condition. It'll be cash and I'll pay by cheque. If you've got a problem with that, tell me now, and I'll go elsewhere." The real estate agent gave a hand gesture indicating there wouldn't be.

For two days, the agent drove Bill Murphy around properties that were for sale in the coastal inlet. In one and out the other. For some reason he was unable to conceive just what it was his client had in mind. Finally, close to despair, the land agent threw caution to the wind.

"There is one other place," he told his prospective client.

"It's been empty for a while. Probably going on three months. I don't have any details, I just know it's there. Long way in off the road... about fifteen minutes south. Backs onto the Hat Head National Park. Only bit of private land left in the area. You want me to grab a key?"

Bill Murphy didn't appear all too enthusiastic. "Why not?" he shrugged.

A short time later, the land agent swung in off the highway a few kilometres from South West Rocks and wound his way in towards the coastline. Ahead, sitting on a small clifftop, the house came into view. White, solid stone walls, tin roof, four old sheds in the immediate surrounds and a garage attached to the house from the eastern side. The complex was semi-circled by bushland, which Bill Murphy assumed was the national park.

The two men got out of the car, and Bill casually sidled away on his own. At the rear of the house were several Sweet William border plants and Glossy Abelia evergreen shrubs. Draped from a wire trellis, their green leaves mottled with yellow, were two Brazilian Bellflowers. A Heath Banksia and several Peegee Hydrangeas stood out from a vast array of shrubs and ground cover. He also noticed a couple of shrubby evergreens known for their fragrant blooms, *Heliotropium arborescens.* Bill preferred to call them by their more common name, Cherry Pies.

He smiled. *By gee I'd like to see them in full bloom*, he thought, seeing in his mind's eye branched spikes carrying clusters of tiny lilac flowers.

In several pots down the side of the garage were Barbados Royal Dutch Lilies. But the coup de grace for Bill Murphy were several Diosmas; these fine, spicy-foliaged South African evergreens had been strategically placed round the house. Some were the white Breath of

Heaven and others were pink. Bill Murphy walked over to get a closer look at some of the the pinks with their tiny, star-shaped flowers.

By gee, I'll bet the people before hated leaving all this,' he thought to himself.

The front yard, which dropped away steeply below, was the ocean. He had to have it. He also knew he had to play down his eagerness to purchase. He looked back to the salesman.

"How much?" he asked dryly.

The land agent, not wishing to look him in the eye because of his slight embarrassment at showing such a place, mumbled, "I think it's about a hundred. But I must say, Mr Murphy, you've caught me on the hop a little with this one. We haven't cleaned it up or presented it any way. I believe it's a deceased estate. The lady who lived here had no family and my understanding is she deemed the proceeds from the sale to the Salvation Army. If it's not sold within two years it will be bought by the government and made part of Hat Head. Don't know how she managed to keep the title, but she did. You want to have a look inside?"

Bill Murphy very much wanted to. With Lonely tucked under his arm, he proceeded to walk around the property.

"A bit over two acres?"

"I believe that to be the case."

The grass was high and there was much debris. Years of discarded tins and bottles, broken implements, part of an old Singer sewing machine. Preserving pots, pans and jars. The rusted front fork of an old pushbike, abandoned car parts, discarded, worn-out tanks, fuel drums, oil cans. An old broken toilet cistern. Casually, Bill forced open the door to one of the sheds. Inside was crammed full of discarded junk. On one bench, a pile about two metres high of women's magazines, some of them dating back forty years. He pulled the door shut and looked around to see if the real estate agent was following.

He wasn't. He went to another shed. Then another. Each time the story was the same. It soon became obvious the old lady who lived there was a compulsive hoarder. When one shed was filled, she simply built another. The land agent saw Bill Murphy walking towards the house and went to meet him. He put the key in the front door and both men walked inside. A small passageway with four rooms leading off it, the kitchen on the end with a bathroom and toilet to the right. From a few quick glances, Bill could see the place was old and tired and very neglected. He turned to the salesman, a flippancy in his tone.

"I suppose this is the sort of place you blokes call a handyman's delight?"

Trying to conceal his discomfort, he replied, "Well, yes, Mr Murphy, I will concede it could do with a bit of sprucing up."

"What about a full-blown make-over? Bill replied, trying to talk down the value of the place. "A hundred grand, you reckon?"

The estate agent cleared his throat. "That's somewhere near the mark, yes," he told him, half turning away.

"Well you better ring your office and get right on the mark because I want it, but I'm not paying that sort of dough!"

Little did the real estate agent know, but Bill Murphy would not have even baulked at $150,000 if he had been firm with the price.

* * *

Three days later, Bill Murphy walked out of the real estate agent's office with the keys to the house. A cheque for $79,000 had just been cleared by the bank and he was like an excited schoolboy. He finally had a place of his own, and right now there was much to do.

Five weeks later, all the rubbish had gone, the grass had been cut and the sheds cleaned out. Part of the roof on the house had been replaced. All new electrical wiring. New plumbing. A new rainwater tank had been installed and a new pine railing fence lined the boundary. His ravaging through old second-hand dealers' showrooms had also produced a near-new hot-water service, Chef stove, oil heater, two room air conditioners, a washing machine and a scattering of furniture. The curtains were make-do, which didn't bother him too much. The bed was a queen size and new, as were all his sheets and towels. So too was his recliner chair and big-screen TV. One of the bedrooms he'd even turned into an office.

I've found my bloody Shangri-la!

Out the backdoor leading from the kitchen was a small veranda, then a large grassed block bordered by a small area of government land which led to a small cliff face. From Bill Murphy's kitchen it was only a short walk to the water's edge. To get there, a small cliff face of about 20 metres had to be negotiated. It was dotted with boulders and traps for the unwary, but nonetheless spectacular. This then gave way to a very clean, white, sandy beach. This tiny patch of coastline was secluded and mostly went unnoticed as people went sailing by.

It's as though no-one's ever been here, he mused.

Bill Murphy stood observing his good fortune. The waves rolled in and, when they broke on the shore, the sound amplified as it bounced off the small cliff face. He glanced round, subconsciously looking for a place to prop. Somewhere he could be alone, undisturbed and out of the wind. A few metres off to his left, and about three-quarters of the way down the face, he spotted what appeared to be an armchair. It was a solid piece of rock, worn away by millions of years of exposure to the elements. Bill went to it and sat down. Stunned at how perfectly his backside fitted into it, he laughed out loud.

"It's even got bloody armrests. Thank you God," he said, casting his eyes to the heavens.

* * *

Bill Murphy sliced the donut in two and handed a piece to Lonely. The young kelpie devoured it with one quick gulp and stood looking at his master.

"You've got to savour it a bit," he told him. But Lonely ignored the remark and continued to sit looking at him.

"Yeah, like hell! You're not getting mine!"

Lonely then started to whine quietly. Bill could see the saliva building round his mouth. As he took a bite from the donut, the dog's eyes popped open just that little bit wider.

Bill laughed. "You're a pain in the arse!"

But Lonely won the moment. Within the blink of an eye, he had devoured the remains of the donut handed to him by his master.

"What do you think, boy? Two years this week since we moved in. Not too bad is it? The old joint's all right. Doesn't leak. Having the ocean right out front is pretty damn good too, eh? Beats the hell out of hi-rise and peak-hour traffic doesn't it?"

He got to thinking of the past couple of years, which had been good for Bill Murphy. He'd taken a post office box in South West Rocks and usually went into town about once a fortnight. Curious locals would sometimes comment about his presence, but no-one really took a great deal of notice when he loaded his groceries into the back of the utility. The odd comment would centre on, 'that's that writer bloke isn't it?', but he was pretty much able to maintain his anonymity. And that's exactly the way he liked it. He knew word would get out soon enough that he was one of the world's hottest authors. He had the phone connected to his house, but only his publisher in London had the number with instructions to ring only between eight and nine a.m. He also had a fax line, but again very few people were given the number. His post office box number, was given only to those on a 'need-to-know' basis. His closest neighbours were two kilometres away and, even after two years, he still hadn't met them. Day-to-day life was very much routine.

He wouldn't rise till around ten a.m., having been up most of the night writing. And Bill Murphy liked to write at night. He felt he was at the peak of his powers when the skies were clear, a gentle breeze wafted in off the ocean and he could hear the sound of the waves rolling in on the beach, far below.

Lonely also had his own special place. It was right by the side of Bill's desk. He'd just prop there, hour after hour, undisturbed by the click-click-click of his master's keyboard.

The sound of an approaching vehicle diverted his attention for a moment. He walked to the front door and watched a car proceed past his driveway and continue on down the track.

Wonder who the hell that is? There's nowhere to go. Just leads into that national park and that's all scrub. Never see the bugger come back either.

Bill Murphy watched the vehicle disappear from view and half shrugged, returning to his thoughts. The past two years had also been very productive for him. He was now about four weeks from completing *The Corridors of Injustice*, a one-thousand page saga of love, lust, power, greed, creativity, and treachery.

The hour was late and he was toying with the idea of going off to bed when the phone rang. His eyes shot to the clock on the wall.

"Hardly eight a.m.!" he snarled as he picked up the receiver. "This better be good!" he said.

"Mr Murphy?"

"Who's calling?"

"I have Felicity Nobleman-Spinks from Lysaught Publishers on the line from London. Please hold."

"Hello... Bill?"

"Felicity..." he began, reaching for a smoke.

"Sorry to break the rules," she began urgently, "but I thought you'd like to know *Fires* went into its sixth print run today. This thing is through the roof..."

Bill Murphy suddenly forgot about the embargo he'd placed on his phone line. "Good heavens! *six*?"

"Isn't that marvellous?" she gushed. "It's now into 27 countries. Hollywood wants an option. What do you think?"

"Do I have to do the screenplay?"

"Do you want to?"

"No way!"

"Then I'll tell them that."

"What do you think? he asked, putting the question back to her.

"Oh, come on, Bill! It's your book, your success. What price?"

"You do it, babe. Nothing's changed from when we first spoke. If you're doing it on behalf of Lysaught, then negotiate a fee and take fifteen per cent off the top for the company. If you decide to accept my offer and be my agent, then go for 20 per cent off the top. Load up the price accordingly. It's up to you. You can stay employed if you want to or you can be my agent. See what the gurus are prepared to pay and have a think about it."

Bill Murphy had asked Felicity Nobleman-Spinks before to be his agent, but she declined, preferring the security of a regular pay cheque. But now, with his increasing success, he tried his luck again. And the irony was, the two had never met. He just liked the way she dealt with him and, as Bill Murphy had a way of taking people at face value, the relationship had blossomed.

"What about the deal with Lysaughts?" she asked.

"This won't affect that. There's nothing in the contract about movie deals. If you get one, it's a bonus. Now that bonus can either go to your employer or to you. It's the same with *The Corridors of Injustice*. The contract is for a book deal only. My contract with Lysaughts runs out as soon as *Corridors* hits your desk. Get me seven figures up front for my next three books and 20 per cent is yours... plus the same with any movie. I don't want to do all that stuff Felicity. If you think you can, draw up the paperwork and I'll sign it. You keep selling me and keep the cheques coming in and you could make a pretty good life for yourself. Screw with me and I'll cut you off. Do you want to do it?"

"Oh, for goodness sakes, I'd love to. But you don't even know me. We've talked over the phone, but we've never met. Are you sure you want to hand a woman 20,000 kilometres away a comfort zone until time immemorial?"

"OK... let's do it your way. You married?"

"No."

"Engaged?"

"No"

"Spoken for?"

"No"

"Ever been in jail?"

She laughed. "No."

"Anything about you I should know but don't?"

"Well, I'm not Mother Theresa!"

He chuckled. "So does that mean a packet of paper clips or a bounced cheque?"

Again she laughed. "The paper clips. But only a few off the top."

"You want the job?"

"I think you're wonderful."

"No you don't. You like money like I do. See a solicitor and fix it up. Take this as a handshake over the phone," he told her.

"And that's it?"

"What else do you want?"

"Will you put it in writing?" she asked hesitantly, not wanting to appear over-pushy.

"It'll be on your fax today. You need any money to start up?"

"Well, I'm certainly going to need a few things..."

"I'll get a cheque off to you as well... oh, Felicity?"

"Yes, Bill."

"Thank you."

Bill Murphy hung up the phone and picked up a copy of *The Fires of Midnight* and held it to himself.

"So now it's going to be a bloody movie! You hear that, Lonely? They're going to make a movie of my book." He walked around the room throwing his arms in the air. "Could there be a greater thrill? My God! What a hoot! You've read the book, now see the movie. *Yeees!* " he yelled. "So who the hell are they gonna put in it? Don't know! Don't care! Look at that!... up there on the screen!... written by Bill Bloody Murphy... *Wow*! Just send me the money you bastards... just send me the money!"

Bill Murphy was still beaming with excitement when he drove into town to post a cheque to Felicity. He checked his mail box and looked inquisitively at an envelope marked for his personal attention.

Chapter 8

Senior Sergeant Ken McLoughlin and Senior Constable Dave Bourke got an early start from Mildura and headed for Sydney. McLoughlin, upon leaving Gabe and Katie Caplin, headed for the beach resort of Robe where for three days he took in walks along the beach, an afternoon in a charter boat fishing for snook at Pink's Beach and just generally taking the time to smell the sea air. But he was preoccupied.

Preoccupied with John James McGregor-McWeasely.

How the hell am I gonna catch this little mongrel?

On the morning of the fourth day, McLoughlin packed his car and drove to Melbourne's police headquarters. It followed his call to the armoury that he would be dropping by to pick up the weapons and accessories he wanted. After checking all was in order, he called Dave Bourke and told him he would pick him up in Mildura early the next morning.

During the trip to Sydney, McLoughlin briefed his partner on the assignment ahead.

"What makes them think you can grab him?"

"Not me, mate... we. *We* can grab him. Jesus, they wanted to load me up with all these pricks I didn't even know. So I just told 'em straight... no Dave Bourke, no Ken McLoughlin."

Bourke laughed. "Yeah! and my heart pumps piss for you too! Who is this prick anyway?"

"Someone who's too damn clever to be caught. So if he's that good, he must have a few things going for him. I don't know if he's a sole operator. I think he is."

McLoughlin went on to explain the ins and outs of the credit cards, the mobile phones, the special police badges and the weekly phone call required to the Police Commissioner. He gave Dave Bourke the names and phone codes of the two Police Commissioners and the two Police Ministers who would be available at all times.

"Bloody hell," he said, "I don't know where to even begin with something like this. It really is the great unknown."

"Start at the start I guess."

"Meaning?"

Bourke looked at him. "Homicide and armed robbery used to drink at the Sussex. What do you think?"

"Yeah, as good as place as any to begin with, I guess."

Senior Sergeant Ken McLoughlin and Senior Constable Dave Bourke were about half-way between Liverpool and the city of Sydney, travelling in an unmarked car, when an announcement on the radio interrupted their conversation.

Minister if you wouldn't mind waiting a moment, I just need to cross to the newsroom. Thank you, Craig. I'm John Emery in the ABC newsroom. There's a major police drama being played out in the city right now. Peter Oliver is there...

"Hang on!" McLoughlin said, leaning over to turn up the volume, "What the hell's all this about?"

McLoughlin pulled the vehicle into a loading zone to fully comprehend the immensity of what he was hearing. Both men sat staring at the radio.

The drama began just after ten o'clock this morning and ended a few moments ago right here on the corner of George and Liverpool streets in the city. Five men have been shot dead by police and two police officers have been wounded. One, I'm told, has a bullet wound to the head. Earlier today, at eight minutes past ten this morning, an Armaguard truck carrying a $150,000 payroll pulled into the Grenco Meatworks in Fyfe Street, Marrickville.

As I speak, the place is crawling with police officers. The bodies of the dead are being stretchered into ambulance vehicles and firemen are hosing the blood off the street. Bags, allegedly those taken from the Armaguard truck, have been collected by detectives and the entire area has now been sealed off. Bullets have shattered several nearby shop-front, plate-glass windows. But, right now, the atmosphere is a little surreal. People seem to be wandering around... almost in a daze. Did this thing really happen here?

You can almost hear them asking the question. Of course the answer is, yes it did, but I don't think those who witnessed it can yet fully comprehend what took place. Police have just released two names of the deceased robbers; one was Lester James Abbott, another was Edward Albert Lansing. Both men were known to police. At this stage, the names of the other three are not known."

McLoughlin and Bourke looked at each other in dismay. They turned the radio off, not waiting for the end of the report.

"Well I'll be fucked!" McLoughlin said. "Edward Albert Lansing! Teddy bloody Lansing! He only got out last week."

"Really?"

"Yeah, they're the two who did that druggie over in Adelaide. Got twelve years."

"And that was these pricks?" Bourke said, trying to recall the incident.

"That was these pricks," McLoughlin said, still staring at the radio. Then he smiled lightly. "Another notch on the belt for Branson."

Dave Bourke offered a puzzled look.

"You don't know about him?"

"He's New South Wales, but what he did gained a fair bit of notoriety."

"I'm intrigued."

"He got a graveyard confession. A young girl was murdered at Gosford... oh Christ, years ago. Everything led back to her uncle, but his alibi was watertight. No matter what the coppers did, they couldn't pin it on him. The coroner returned the usual, 'murdered by a person or persons unknown' but Branson wouldn't let it go. He was a bit of a bookworm. Liked to read a lot. He found, even going back hundreds of years, that killers liked to not only return to the scene of the crime..."

"Yeah, well, we know about that..."

"Hang on, it goes further. If they hadn't been caught and they were close to the person they killed, they liked to actually visit their graves."

"Jesus, how sick's that?"

"Apparently it happens. Well Branson got onto this little theory and thought he'd like to try it out. So on the fifth anniversary of the girl's death, he set up surveillance of the grave, aimed a directional microphone at it and rolled a tape. Bugger me dead if the uncle doesn't turn up and go into this great long spiel of confession. Branson had it on tape, but he knew he couldn't use it in court. So he waited till the bloke got home and knocked on his door. He played him the tape... the bloke shit himself and spilled his guts. He got life, and that's how Branson got famous... in New South anyway. He's an inspector now, I think."

"Then he grabbed this joker?" Bourke said, nodding at the radio.

"Yeah... clever bugger, Branson. Want to go and have a look?"

"It's all over isn't it?" Bourke replied.

"Crime scenes attract, Dave. Never know who you might spot in the crowd," McLoughlin grinned.

Forty minutes later, the two detectives parked their vehicle and made their way on foot to the corner of Liverpool and George. The crowd around the scene of the shootout had swelled to several thousand. Policemen on point duty had the unenviable task of trying to move people on, but it was pointless. People came to look and wouldn't leave until they had. McLoughlin and Bourke eased their way through the masses, with McLoughlin scanning the faces. Then something caught his eye. Briefly. It was on the other side of the road.

What the hell was that? he asked himself, darting his gaze back.

Bourke noticed McLoughlin's anxious change of expression. "What's happening?"

"Dunno, mate. I just saw something and I don't know what it was. But it was something."

"What... a thing... a bloke?"

"A bloke... I think," he replied straining his eyes to pick up on it again. Suddenly it reappeared, only this time moving quickly away from them. With no explanation to his partner, McLoughlin took off as best he could through the mass of people. Bourke followed.

"What, Mac?" he called after him.

"It's him, mate, it's our man for Christ sakes! It's the fucking Weasel!"

"Bullshit!"

Still forcing his way, McLoughlin quickly turned his head. "No bull-shit! I'd recognise that prick's walk anytime... come on."

But by the time McLoughlin had got through the crowd to the other side of the road, John James McGregor-McWeasely had disappeared.

"You sure it was him?" Bourke queried.

McLoughlin turned to him, a knowing grin falling across his face.

"Believe me. It was him. You wait here in case he doubles back. I'm gonna have a real good look. He can't have gone far."

"Did he see you?"

"Dunno. If he did, I'm a dead duck 'cause he'll know we're onto him. Why else would we be in Sydney?"

"But that other stuff you told me about was a long time ago."

"To blokes like that? Yesterday! They never forget."

"How much of a look at him did you get?"

"Tell you when I get back... wait here for me... and watch out for him. He's as cunning as a shithouse rat!"

McLoughlin hurried away, taking care to eyeball as much as he could. Every nook and cranny. Every face. But he knew it was a hopeless task with so many thousands of people present. Eventually he returned to Bourke.

"Nothing doing?"

McLoughlin shook his head.

"So how much of a look at him did you get?"

"Not so much a look, but rather his walk."

"His 'walk'?"

"Yeah, I told you about it. He sort of takes short steps and hops a bit. Mate, no-one else in the world would walk like that. I did get a glimpse of him side-on."

"So if you were a betting man, did he see you or didn't he?"

McLoughlin thought deeply and bit on his bottom lip. "He saw me. Would not have scattered like that unless he did."

"So what now?"

"We have to assume he's onto us. Probably even watching us right now. But he'll go to ground now, the prick! So we find a motel and start tomorrow."

They were just about to move away when a young female voice challenged McLoughlin. "Excuse me, but aren't you a detective?"

McLoughlin turned in the direction of the voice and was a little taken aback from the person it was coming from. "Who are you?" he asked the stunning young woman before him.

"Hi. Georgette McKinley, RTN ELEVEN," she smiled, holding out her hand.

"A bloody television reporter. That's all I need!" he muttered. Cautiously and hesitantly McLoughlin accepted the woman's hand.

"My, we are a long way from home aren't we?" she said.

"Hi... just on holidays really," he told her unconvincingly, still a little off balance from being caught unawares.

Georgette glanced at Bourke. "You guys always holiday with your partners?" she asked, a note of sarcasm in her tone.

McLoughlin, quickly regaining himself, responded, "Ah, only if inseparable," he told her, coyly. "Go away, lady" he heard himself urging.

"Somehow you don't look the type. You are a detective aren't you? I've just been putting together a one-hour special called *Crimes of the Decade*. This week I cut up the footage from that Mildura bunfight a few years back, and I could swear that you are the man who features in it prominently. Tell me if I'm wrong... er Sergeant McLoughlin. Yes, Ken McLoughlin."

McLoughlin's eyes flashed at Bourke then back to the young woman. "Ahhh... so you've got me," he conceded, half throwing his arms in the air. "What can I do for you?"

"What are you doing here?"

"On holidays."

"No you're not. Where's your beach towel?"

"In the car."

"Is this man your partner?" Not waiting for an answer she stepped in front of Dave Bourke. "Hi... Georgette McKinley."

Bourke took hold of her out-stretched hand.

"And you're a long way from home too, aren't you?"

"And you ask a lot of questions!"

"I'm a reporter. That's my job. Don't worry, detective, I'm not going to stuff your brief..."

"You don't know what my brief is," he cut in.

"I reckon I could take a guess," she answered thoughtfully.

"You wouldn't even get close," he responded.

"So tell me what you're both doing here?"

"Listen, lady," McLoughlin began, his patience tested.

"Uh-huh... don't get mad. I won't blow your cover. It's just unlucky for you I recognised you," she told him. "What do you know about this lot?"

"We just stumbled upon it... besides, as you say, we're a long way from home... now if you'll excuse us?"

"So you won't even give me a clue?"

McLoughlin leaned over into the woman's ear. "Darling, if we did that, you'd piss yourself with excitement and blow our case. We're just passing through and dropped in here to have a look after hearing about it on the air. So it's goodbye from us."

McLoughlin jerked his head to Bourke indicating they were out of there. Out of earshot, it was Bourke. "Bloody hell! How pushy was that?"

"They're all the same, mate. Don't let the glitz and glamour fool you. Most of 'em have got balls. She wouldn't be any different. Pretty faces like that have sunk many a good copper."

Inside though, he knew Georgette McKinley wasn't convinced. *She may well have been onto a monster story here today, but she knows we're onto a bigger one.*

He turned to look over his shoulder and caught her watching them from afar as they disappeared from her line of sight.

* * *

Unbeknown to Bourke and McLoughlin, John James McGregor-McWeasely had also been watching their every move. It was only by sheer chance he had been in the city. John James was responding to a newspaper advertisement for 'half price jeans for a half day only' at a major department store near the corner of Liverpool and George. He checked the address and saw the store was close to the Town Hall Station which was also near Liverpool and George streets. This meant his face wouldn't be publicly exposed for any length of time. And he did need clothes. He sat in the rear carriage of the train on the way into the city and held a newspaper up to his face. When he got off at the Town Hall, the police shootout had just come to an end. Like the rest of Sydney's shoppers, he couldn't resist seeing what was going on.

As he made his way to the front of the crowd, he looked up and saw McLoughlin on the other side of the road.

For that bastard to be here, he would have to be after me... have to be. Why else would a Victorian copper be in Sydney?... especially that one... he's the only one who knows me.

At that point, McLoughlin hadn't spotted him. Quickly he backtracked, but not before McLoughlin caught a glimpse of him and his very recognisable walk. But it was too late. John James scampered away and was actually able to hide behind a stone wall leading down to the underground railway. McLoughlin's search took him in the opposite direction. Keeping an eye on what was behind, John James waited until McLoughlin returned to the scene of the shooting. Then he saw him talking to his partner.

Haven't seen him before. Yep. He spotted me all right. And that's why they're here. And he's just been trying to find me. They're gonna try and nab the fucking Weasel! Yeah, well you fucking-well try, you mongrel bastards, and you'll get a whole lot more than you're bargaining for.

John James watched the policemen talk with Georgette McKinley before walking away. He followed from a lengthy distance and saw them stop just short of their car. He couldn't hear the conversation. He didn't need to.

"Can you feel it?" McLoughlin said to Bourke.

"What?"

"He's following us"

"Bullshit!"

"Uh-uh... it's true. I can feel it. The prick is watching you and me right now."

"Jesus, boss, you're getting bloody paranoid!"

"Maybe," McLoughlin replied, turning his head to look back over the distance they'd walked, straining his eyes to see in the distance.

"Why would he even suspect we'd be looking for him, even if he did see you?"

"For the same reason two goddamned police forces in two separate states haven't been able to nail the son-of-a-bitch."

Bourke's eyeline followed McLoughlin's. "I'm buggered if I can see anything."

"I can't either... that's not to say he's not there... and I'm telling you, I know he's watching us right now."

From his vantage point a good distance away, John James knew, deep in his gut, that he was the topic of conversation.

Yeah, they're after me all right, he told himself, *they're certainly after me.*

Chapter 9

Gina knew she had a problem. Not with Sebastian McAlister. She already had him just where she wanted him. Her problem was Franco. She knew she simply couldn't waltz into Lay Lady Lay and say, "Hi Franco, want to rob a safe with me?" He would dismiss her comments as those of a silly, scatter-brained woman. She had to be clever. Most of all, she had to win his respect and trust. She also knew from previous experiences that Italian men were loathe to place all their trust in a woman. Trust wasn't part of their genes. She would have to be alluring and aloof. She'd have to get angry, thus giving him the impression she didn't need him... then hope beyond hope that the carrot of greed was too strong for him to ignore. She decided upon a plan of action.

Ring me at the Hilton. Room 797.

Franco looked at the message handed to him by one of the bar staff at Lay Lady Lay.

"What's that?" Luigi asked casually.

"Gina. She wants me to ring her."

Moments later he was dialling the number. "Gina?"

"Franco!"

"What the hell are you doing there?"

"Will you come in? We need to talk."

"To the bloody Hilton! You must be jokin' Gina! Why the hell do we have to meet in there? We talk one, two, three times a week. What's so different about tonight?"

"Will you come?"

"You're serious, aren't you?"

"Never been more serious in my life," she told him solemnly.

"Something wrong?"

"Not at all."

"Someone got a gun to your head?"

Gina laughed. "Don't be ridiculous!"

Twenty minutes later, Franco was knocking on her door.

Gina checked the security-eye then released the locks. As the door opened, Franco was suddenly confronted by a woman he hardly recognised. Gone was the 'cheap' look. Her hair was freshly shampooed and shining. The brassy red lips and dark eye shadow had given way to soft tonings which complemented her features and there was no more tight leather mini-skirt, fish-net stockings and excessively high heels. Franco was literally frozen to the spot.

"G... Gina... Jesus Christ... is this you?"

The Sicilian redhead scoffed lightly. "You never would have guessed, would you? Now you know why I wanted you to come in. I could hardly turn up at Lay Lady Lay looking like this."

Franco closed the door behind himself, totally nonplussed and wondering whether this woman had been conning him all along. "So who the fuck are you? Is *this* the real you or is what I get at the club the real you?" he asked with a degree of annoyance in his tone.

"Which do you prefer?"

Franco was still suspicious. He checked inside the wardrobe and behind the bathroom door. Even the shower alcove.

"I *am* alone," she stated, again trying to convince him.

"Jesus, Gina! You're two bloody people. If I saw you in the street looking like this I wouldn't recognise you. What's going on?"

"Like a drink... ?"

"No, I don't want a fucking drink. What the *fuck* is going on?" his anger beginning to build.

"OK." Suddenly she took on her character from the club. "Just sit the fuck down there and I'll tell you. Jesus Christ! What's the matter with you?"

"How the hell am I supposed to react? You call me in here and suddenly I'm greeted by some bloody sheila like she's straight from the pages of Vogue magazine!"

Gina allowed Franco to take a seat and deliberately maintained a silence for several seconds hoping to calm the situation. She pulled up a chair and sat directly in front of him. "Two years, Franco... is that how long it's been?"

"So?"

"And in that time, I haven't asked you any questions and you haven't asked me any... right?"

"OK... right... I don't..."

"Just listen to me. You asked me if I'm two people. Maybe I am. But no man has ever turned me on like you do."

She saw his defenses drop a little. *Thank god for that.*

"That's probably why I keep seeing you. No demands. No forevers. Not a hell of a lot of conversation. No questions. Just sex. Right?"

Franco shrugged his reply.

"But the time has come for you to know a few things about me. I won't bore you with all the family crap. We've all got our skeletons. But what I will tell you is that I am a fully-grown woman with feelings, ambitions and dreams."

"Gina, this is crap..."

"Franco this is not *crap*!" she told him firmly, raising her voice and getting out of her chair to pace the room.

Franco became ill-at-ease with Gina's change of temperament.

"Bloody hell! You want to tell me what the hell this is all about?"

"I'm trying to, all right? I'm trying to! It might also surprise you to know that by day I have a very good, very responsible and highly professional job. It gives me the opportunity to meet people from all walks of life... and I do mean *all* walks of life. From the high-powered to the blue collar. It may also surprise you to learn that your little Gina here has always dreamed of being very wealthy." She laughed at her own words. "Not much chance of that I guess... at least not until now, and that's where you come in."

Franco looked hard at her. "Don't look at me?... Jesus, babe, I'm not wealthy... !"

She spun round, again placing her hands on his knees and stared straight into his eyes.

"But how would you like to be... and I mean *really* like to be?" she asked, her clenched teeth muffling a tone of deep-seated bitterness.

Franco shifted uneasily in his seat. "I've never seen you like this before. What the fuck do you want me to say? Of course I'd like to be rich. Everybody would like to be rich. What are you saying?"

"I'm saying we can be."

Franco pushed Gina's hands off his knees and stood up. "What's this 'we' shit?"

Again the Sicilian woman looked hard into his eyes. "As I've said, Franco, I've never asked you any questions. But I also don't need to be bloody Einstein to know that you and your brothers are into all sorts of shit. And I mean the kind of crap that gets people locked up."

Franco spat out his reply. "You're fucking full of it, Gina..."

"Enrico gets pissed, Franco. He doesn't say much, but I can add up. You know what they say about loose lips? In fact if anyone had've been game enough to speak up, he'd already be inside for what he did to that woman."

"What woman?"

"Close your mind to it if you like, but you know as well as everybody else in the joint that he's the one who fucked her. Now the poor bitch is in a wheelchair."

Franco's eyes dropped. Gina knew she'd hit the mark.

"But don't worry, sweetheart, no-one's gonna spill their guts."

"So what's the story?"

"Do you trust me?"

"I don't trust any bastard!"

"Wrong answer. Let me try again. Do you trust me?"

"If you're asking me if I would trust a woman, the answer is no."

Gina glared at him. "Not just any woman. After seeing me for two years, do you trust me?"

"I would never trust a woman," he told her coldly.

Gina flew into a rage.

"Get the fuck out of here! *Get the fuck out of here!* Do you hear me, you arsehole! Go! Get! Go on, *Get out!* I knew this wouldn't work. And as you're leaving, ask yourself if there was twenty million bucks on the end of it, would you trust a woman then? Now piss off, you sonofabitch."

Gina grabbed Franco by the arm and hustled him to the door.

Normally Franco would have stood his ground and delivered a backhander. But this time it was Gina who held the trump card and she knew it.

"Come on, babe... ," he protested.

"Go... *out*!"

She reefed open the door, shoved him outside then slammed it shut. Regaining her composure, she lit a cigarette and sat down. "If that prick doesn't ring me back within the hour, I'm done." She knew she had to play the heavy hand to win Franco's respect. By seeing him off from her room, she now had to wait to see if the bait was big enough to lure him in to returning. She knew if he did, it would have to be on her terms. Gina knew the stakes were high. But this was a high-stakes game she was playing. She couldn't be a player without Franco. She hoped he didn't realise that. She also hoped her Italian friend was sufficiently motivated by greed to call her back.

Forty minutes later the phone rang.

"Gina?"

"So?"

"So what the fuck got into you?"

"I asked you a question and you lay that sort of shit on me? Jesus Christ, Franco, we've been balling each other for two years... and you tell me you would never trust a woman?"

"OK. I'm sorry. I didn't mean for it to include you."

Gina smiled to herself, knowingly. Franco knew as well as she did what he had said, but he'd obviously gone away and thought about the twenty million bucks. The power of greed was just too strong.

I'd hoped it would be. Thank god, I was right.

She knew, too, that from now on he'd be amiable and easy-going with the money his sole motivation. She also knew that come time to divide it up he'd show his true colours and if she wasn't careful, he'd either kill her or leave her out in the cold. Twenty million dollars was a lot of money.

"Let me ask you again. Do you trust me?"

"Do I trust you? Of course I trust you. With my life, for Christ sakes!" he told her.

Lying bastard! she said to herself.

"Come back up."

As she opened her door to Franco, he smiled. "Hi babe," he smiled. "Take two?"

She put her arms around him. Within moments, the two were locked together, pushing each other to exhaustion.

"Don't fight with me," Franco pleaded, as he sat on the side of the bed lighting two cigarettes. Gina accepted one.

"Then don't fuck with me!" she told him, with no hint of emotion.

"You've really got a plan, haven't you?"

"I have. You in or out?"

"Tell me the plan."

Gina produced a folder and laid its contents on the floor. "What you're looking at is a villa and its interior. It belongs to Bruno Formicella."

Franco's eyes opened widely. "Bloody hell! People actually 'live' like that?"

"This little turkey does."

"So who the hell is this guy?"

"The House of Bruno in Milan. Fashion guru extraordinaire."

Gina went on to tell Franco everything she knew about the man police and governments regarded as untouchable.

"So how did you get on to this?"

"That's why I asked you if you trusted me," she began. "It was a work function dinner and I happened to sit next to a man with a real big job..."

"Did you fuck him?"

Gina's temper flared. "Jesus, Franco! How come everything comes down to that with you?" hoping her outburst would cover her guilt.

"Did you?"

"And if I did?"

"If I found out you did, I'd kill you," he replied unemotionally.

"As it turns out, no I didn't. Jesus Christ, Franco. Do you fuck anyone else besides me?"

"Need to know... you don't need to know."

She flashed her eyes at him. "I bloody well *do* need to know. If you are, I'll kill you!"

"Piss off, Gina!"

"How do you like it? Not much fun having someone say shit like that to you is it?"

"Who's the guy?"

"Need to know. You don't need to know," she told him curtly, turning his words back onto him.

"Get on with it."

"In five months' time, little Bruno, his darling wife and their children will be away from the villa for two days and two nights. It's the only time of the year the place is unoccupied. My source assures me there will be around twenty million bucks in his safe. There's no security and that's because no-one's game to touch him."

"So he goes off and leaves twenty mill in a safe with no security? Bullshit!"

"True story. But there's one catch."

"Which is?"

"The safe door weighs a tonne."

She could tell Franco's mind was already in overdrive. "Not a problem. And you want me to go and knock it off? Whereabouts is the place?"

"Portofino, on the Italian Riviera."

Franco laughed. "And just how the hell do I get there, clean the joint out and get home again with twenty million bucks in my back pocket?"

"In $1000 bills US, two bags is all you'll need to hold twenty mill."

"OK, how am I supposed to pull off this little miracle?"

"Would you be prepared to?"

"If I say yes?"

"There'll need to be a shit-load of planning. You'll need your brothers to help. We'd need to buy a plane, find a pilot, a deserted landing strip in the Northern Territory, the right weather conditions and about four hundred grand to fund it..."

"Four hundred grand... ?"

"It's on the other side of the world. We'll need fuel, black money, a vehicle to meet us at the plane on our return. You think it's too big?"

Franco paced the floor. He began to chuckle. "Got to hand it to you, babe. You don't do things by half measures. How good's your information?"

"Good enough to say I want to come with you..."

"Pig's arse!"

"If I can't come with you, then I'll call it off right now," she told him firmly.

"You want to be part of all the shit? Christ, you could get shot! The bloody plane might crash. Flying under radar, we might even get shot at..."

"I might also be very handy to have by your side in Italy. I am fluent, you know."

"So we just go out and buy a fucking aeroplane, hire a pilot and take off. What about flight plans, fuel stops, landing rights. Christ, Gina, what are you thinking about?"

"Twenty million dollars," she replied determinedly.

"All right, when?"

"Five months from now. If we do it, we do it five months from today. That's when our little turkey nicks off for a couple of days."

Silence fell between them for a considerable length of time. Franco smoked two cigarettes before he spoke. "How much do you get out of it?"

"Five mill each."

"You reckon there's twenty in the safe?"

"More or less."

"Come on, Gina. Twenty or not?"

"Could be less. Could be more. Christ, I can hardly ring and ask him!"

"No security?"

"That's what I'm assured."

"How much are we paying your snitch?"

"Don't give up, do you? He doesn't even realise the implications of what he said over dinner at the function. Once he mentioned the magic figure, several of us hit on him for detail. All the others were doing it out of sheer curiosity. Not me. But all I'm prepared to tell you is the guy telling the story was a high-ranking officer with the government. His source was the Italian government. OK? It's a risk. It might be bullshit. The bloody safe may be empty when we open it. I know all that. If it turns out that way, we'll pinch the bastard's steak knives so we don't leave empty-handed."

"How long?"

"We'll all need to lose a week out of our lives."

"Four hundred grand! Where the hell am I gonna get that sort of dough?"

Gina smiled. "Cut up some Mercs," she told him, handing him her phone. "You want to call your brothers and ask them to come up?"

Franco shot his glance at Gina. She gave a half-way grin as he dialled Luigi's number. "Luigi? It's me. Enrico with you?"

"Yeah, he's here."

"Listen to me. Tell Enrico to put his dick back in his pants and both of you get in here now... to the Hilton. Room 797. Don't be long."

"You OK?"

"I'm fine. Just get in here."

Franco turned off the phone and handed it back to Gina and sat down. "You might have convinced me, but I'm fucking you, they're not. Convince them, and we'll do it."

* * *

Ten minutes later came a knock on the door. The reaction of Luigi and Enrico was similar to that of their brother's when they saw Gina. They too had to look twice to convince themselves it was really her.

"I'll explain all that to you later," Franco began. "Sit down." Then to Gina, "Gina, four coffees."

"So what's the story?" Luigi asked.

"Gina will tell you in a moment."

A minute later Gina handed each of the three brothers a coffee. "Milk and sugar's on the table if you want it." Then she began to tell them her plan.

After an hour of explanation and intensive questioning, silence fell amongst the group.

"Could be a pig in a poke Franco?" Luigi said.

"Could be a shitload, could be nothing. She told you that. Somehow

I don't think it will be nothing," he answered thoughtfully, gesturing towards the computer printouts of the villa. "Not in a joint like that."

"And the safe door weighs a tonne?" Enrico put in, glancing at Gina.

"That's what I'm told."

Enrico grinned. "And we've got just the gadget to fix that bastard," he sneered.

They smiled in agreement and Luigi began to pace. He rubbed his chin, speaking his thoughts out loud. "Five mill each? I say five and half for us, three and a half for Gina. Any extras, she pays for them."

"Piss off," Gina interjected. "An even split or it's not on. Jesus, Luigi, you're fucking unreal! Franco, tell him!"

Luigi looked at his brother.

"Any room for negotiation, Gina?"

She was suddenly filled with anger. Deliberately calming herself, she gave a gritty and determined reply. "There is no room to negotiate."

"Even split, then." Franco turned to his brothers. "Any expenses go four ways. Anyone got a problem with that?"

All agreed.

"OK. So what's your answer. Do we do this thing, or don't we?"

"Gina," Luigi began, "so how do you plan to launder the stuff back here?"

Franco laughed. "Carefully! Let's just get it first and we'll worry about that later. But I don't see it being a problem."

"When do you need to know, Gina?" Enrico asked.

"Now. If you guys say yes, there's a truckload of detail to be worked out and we've only got twenty weeks. In that time we have to find a pilot and buy a plane. Over to you."

Luigi rolled his bottom lip under his top front teeth. "How do we know we're not being sold a pup?"

It was Gina who spoke. "If we've been sold a pup, then I go down with you, because I will be coming along. Is that guarantee enough?"

Her reply seemed to ease his concerns. "I'd say it's worth a shot," he said.

"Yeah, me too," Enrico agreed. "Franco?"

Franco nodded.

"OK, where do we go from here?" Enrico wanted to know.

Gina took over and rolled out a map of Italy on a table. She pointed to Portofino, and stressed the first priority of hiring a pilot and purchasing the right type of aeroplane.

"Enrico, tell Gina about the time you took a trip through north Queensland. What was that town you went to? You know, the place that's full of blokes escaping wives, maintenance, the law and Christ knows what?"

"You mean Karumba?"

"That's it! Cairns sits on one side of the gulf. Karumba sits on the other, almost directly opposite."

"Tell me about it?" she asked.

"It was a fair while ago. If you head out that way, first you go to Normanton and the thing that hits you about that place is the really weird paint job on the 'local'. That's called The Purple Pub. Not much there. Couple of shops. A post office. Camel trains used to run up to the Cloncurry copper mines. Seventy kilometres away on the coast is Karumba." Enrico laughed. "The bloody joint is so remote, even the paper's two days old when you get it. You'll get plenty of Grunter, king salmon and blue salmon up there. It's also the home of the barramundi and the centre for the Gulf prawning industry.

"There was a time when they were going to establish a telegraph connection with Asia, but somewhere along the line that died in the arse. Not a lot of Aborigines. They tend to shun the joint pretty well. Apparently there was a huge shitfight with the whites at one time. Many Aborigines died, so they give the place a wide berth. Mind you, down the road a bit is an all-black roadhouse. If you're white, you don't go near the place. But the local is called The Animal Bar. Enter at your own risk. I reckon it would have to be the roughest pub in the country. To the extent that a couple of tourists had the audacity to take a photo of the place. They had their heads kicked in, their camera smashed and their car totalled.

"In fact I don't reckon you'd find a more diverse group of blokes. Anyone and everyone from crooked lawyers to bent coppers to druggies to the straight out mean sons of bitches."

"Would it be a good place to find a pilot?" Gina asked.

"Probably as good a place as any... especially one who might be a bit of a shonk."

"Could you go there?"

Enrico looked at Franco. "Bloody long way to go on a maybe!"

"Yeah, well we can't run an ad in the paper either."

"Luigi?"

"Don't you think we should get the dough together first, then look?"

"How long will that take?" Gina wanted to know.

"Eight weeks, if we start now," Franco told her.

"So in eight weeks, can one of you go to Karumba?"

"One of us will go," Luigi told her.

* * *

From that moment on the weekly meetings at the Lay Lady Lay took on a different genre. Instead of all the laughing and carryings-on, mostly all four sat in deep conversation and away from the rest of the patrons. Sometimes the mood would lighten, but now there was a different and more compelling motivation behind the weekly get togethers at their favourite haunt.

Gina was pressuring the brothers to raise the funding. The brothers kept pressuring Gina for more details. It was a juggling act for Gina, keeping Franco happy and always being there for Sebastian McAlister. She kept up the subtle pressure on her political friend, constantly reassuring him she was doing it 'for them'. Franco still wanted to know the source of her information. Gina continued her wall of silence. After several weeks of keeping to themselves at Lay Lady Lay, Marcella, a casual acquaintance of Gina, cornered her in the washroom.

"What the hell is it with you guys? You used to be the life of the party. Now you just sit in a huddle all the time?"

Gina tried to dismiss the question. "Oh you know what guys are like. Sometimes they just want to talk."

"That's crap, Gina! I fucked Enrico the other night when he was half-pissed and he said there's something big going down."

Gina laughed. "Oh Jesus Christ, you believe that? Marcella, he's a bloody dickhead and full of shit!"

Inside, Gina was fuming. *That bloody useless, big-mouthed sonofabitch. He may have blown it.* Then came the words which ripped into her gut.

"He even told me the date," Marcella added in a knowing tone.

Gina wanted to explode. Somehow she kept it together. She looked at Marcella. "The date... what date?"

"For whatever the fuck it is you lot are planning."

"Oh, Christ, Marcella, you mean that extravaganza in three or four months' time?" she answered rapidly, collecting her scrambled thoughts to create a convincing lie.

"Uh-huh."

"Sweetheart, he's having a lend of you. It's just a surprise party for Franco... here, too... forget about it. Enrico just loves mouthing off to impress."

"Oh shit, Gina! I was thinking you guys must have been planning a fucking heist or something," she replied, disappointedly.

Gina hoped she'd successfully extinguished the words from Enrico's loose lips, hoping Marcella wasn't foxing her. She went back inside the club, content somewhat that she'd prevented any damage. She just hoped that Enrico's loose tongue wouldn't jeopardize the futures of all of them.

When she got back to the table she looked at all three brothers. "Can we go out to my car for a few minutes, please?"

She left without waiting for a reply. She reefed open her driver's side door, then slammed it shut after climbing in. Moments later the three brothers all joined her.

"This is all very mysterious..."

She didn't wait for the sentence to finish before she exploded. "Franco, I've just been stood up in the bloody wash-room by Marcella telling me she fucked Enrico the other night and he told her something big is going down. Now for Christ sakes! Enrico, what the fuck did you tell her?"

"Piss off, Gina..."

Next thing, Franco's elbow caught him hard in the face. "Jesus, Enrico, did you spill your guts?"

"That's bullshit!" he protested. "Fuck you, Franco! You do that to me again and I'll fucking kill you!"

Franco again struck his brother.

"You sonofabitch!" he screamed, holding his face, blood now oozing from a cut over his lip.

"What did you tell Marcella?"

"I didn't tell her shit!"

"Then how come she knows the fucking date of the heist in Portofino?" Gina yelled at him.

Enrico was wiping the blood from his lip and now his nose, on his shirt sleeve. Luigi and Franco both cursed loudly, throwing their hands in the air.

"We're buggered then!... Well done, little brother." Again Franco jammed his elbow into his brother's face. "You sonofabitch! Can't you keep your cock in your pants? Jesus Christ! now what?"

Gina went on. "I was able to smooth it over with Marcella. I told her Enrico was referring to a surprise party we are having for you, here at this place. Enrico was just mouthing off. I hope she bought it."

"So do we stay on track, or do we abort?" Luigi asked Gina.

"It's up to you guys. It's your call. I say it's OK. You may think differently."

Franco spoke. "You're a bloody dickhead, little brother. An absolute and total dickhead. I say we keep going."

"Then we keep going," Luigi added.

"And right now, little brother, you can get going. Home! All right? You go home! You hear me?"

"Fuck you!"

"You go home, all right? We'll talk again in the morning. Meantime, you talk to no-one. You hear me! You talk to no-one."

"Jesus Christ, all right, I bloody hear you, all right?"

"All right! We talk again in the morning."

All four alighted from Gina's car. Three of them watched Enrico drive away.

* * *

When they re-entered the club, Marcella walked up to Gina. "Where's Enrico?" she asked smugly.

"He's not feeling well," Franco told her coldly as he brushed past. "You'll have to fuck someone else tonight."

Marcella moved away, and watched the trio from a distance. *By Christ, I know I'm right. They're into some damn thing. I just know they are.*

She found herself a place at the bar, not taking a great deal of notice of where she chose to sit. As she spun her backside around on the stool, she accidentally bumped the person on the next seat.

"Sorry," she said, casually.

The person on the other seat was a slightly built man who appeared a little nervous, a little edgy. Marcella glanced at him, then took a second look. She took a cigarette from a packet. "You got a light?" she asked him. "I haven't seen you in here before."

The man nervously lit her cigarette. "I haven't been here before," he replied.

"Jesus, you're in for an education! Where do you fit in? You gay? You a pimp? You fancy little boys? You a bloody crook? You a drag queen? Everybody in this joint fits in there somewhere."

He forced a small grin and shrugged. "None of them, I guess. I just called in for a beer."

"What's your name?"

"Peter Heatherington," John James said.

"Nice to meet you Peter, I'm Marcella."

He turned to Marcella. "Do you think I'm ugly?" he asked.

Marcella looked each side of herself, then came back to him. "Jesus, are you asking me that?"

He nodded, now appearing more nervous than ever.

Marcella looked at him. She tried to remain expressionless as she took in his unfortunate face. She tried to make light of the question. "Well shit, Peter! There's those out there who say my face is one only a mother could love. Maybe yours is the same."

"But you have a beautiful face."

Marcella was embarrassed. "Whoa there! Next thing you'll be asking me to marry you. Let me buy you a drink."

Suddenly, John James felt an overwhelming desire for the woman. "You order and I'll pay." He noticed that Marcella appeared enormously impressed with the roll of notes he took from his pocket.

"Christ! you're not broke, are you?"

"You live around here?"

"Pretty close."

"You married?"

Marcella shook her head. "Got close a couple of times. Left my run a bit late I think," she replied, taking a sip from her drink.

He put her hand on the roll of notes. "Don't get mad, OK. There's about a grand there. You can have it if I can spend the night with you."

Marcella didn't flinch a muscle. "I don't drive. I'm two blocks away. You want to walk or get a cab?"

"Walk."

Chapter 10

McLoughlin and Bourke retained their room at the University Motor Inn on a week-to-week basis. Since McLoughlin's initial spotting of The Weasel, the trail had gone cold. Dead cold. Night and day they would cruise the streets of the city and the suburbs. McLoughlin maintained the regularity of the weekly phone call to Victorian Police Commissioner Jack Rowland and each week the report would be the same.

"No sign of him, sir."

"Keep on it, and keep in touch," would come the reply.

In the four weeks the two detectives had been in the harbour city, they had wandered in and out of scores of gambling dens, strip joints, night clubs, leagues clubs, RSL clubs, hotels, bars and restaurants. During that time there wasn't the slightest indication they were anywhere near their man.

"The prick's gone to ground, mate, no doubt about it," McLoughlin said to his partner.

"You'd reckon after showing his picture a thousand times, some bastard somewhere would have seen him," Bourke answered.

"I've always believed he was a loner. Now I'm totally convinced. I didn't want to do this but the time has come to put the prick's photo in the mail tray of every cab driver and into every patrol car. I'll get onto Johnson, the New South Wales commiss. Sure as hell we're not going to turn him up this way."

McLoughlin spoke with Colin Johnson and explained what he wanted. Commissioner Johnson told the Senior Sergeant that the operation would be up and running within twenty-four hours. It was.

Ken McLoughlin had decided to issue a mug shot of The Weasel for display in every police patrol car across New South Wales, with specific instructions that under no circumstances was he to be apprehended. Instead, if spotted, The Weasel was to be kept under surveillance and the number supplied with the photograph be phoned immediately. The same request was sent to every cab company in the state with the instructions the photograph not to be displayed in the vehicle. Should The Weasel hail a cab and see his own picture displayed it could well jeopardise the safety of the driver.

"Why don't you want the coppers to grab him?" Bourke asked. "Might save us a lot of bloody grief."

McLoughlin shook his head. "No way. I reckon he's such a secretive bastard that, if we pinch him, we'll get nothing. He's got to have a stash. He's got to be linked to all those bloody robberies. We drop down on him, we'll never know. No mate, we've got to find him and stake him out. And I just have this gut feeling we're in for a bloody long haul. But by Christ if somebody spots him, we'll have to keep our distance because he already knows we're onto him. I just hope some trigger-happy bloody copper doesn't piss himself with excitement if he spots him and tries to make a hero of themself."

"So this time tomorrow it's full on?"

McLoughlin looked at Bourke. "This time tomorrow, when we leave that motel room, we better be prepared to go. Anywhere. Keep that elephant gun well oiled. Check the triple twos. Keep the vests in the car. Wear your bloody Glock like it's a second skin. Don't forget your spare clips and strap those back-ups onto your ankles. I reckon we'll get just one go at this bastard. If he spots us, and we lose him again, it'll be goodnight nurse. He'll go to ground. And that's the bloody thing, Dave. Finding exactly where the bugger does go."

"Haven't you forgotten something?" Dave Bourke asked his boss.

McLoughlin's expression changed. "Christ, I hope not... what?"

Bourke was grinning. "Didn't you want to find a post office?"

"Oh shit! That was yesterday. Why didn't you remind me?"

"I did. Three times. Must be a pretty important letter?"

"Postcard, actually. Mind your bloody business," he grinned.

* * *

Bill Murphy parked his Commodore utility in front of the South West Rocks post office and checked his mailbox. There was the usual array of bills and other paraphernalia, except for one. It was marked 'personal' but he couldn't determine who it was from either by the PMWG on the envelope or the post mark. He didn't wait until he returned to his vehicle to open it. It was from the Port Macquarie Writers' Guild inviting him to be guest speaker at a gala dinner to mark the fiftieth anniversary of the organisation. The State's Premier would also attend and officially open what would be a week of celebrations. An attached list named other VIPs invited to attend, along with some of the country's biggest stars in the entertainment industry.

Our congratulations for the continuing success both locally and internationally of The Fires of Midnight. *Accordingly, we would be deeply honoured...*

Bill Murphy shook his head in disbelief. "Bloody hell! They want *me* as the guest speaker. With all those whackos there! Good god! They want *me* ! Why the hell would they want *me* ?" he asked out loud. "Two years ago, no bastard wanted to know me! How times change!" he laughed. "How bloody times change!"

He was tempted to discard the letter into a nearby garbage bin, but then had second thoughts. "Bugger it! Why don't I do it?"

He checked the bottom of the invitation for the RSVP and a phone number. Taking his phone from his pocket, he dialled the number.

* * *

Franco, Luigi and Enrico had moved into top gear. Their attendances at Lay Lady Lay had reduced to about once a fortnight as they mounted a concerted effort to steal high-priced, late model Mercedes Benz cars. In six weeks their early morning raids were carried out in Albury, Newcastle, Gosford, Goulburn, Wollongong, and Katoomba. Only three vehicles were stolen from the Sydney metropolitan area. The procedure was always the same. Steal the car, take it back to the workshop and completely dismantle it.

They soon discovered there was a ready market, willing and able to deal in 'midnight spares'. The compliance plates were as good as currency, as too were the log books.

On two occasions the vehicles were driven straight from the workshop at a price tens of thousands of dollars under book value. All deals were in cash. No paperwork. No names. No identification. At Gina's insistence she was always the one to call Franco. She couldn't risk his calling her should she be in the company of Sebastian McAlister. She knew he didn't like it, but he went along with it.

"We've got three hundred," Franco told her. "Will that get us started?"

"Can you spare Enrico to go to Karumba?"

"It'll be pushing it, but yeah, he better go I think."

"Does he know what to look for?"

"I spoke to a bloke the other day," his voice broke off as he offered a slight chuckle, "a sort of client, if you get my meaning? He's a bit of a flyer, so I made up a cock and bull story about a couple of blokes I know who want to buy a plane and fly it round the world. Had to be cheap. What should they look for? All that crap. He said to go for an old Cessna C441 turbo prop. Very reliable and you can get them for a couple of hundred... if you know where to look. So I've told Enrico we should aim for something like that."

"When do you think?"

"We knew it was coming up, so he can go. We've acquired a vehicle for the trip. We'll pack him up and send him on his way in a day or so."

"Fine."

"What about the money?"

"Take ten with him. That should be enough to get the ball rolling. You sound tired."

"Stuffed, Gina... but not too stuffed that I can't see you," he said.

She thought quickly. Sebastian was in Perth for three days. He had spoken to her only two hours earlier, so there was no danger of any paths crossing. She knew, too, she must always be there for Franco.

"Don't be long. It's late and I'm a working girl, remember."

* * *

Katie Caplin had just arrived back at the farm from shopping in Naracoorte. Joker, now slowing down somewhat, hauled himself off the verandah to go and greet her as she got out of the car. He always seemed to know when she'd been shopping. Brushing up against her, his tail wagging furiously, Katie stroked his head and laughed.

"All right... all right... here you go, taking out a large bun from a packet. It was oozing with cream and Joker woofed it down.

"Good lord, anyone'd think you haven't been fed for a week. Where is everyone?"

"I here, Miss Katie," Kazumi called. "You want help with shopping, yes?"

Kazumi was taking care of the last of the bags as Gabe arrived home from the paddock. "Hi babe," he called to Katie. "Many in town?"

"The usual." Katie's face broke into a broad grin. She beckoned Gabe, who gave her a puzzled look. "Watch this," she whispered in his ear. "Kazumi," she called.

Kazumi appeared from the kitchen.

"Look what I've got," she said, waving an envelope.

Kazumi's eyes lit up. "For me. A letter for me?"

"Who the hell's that from?" Gabe wanted to know.

"Guess?"

Kazumi looked at the letter and hugged it to her breast. Her face went bright red and she spun on her heel and rushed back into the kitchen.

Katie looked at Gabe. She could see he still didn't have a clue. "Ken McLoughlin, dummy!"

"I'll be buggered! I didn't think he'd give her another thought."

A few moments later, Katie poked her head around the kitchen door. "Everything all right, Kazumi?"

Kazumi's face was lit up like a beacon. "It's from Sergeant Ken, Miss Katie. He say hello to everyone and thank you for lovely day. He tell me he very busy, but he tell me again to keep the fires burning. He say he come back one day. Oh, Miss Katie..."

"How come no bugger tells me anything around here?" Gabe cursed.

* * *

Georgette McKinley walked into Jack Rider's office. "Port Macquarie! What do you think?"

Not wanting to appear that her request to interview Bill Murphy was 'cut and dried', he leaned back in his chair and gave her an inquiring look. "You reckon you can get him?"

"Doesn't hurt to ask."

"Have you got onto his publisher... ?"

"Stop the bullshit, Jack! Yes or no?"

Rider had to bite his tongue. This was the part of the job he hated. Sacred cows. If any of the other staff spoke to him like that, he'd show them the door. But there was nothing he could do about this one. He'd also grown to detest the woman. Scoops or no scoops, he hated even having to talk to her.

"Why do you bother to ask?" he told her curtly. "Obviously, if you want to go to Port Macquarie, you will, irrespective of what I say."

"So it's OK?" she asked sarcastically.

Rider looked at her, about to say something when his boss entered his office. "No problem, Georgette," Hanks answered for him. "Port Macquarie's fine. When do you want to go?"

Georgette explained the situation saying it was writers' week and it may take a day or two to corner Bill Murphy.

"Go early Friday and come back Sunday. You happy with that?"

"Yes, that'll be fine. Thank you, George." She turned to Rider. "See! quite painless wasn't it Jack?" she said as she walked from his office.

Rider sat there seething. George Hanks moved over and put his hand on his shoulder. "Mate, I told you. Let it go. You're not going to change it. If you take her on, you'll lose. Forget it. She's not worth it."

Rider spun round to face his long time friend and boss. "Do you know how embarrassing it is to have her walk jack-shit all over me?"

George Hanks looked around himself. "No-one saw, Jack. It pisses me off, too. I can't change it. You can't change it. But you better get yourself together or she'll see you out of here. I can only smooth things over so far. So mate, come on. Christ, I love you like a brother, don't let some piece of arse get the better of you. We've both been around too long for that."

"Fuck the bitch! OK. It's forgotten."

George Hanks patted his good friend on the shoulder. "Good on ya, son! Worry about every other bugger."

* * *

John James McGregor-McWeasely was frightened out of his wits. After being spotted by McLoughlin in the aftermath of the George Street shootings, he had watched the policeman and his partner from a distance. After they drove away he caught a cab to Lane Cove, a neighbouring suburb of Ryde. He purchased several weeks' supply of food and groceries, then caught another cab to his flat. He scrambled inside the front door, spilling packages all over the floor in his haste. John James hated McLoughlin, but even more he hated the thought of being captured. For two weeks he didn't venture outside his front door. He slept lightly, ever expectant of the knock on the door. When it didn't come he began to breathe more easily. As effortlessly as he inflicted death and injury on others, the very thought of any harm coming to himself reduced him to a trembling mess. Cautiously, very cautiously, he began to venture out. Usually late at night and into the early hours of the morning, and only once a week. He learned of the all-night book and paper shops in King's Cross and would return home laden with reading matter. He also learned of the Lay Lady Lay night club. Nervously, he entered and took a seat at the bar. A chance meeting with a woman at the bar led him to believe he may at last have found a female friend.

A woman that may be interested in spending time with him. He wasn't sufficiently versed in male-female relationships to realise the only interest the woman had in him was his access to what seemed an endless supply of cash.

The woman's name was Marcella. About 35 years of age, Italian, olive skin with long black hair and far too much cheap make-up. Her breasts were firm, her stomach flat and it was obvious she was very proud of her great legs, which she showed off mercilessly. When John James, who introduced himself as Peter Heatherington, offered Marcella, within minutes of meeting her, a thousand dollars to spend the night with him, she didn't hesitate.

Marcella lived only two blocks from the club. They covered the distance on foot and when they entered her apartment, she turned and smiled. "OK, lover boy. You want a coffee first or do you want to get right down to it?"

John James was incredibly nervous. He had no idea what to expect or what to do.

She could see he was more than slightly embarrassed. She moved to turn out the light, throwing back the curtains as she went to allow the reflections of the city to light their way. "Feel happier now?" she asked softly.

John James didn't answer.

Marcella looked at him in the dimly lit room and was unsure what to do next. She decided to sit down. "You change your mind?"

"No, no," he blurted with great urgency.

"What then? You want to sit and talk?"

"I just want to look at you."

Marcella laughed. "Oh, Jesus, a fucking weirdo... !" she exclaimed before John James abruptly cut her off.

He shook his head frantically. "I'm not a weirdo!" he protested, a high-pitched panic in his tone. "I've... I've never been with a woman before," he told her, ashamedly.

"For Christ sakes!... really?"

John James shook his head. "Hardly ever spoken to one," he went on, his voice dropping away to almost a whisper.

"Well, you're alone with one now. You wanna fuck me?... or do I have to show you how? Bloody hell, for the dough you're paying I'll do fucking hand stands on you. You say."

John James by now was most uncomfortable. "I... I only want to look at you," he mumbled.

"You do that at the bar. You want to see me naked?"

John James dropped his eyes, too embarrassed to face her.

Marcella gave a slight chuckle. "If you want to do that, you'll have to take my clothes off," she told him. "Come on, I won't bite."

John James hesitantly made his way to Marcella. He tried undoing the hook and eye at the back of her dress but was all fingers and thumbs.

"I'll help you."

Within moments, Marcella was standing naked in front of John James. She took hold of his hands and ran them over her breasts then down to her patch. "What do you think?" she asked him.

Suddenly he undid his trousers and began to masturbate.

"Jesus, don't waste it!" Marcella cried out, grabbing his hand and leading him into her bedroom. She was quickly on her back.

"Jam that fucking thing inside of me... Christ, don't just bloody jerk off."

John James hadn't even got inside of Marcella when it was all over. She laughed. "You're gonna be here all night, so there's plenty of time to try again," she told him.

In the weeks that followed, John James would turn up at Lay Lady Lay once a week, always unannounced. He'd immediately look for Marcella, hand her a thousand dollars and the two would be gone. He spoke to no-one else.

Gradually, after their third or fourth time together, John James began to talk a little. Not very much, but enough for Marcella to learn he didn't have a living soul in the world who cared for him. If she asked any questions, he totally ignored them. Except one.

"Peter... how would you like to be really rich?"

Suddenly his eyes came to life and the whole of his face became animated. Marcella was a little taken aback at the visual response to her question.

This guy might be my man, she thought.

"I wish I had all the money in the world. That's all I want. To become richer than anyone else on earth."

"Why?" Marcella asked him.

John James looked at her. All he could offer was a puzzled expression. "I've never asked myself that," he told her. "All I know is that's what I want."

"I may be able to help you get at least some of it," she told him coyly.

"How much is some of it?"

"Can't say. But I've got a gut feeling that some people I know are planning something big — *really* big — in September."

"What sort of something?"

"I've tried to find out, but I can't."

"Who are the people?"

"They come to the club. You may have noticed them. There's three brothers and a woman, Gina. She's Sicilian. They always sit in a tight group over by the far wall. They used to be the life of the joint. Now they only sit and talk all night. They used to be here up to three times a week. Now... maybe they turn up once a fortnight. One of the brothers, he told me the other night they're gonna do a big job in September. So I challenged Gina. She was pretty pissed at being asked about it. Tried to laugh it off. The guy was just mouthing off about a suprise party for one of the brothers. Well, I say bullshit to her. I reckon something's going down and I'd like to be part of it. It may be jack-shit, but my guts tells me different. You want to be part of it, Peter?"

"I... I've never done anything like that," he lied, trying hard to sell his innocence to the Italian woman. "You don't know me, Marcella. Why would you want to cut me in on something that could be worth a lot of money to you?"

"'Cause I can't do it on my own. I can't follow those sons of bitches to see what they're up to. But you gotta promise me. If you stake them out and grab what they get, you gotta promise to look after me, OK?"

John James looked at her and offered a wry smile. "Half, Marcella. I'd give you half," he said.

"Do you mean that?" she asked excitedly.

"I mean that," he told her, a firmness in his voice.

"Take your trousers off again, baby, that's worth one for the road."

The last thing on John James mind was the woman he was with. The first thing was what the woman had told him. They sat and talked again for a lengthy period.

"Tell me all you know."

"I have," she replied. "But if I know Italian men, one will go missing from the group a few days before the others take off. He will be the organiser. So we better try and find out where each of them lives. The night one doesn't turn up, we go to his joint and wait. When he takes off, we follow."

"You reckon that's how it will work?"

"I *know* that's how it will work."

John James pulled another wad of notes from his pocket. "Cab fares. You follow and find out where they live."

Marcella took the money. "Might take a few weeks."

"We've got plenty of time. September, you say?"

"Apparently."

"I can't see why you think it's something big."

"A woman's intuition," she smiled. "This guy, Enrico, he was a bit pissed, but it was the way he said it."

"Has he got a mobile phone?"

Marcella told John James he had.

"Can you get the number?"

"Jesus, that's a tough one. I'll try."

"If you get it, arrange to get him pissed then ring him up and pretend you're... Gina, was it?"

"Yes, Gina."

"Phone him and ask what's the agreed split again. They would already have worked that out if something's on. He'll probably just blurt it out without thinking."

"I'll try."

"I'd better go. See you in a week."

* * *

Again John James didn't leave his flat over the ensuing days. His mind was racing with the possibilities of what Marcella may have turned up. The following week, in the early hours of the morning, John James walked into the Lay Lady Lay. He saw the group of four huddled together by the far wall, then he saw Marcella seated at the bar.

"Hello," he said softly as he sat next to her.

Marcella didn't look at him. "Something wrong?"

"Get a good look at the group of four if you can, because we can't come back here again. They could be on to me. Take a piss or whatever. But get a look at their faces. I'll get a cab and meet you outside."

John James eased himself off the stool and went to the men's toilet. As he was standing at the urinal, the three brothers walked in after him.

Panic took hold of John James' gut. *Have they worked out I put Marcella up to calling Enrico? Has Marcella told them I might be a threat? Was she playing a double hand and really belonged to one of them anyway? Am I about to be dead over this September thing?*

These questions raced through his mind as his breath shortened and instinct told him the shit was about to hit the fan. He stood at the urinal trying to pee, but nothing would come. Nobody spoke. Instead, the brothers just stared at him. Then Franco made his move. He lunged at John James, grabbing his trousers and reefing them hard up through the cheeks of his backside, pushing his head against the wall.

"Who the fuck are you, pally?"

"Jesus Christ, what have I done?" he squealed.

"That broad at the bar. The one you seem to be very cosy with every week. She's my brother's head job when he says so. OK? You understand what I'm saying? That means you stay the fuck away from her or we'll cut your cock off and feed your balls to the rats. You get the message? You get the message, you little worm?"

"Oooh, Christ!" John James stammered, feeling his warm urine run down his leg. "How was I supposed to know? She didn't say! You want me to stay away? OK, I'm staying away. Fucking hell!"

Franco released his grip on the slightly built man. John James felt relief run through his body.

Shit! And I was thinking all that other stuff!

But it wasn't over. Enrico spun round and jammed his knee into John James' groin. He screamed in agony, collapsing in a heap onto the toilet floor.

"That's in case you change your fucking mind, arsehole," he said, joining his brothers as they returned to the bar. He fought to regain his feet, but was unable to stand erect.

Outside, Marcella was seated in a cab waiting for him. She was beginning to panic when suddenly John James literally ran from the premises, his eyes wide open in expectation she'd be there. He fell into the cab.

"Go!" Marcella yelled to the driver. "What the bloody hell happened to you?" she asked John James, knowing it may take him a while to answer. He finally caught his breath.

"I just met the brothers," he groaned, the pain still causing him to double up.

Marcella quickly gave the cab driver the address of a motel. "I booked a room tonight in case there was trouble," she said. "With what I found out, there might be."

The two didn't speak as the cab driver drove to their destination. Inside the room, John James still couldn't stand properly.

"What the fuck was all that about?" Marcella asked with genuine concern.

"Those bastards grabbed me in the can. Told me to stay away from you as you belonged to Enrico when he said so."

Anger rose in Marcella. "They're mongrels, those bastards. I told you, I fucked Enrico once and that was it. I don't belong to anyone," she said fiercely.

"They say you do."

"Believe me. I don't. But I'll tell you one thing. I thought that little shakedown might have been about the phone call."

"You rang Enrico?" John James asked, brightening up a little.

"Cost me five hundred to the barman, but yes, I rang the prick."

"Tell me?" he urged, still trying to overcome the pain in his groin.

"Two nights ago. The barman loaded him up with triple Jacks. I waited till they all left. Worked well, actually, because Gina wasn't there that night. So I dialled the number. Enrico slurred some sort of hello and when I said, 'Enrico, Gina, tell me again the split we agreed upon.' He came out with a mouth full of abuse about being phoned on his mobile. Said it pissed him off that she was even going and if she wasn't such a shit-for-brains wog Sicilian, she would have remembered it was five mill each. 'Now go away and leave me alone.'

"He would had to have been pissed to speak to her like that because, from what I've observed, Gina calls the shots... make no mistake about it. But when you see them in the group, he's all over her. He obviously hates her guts, but because of what's going down, he's sugar sweet when face to face with her. What an arsehole! But what about that, Peter? Five mill each? Surely that can't mean five *million* dollars each?"

John James was nearly beside himself with excitement. "Tell me again? Enrico said her share was five mill?"

"I can still hear his voice."

"Bloody hell, if that's the case, it's a twenty million dollar heist? In this country? In September? No way! They're going overseas. Have to be. And Gina's going with them?"

"That's what he said."

John James paced the room of the motel. Thinking. "Do those guys know where you live?"

"Wouldn't be hard for them to find out."

"Have you followed any of them yet?"

"Just Franco," she told him, opening her handbag and handing him an address. "That's where he lives. Quite a joint. Wife. Kids. Two cars."

"Turramurra?"

"Top suburb."

"OK." John James pulled another wad of notes from his pocket. "Stay here tonight. Give me your mobile phone number. Move somewhere else every day. This will cover it," he told her, handing her a bunch of $100 bills. "Don't go back to your place for five days. If you need anything, buy it," he said, handing her more money. "I'll go back to your place with you when you go so you can get what things you need. You'll need to find another place to live. I'll pay for it. I think once they get their head around that phone call, they'll know it was you, and your life will be in danger."

"I reckon Enrico would already have figured that. He'd be too scared to tell his brothers and he'd be racking his brain trying to remember just what he did say on the phone. I don't think I have to worry about the other three. It's Enrico who'll want me out of the way. And he'll think I've told you, so that means he'll be after you, too."

John James gave a shallow grin. "I'm not worried about him. He won't get near me. But I am worried about you. I'll go now..."

"Can't you stay?" she pleaded.

But John James had enough problems of his own, namely one smart cop who was on his trail. He felt exposed being away from the security of his flat. He looked at Marcella. "I'll ring you tomorrow. Lock the door when I leave."

Marcella placed her hand on his crotch. "You sure I can't convince you to stay?" she asked softly.

But the pain of Enrico's knee was still most apparent. "That prick might have fucked me for all time," he told her.

"You sure you'll be all right?"

"Just lock the door, Marcella. I'll ring you tomorrow."

* * *

When Enrico awoke the next morning, recalling the phone conversation, his stomach twisted into a knot and his mouth filled with bile. He went to the bathroom and gargled.

That wasn't bloody Gina. No way that was Gina. Jesus Christ, what the hell have I done? It had to be that Marcella bitch! But why would she suspect? Surely she didn't believe that shit I told her the other night. Obviously she did. But how would she have got my mobile number? And who's that prick she's with? That scrubby-arsed, ugly little mongrel surely couldn't be a threat to anyone! One thing I do know, if bloody Franco or Gina hear about this I'm fucked. Jesus, I've got to stop mouthing off when I get on the piss. But right now I've got to stop them from mouthing off or getting in the way of September.

But Enrico also knew he had to play it cool. What if it *was* Gina on the phone? He knew the answer to that question would be forthcoming as soon as they all met again. But that guy had him tricked. He didn't know what the story was with him.

Maybe I'll just kick his head in and see what happens. He'll probably just disappear.

Enrico found out where Marcella lived and sat waiting for her every night. But to no avail. He checked with her neighbours. No-one had seen her, but no, she hasn't moved out. All her stuff was still there, they assured him.

Her continuing absence frustrated him to the point of extreme anger. But he had to contain it and not show his hand to his brothers or to Gina. This was a problem he had to fix himself.

* * *

After his call to Marcella on the fifth day, John James picked her up at her motel at his favoured time of ten minutes to four in the morning.

"Hell of a time to get a girl out of bed," she told him.

"It's the safest time of the day," he told her. "We'll go to your place. Grab the things you need and come back here. Keep changing motels for another week then we'll find you a place. Any luck with where the other bastards live?"

"All three."

"Jesus, that was quick... how did you manage that?"

"Don't ask," she replied, handing him the addresses of Gina, Franco and Luigi. "I have my ways."

When John James got into the cab he'd hailed to take the two of them to Marcella's place, he was careful the cab driver didn't get a look at him. He sat directly behind him, almost in a crouched position. If Marcella noticed his over-cautious behaviour, she didn't comment. John James had the driver circle Marcella's place three times before he was happy to pay and let him go. Moving as quickly as his irregular gait would allow him, he and Marcella were soon inside her apartment. John James was also confident no-one had seen them enter.

"We better be quick," he told her. "There's no telling if those bastards are onto you... or me."

Marcella went quickly to her bedroom and took a suitcase from a wardrobe. She was busily packing her clothes into it when John James walked in to join her.

"I have something for you," he told her.

"Oh, Peter, you've already given me so much... and when this is all over, *wow*, it looks like it's going to be millions."

Marcella could see John James was holding something behind his back. Her eyes opened wider in anticipation. "Oh, you really are spoiling me."

"Turn around and close your eyes."

They were the last words Marcella would ever hear. The moment she put her back to John James, he jerked his pen-gun from his shirt pocket, pressed it to the back of her head and released the firing pin.

Marcella never uttered a word as she fell, dead, onto her bed. John James had watched carefully to see where the bullet would lodge after passing through her skull. But this was one bullet he wouldn't retrieve. It had gone through her bedroom window. Coldly he looked at her. He foraged through her handbag and withdrew the remaining $100 bills he'd given her. He went to the kitchen, soaked a tea towel and rubbed it over all the places where he felt his fingerprints could be found. He checked around the rooms to see if by chance there was anything that could identify him. He returned to the bedroom and placed a finger on her neck to make sure the woman was definitely gone. She was.

"Sorry, babe. You were a loose end. I can't afford loose ends."

As he hurriedly, but cautiously, left Marcella's apartment, his mind was spinning with the thought of such a massive booty. It might be nothing, but it might be all the money in the world.

Now I know where these sons of bitches live I'll just take my time. When the move is on, I'll be there. Then we'll see who gets kneed in the balls!

* * *

McLoughlin and Bourke were having breakfast in their room when the news came on the radio. The death of the Italian woman was being widely reported, but no different to any other murder.

Homicide squad detectives are investigating the death overnight of a woman in her King's Cross apartment. Believed to be aged in her early thirties, the woman is thought to have been alone at the time and was killed by someone known to her. Detectives say there are no signs of a struggle. She died after being shot in the head at close range by a small-calibre handgun or possibly even a pen-gun...

McLoughlin nearly dropped his coffee cup. Bourke looked at him. "It's the fucking Weasel... the bastard's done it again!"

"What the hell are you talking about?"

"The pen-gun! The fucking pen-gun! He knocked a sheila off in Melbourne years ago with a *pen*-gun."

"I thought they went out with the ark?"

McLoughlin shook his head. "They used to be big in the jails, but they managed to clean that up. But some of the crims still use them. By Christ, they're effective. But this sheila? I'm telling you. It's the fucking Weasel, believe me," he said reaching for his phone.

"Who you ringing?"

"Johnson," he said and he moved away from the table. "Sir, good morning, sorry to bother you. It's McLoughlin..."

The police detective then explained to the New South Wales Police Commissioner what his suspicions were about the overnight killing of the Italian woman.

"This bastard's got form with a pen-gun sir. I need everything there is on this investigation."

"I'll see to it right now you are called within the hour by Inspector Harry Springer. Springer heads up homicide."

"Thank you, sir."

* * *

John James remained holed up in his flat for nine days before he went outside. He listened constantly to radio news bulletins, and television newscasts became compulsive viewing. The death of Marcella received heavy coverage in the twenty-four hours after her body was discovered. As it turned out, that was three days after her death. A local council employee, topping a nearby tree, reported seeing a bullet hole in her bedroom window. Before killing Marcella, John James bought three second-hand VCRs from pawn shops so he could tape everything that went to air.

When the initial surge of reports had run their course, the death of the Italian woman received little or no coverage after 48 hours. Within 72 hours, all coverage of Marcella's death had dried up. Still, John James persisted in listening and watching for any indication that police were on to him.

* * *

It was only a matter of hours after Marcella's body was found that homicide detectives were climbing all over the Lay Lady Lay nightclub. Yes, Marcella was a regular. No, she didn't mix very much. Yes, Enrico was forced to admit he'd had sex with her and that was as far as their once-only association went. Yes, the barman was forced to admit he too had had a sexual encounter with her. Gina admitted she was a casual acquaintance, other club patrons said they knew her to say hello to with Franco and Luigi telling police the woman wasn't known to them. But the common thread emerging from the inquiries was the man she met casually and infrequently in the early hours of the morning. All gave a common description of a slightly-built man, of unfortunate looks with a peculiar hopping gait. No-one knew his name or anything about him, much less where he lived.

McLoughlin's phone rang. It was Inspector Harry Springer.

"Commissioner Johnson has spoken with me, what do you need to know?"

"I need to know if the prick who knocked the Italian sheila is the little germ I'm after."

Springer told McLoughlin what was known of the case at that stage plus a description of a man she was seen with at irregular intervals.

"Yeah, that's the bastard."

"Not much to go on is it?" Springer retorted.

McLoughlin gave a slight grunt. "Definitely a pen-gun?"

"That's what first reports indicate... need the lab report to be sure."

"And germ-features walks with a kind of hop and is as ugly as sin?"

"Seems to be the case, yes. The commiss played this one pretty close to his chest, Sergeant. What's going on?"

"Can't tell you that Harry. Sorry. But I do need to be kept in touch with everything about that woman's death. What I can tell you is that it's priority, right to the top. I have to catch this bloke."

"We'll do our best. This the only number?"

"Twenty-four hours, Harry. Ring it anytime."

* * *

John James counted down the days to September. He knew there was a lot to do to single out which of the brothers would be the runner. His persistence paid off. After continually staking out each brother's home, suddenly a four-wheel-drive appeared in Enrico's driveway.

Him. It's got to be him.

In the days that followed, he noticed bigger tyres had been fitted to the vehicle. A large front-to-rear roof rack. Several jerrycans were lined up along the front of the rack. A bull bar was added, which in turn had been fitted with a winch and high-powered driving lights.

Two large radio aerials. A hi-lift jack mounted on the rear. A large car fridge then went in. The vehicle's seats were replaced with custom-made highly expensive Recaros.

From a distance, John James watched as the vehicle was transformed over a period of two weeks. Every day something else was added.

These pricks are planning a very, very long trip. But when? And where? Whatever it is, it's big. Damn big. Maybe Marcella was right. Maybe the hit is for twenty million. That's even too much to dream about. But you'd hardly do up a bus like this if you're not going somewhere. And, by hell, they're going somewhere!

John James began to wonder about his own vehicle. If he suddenly had to take off and follow, which is what he was expecting to do, he would also need to carry extra fuel. His mind went to the car he seldom drove, locked safely away in the garage at his flat. He felt confident he could go anywhere anytime in it, and with safety.

Better get a couple of jerrycans, I think.

The installation of pen-guns in the air-conditioning ducts in the dashboard also gave him an added-feeling of personal security. Fearing anything might happen, John James loaded his vehicle with everything he'd need for a long journey. As he sat outside the Italian's house in the early hours of the morning, the stillness of the night was broken with the arrival of three vehicles in quick succession. Enrico emerged from his front door, hugged his brothers, shook hands with a woman (*That's Gina, has to be... bit hard to tell from here though, but it has to be!*), climbed into his vehicle and drove off. John James waited for a few moments, then followed.

Remaining at a lengthy distance behind, he followed Enrico as he made his way up the freeway to Newcastle and beyond. Because the four-wheel-drive looked so much like so many others, John James sometimes thought he'd lost his quarry. It meant he had to remain doubly alert. On through the morning, the day and into the night, Enrico only stopped briefly to take on fuel. John James was grateful the Italian was so pre-occupied with the job at hand, he didn't even bother to check to see if anyone was following. For three days, Enrico kept up a frantic pace behind the wheel. John James was near exhaustion. His eyes felt like balls of sandpaper. He knew if he stopped to sleep when Enrico stopped to sleep, he'd wake to find him gone.

So he forced himself to stay awake. Enrico continued to travel north. John James would check the map.

Bloody hell, if he keeps going like this he'll end up in the ocean.

Finally, the waiting was over. John James backed off considerably when he followed the Italian through Normanton.

Karumba, he thought. *There's nowhere else to go.*

Satisfied his assumption was correct, he drove his car over salt-pans to a bushy area, a long way in off the road, south of Walkers Creek camp. Checking that he was safe from hijackers, muggers and car strippers, he switched off the engine, locked all his doors, left his driver's side window open a little and tilted his seat back. He put a pen-gun in his hand and a cushion behind his head.

He didn't wake for ten hours. When he did, it was with a start. He turned the ignition key to accessories and lowered the windows in the two front doors.

I bloody heard something! I know I did.

As he strained his ears for the slightest sound, it came. Quickly he opened his door as silently as he could, knowing if someone was approaching it would be from the passenger side. He rolled onto the ground from his seat and crawled on his belly into nearby bush. In a few seconds he had cleared his car and become invisible. His heart began to race. As he peered through the bushes, he saw two men approaching. They were nervous and fidgety. They were also in a hurry. As they closed in on John James' car he heard their conversation.

"Get a load of this! Jesus, is this Christmas day or what?"

"Can you see anyone?"

"Nah. Must have broken down. Poor bastard will be in for a shock when he gets back eh?"

John James watched as a tool box was opened and a spanner placed on his vehicle's wheel nuts.

The mongrel bastards! They gonna strip my bloody car.

Crawling on his belly he wondered how he was going to deal with two of them. One wasn't a problem. Two were. He would take the first one by surprise with the pen-gun. But both were much bigger men than himself. Especially the one on the other side of the vehicle. One wrong move and he knew he'd be dead.

John James moved as silently as a cat. When he was only a few metres from the man on the driver's side, he leapt to his feet and lunged. His leap landed him right next to the man removing the wheel nuts from the vehicle.

"Happy Christmas, arsehole," John James sneered.

His victim didn't know what hit him. The pen-gun was jammed into his ear and the firing pin released. The would-be thief slumped forward, dead. Hearing the Happy Christmas greeting and a shot from the other side of the car, his accomplice raced around the vehicle. He caught John James by surprise, still on his haunches, landing a vicious blow to his head. John James slumped to the ground, almost senseless.

His attacker was yelling and screaming as he threw himself on top of him, wrapping his arms around him in a vice-like bear-hug. John James thought he was going to pass out with the pain of such a hold. Gradually, he was able to move his hand across to the top of his belt and jerk the rip cord. It was attached to a pen-gun he wore on his belt but was pointed to the rear to cover him for just such an attack. He heard the gun go off, a screeching "Aaaah!" and then felt the big man's grip on him loosen. The bullet failed to find its mark but it gave John James sufficient time to free himself and push his attacker on to his back. As he did, he threw himself directly on top of him and jerked a second rip cord.

This one was attached to another pen-gun which was aimed to annul any attack from the front. Again John James heard the little weapon fire. This time the bullet did its job, penetrating the heart of his attacker. He watched the big man's eyes roll back into his head, a look of total surprise on his face. Covered in blood back and front, it took John James all his strength to drag the two bodies into nearby bush. He took their personal effects to prevent immediate identification, then covered them. He was grateful at being so far off the road.

At least there's no one else around, he said to himself, fighting to stop his body from trembling.

He reloaded his pen-guns then took a can of water and a bowl from the boot of his car. Then John James took off his clothes and washed himself down. He grabbed a clean shirt and trousers from an overnight bag and placed what he'd taken off into a plastic bag.

Jesus Christ, I better bury that lot really deep... but not here.

Suddenly, the shock of what he'd endured and the action he took hit him like a tonne of bricks. His face was on fire, pains gripped his stomach and he shook uncontrollably.

Get yourself together, John James, and get the hell out of here,' he told himself.

He checked his car's wheel nuts, climbed in behind the wheel and drove back to the main road. A short distance away he came across an old Holden utility.

That's their bloody car, he thought, slowing down as he approached it.

He checked the road behind and ahead. There were no other vehicles. He pulled up and grabbed a screwdriver from his glove compartment. He hurriedly removed the vehicle's number plates, used his pocket knife to disfigure the registration disc, piled what belongings were in the cabin into one corner and soaked the car's interior and exterior with petrol. He then ran a trail of fuel several metres long, up the road. John James raced back to his car, drove a short distance, ran back, threw a lighted match into the petrol trail and rushed back to his car. The flames quickly snaked their way to the old Holden. He saw it erupt into an inferno in his rear vision mirror as he drove away.

"OK," he yelled loudly as he held one hand to his bruised cheekbone. "So where the fuck are you, Enrico?"

* * *

McLoughlin was becoming increasingly frustrated. "Mate, he's gone to ground, the prick. Nothing surer," he said to Bourke."Nothing from Springer?"

"Only that it's a dead cert The Weasel's our bloke, but Jesus, he's just disappeared into thin air. No bloody sightings from the cabbies. Nothing from the coppers in their cars."

"I meant to tell you, his bloody picture's at the airports, too. And nothing from any of them."

"So what now?"

"We just have to wait. I'll get on to Johnson again and ask him to prioritise The Weasel's picture. Send it out again if he has to. Somebody, somewhere must have seen him."

Chapter 11

The place has changed a bit since I was last here, Enrico thought as he drove slowly around Karumba. Television aerials peeped out of rooftops and there appeared to be more front gardens than years before. He pulled into the side of the road and again checked his map which also gave a brief outline of what amenities were on hand. Three caravan parks and six sets of holiday cabins. He looked ahead and saw a sign.

That one will do. Units are cabins, I guess.

He booked and paid for three nights. He didn't want to be in Karumba any longer than he had to be. After three days and nights on the road, the shower and a change of clothes was most welcome to the city-raised Italian. Deciding not to lose any time in trying to find a pilot, he chose to leave the cabin and go for a walk. He recalled how the one place you didn't go was The Animal Bar, regarded as being the roughest pub in Australia. Cautiously, he approached the establishment and did something of a double-take when he saw two women standing behind the bar serving.

By hell, that joint must've changed, he thought. *In the old days, you wouldn't have found a woman near the joint.* He paused for a few moments. *Hell, if there's women barmaids, the place can't be too bad. I'll see how it goes.*

Enrico walked into the bar and sat down on a stool. A sprightly woman, probably in her thirties, approached. "Howdy... what'll it be?"

"Just a beer, luv... bloody hot isn't it?"

She laughed and said, "You must be a tourist. Most of you lot have emptied out by August."

Enrico laughed back. "That obvious is it? Tell me then, what do tourists do around here for leisure?"

"There's two TV channels, that's it," she said. "You can't swim here because of the crocs. Bloody big salties, so you need to be aware of that. Know it and respect it. Leave them alone... they'll leave you alone. They were here first. And if you go walking through the bush," she continued with a wry smile, "then watch out for the taipans, the pythons, the blacks, the browns, the tree snakes and the goannas."

Enrico finished his beer. "Anything else to be aware of?" he asked with a wink. "The man-made kind."

"Oh," she smirked. She ran a damp cloth along the top of the bar and leaned over to speak quietly to Enrico. "A couple of coppers with about a thousand orders and warrants and Christ knows what else for people who don't exist."

It was just as he expected. "Got an airport?" he asked casually.

"Not an airport as such... more like an airstrip. If you want an airport you have to go to Burketown."

"So where's the strip?"

"About six kilometres out of town at Karumba Point. It runs parallel with the beachfront, facing west towards Mornington Island."

"Is it sealed?"

Helen gave a brief chuckle. "You gotta be joking! Red soil and gravel. Planes can't even be serviced here. They have to be taken to Mount Isa, Mareeba or Cairns."

"Many planes come in?"

She served him another beer as she spoke. "No big ones, but heaps of small ones. Especially at the height of the fishing season. There's even a couple of pilots who live here on the off chance of getting a gig when they can."

Enrico suddenly became very interested.

"One poor bugger," she went on, "Jesus, I feel sorry for him. Actually, he comes in here now and again. Josh Emery. Came up here with his girlfriend and kid on a promise to fly some guy around. Turns out he was a bloody shonko. The coppers cart him away. Josh then has to send his bird and the kid back to Bathurst in New South Wales to live with his mother 'cause they've got nothing. And he's out there shovelling shit on prawn boats and grabbing what pilot jobs are going."

"Shit happens!" Enrico said as he drank some more.

"Yeah, shit happens," she added dryly.

Enrico looked around. "Always this quiet in here?" he asked, noticing there were only a few other people in the bar.

"You've just happened by on a quiet ten minutes. Most of the time I don't have time to spit, let alone have a yarn with a customer. That's total luxury." She looked up as another customer entered the bar. She nodded to him and said, "Josh Emery's just walked in. You want to meet him?"

"The pilot bloke?" Enrico couldn't believe his luck. "If you like," he replied casually.

"G'day, luv," Josh called to the barmaid as he walked to the bar.

She noticed a forlorn look on his face. "G'day Josh. Still nothing?"

He shook his head.

She pulled a pint and put it in front of him. "On the house. Guys, why don't you have a chat," she said and introduced the two of them. She looked up as more people entered the bar. "Seems my ten minutes is over, fellas. You'll have to excuse me."

Josh unenthusiastically held out his hand. "Nice to meet you," he said as Enrico took hold of it.

"Yeah, good to meet you, Josh. I'm told you're a pilot?" Enrico put in, looking to make conversation.

"Trying to be," he answered glumly, "but all those plans appear fucked and burned."

"Not necessarily," Enrico told him with just enough enthusiasm to give the young man hope. "How old are you?"

"Twenty-six going on fifty," he replied offering a hollow laugh.

"How good are you?"

Josh turned to Enrico. "I could fly through the eye of a fucking needle."

Enrico took a $100 bill from his pocket and put it on the bar in front of him. "I'd like to buy an hour of your time. Will that cover it?"

Josh grabbed it and stuffed it into his pocket. "So... what do I have to do?"

"Talk to me. Is there somewhere we can go?"

Josh's temper suddenly flared. "You come on to me with any crap and I'm gone."

Enrico looked around the bar. He spotted an empty table in a corner. "OK, we stay in here," he told Josh, then ordered another two beers and moved to the vacant table. "What can you fly?" he asked.

"Pretty well anything... except jets and helicopters."

"No jets or helicopters," he assured him.

"So what then? You haven't driven all the way up here to find a pilot if what you're doing is legit. I would suggest to you that you're looking to do a one-off fucking drug haul in a plane that's not your own. You'll pay the pilot with an ounce of lead behind the ear once the job's done and walk away with a million bucks. Tell me if I'm getting warm?" he said angrily.

Enrico hardly flinched. "Not even plugged in, young man."

"What then?"

Enrico liked the man's attitude. He also knew he'd have to be very convincing to prevent him walking out the bar room door. "OK... I want a pilot. It's a one-off job. A big job. It'll also involve a plane which won't belong to somebody else. I intend to buy one..."

"Jesus Christ, mate, it must be some sort of bloody deal!"

"All I'm prepared to tell you at this point is that if you're interested, the job will require two weeks out of your life. One week to prepare and one week for the actual job. It will be dangerous, I won't lie to you about that. You'll need to know your way around the aviation industry and that means flight plans, fuel, runways. You will be paid $200,000 for those two weeks and if you get us home safe and sound, you can keep the aeroplane."

"Whoa, now just hold on a minute! Who the fuck's '*us*?"

"You will have three passengers. Two men and a woman."

Josh Emery looked at Enrico for a lengthy period without speaking. He got up from the table and walked away. When he returned, he sat down and again glared hard into Enrico's eyes. "What sort of plane?"

"We'll get to that."

"Is it drugs?"

Enrico shook his head.

"Bullshit man! It's fucking drugs. Has to be. No way! There's no amount of money in the world that'd ever get me to do that shit."

Enrico held up his right hand. "On the life of my children, I promise you it is *not* drugs."

"What then? Stolen bloody paintings? Whatever it is, it's obviously not very big and is worth a shitload."

"If you decide you'd like the job, we'll talk more and you'll be told more. How long do you want?"

"If I decide to take it, when do I start?"

"If you decide to take the job, it starts now and so does the pay. It's up to you. Right now, I'm pretty stuffed. I'm going back to the cabin to have a snooze for an hour or so. If your answer is yes, be back here in three hours. And Josh. Think long and hard. If you commit, there's no turning back. Remember that. My partners wouldn't take too kindly to a walk-out halfway through."

"Is that a threat?"

Enrico leaned into him. "That's business," he answered in a voice as cold as the beer he'd been drinking. "You can't wear new boots if you're planning to take them back. Think about it. See you in three hours."

* * *

John James McGregor-McWeasely was still holding his face as he drove into Karumba. Slowing right down, he scanned the streets trying to pick up Enrico's four-wheel-drive.

He went past one group of cabins. It wasn't there. As he got opposite another he saw a similar vehicle.

Shit!, that's it, he said to himself, drawing to a halt. He was about to back up and take a better look when up ahead he noticed a man walking towards him. *Fuck!... it's him!*

Quickly he checked his mirrors and backed up before doing a U-turn. He drove a short distance and looked into the rear-view mirror. Enrico gave no indication he had seen him.

That bloody prick doesn't even know I'm on his arse, he thought, grinning.

When he saw Enrico disappear into a cabin, he did another U-turn and parked opposite, about 60 metres from the entrance to the accommodation complex.

Now I'll wait and see what he does next, he thought as he slipped the driver's backrest a couple of notches and made himself comfortable.

Three hours later, he watched Enrico leave the cabin and approach The Animal Bar. A man he didn't know was standing out front waiting for him. They exchanged words and then headed back to Enrico's cabin.

As the two walked together, John James noticed one of the locals speak to Josh Emery. After the two had disappeared inside the cabin, John James turned over the engine and drove up to the person who had spoken to him.

"Excuse me, mate, that bloke you just spoke to, Jesus, I know him from somewhere... can you tell me who it was?"

"Yeah, that's Josh, mate. You know him?"

"I reckon I went to school with him. Haven't seen the bugger in years. Josh eh! Bloody Josh," John James laughed. "What the hell's he doing here?"

"Came up here to fly planes but got left high and dry by some bastard. Top bloke, too..."

"Josh... Jesus... what's his other name... Josh Smythe is it... some name like that?"

"No, no. Josh Emery. Dunno who the bloke is he was with."

"Small world isn't it... bloody Josh Emery. He used to date my sister. Thank you. Thank you very much."

John James' mind went into overdrive. *That bastard has come all the way up here to find a pilot? What the fuck are they into? Marcella was probably right. Twenty million bloody dollars. It's gotta be that big for them to go to this trouble. Better see what happens from here.*

Again John James drove back along the street and parked at a discreet distance but within full view of the entrance to the holiday cabins. He was desperate for sleep and a good meal. He was low on fuel, but he knew he couldn't risk being seen by too many people. He was also keenly aware that once he got out of his car, people would be quick to spot his unusual gait. He'd already risked his identity in finding out about Josh Emery. He accepted that such was a totally unavoidable risk.

John James was in two minds. He had now established that Enrico had driven all this way to recruit a pilot. Did he leave now, return to Sydney, stake them out and wait, or hang around for a day or so, wait for Enrico to leave and see what he could find out? He chose the latter. There was also the matter of a couple of stiffs he'd left out on the side of the road. A chill shot through his body as he recalled how close he came to being killed himself.

An even bigger chill froze him to his seat when, a couple of hours later, still waiting to see the result of the meeting between Josh Emery and Enrico, a tow truck pulling a trailer went past his parked car. John James only paid it scant attention until he noticed the burnt-out remains of a Holden ute on board the trailer.

Shit! he exclaimed silently. *Not much left of that.* He glanced at the rear-view mirror, then over his shoulder and all around himself. *Something is telling me to get the fuck out of here. Soon, me-boy... soon.*

He couldn't help wondering if the bodies of the two men had been found. Noticing no increased activity in the town or a sudden mass exit of vehicles to the spot, he figured they hadn't been.

The meeting between the two men went on past three hours. Finally Josh Emery emerged alone from the cabin wearing a grin from ear to ear. He kept one hand in his pocket. John James had his suspicions.

He's holding a shit-load of cash in that pocket. I know. I used to do the same. The first time you get your hands on a heap of dough, you just want to hold onto it. Right now Josh Emery is holding onto it.

He also knew that if Josh Emery had just been given some sort of lifeline, he'd want to talk about it... even if he'd just made a promise to Enrico not to, which he was sure he had. That was human nature. *He* always wanted to, but didn't know anyone.

He watched as the young pilot made his way up the street into The Animal Bar, figuring he had to take another risk. As unobtrusively as he could, he walked slowly into the bar, his head down, but his eyes ever alert. He spotted Josh sitting at the bar. There were two empty stools next to him. He climbed onto the one furthest away. The barmaid approached him and asked him what he wanted.

"Just a beer."

He watched her approach John James, sitting alone with a stupid grin on his face.

"Jesus, you look like the cat that swallowed the canary." she beamed.

Josh looked around, offering only a passing glance at John James.

Speaking in a voice just above a whisper, but still loud enough for John James to hear, he told her, "That guy you introduced me to earlier today just gave me a job. Paid me a shit-load up front, but swore me to secrecy."

"What sort of job?"

"Flying."

"What... out of here?"

"Sssh. No. Got to work that out yet. Probably from a deserted airstrip in the Northern Territory somewhere."

"Where to?"

"You wanna come to Italy?"

"*Ita...*"

"*Sshhh...* fucking hell!"

"Sorry... when?"

"September. The twenty-third."

John James half turned on his stool to put more of his back to them. Again his mind went into overdrive. He couldn't believe his good fortune. The pilot, the destination and now the date. Even the approximate departure location.

Thank you very much you total bloody idiot.

He finished his beer, picked up an abandoned newspaper, held it to one side of his face and walked from the bar. He walked down the street, ordered three steak sandwiches and a giant coke, climbed in behind the wheel of his car and headed back to Sydney.

This is big, this one. I can really feel it. You don't drive all this way to recruit a pilot if it's not. Twenty mill! Starting to look better all the time.

As he cleared Karumba and sped off back to the harbour city he slowed a little as he went past the site of the double killing. He breathed more easily when he saw no activity around the area where he'd covered the bodies. He caught a whiff of something smelling.

Jesus, I need a bloody shower!

* * *

McLoughlin reached for his phone. "Hello."

"Harry Springer, Ken."

"Whaddaya got, Harry?"

"Jesus, I didn't know whether to call you on this or not..."

"Go on."

"The bodies of two blokes have been found way the hell up in North Queensland..."

"No, my bloke's here..."

"You sure?"

"No, I'm not sure. If I was, I'd nail the prick... tell me?"

".22... point blank. Looks like a pen-gun."

"Bullshit!"

"I was just going through the sheets of what's been going on around the place. Forensic in Brisbane had a look. They couldn't find one of the bullets. Went clean through one joker's head and out the other side. But two others lodged inside the other bloke. Powder burns show the bullets entered the body as they left the barrel. But get this. No rifling on the bullets."

McLoughlin was stunned. "Whereabouts?"

"Karumba... it's up on the gulf, opposite side to Cairns."

"Jesus Christ, way up there?"

"What do you think?"

"Motive?"

"Doesn't seem to be one. Whoever did it also torched their car. It was ten days before they were found."

"Nice one!"

"Still no ID on them. The hitter took their wallets and stuff. Ripped off the number plates. Defaced the rego label. The local blokes up there say they weren't known. The engine in their car was stolen according to licensing. Probably a couple of transients off the prawn trawlers. They're still checking."

"Looks like a quick trip to Karumba. Thanks Harry. Stay in touch." McLoughlin pushed another button on his phone. "Commissioner Johnson." He waited to be put through. "McLoughlin, sir. I need a plane to get me to Karumba in North Queensland ASAP."

"I'll call you back as soon as it's ready," came the reply.

Bourke looked at him. "Karumba?"

McLoughlin briefed his partner on the conversation he'd had with the homicide squad chief. "I reckon I better go, just to be on the safe side. You stay here. I'll leave you my phone in case we get a call. Can't see the fucking Weasel going all the way up there, but this bloody penguin shit! Christ, they're not that common."

McLoughlin was met at Karumba airstrip by the local Senior Constable. They quickly exchanged greetings and McLoughlin handed him a photo of John James McGregor-McWeasely. "Seen this prick?"

The Senior Constable shook his head.

"Where're the bodies?"

"You serious?"

"Yeah, I'm serious."

"Shit, Sarge, they've been cremated."

McLoughlin nearly choked on a laugh. "Wh... what? Who ordered that?"

"Dunno. Just happened. About a week ago. Forensic in Brisbane said they had all they needed. Go ahead and fix 'em up. So the local funeral bloke did."

McLoughlin was too dismayed to comment. "Take me out to where they were found."

A short time later, the two policemen were walking round the area where the two bodies had been located. McLoughlin made his way to the spot. "Been raining up here?"

"Had about thirty mils two days ago," he replied.

Realising it was pointless trying to find anything of substance, he told the Senior Constable to take him back to the town.

"Go up to the end of the street and pull over." When they alighted from their vehicle McLoughlin handed him a picture of The Weasel. "You go down that side... in and out of everywhere. I'll do the same on this. Try for a positive sighting. See how you go. Meet you back here."

McLoughlin walked a few metres and stopped. Suddenly, a strange feeling came over him.

He's been here. Jesus Christ, the prick's been here, I can bloody feel it. But why? Why the hell would he come up here? And I just bet a pound to a pinch of goat-shit no-one saw him.

Two hours later the two policemen met back at Clark's car.

"Don't tell me. No-one saw him."

"Beats me, sarge. Everybody who comes here always goes to The Animal Bar. I spoke to the barmaid in there. She doesn't miss a trick. She hadn't seen him. The bloke at the service station said he hadn't either."

"He's got an unusual walk. Sort of hops a bit. Anyone comment on that?"

"No, Sarge."

McLoughlin walked up the street a little and turned to face the town. "Oh, you're good, you bastard. You are real good. And I just know you were here. Don't ask me how I know, but I know."

Chapter 12

"So I guess what I'm saying to you," Bill Murphy said as he began to wind up his speech to mark the opening of Writers' Week at Port Macquarie, "is if you dare to dream, don't dare to write. People love stories. People love people who tell stories well. I don't know that you can be taught to tell stories. I think that has to come from within. It has always surprised me somewhat to see some Young Turk gain worldwide fame as an author at an early age. To me you have to have lived a little before you can sit down at a keyboard.

"Then again, everybody's different. I just didn't want to get to age 65, look back and think I didn't have a go. And the marvellous thing about writing is that there are no rules. There is no right or wrong. If I want to have five thousand jet aeroplanes fly over a mountain of ice cream and custard, I can. Hell, I just sit there and write it. If I want to have the best-looking woman in the world flutter her eyelids at the ugliest-looking bloke in the world, I just sit there and write it. If I want my heroine to sweep some great hunk off his feet and keep him as her sex slave, again, I just write it in.

"As I say, there is no right or wrong. Where it becomes tough... after all the reading, re-reading, editing and re-writing... is finding someone who has the same enthusiasm about your work as you do—or, at least, enough to actually pick it up and read it. Your friends will. Your acquaintances will, but with over 240,000 books hitting the bookshelves in this country every year, it's particularly difficult to even have a letter or a phone call acknowledged from a publisher or a film company. If you get lucky, you'll invariably get the standard photocopied reply: thanks, but no thanks.

"If you hear back from a film company the call will probably come from some damn kid who wasn't even alive when you conceived the original concept of your story. You'll be told, 'Oh, we have your book. Not for us. There's no central character driving the plot'.

"Purely from such a comment, you know full well whoever it is who's phoning you certainly hasn't read what you've written. If they had they would know such a comment was absolute crap. But there's no point in arguing. The little darling on the end of the line probably had another 20 authors to phone that day and what better put down than: there's no central character driving the plot. And that's despite the fact you may have chosen to put your main character in about three-quarters of your 500-page novel... including the first page and the last. That's the sort of crap you're up against. I am constantly asked how can I get read? The simple answer to that is, I don't know how you can get read. If you go to med-school and pass, you can hang a shingle on your door and say, I am a doctor. An accountant, the same; and so on. You can spend your life trying to be a writer, and the only shingle you'll hang over the door is the success of your last book... that is, of course, if you're able to find someone in the first place with enough belief in you to actually sit down and read the bloody thing.

"I thank you all, most sincerely for making *The Fires of Midnight* the success it is. And I thank the directors of Writers' Week for allowing me the opportunity to speak with you today. And finally may I say, if you want to write, don't dare to dream, because it's within your dream so many people look to for an escape. That's why they buy books. Thank you. Thank you all very much indeed."

The auditorium of the Port Macquarie town hall suddenly filled with applause. Not just a round of polite clapping but, rather, a sustained, lengthy and most enthusiastic thank you which evolved into a standing ovation. Bill Murphy was gobsmacked. Innocently, he looked to see if someone else of note had walked onto the stage. When he realised that the applause was for him, he felt his knees go weak and he lifted a hand to the rostrum to steady himself.

The Writers' Week director stepped onto the stage and approached the microphone. "Ladies and gentlemen, Mr Bill Murphy."

Again the applause was loud and long. Slowly Bill Murphy made his way back to the VIP table where he was previously seated. A surge of people rushed forward with a copy of his novel in their hands hoping for an autograph. He was about to resume his seat when a voice came over his shoulder.

"Excuse me, Mr Murphy. Georgette McKinley, RTN ELEVEN. Mind if we have a quick word?"

"I'd rather not," he told her politely, withdrawing his chair.

Expecting such a reply but still taken aback by it, Georgette politely backed away, deciding to wait until she could grab a moment with him alone. Because she was very well known due to her high profile on television, Georgette was constantly surrounded by people at the event eager to speak with her and touch her. Some even sought her autograph. But her gaze was constantly focussed on Bill Murphy. She knew she'd cop a fair bit of ridicule if she didn't get a comment from the author, and that ridicule would come from Jack Rider.

Gradually the crowd which packed the town hall began to disperse and her one fear was that Bill Murphy would leave as well. As she watched, she felt he had made a decision to depart. Again she made an approach. "Excuse me, Mr Murphy... ?"

Bill Murphy looked up. "You're still here?"

"Yes, and I'm not leaving till you speak with me," she answered, offering the best and most gorgeous smile she could muster.

"At ELEVEN, you say?"

Georgette nodded, thinking she'd broken through.

Bill Murphy spotted a mobile phone in her hand. "That's George Hanks isn't it?"

"Oh, my boss! You know him?" she gushed.

"Yeah, I know him. Used to work together. Get him on the line for me."

Georgette quickly dialled the number. "Hello... Hanks."

"Hi babe, did you get Murphy?"

"About to, I think. He's with me now... wants to talk to you."

"Sure, whack him on."

Georgette handed Bill Murphy the phone. "George?"

"G'day maaaate... Jesus, it's been a long time?"

"Certainly has... Listen George, sorry to get to the point so quickly, but have you got a reporter up here doing a story on me?"

"Yeah."

"Tell her to leave me alone will you. The last thing I want to do is stick my head on a TV screen. Christ, I used to work in the business, remember?"

"Well, you're a bit of a recluse, old son... she only wants a grab."

"Piss off, George. No! Not even for old times sake."

Bill Murphy didn't wait to hear any further conversation. He handed Georgette back her phone and walked away.

George Hanks was still wondering if there was anyone on the line and kept calling into his phone. Georgette didn't put it back to her ear. She was too embarrassed to continue the conversation. Instead, she pushed the 'off' button.

"Jesus, he's got a mind of his own," her cameraman commented.

Georgette was fuming. "What an arsehole! That prick really humiliated me!"

"Forget it," the cameraman responded. "At least you tried."

Bill Murphy climbed into his utility. "Fixed her bloody wagon," he laughed out loud, as he drove back to his motel. Back in his room, he showered, shaved and changed.

Georgette McKinley, he thought. He reached for the phone and called RTN ELEVEN. "George Hanks, please"

"Jesus, Bill, you could've given us a grab for fuck's sake!"

"Don't do interviews, Bill, you know that. Besides, didn't you and I once sit down *all day... all bloody day* discussing the fact that if ever we became famous we'd tell the media to piss off?"

"Don't remember!"

"Bullshit, George... anyway, where is she?"

George Hanks laughed. "So she's got under your skin?"

"Pig's arse! Is she still here, or did she leave?"

"Got a pen?"

"Yep."

George Hanks gave Bill Murphy Georgette's mobile phone number. "And she's still there... thirty seconds Bill?"

"Don't be an arsehole... talk to you."

Bill Murphy dialled Georgette's mobile. "Georgette? Bill Murphy... Got time for a drink?"

"You're joking! After what you just did to me?"

"Yes or no?"

"I'd prefer dinner. How did you get my number?"

"Ways and means... I called George back."

"So why are you ringing me if you're not feeling guilty?"

Bill Murphy was on the verge of hanging up. "'Somehow I don't think this was such a good idea," he told her his voice trailing off.

Georgette could sense she was about to lose him. "OK. Dinner. Seven o'clock at the Whalebone Wharf Restaurant. It's on Hastings River Drive. You'll find it. See you then."

Bill Murphy put his phone back into his pocket wondering why he even bothered to call her. "Mate, she's everything you detest in a woman. You only have to look at her to know she's got balls. Pretty face. Great tits. Call her back you idiot. Bail out. You don't need it'."

But he couldn't make the call.

* * *

"Good evening sir, welcome to the Whalebone Wharf Restaurant, do you have a booking?"

"Hi, yes... for two... Murphy. Did you get my message... ?"

"Indeed we did, sir."

"I am expecting a young lady to join me. When she does, would you kindly oblige when I give you the nod?"

The waiter smiled. "We thought as much sir... of course."

Bill Murphy had arrived a few minutes before seven and ordered a beer while he waited for his guest. At ten minutes past seven he saw Georgette McKinley walk in the door. He noticed she hadn't seen him, so he dropped his eyes and pretended to read the wine list which was already on the table. Moments later, the waiter approached his table.

"Mr Murphy, your guest has arrived..."

Georgette offered the waiter an artificial smile. Bill Murphy rose from his chair and held out his hand.

"So... here we are," she began, taking her seat.

"Looks a nice place," Bill Murphy commented, attempting to break the ice.

"So why the phone call... did you change your mind?"

Bill shook his head. "No, I didn't change my mind. Did you think I would?"

"I was hoping."

"I worked in the industry for 30 years. I don't want my head on television."

"Come on... is it still Mr Murphy?"

"Depends."

"On what?"

"Is this Georgette McKinley, journo or Georgette McKinley, private person?"

"Does it make any difference?"

"You better believe it does."

"How?"

"I despise women journos."

"Then why are you here?"

"I thought it might be interesting to see if you had a private side."

"Why do you despise women journos?"

"Another story for another day... if we get that far."

"Not looking too flash at the moment is it?"

Bill Murphy shrugged his shoulders.

"Word out there is you're a recluse. Are you?"

"Is this the journo asking or the private person?"

"OK. The private person."

"Where's your phone?"

Georgette opened her handbag and held it up.

"Switch it off."

"I can't do that..."

"You working or not?"

Georgette huffed and puffed and grumbled. "What if someone is looking for me?"

"Here in Port Macquarie?"

"Pushy bugger aren't you?" she remarked, pushing the 'off' button.

"Never get told what to do, do you?" he retorted.

"No... but it took a lot of hard work to get to that."

"And you're spoiled, too."

"Jesus! anything else?"

He simply smiled his reply. Out the corner of his eye Bill Murphy could see the waiter standing a short distance away, watching him. Without moving his eyes off Georgette, he signalled with his hand. Almost immediately, a bottle of Dom Perignon and two crystal flutes appeared in front of them.

Georgette tried to cover a faint smile with her hands. "If I'd remained Georgette the journo, I suppose it would have been a mineral water?" she asked with a slight sting.

"If you'd remained Georgette the journo, I guess I would already have made my apologies and left," he told her.

"So what do *I* have. Murphy the writer, or Murphy the recluse?"

"They're one and the same."

"So you don't like people?"

"Would you like some of this?" he asked, almost off-handedly.

"Yes, of course, but I'd also like an answer to the question."

Bill was about to reach for the bottle as he'd specifically asked the waiter on the phone earlier not to pour it in case his guest didn't partake. But he was beaten to the punch. The waiter was quickly at the table.

"Oh, please, allow me."

Both watched as the flutes filled. "So what do we drink to?" she asked.

"Women journos," Bill replied facetiously.

Georgette raised an eyebrow. "So why don't you like people?" she asked again.

"I didn't say that."

"As good as."

"I'm just happy to live my life away from them."

"Without people you wouldn't be a successful author."

"Now you're being a journo."

"And you're evading the question."

"There shouldn't be any questions to evade. You want to talk about the weather or something?"

"Is it Mr Murphy or Bill?"

"Are you working, or aren't you?"

"I turned my phone off."

"Bill," he said, holding out his hand to her a second time.

She took it, but both knew it did little to smooth the way.

"So why do you write?"

"Do you read?"

"I haven't read your book, if that's what you mean."

"You're lucky you didn't roll the camera because that would have been the first thing I'd have asked you."

Georgette smiled. "Had that one covered," she replied confidently.

"I'll bet you didn't."

"I'll bet I did... try me." Georgette opened her handbag and withdrew a copy of *Fires*. She opened it to a specific page and was about to ask a question when Bill Murphy interrupted.

"That's the oldest trick in the business," he laughed. She looked at him. "When you interview an author, you always have a copy of their book with you and ask about a specific passage. That's supposed to convince the writer you've read it. If you'd have done that to me, I'd have asked you to explain to me what was written on the ten pages before."

"That's very clever, Mr Murphy."

"So you *are* working?"

"OK... Bill."

"Hey, listen, I did the same job as you for 30 bloody years. I've interviewed a truckload of authors. Most of 'em I found were better read than listened to, but one day I damn near got caught out on the exact scenario I told you about. It just so happened I had read the book and could tell the guy about the previous ten pages. You should be careful of that. If you reckon my phone call embarrassed you, that would have been a whole lot worse. On camera, too. And what's more I would have done it."

"Why?"

"Because you didn't come all this way to further my career. You came all this way to further your own. You see, for some reason, everybody reckons I'm hot property. Incredible isn't it? Two years ago, nobody wanted to know me. Two years ago I would have driven down to see you for a 30-second grab. Amazing how things change, isn't it? Like to order?"

Georgette scanned the menu and chose a small entrée and a main course of John Dory fillets. Bill followed suit. After each had given their order, an uneasy silence fell between them. There was something about Georgette that Bill Murphy found particularly attractive. If nothing else, he knew he was proving a difficult challenge for Georgette. Neither was prepared to give an inch and both knew it. He also knew she didn't like the fact that he, Bill Murphy, without a doubt, knew more about her job than she did. And in the area of writing books, again she was forced to admit defeat.

He also made damn sure he gave nothing away in regard to how he felt about her. No compliments. No double-meaning remarks. Not the slightest indication that she was even female. He was sure this was an entirely new experience for her. He was also sure it bothered her that she couldn't pigeon-hole him. He knew that a day in the life of a woman like Georgette McKinley would be filled with compliments, passes and one-liners. Such was her glamour. But he'd be damned if he was going to say so.

She was attractive, but not irresistible, and he wasn't convinced that he'd pierced her journalistic skin to expose the real person anyway.

Their chit-chat continued, though it was strained at times.

Their entrées arrived. Both agreed they were delicious. Bill Murphy seemed happy enough. He was content to chat away the evening and for each to go their own separate ways. That was until their next exchange. Georgette leaned across the table and asked him in a voice a little above a whisper.

"You rang me, remember? Now what the fuck's the problem? Have I got three heads or something? Open up a bit will you? I know you despise women journos but, for god sakes, I do have feelings!"

Bill Murphy's eyes popped like saucers. "What the hell did I do?"

"It's what you *haven't* done. We're not having dinner. We're going through the motions. The Dom's a delight. The food exquisite, but there's something missing here."

"Jesus, you're full-on aren't you? I thought we were having a pleasant couple of hours..."

"Do you know the difference between a husband and a lover?" she asked pointedly.

Bill was taken aback by the question. "Why would you ask that?"

"A famous line from Helen Rowland. Quote: A husband is what is left of the lover after the nerve has been extracted: Unquote. To me, you're acting like a husband. Am I that boring?"

It seemed to be the icebreaker both were seeking. Bill Murphy seemed happy that Georgette had vented her feelings. It was as though someone had come along and released her pressure valve. Whether it was because she was expecting him to hit on her (which he had no intentions of doing) or the built-up anger over his phone call to her boss, he couldn't tell. But the atmosphere certainly began to ease as more conversation flowed. Bill Murphy smiled.

"And Jessamyn West wrote, quote: It's better to learn to say good-bye early, rather than late. Unquote."

"So are you looking at good-bye already?"

"Hell, I'm still trying to get past hello."

"OK," Georgette went on, "who said this? Quote: As long as you know that most men are like children, you know everything. Unquote."

He gave a slight chuckle. "That's the number five girl. Coco Chanel."

"I have another. From Joan Rivers. This is one of my favourites. She came out on stage and said, quote: Last night I asked my husband his favourite sexual position and he replied, 'Next door'. Unquote."

"Yeah, that's good. Another one I remember is from Zsa Zsa Gabor, quote: A man in love is incomplete until he has married. Then he's finished. Unquote."

Georgette laughed lightly. Both enjoyed the lightening of the moment.

"You like all that stuff... the quotes of the famous and so forth?"

Georgette nodded. She now found herself more relaxed as the tension between the two began to dissipate. "And the original meanings of words."

"Such as?"

She sipped from her crystal flute, trying to recall examples. "Oh, well, take the name 'Todd' for example. If someone's called Todd, he probably should be cunning because in medieval times a 'Tod' was a fox. It's based on the word 'Todde' and that means a bushy mass, which of course is the fox's tail."

"I didn't know that," Bill commented, surprise in his tone.

"Or there's 'Ragamuffin'. Used to describe a disreputable or untidy boy. Don't hear it much anymore and that's a pity. Has a nice ring to it. That goes back to the fourteenth century and comes from 'Ragamoffyn', the name of a demon in the *Piers Plowman* poem by William of England."

"Not just a pretty face, are you? Got a favourite?"

Georgette thought for a moment. "Clodhoppers is interesting."

"Oh?"

"Comes from old England. The Lord of the Manor rode on horseback as the peasants followed along behind on foot, hopping over stones and clods of dirt."

"Just goes to show doesn't it? There's always another side to a person. I said earlier I wondered if there were other aspects to you. Listening to all that, obviously there is. You're very bright, aren't you?"

Georgette dismissed the compliment lightly. "I don't think knowing the origins of a few words sends my IQ into the stratosphere. Anyway, enough of that. What now for Bill Murphy?" she asked.

"More of the same I suppose. I guess I'm living the dream I've been striving all my life to create."

"Which is?"

"No big deal. A house. Pet dog. Bit of a beach and total privacy."

"The privacy thing... that's important to you?"

"Very much so, yes. The wind in the trees, the waves on the beach, only a handful of people have my phone number. I get up late. I work late. And I'm not answerable to one single living soul."

"Sounds like bliss?"

"I'm where I've wanted to be for 25 years."

"Are you married?"

"Was once. Long time ago. Wouldn't even know where she is now."

"Any family?"

Bill pondered the question and chose the simple answer. "Not really. You?"

"Just me. All alone out here in the big bad world," she smiled. "So where to from here?"

"Back home in the morning and back to the grind."

"Another book?"

"Another book."

"What's literary fame really like?"

"Jesus, I don't know, Georgette. I don't seek it out. I just like the cheques that come from it."

"So who are you really?"

Bill Murphy looked at his glamorous companion, wondering at the question. "So who am I really?" He paused for a lengthy period. He drank from the crystal flute. Georgette sat in silence. "I guess all I've ever been was the dream I was chasing."

"And now you've caught it?"

"Yes, I suppose I have, haven't I?"

"So are you still on the run?"

"I can't answer that. How do you know when to stop?"

"When you're content, I suppose. Are you content?"

Bill took another sip of Dom and nodded. "That I am," he replied.

The waiter came by and topped up the flutes with the last of the Dom Perignon. He looked at Bill.

"It's up to the lady?"

Georgette smiled. "I'll tell George we ordered the second one and had a drink for him on his behalf," she giggled.

"I thought I was paying?"

"It's OK. I'm sure ELEVEN can handle dinner for two, even with a couple of bottles of Dom."

Bill Murphy wouldn't hear of it. "No, I'll pay. I'll tell 'em to sell a few more books."

"You want to make a deal?"

Bill raised his eyebrows. "You better tell this man 'yes' or 'no'."

She looked at the waiter and nodded.

"Jesus Christ, we'll be on our bloody ear. What's the deal?"

"That stuff's about $200 a bottle. The bill for tonight will be around 600 bucks. Give me a 30-second grab?"

Georgette didn't continue when she saw Bill shaking his head.

"You don't give up do you?"

"Did you?"

He smiled. "Got a point, I guess. But no, I didn't give up."

"Who was the hardest interview you ever got?"

"Rudolf Nureyev."

"How many times did you ask?"

"It wasn't like that actually. When I fronted him, he didn't speak English very well. He pretended to be in a big hurry. So I thought, bugger it, I'm not leaving empty handed, I'll get his autograph. So I did. Still got it, too."

"So you can't blame a girl for trying can you?"

The second bottle of champagne arrived and the waiter filled the flutes.

"OK. Now I've got a question for you," he said. "I didn't spend 30 years in your business to not know how things work. How is it you keep coming up with the big ones?"

Georgette knew her answer would have to be good or else he'd see right through it. "You know about contacts?"

"You've only been around five minutes. Thirty-year veterans don't get the drop on the sort of stuff you turn out."

Suddenly she felt terribly inadequate, almost an imposter. She knew she could hardly sit there and tell Bill Murphy the real cost of her scoops. She decided to tell him a half-truth and make light of it.

"Oh gee, Bill," she began comically, "you guessed already! I sell my body. One scoop, one screw," she laughed. "God, I don't know! Contacts I guess. I really, really work hard on my contacts. I try and make a good one each week. But I'm careful where I cast the line. You know as well as I do that the main game is federal politics. That's followed by local government development, the bread-and-butter lines which affect peoples' hip pocket. And of course when big business makes a move, many peoples' lives are also affected. So I just work on all that stuff." She hoped more than anything that her answer would satisfy him. It did.

"Don't know how the hell you do it, but I take my hat off to you. Some of that stuff makes it look as though you've got a direct bloody line to the Prime Minister."

Georgette felt a slight tinge in her stomach. "You must have had your scoops?" she asked, trying to turn his attentions away from her.

"Oh, sure. But nothing like you turn out."

Georgette felt uneasy with the questions, so she retreated. "OK... so what do we do about the bill?"

"Thirty seconds?"

"Thirty seconds."

"Your news comes up here, doesn't it?"

"On relay right up the coast and inland as well."

"I'll give you your 30 seconds, but I don't want it to go out on the relays. I enjoy being anonymous. Put me on the telly up here and I'm buggered. If you can guarantee that it will only be shown in Sydney, I'll do it for you. OK? Nothing on relay."

"Do you mean it?"

"I mean it," he told her reassuringly.

Georgette's face lit up with excitement. "Thank you. I'll call George first thing and arrange it. The relays will need to alter their schedules. They won't like it, but that's their problem."

"Don't let me down."

"I won't let you down... promise"

"If you do, I'll just be someone you once met."

Georgette knew exactly what he meant. "What changed your mind?"

He laughed. "The second bottle of Dom. Hell, I don't know. Come the morning I might even change my mind."

"Please don't do that."

"OK. I won't do that."

"Will there be anything else Mr Murphy, Miss McKinley?" the waiter asked.

The two looked at each other. "No, we're fine thank you. Just the bill."

"Indeed, sir."

Moments later the waiter returned with a small folder containing the account. Bill picked it up and Georgette took it from him. "A deal's a deal," she told him.

"When that hits George's desk, he'll sack you," Bill put in.

"Oh no, he won't," came Georgette's over-confident reply.

For some reason the comment smacked Bill Murphy in the face. *She's certainly got the goods on somebody there*, he thought.

"Well, it's been quite a day hasn't it? Like to make a move?"

Georgette smiled. "If you like."

"Can I drive you back to your motel?" Bill asked Georgette.

"Thank you."

The two continued in conversation as Bill Murphy made the very short journey to Georgette's motel. For the last two hours she had been bracing herself for when Bill would ask her back to his room. Even now in his vehicle, he still hadn't asked. She then even surprised herself when he pulled into her motel.

"Would you like to come in?" she asked, amazed at her own words.

Although staggered at the invitation, Bill Murphy gave nothing away. His facial expression didn't change. "It's pretty late," he told her.

"If you'd rather not ..."

He looked at her. "Georgette, I might be twice your age, but the blood in my veins still runs bright red. You are not someone I could say 'no' to very easily..."

"What about if you just walk me to the door?" she asked him.

He turned in his seat, took hold of her hand and looked into her eyes. "After we get through in the morning, what do you have to do then?"

"Go back to Sydney."

"Straight away?"

"Not necessarily. Why?"

"I thought we could have lunch and tour around the place. Flynns Beach, Peppermint Park, Sea Acres Rainforest Centre, the Koala hospital. Lots of places to see... whip up to Nambucca Heads if there's time. That's about an hour up the road."

"That sounds lovely. Don't know about Nambucca, though. We'll need to be gone by about four."

Bill Murphy thought for a moment. "What about if I drove you back to Sydney?"

Georgette looked at him in amazement. "You're kidding. But you despise female journos..."

"There's another interesting side to this one."

"I don't think that's a good idea," she told him. Georgette knew she couldn't afford to interrupt her routine. If she allowed Bill Murphy to drive her back to Sydney, he could well end up staying at her place and that was a luxury she couldn't afford. Especially as Prime Minister John Talbot expected her to be at his beck and call. Then there were the corporates. Port Macquarie was a different ballgame. Port Macquarie wasn't Sydney.

"I couldn't allow you to do that," she told him. "It's too far and I wouldn't feel comfortable about it." Georgette knew her statement wasn't the truth, but she felt she had little choice.

Outwardly, Bill Murphy wasn't affected by her decision one way or the other. Inwardly, he took her response as a rejection. He also had the feeling that she wanted him to take her back to Sydney, but that something was holding her back. He decided not to force the issue.

"Come on, I'll walk you to your door." Again he held her hand. "Dinner was wonderful. Thank you," he told her, pressing her fingers to his lips.

"And thank you."

"I'll see you in the morning," he told her as he watched her walk inside and close the door.

* * *

Bill Murphy kept his part of the bargain and met her at eleven a.m.

She also honoured hers and kept his face off the relays. In the four hours he spent with her during that afternoon, it was as though he'd stepped outside of himself. He wasn't a good walker at the best of times, yet he spent most of the afternoon doing exactly that, not realising he'd even taken a step.

After recording her interview with him Georgette returned to her room, removed all her makeup and dressed down into jeans, T-shirt and Nike walking shoes. Bill did a double-take. He enjoyed the scrubbed look in a woman, never having much time for all the hair and make-up rigmarole. He tried not to show it but he was overjoyed at the transformation of the television journalist.

"There you go," she said, throwing her arms open, "the real me."

The hours that followed were enjoyed by both with no surfaced animosities or prejudices, an afternoon totally free of angst. Conversation was trivial covering places each had been to, places they'd like to go. Bill Murphy was trying to come to terms with why he'd found himself in such a situation. His words kept coming back at him.

I despise women journos.

But something was happening. He knew it. She knew it. But, like the first part of their evening at the restaurant the night before, neither was prepared to give an inch.

Checking her watch, Georgette said, "It's past three-thirty. I should be getting back."

"Went pretty quickly didn't it?" he said, a sadness in his tone.

They shook hands at the RTN ELEVEN Newscar and Bill watched as the vehicle disappeared from view. Driving back to his house he still felt as though he was walking outside of himself. It was a strange sensation, and one he'd never experienced before.

Interesting, was the only word he'd allow himself to describe his meeting with Georgette McKinley.

* * *

Later, when driving back to Sydney with her crew, the radio was on in the background. Georgette's ears pricked when, in the middle of the program, she heard a very familiar news theme. She leaned over to turn up the volume.

We'll return to our normal program in just a moment. Right now, here's Cecily Pridham in the newsroom with a newsflash.

As she listened, her jaw dropped open, as did those of her cameraman and sound technician. What was coming over the radio at that moment would throw her entire world into absolute turmoil.

"Bloody hell! Now what?" her cameraman blurted.

"Bugger me dead! How big's *that*?" the sound technician exulted.

Georgette sat glaring at the road ahead, too stunned to speak.

Chapter 13

Enrico Mogliotti's mobile phone rang. "Yep."

"Gina... Josh Emery's now had five weeks. We're due to leave in three. What's happening. Is tonight's meeting still on?"

Enrico had to bite his lip whenever Gina called. He couldn't stand the woman. And as the intensity of the heist continued to build, she began to pressure him more and more for updates on their current situation. He found himself subconsciously counting down the days to when he'd no longer have to deal with her.

"Hi, Gina," he chirped with false enthusiasm, knowing he wasn't fooling anyone, least of all the Sicilian redhead. "I'm on my way out to Bankstown airport now to get Josh. Yes, the meeting's still on."

"Eight o'clock, right? Your room."

In the five weeks since Enrico had enlisted the services of Josh Emery at Karumba, the Mogliotti brothers and Gina had to cool their heels and wait for him to implement their plan of action. Josh and Enrico spoke on the phone every day. Josh said he was making good headway in purchasing a plane but he would need about $200,000 to secure the deal.

"I'll get it to you," Enrico had told him.

Gina kept up her contact with Sebastian McAlister, although at times she felt he wished he hadn't conceded to her demands. It took all her sexual prowess to have him continue with the façade to the Italian minister. The entire operation hinged completely upon what information he could pass on to her. She too, was counting down the days when she could sever her ties with the minister. Sebastian was living on the dream that, because of the money she stood to gain, he would have Gina just where he wanted her.

Enrico was particularly nervous as he drove into Bankstown airport to the area where Josh said he'd be waiting for him. When Josh saw the Italian approaching, he waved his arm and pointed.

"There she is me boy... what do you think?"

Enrico looked across the tarmac and shook his head. "I don't believe you actually got it."

"Mate," he grinned, "told you I would."

"Amazing! And you got here OK?"

"Mate, she's a bloody dream."

"And it is a Twin Turbo, I take it?"

Josh glanced back at the aircraft. "What you have here is a Cessna C441 Conquest Twin-engine Turbo Prop which will run on Jet A1... or, for your purposes, kerosene. I've gone over her thoroughly and..." his voice tailed off. "Let me put it this way; she's good for, say, two trips from here to London and back again before being due for a major service and overhaul. You only want to do a smidgen of that."

"And the registration number. How did you get that?"

"Don't look too closely. The paint's still probably wet. It's all bullshit, but no-one will know. I went through the Australian Aircraft Registration list to make sure no other bastard's got the same. You'll be fine."

Enrico chuckled lightly. "Any luck with a strip?"

"Yep... meeting still on tonight?"

"It is."

"I'll tell you all about it then... plus all this other stuff. Talk about a bloody marathon. Mate, about four hours sleep a night, but I reckon we're organised. Where have you got me?"

"The Hilton, Josh... under the name of Sam Oaks," Enrico told him, opening the envelope and withdrawing a pile of notes. "Here," he said handing him a stack of $100 bills.

"That's for being honest. You'll get another 50 G's tonight. Meantime, I'll drop you off. Get room service, have a sleep... do what you like. Room 850 at eight p.m."

Josh looked at the money. "Jesus, you don't have to do that. A deal is a deal..."

"Our pleasure. You earned it. Again, thank you."

Enrico dropped Josh Emery off at the Hilton, parked his car then made his way to the room he had booked for himself.

* * *

Josh Emery's head was spinning. In five weeks his life had gone from complete despair to the anxiety of living on the edge. He had no idea who his employers were or what they were up to. As far as he was concerned, he'd been hired to fly a plane to and from Italy.

Some of the flight would be on legal flight paths. Some of it wouldn't. If he got caught he could go to jail. Such a thought frightened the living daylights out of him. To the extent that when speaking to his wife about his change of luck he failed to mention he was in all probability dealing with a bunch of crooks. If his passengers were bailed up by other people of a similar ilk there could be guns, there could be shots and there could be people dead. He just knew that in order to fulfil the requirements of the job he needed to pull on every ounce of learning he'd achieved. Especially when it came to the big three of flight plans, fuel requirements and landing permits.

He had a mate at Darwin airport. They'd attended flying lessons together. Josh only ever knew him as 'Spanners Hudson'. He recalled Spanners telling him once that if ever he got onto a shonky deal and needed help with flight plans, fuel stops and landing rights, he'd help him. It only took three phone calls and he had Spanners on the phone. After he'd explained what he needed, Spanners told him the price. Josh spoke to Enrico. The money was sent in three separate padded bags to Karumba. Josh re-addressed them to Spanners at the Darwin post office. Upon pocketing the money, Spanners went to work on his promises.

* * *

Within a few minutes of eight p.m., everyone had gathered in room 850. Josh was particularly tentative about the meeting, mainly because he didn't know anyone apart from Enrico.

Introductions were made and Josh immediately spotted the tension between his man and Gina. He was also quick to pick up on the body language between Gina and Franco and was soon to learn it was the Sicilian woman who was running the show. Although he felt inwardly that there was a connection, at no time was he told the three men were brothers.

Enrico served coffee and, after brief formalities, it became apparent that Gina wanted to cut the small talk.

"So... what do you have for us?" she asked.

Josh looked around the hotel room. "Probably best if we can sit at the table so I can lay a few things out."

A shuffle of chairs followed.

"All right," he began, "Australia, Italy return in a Cessna C441 Con-quest Twin-engine Turbo Prop. Take-off date, September the twenty-third. Here's the state of play. I've found a deserted airstrip a little north of the Durack River, to the north-west of Kununurra in Western Australia. By air, 148 kilometres in from the coast. It's in very open country. In fact the closest bush, undergrowth and scrubland is about a thousand metres away. So there's not a snowball's chance in hell of an ambush, if that is of concern to you. Someone told me it was built for the Second World War but never used. I've been out to it and had a look. Through the good grace of Enrico or, for that matter, all of you I guess I was able to hire a plane, fly out to it, land on it and take off OK, so it'll be fine. That's our starting point. I take it Enrico will bring you all out to meet me on the day, and be there to meet you when we return?"

Josh raised his eyes and scanned the faces. All nodded their agreement.

"Actually there's been a change of plan on that," Franco piped up. "Luigi will now be the greeter and Enrico will make the trip."

Josh looked at Luigi, not that it mattered to him who was on the flight and who wasn't. Luigi shrugged.

"I hate flying, man. It's been bothering the shit out of me."

Josh's body language indicated there wasn't a problem.

The truth of the matter was that Gina so mistrusted Enrico, she convinced Franco to switch the brothers. At least if Enrico was with them she could keep an eye on him. The switch also suited Franco. The thermal lance was really Enrico's baby. He would feel happier with him using it than having to master it himself.

Josh Emery continued. "Now the flight plan is long and complicated. Do you want me to go through it with you?"

Again he scanned the faces and was met with great enthusiasm.

"After we leave Kununurra, I'll have to land at Darwin to get the ball rolling legally. I'll top up with fuel and we'll head off to Changi in Singapore. Now you need to be aware this entire trip will mean a lot of time in the air. To Changi will take six hours 47 minutes. It's 1833 nautical miles and during the trip we'll use 2290 pounds of fuel cruising at 31,000 feet.

"There's other stuff here like the route from YPDN which is Darwin via J61, IKUMA, A464, TI, and TAN4B to WSSS which is Changi airport in Singapore, but that's pilot-speak, so I won't bore you with all of that. When we land at Changi it'll be runway Zero Two Left... again you don't need to know about that. It's not usual for small planes to land at Changi and you may notice when we touch down we'll be in the north remote apron. Mostly, small planes land at Seletar in the north of the island on the The Johoree Strait. Military aircraft land at Payar Lebar Airport between Seletar and Changi. But we've had a stroke of luck on this occasion. Because there's an air pageant at Seletar the day we arrive we've been given permission to land at Changi. OK.

"From Changi we go to Calcutta in India. Bloody godforsaken place. It'll take us six hours 25 minutes to get there. We'll go up to 31,000 feet, use 2179 pounds of fuel and travel 1603 nautical miles. Do you want the route number... like WSSS via VJR7B..."

"We can skip that," Gina put in, "as long as you know," she smiled.

Josh nodded. "It's all here, ma'am. From Calcutta we're into the third leg, and, that's to Dubai in the United Arab Emirates. Now this is a long bugger. One minute short of nine hours."

"Is there a loo in this thing?" Gina interrupted.

Josh gave a slight chuckle. "Not in the true sense of the word," he told her. "It's more of a potty chair which fits into the regular passenger seat like a commode. So whoever is sitting in it at the time will need to stand to make way for the user, but it can be curtained off."

"Well I'm pleased to hear that," she smirked.

He continued on. "From Calcutta to Dubai is 1960 nautical miles. We'll burn just on 3000 pounds of fuel. This leg cuts things a bit fine. Once we land we'll only have 300 pounds left in the tank, only thirty-nine minutes' flying time.

"Jesus, that's tight!" said Luigi.

"Yeah, too tight for my liking," Josh added. "Doesn't leave any reserves. So I've set up an alternative. Which way we do go will be decided upon by the weather. We'll learn that before we leave Calcutta. If there's a tail wind, the first route will be OK. If not, we'll have to go for VECC via G450, BBB... again, none of that stuff will mean anything to you. Now the next bugger is no picnic either. Again it's nine hours in the air and 1804 nautical miles to Iraklion in Crete. Much the same as the previous leg... shorter by 156 nautical miles actually. But, legally, we're not left with enough fuel in reserve. This time we'll be at 33,000 feet. I'll need to keep a close eye on these last two legs, but we'll be OK. From Iraklion to Italy is a hell of a distance. Too far for us in one hop without refuelling. So we'll continue at 31,000 feet to Malta. That'll be about two-and-a-half hours and 600 nautical miles. Gets a bit tricky from here. I don't know if Enrico told you all, but I've enlisted a bit of outside help. He's a mate of mine in Darwin. He knows nothing of any of you or what you're about.

"Then again, how could he? I don't even know myself. In working this flight plan through with him he's advised me of trouble spots in obtaining fuel. We'll need graft money, because to get some of these pricks to look the other way can amount to a shitload."

"What are the fuel costs?" Gina wanted to know.

Josh thought for a moment. "It's a bit like asking how long's a piece of string? Fuel costs, ma'am, can vary dramatically... very, very dramatically. But if we try and look at the overall picture it works out at around 90 cents a gallon, US. In our currency about one dollar fifty. A gallon of fuel weighs eight and a half pounds. On the trip from Darwin to Changi, we'll use 2290 pounds of fuel. That's roughly 270 gallons. In our money, a bit over $400 in round figures. But in some places where we'll have to refuel it could be double that. You need to be aware of this and have sufficient cash to cover yourselves if need be."

They all nodded.

"Through Enrico, and obviously all of you as well, I've loaded my contact up with the appropriate cash reserves and plastic to get us over those hurdles smoothly... including landing costs. He'll leave a week before we do to set things up. Anyone got a problem with that?"

No-one spoke up.

"It appeared to me that you are all going so far in such a short time, the last thing you needed was a hassle over refuelling... being, as I take it, time will be of the essence. My contact will work ahead of us all the time..."

"What's he costing us?" asked Franco.

"Twenty grand, and that includes the fuel in Italy," Luigi said. "Twenty-three with the car hire."

"What car hire?"

"When we hit the ground near Portofino, I'm not walking," Enrico cut in. "This guy will have a car for us. To hire a car over there that shows no record of it being hired costs three grand."

"OK," shrugged Franco.

"We'll need to leave Malta at night, then head to a little landing strip that lies between Sori and Cicagna. My contact will take you to the car he's hired for you then return to refuel the plane. It is Portofino, right?"

"That's right," said Gina.

"Yeah, well that's about as close as I can get you to the place without raising a whole heap of curiosity. For safety's sake I'm inclined to go along with Enrico. No longer than twelve hours on the ground before we take off... ten preferably. How long will you guys need?"

Franco looked at Enrico, but it was Gina who spoke. "Two hours out, you say?"

"Approximately."

"So two to get in. Shit, I'm hoping no more than... what do you think Enrico, an hour, two hours?"

"Two max."

"So probably six hours. Maybe seven. How long to refuel?"

"About an hour."

"OK, so we should be set to leave in seven hours."

"Sounds good to me. You must remember that from Malta to Italy and return, we'll fly low level. Turbines don't perform economically at low level, so we'll use a shit-load of fuel, but it's not a big distance so we'll be all right. Then we'll come back the way we went."

"In order to get around not landing first up in Darwin we'll need a bit of the old smoke and mirrors routine. After passing Kupang in West Timor I'll radio that I have a pressurisation problem. I'll tell them everything is OK, but that I will need to descend to a lower level because of it. This will allow us to drop below the radar and sneak in over the coast to the airstrip near Kununurra. So there you have it," he smiled. "Any questions?"

"Where the hell did you find this guy?" Luigi asked his brother.

Enrico's face lit up. "I told you he was bloody good."

It was Franco who was unashamedly impressed the most. He rose from his seat and put his arms around Josh. "Mate, I gotta tell you. You just blew me out of the water. How the fuck did you put all that together? That is nothing short of incredible. Christ, you've got it down to the last little detail haven't you?"

Josh Emery was fairly chuffed by the response, which he took as genuine. He shook his head lightly. "I've tried not to forget anything... you know, forewarned is forearmed. I hope I've covered all the bases, but of course we won't know that till we get going." When nobody else was forthcoming, he said, "I guess I'll see you all on the twenty-third at six a.m."

Enrico took an envelope from his pocket and put an arm around his shoulder, leading him away. "Don't spend it all at once. Fifty grand, right? But more than anything, you'll need to shut the fuck up about it. And I mean really put a zip on your tongue. If this leaks we're all totally and absolutely rooted. You understand?"

He walked Josh Emery to the door and shut it behind him.

* * *

After the door closed, Gina sought an immediate response from the three brothers. All agreed he was perfect for what they wanted.

"Do we let him walk?" Enrico asked.

Gina flew into a rage. "You really are an arsehole, Enrico! What do you want to do? Shoot the poor bastard? For fuck's sake, without him we're nowhere. He's put his arse on the line over this... for people he doesn't even know..."

"He's being paid heaps..."

"And so are you. If he gets onto the fact he's bringing home twenty million dollars, he might just decide to bloody well shoot all of us. Remember, at 31,000 feet we're totally at his mercy. And you want to waste the guy? How much would ever be enough for you, Enrico?"

"Cool it, Gina," Franco put in.

"Fuck you, Franco! You want to waste the guy, too?"

Franco rose to his feet and put his hand on Gina's shoulder. "No-one's gonna waste anyone."

"How come I don't believe that?"

"Tell her, Enrico."

"What?"

"Tell her you're not gonna kill the fucking pilot."

"OK. I'm not gonna kill the fucking pilot, all right? Jesus, Gina!"

Gina sat down, but she was far from convinced. Franco and Luigi didn't bother her. Enrico certainly did. She not only feared for the pilot's life, she now feared for her own. If Enrico was having thoughts of wasting the pilot she would almost certainly be on his list, and that's despite her association with his brother. She really couldn't see him letting her walk away with all that money.

Gina had suspected all along Enrico would be trouble. Weeks before she very quietly and very anonymously joined an outer suburban pistol club. Such a membership then legally entitled her to own a pistol and she wasted no time in visiting a gun shop. After meeting all the legal requirements, she purchased a small .22-calibre six-shot Remington semi-auto. As she always liked to carry the same large leather handbag, she had a bootmaker sew in a special pocket inside its lining. He didn't ask what it was for and she didn't tell him. She had taken care to place the pocket on the side of the bag which she carried next to her body.

Anyone opening her bag by mistake wouldn't see the gun, but at the same time it was very easily accessed. She told no-one she had it.

Out of the blue Luigi asked a question. "So what's Josh do now till we go?"

Enrico told him he'd stay at the Hilton for a week, move to a motel at Bankstown for a week, then take off for Darwin three days before the flight to Italy. He'd refuel in Darwin, stock the plane with food and drinks, then fly out to Kununurra and wait.

"OK," said Luigi, "is everybody happy?"

"Getting close now isn't it?" Enrico said.

"Gina, your info still on track?" Franco asked.

She told them the next update was due in a day or so and would continue to be that way.

"So we just sit tight?" Enrico asked.

"We just sit tight," Franco told him. "We work as usual. We carry on as normal, then we take off. Luigi will run us up there, camp in a caravan park for four days then come and get us. The best thing is to move each day if you can, Luigi."

"I'll move each day," he reassured his brother.

"So allowing for a bit of sleep time, 48 hours there, 48 hours home, seven on the ground. We leave Wednesday six a.m. Depending on what time we're on, it's nine thirty or ten o'clock the night before in Italy. Forty-eight hours later will get us into Italy at nine thirty or ten on the night Bruno and his family leave the Villa. Two hours for us to get into Portofino. That means we should be able to hit the joint round midnight-one a.m. on the Thursday."

"Two hours after we leave, we're back in the air and home 48 hours later. Luigi should see us coming over the horizon around ten a.m. on the Sunday."

"So, all over in five days," Gina said, taking a deep breath.

"Franco, what have we forgotten?" Enrico asked urgently.

"What haven't we covered? Christ, do we just take off, burn a hole in Bruno's safe, pick up $20 million and come home? Surely somewhere, someone is going to be pretty pissed about all this? Do we walk away scot-free?"

"Think about it," Franco said to him. "Who in their right fucking mind would even attempt it? I think that's our strongest ally. It's just so outrageous, no-one would give it a thought. If what Gina says is true and there's no security, then what will give us a problem? We might hit bad weather. The plane might blow an engine. The rent a car might break down. Jesus, there's all sorts of stuff like that. But I can't see how we're going to have a problem. Gina?"

She shook her head. "I've asked myself over and over. I'm with you. I think the plan is so bloody outrageous it will work."

"OK. So we wait it out."

"One further thing" Gina added. "Wouldn't it have been easier for us to fly with Josh from here?"

"Too messy," Franco responded. "Too many people on board going into Darwin. And what do we do for a few days while Josh loads up, apart from draw attention to ourselves? No, I think this is best. It also gives Luigi a look at the place first before he comes back to get us."

As everyone departed Gina was still gravely worried about Enrico.

How the hell do I keep him off the piss and away from the women in the time left before we leave? I'll talk to Franco. That can be his job.

She could tell Franco wanted more of her, but she was also expecting a call from Sebastian... and she was already late. She went to Franco's door with him and looked down her face.

"Oh, Jesus, you're not?"

"Started early. During the meeting for god's sakes."

"Shit, Gina!" he cursed.

"Bloody hell, babe, I'm not god. That's one thing I can't control."

"Sorry, sweetheart."

Franco cursed and entered his room alone.

Gina checked her watch. *Now I have to get the hell out of here and hope to god those bastards don't spot me.*

Gina could hear the phone ringing as she tried to open her front door. She made a rush to get it.

"God I miss you... have you been running?"

"I've just been down to the car. I heard the phone ringing as I was trying to open the front door. How long have we got?"

"Two hours," he answered glumly.

"Please hurry," she purred into the phone.

As she hung up, she wondered how many more times she'd have to go to bed with Sebastian McAlister before she could quietly slip away.

Make the most of it, baby, 'cause time's nearly up.

Chapter 14

John James McGregor-McWeasely remained closeted in his flat by day, only venturing out at night to keep watch on Enrico's house. He knew that when that four-wheel-drive left for the Northern Territory he would need to be closely following.

This particular night started out like any other. He parked himself off Enrico's house, then suddenly his stomach went into turmoil as Enrico arrived home in his car without the four-wheel-drive. John James panicked. He drove away quickly, heading for Franco's house. There was no sign of it there.

Shit!

He then made his way to where Luigi lived, only breathing a sigh of relief when he saw the vehicle parked in his driveway.

The bastards have changed tack. They've bloody swapped. Must have. So now it's Luigi who'll be the greeter. Ten days till the twenty-third. There has to be some movement shortly.

* * *

Georgette McKinley sat staring out the window of her unit, still in shock about what she'd heard on the car radio. Now and again she'd glance over at her telephone.

Funny it hasn't rung, she thought.

She poured herself a small sherry, something she'd rarely do, and paced up and down her loungeroom floor. She was so preoccupied that she nearly jumped out of her skin when the phone did ring. Quickly she grabbed it. "Hello," she said urgently.

"Have you heard?" came the question from a familiar voice.

"What the fuck happened?" she yelled down the line.

Georgette was speaking to Prime Minister John Talbot. The newsflash on the radio told of his demise. He'd been rolled in cabinet at a specially convened Saturday meeting.

"Had no idea," he told her in the voice of a shattered man.

"Who?"

"Who do you think?"

"Not Cameron?"

"Uh-huh, Cameron, my closest bloody confidant."

"Jesus, John, he's the goddammed treasurer. What was the split?"

"He got in by five."

"*Five*? And you *really* had no idea?"

"I've just spent a week behind closed doors with him doing the bloody budget. No! Jesus Christ, not a bloody clue. What a fucking germ! I've dedicated my life to that bloody party!"

"So what now?"

"Too bloody shell-shocked to even think about it."

"The budget's this Thursday isn't it?"

"Yes. I have to resign Tuesday morning and he takes over from there."

"Certainly be in his element come Budget Day won't he? What a mongrel!"

"You home tonight?"

"I'm always here for you, you know that," she told him in a voice she hoped would go some way towards consoling him.

"I'll be in Sydney tonight. I have a couple of official duties to cover. I'll get rid of security and come and see you."

"Oh, John, that'd be wonderful, but this is hardly the time. You must be going through hell."

"I am. Don't make any mistake about that. I really, really am. I have something for you. It'll be late, but I'll be there."

"Be careful, because right now you're front-page news. Every journo and photographer in the country will be trying to track you down."

"They won't get anywhere near me. See you soon."

A short time later Georgette switched on the television to catch the news, but the demise of John Talbot was already across all channels.

Bloody Cameron! What a mealy-mouthed, gutless little bastard he turned out to be. Got to hand it to him, though. That's the neatest bloody hatchet job I've ever seen done on anyone!

She cooked herself a light meal, showered and waited for John Talbot to arrive. When it came midnight and there was still no sign of him, she went into her bedroom, she went into her bedroom, took a blanket from her blanket box and curled up on the couch. At two a.m. he still hadn't arrived. Three a.m., still no sign. It was ten past four in the morning when a slight knock at her door stirred her. She checked the security-eye. It was John Talbot. Quickly, she opened the door.

"Bloody hell, you were right about every bastard in the country wanting a piece of me! The buggers are everywhere." He closed the door behind himself and tried to smile as he took Georgette into his arms. "Hi," he said softly.

"John, this is just so awful... ."

"Never know in this game, do you?"

"You sure it was Cameron?"

"Sure I'm sure! He told me."

With that John Talbot put his briefcase on Georgette's lounge-room table and looked at her. "How would you like the most humungous bloody story of your gorgeous young life?"

She looked at him, her eyes opening wider and wider.

"You've got two hours. I'm gonna take a shower and grab a bit of sleep... if I can use your bed... ?

"Of course you can, you know that," she cut in.

"Wake me up at ten to six. If you open my briefcase, you'll find the Budget Papers. The summary's on the top. Don't bother with the other crap. Just use the summary. Defence, health, petrol, beer and cigarettes are the big ones. Write out as much as you like until ten to six. Save it till Tuesday night. I promise you it won't leak. Then drop it at six o'clock. I want to watch Cameron squirm as you totally fuck his day."

"Oh, John, for god's sake's, this is... is..."

He pressed his fingers to her lips. "I'm not bloody naïve, babe. I know that now I'm out of there you'll move on. I'll go about what's left of my life being a former Prime Minister, so I guess this is my way of saying thank you for being part of my life."

"It doesn't have to be like that..."

"Yes it does. You know that. I know that. It's all about power and ambition. I had the power. You have the ambition. My god! you are so damn special to me it hurts. Believe it or don't believe it, but a big part of me will always be in love with you. But I won't hinder you. You have your whole life in front of you. Now start writing and wake me at ten to six."

"No," she said sadly, "I'll wake you at twenty to six." Tears began to cover her eyes as she ran her hand up his shirt.

He pulled her in close to himself. "OK. Twenty to six. I'd like that."

When John Talbot walked from Georgette's unit a few minutes after six, she picked up the phone to the telephone company. She had planned to go to bed, sleep for the day then prepare her story on the budget when she got up. But she found she was on such a high in receiving the hottest story in the country, at that moment sleep wouldn't come. So she switched on her laptop and went to work. By midday she was nearly out on her feet. In her office there was a small wall safe.

She put her story behind lock and key then fell into bed.

* * *

Bill Murphy was having a dreadful time putting the words together to complete *The Corridors of Injustice.* He'd sit down at his keyboard, but nothing would come. He'd spend literally hours in his 'seat' on the cliff face in front of his house. The waves would roll in. Seagulls swooped on anything he threw to them, but the only thoughts to fill his mind centred on Georgette McKinley. He'd light one cigarette, then another while the first one was still burning.

As much as he tried to tell himself he was being nothing but a ridiculous old fool, her image was constantly before him. Even the sea air couldn't dispel her smell from his senses. He'd try to sleep. An hour later he'd be up, pacing the floor, berating himself. Convinced such stupidity was nothing more than a mid-life crisis, he found if he kept himself physically active he was better able to cope. So he'd fuss around his plants and bushes. After spending the Tuesday afternoon in his garden he walked inside in time to catch the six o'clock news. Georgette McKinley led the bulletin with a story that stopped him dead in his tracks. She began:

"Australia's new Prime Minister and Treasurer Lindsay Cameron will hand down his third budget on Thursday.

"And I can tell you this document will not only be heinous and ruthless, it will rip the very soul out of mainstream Australia. Cigarettes will be 25 cents dearer for a standard pack of 20. Leaded and unleaded petrol will jump 15 cents a litre. It'll cost you an extra 20 cents to buy a schooner of beer and there'll be an across-the-board cut of 12 per cent in unemployment benefits. Defence spending will be dropped by 32 per cent meaning there'll be no funding for recruitment purposes over the next year, and allocations to public hospitals chopped by 20 per cent..."

Bill Murphy sat glaring at the television set. "Jesus Christ! That's the bloody budget! How the fuck did she get *that? Nobody* gets that." He rose from his chair and paced his kitchen floor, still glancing at Georgette on the screen. "*Nobody* gets that! This is unbelievable! *Unbelievable*! How the hell did she get it?"

He couldn't stand it any longer. He dialled RTN ELEVEN.

"Good god! Three times in a bloody week!" George Hanks said. "Hey, thanks for the grab. I owe you one."

"And I'm about to call it in, too. What's going on?"

"You mean the budget stuff? Christ, if she's got it right, then she's just scooped every bastard in the business. Every journo in the country has been on the phone to this joint since it dropped. Cameron is screaming but he won't say it's bullshit. The Opposition's carrying on like a dog with two dicks. *The Financial Review* is shitting itself because no bugger in there got the drop on the price hikes and cutbacks. *The Sydney Morning Herald*, *The Age*... mate, *every* bastard's climbing up my arse!"

"Has she got it right?"

"I only hope for her sake she has. If not, I'll have to fire her."

"And if she is right?"

"They'll probably make *her* the bloody Prime Minister."

"Jesus, I don't know. She'll be able to write her own ticket I suppose."

"Mate, when she came into my office Monday and closed the door, I could tell whatever was on her mind was a bit more than a children's tea party. When she laid it on me, Christ, I nearly had a bloody haemorrhage. I asked her where she got it, but she wouldn't tell me. In fact I reckon she'd even go to jail rather than disclose her source."

"So now what?"

"Wait till Thursday, I guess"

"If she is right, is it too late for Cameron to change it?"

"I'd think so. The presses would already have done their job. Anyway why all the interest in our wonderfully gorgeous Georgette?"

"Has she got a passport?"

"Oh really! So she *has* got under your bloody skin?"

"Don't be an arsehole, George. Could you do without her for five days?"

"Piss off! After what's happened tonight? You must be joking. And if her budget stuff is spot on, I'd say she's going to be pretty thin on the ground. Why? What's going on?"

"Nothing's going on... I was wondering if she disappeared for a week, that you'd cover for her?"

"When?"

"About a fortnight's time."

"No way..."

"You owe me one, remember? She'll only be away five days, OK?"

"You're a pain in the arse, Bill."

"Thanks, mate. Just don't tell her you and I have talked."

* * *

Australia's news media and talkback radio shows ran with saturation coverage of the leaked budget. Prime Minister Lindsay Cameron instituted damage control in a bid to run a snow job over the entirety of Georgette McKinley's report. But at no time was anything she stated denied. The pressure for comments from Georgette became so intense, George Hanks ordered all her calls to be screened.

"You want to talk to the media about this?" he asked her.

"Do you think I should?"

"It's up to you. I wouldn't."

At that moment George Hanks' direct line rang. Only a handful of people had the number. He picked it up expecting a familiar voice. It wasn't what he got.

"Is that George Hanks?" bellowed a question into the phone before he even had time to fully announce himself.

"Yes it is..."

"Lindsay Cameron, Mr Hanks. Put Georgette McKinley on the line," he demanded.

George Hanks felt his stomach drop. He looked at Georgette. "It's the bloody Prime Minister... for you."

Without thinking, she grabbed the phone. "This is Georgette McKinley, Prime Minister. Good evening."

"Don't you good evening me, you fucking strumpet!" he roared. "Where the bloody hell did you get your information and don't come the bullshit it just lobbed on your desk?"

Georgette's hands and knees were shaking. "I'm sorry, sir, I can't tell you that..."

"Well, let me tell you something, you goddammed smart-mouthed bitch. This phone call never happened. If it's being recorded I'll see you in fucking jail. And as long as your arse points to the ground you will never ever get anything *ever* again from this office or this government, as long as I'm Prime Minister. Do you understand?"

"Perfectly."

"I demand as Prime Minister of this country that you tell me your source or I'll sue your bloody station for every penny it's got."

"One question?"

"What?" he bellowed.

"Tell me my report was a pack of lies?"

"Fuck you, bitch!" Click.

"He hung up on me," Georgette told her boss.

"What the hell was all that about?"

"You mean amongst all the threats and abuse? He called me for everything. Wanted disclosure or he'll sue the station for everything."

"The mongrel bastard!... And?"

"And nothing. I wouldn't tell him and, what's more, you heard me ask if what I said was a pack of lies and he just roared 'Fuck you, bitch!' and slammed down the phone."

George Hanks looked squarely into Georgette McKinley's eyes. "Jesus, I hope you're right."

"If I'm not, you won't have to fire me. I'll leave."

"Yeah, and you'll be taking me with you. The old man wouldn't let me stay after that. And remember, too, if you are wrong, Cameron will see to it that our names are shit and we'll never work in the industry again."

George Hanks' direct line rang again.

"Monkhouse... put the girl on will you?"

George turned to Georgette with his hand over the mouthpiece. "It's the old man."

"Shit! What will I tell him, George?"

"The PM was a piece of piss. The old man should be a walkover," he grinned.

She took the phone. "Mr Monkhouse?"

"What have you done, girlie?" Georgette *hated* being called that. "I've just had bloody Cameron screaming blue bloody murder on the phone. You as sure about this one as you were with all the others?"

"Probably more so, I'd say," she told the station owner.

"Give me a 'yes' or a 'no'. Have you got him by the balls—figuratively speaking, of course?"

"With both hands, and I'd say very tightly," she replied.

Monkhouse roared with laughter. "Jesus, girlie, you'll do me. You know if you're wrong I'll have to sack you, don't you?"

"And if I'm not?"

"I'll give you a new contract, and I'll draw the bastard up myself. So now we wait till Thursday?"

"We wait till Thursday," she told him.

* * *

The Wednesday morning papers were full of the Georgette McKinley story. The proposed price hikes and cutbacks sparked outrage across the nation. Prime Minister Lindsay Cameron went from one interview to another all day and into the night. At times he struggled to remain calm, but in every interview he tried to dismiss McKinley's report as pure speculation and urged people to wait until the budget was read in full to the House on the Thursday. When asked over and over to stamp McKinley's report as a pack of lies, he held to the political line of saying he wouldn't give the woman credibility by commenting on her.

But by Thursday morning, because of the lack of government denial, public comment and outrage was at fever pitch. At two o'clock in the afternoon a clearly bedraggled Prime Minister rose to his feet in the House of Representatives. Australia's public, within earshot of a radio or television, held its collective breath. Was the leak the truth or just some glamour-puss trying to make a name for herself? Cameron tried to delay the inevitable as long as he could, outlining to the House the need for stringent cost savings in order to maintain a robust economy.

"Get on with it," George Hanks urged, sitting in his office watching the speech on television.

His office was packed with staff as everyone waited on tenterhooks to hear if Georgette McKinley had blown it. There were many who were prepared to bet she was wrong and they'd be seeing the last of her before day's end. Finally, the Prime Minister got to the key points of the budget. As he slowly and precisely read out the price hikes and cost-cutting measures, there was suddenly a thunderous round of yelling and applause. Georgette McKinley had got it right to every last detail. The House was in uproar. The Speaker was at his wit's end trying to control so many angry politicians.

George Hanks got out of his chair and wrapped his arms around his star reporter. "I don't know how you did it, but by Christ that puts you right up there now, young lady."

She looked at him. "I was once told if you want to run with the big boys you better learn to piss in the tall glass. Does this mean I'm now pissing in the tall glass, George?" she asked, with more than a sense of déja-vu.

George Hanks' direct line rang again. Before he had time to announce himself a voice said, "Monkhouse... Come upstairs and bring the girl with you." Click.

He turned to Georgette, pointing up towards the ceiling. "He wants us upstairs... now."

The first person Georgette saw when she entered the office of Sylvester Monkhouse was Tom Ricketts. Whenever she saw him, she physically wanted to vomit. This occasion was no different. As he approached her full of gush, she nearly did.

"Sit down, Tom; let me get to my star reporter," Monkhouse bellowed, taking hold of Georgette's hand. "Well, you really did it, girlie... g'day George... this'll just about make her a legend, won't it?"

"Er, the PM's going to sue, sir."

"Fuck him! Word I get tonight is there's a meeting at midnight of the cabinet. And by the Jesus, they just might tip him over. Never been done before. Always a first time I suppose."

"In favour of whom?" asked George Hanks.

"You won't believe it. Bloody Talbot. Apparently he's got the numbers. Cameron's supporters are so pissed about the leak, and the fact that it was right... most of 'em didn't even know what was in the damn thing themselves, you know, and they're spewin'. Then to have some bloody sheila get on television and blow the lot embarrassed the fuck out of them. Politicians don't like being embarrassed. George. Yeah, it just might be that Lindsay fucking Cameron goes down in history as the shortest-serving Prime Minister to date. What did he get? Two days, for Christ sakes. What's the time?"

"Eleven p.m. Mr Monkhouse," chirped Tom Ricketts.

"Couple of hours should do it."

"Are we on it?" George Hanks asked.

"No, we're not on it. Should we be?" Monkhouse retorted.

Some of you bloody media owners wouldn't know a story if it jumped up and bit you on the arse, Hanks thought.

"How strong is your information?"

"What if I told you it was from a minister who's called for a spill and will be at the meeting?"

Georgette's eyes lit up even brighter. "Can we use that?"

"Pretty bloody late... won't catch the papers," Monkhouse replied.

"No, but it'll catch everything else," George Hanks told him.

"Well use it... go on, get on it for Christ sakes! You want to go on camera, girlie?"

Georgette's eyes flashed at George.

"Why not? You've gone this far," he told her.

She gave the station owner an inquiring look. "So I can interrupt program with a newsflash saying an emergency meeting of cabinet is about to get underway in Canberra and the strong word is that Prime Minister Cameron's job is on the line?"

"That's all you've got to say. That's all there is to say. Oh, you can drop in the bit that former Prime Minister John Talbot is tipped to have the numbers to restore him to the Lodge. That'll get right up Cameron's fucking nose." Monkhouse looked at the clock on his wall. "You're running out of time," he told her.

Quickly Georgette grabbed an A4 sheet of paper off the station owner's desk and began to write frantically. "No time for auto cue. I'll just do it from this," pointing to the script she was writing.

"In there, girlie. Use the suite," Monkhouse told her. "Put the newsflash on this, Tom. You want to use the phone?"

Tom Ricketts picked up the intercom and called the studio director. "When's the next break, Ian. It's Tom."

"Er, seven minutes," he replied.

"Pull out the newsflash. Georgette will be going live. Where do you want her?"

"Two. It's still set up from the game show."

"Get rid of the backdrop. Put in the News logo and keep Georgette tight. She'll be on for about thirty seconds."

"Righto, Tom. Six minutes forty till the break."

"She'll be there."

Georgette was busy doing a quick makeover when she heard the phone on the old man's desk go.

"Really!" Monkhouse exclaimed. "So he's fucked? You're telling me the numbers are there to roll him?" He paused. "You bloody certain of this? Christ, if I drop that and it's wrong, I'm fucked too, along with a lot of other people in this place. OK... Cameron's gone... for sure. Jesus, that's the first time since federation. Talk to you soon." Click.

"Georgette," he boomed.

She stepped into his office.

"Cameron's fucked. Talbot's got the numbers. I don't know how you want to handle it, but that's the go."

"I'll work around it," she told him.

"Three minutes, Georgette," Tom Ricketts told her.

"OK. Let's go."

The entire staff of the newsroom was still gathered discussing the enormity of the McKinley story when suddenly someone made a dive for the volume control of a television set. The theme from the newsflash killed all conversation. Georgette McKinley, yet again, scooped the rest of the country.

"In about thirty minutes from now," she began, "an emergency meeting of cabinet will take place in Canberra. Major unrest and in-fighting has taken centre stage with ministers in the forty-eight hours since news of the Cameron budget first leaked. I am told several ministers are prepared to change their preference in a vote of no confidence against new Prime Minister Lindsay Cameron. If that's the case, and I do believe it to be the case, then within the hour John Talbot will again be Prime Minister of this country... er, excuse me a moment please," Georgette said as she picked up the phone that was ringing on her desk.

"Don't say anything. Don't change your expression. It's Monkhouse. Talbot just rang me. He won't accept the job."

Georgette replaced the receiver and returned to camera, "Apologies for that. As I was saying, I do believe John Talbot will have the numbers to unseat Lindsay Cameron, but I also believe as a person he was so devastated at being so ruthlessly dumped by the party he'd dedicated his life to, he won't accept the position. As soon as there's a result, we'll certainly bring it to you right here on RTN ELEVEN."

The red light of the camera went off. Georgette slumped in her seat. Immediately the phone rang again. It was Monkhouse.

"Jesus, girlie, that was bloody magnificent. Top job."

"You say John Talbot rang?"

"Yes," he roared. "Christ, you're about into your spot, so I said you better hurry. He said 'fuck 'em, I won't do it, they're a bunch of arseholes', so bugger it, thought you better tell 'em that too. Goes to show, eh? Come back to the office. Might be a long night. As soon as we know the result, for the record, you better go back on."

Georgette re-entered the room a minute later.

"Bloody hell! This is seat of the pants stuff, isn't it?"

"How many scoops is that this week?" Monkhouse asked, turning to Ricketts. "Can we afford this girl any more?"

"I did tell you I thought she had wonderful potential."

Georgette glared at him, but nobody caught the moment except Ricketts.

"Potential?" Monkhouse bellowed. "Come on, Tommy me boy, she's pissing in the tall glass better than most of the blokes. Good on you, girlie, bloody good on you... stick it up 'em."

The office banter continued until twelve forty a.m., when Sylvester Monkhouse's private line rang. "Malone in Canberra, sir. It's as you called it. Cameron's out. Talbot got up by seven but has declined."

"So he won't accept the job as leader second time round?"

"No, sir."

"So who's in?"

"Talbot's original deputy, Sebastian McAlister."

Monkhouse hung up and turned to Georgette, "Well it's all go, isn't it? Cameron's out. Talbot got the numbers. Got in by seven. Turned it down. Our new prime Minister is now Sebastian McAlister. Now just who the fuck is Sebastian Bloody McAlister? Go for it, girlie. Get that on the air and I reckon you'll have earned yourself a good night's sleep. Come into my office at five o'clock tonight and I'll give you a new contract. Christ knows, you've earned the bastard."

For the next seven days, the turmoil within the government grabbed every front page in the country. Mentioned right along with it were the efforts of Georgette McKinley. All areas of the media couldn't get enough of her, but, try as they might, nobody could gain an interview with her.

RTN ELEVEN bled it for all it was worth, but guarded her privacy with an iron fist. Sylvester Monkhouse gave her a new five-year, seven-digit contract. John Talbot made no further attempt to contact her, nor she him. She knew, he knew, it had run its course. At the beginning of the third week, as the dust began to settle on the enormity of what she had been involved in, George Hanks approached her desk.

"This came for you today," he told her, handing her an envelope.

Chapter 15

Josh Emery had the engines running on the Cessna C441 as the four-wheel-drive with his passengers for the flight to Portofino came into view.

Even as the sun began to break into the dawn, it was obvious temperatures would rise. *Be a stinker today, I reckon*, Josh thought as he watched the dust thrown up by the vehicle rise into the early-morning air. Within minutes, Luigi had pulled the four-wheel-drive in close to the plane. Each had only the clothes they were wearing and a small piece of hand luggage which gave them a change of clothes and basic toiletries. The main cargo was two large suitcases. Josh watched as Franco and Enrico loaded the bags.

Bloody hell! There's some weight in them, whatever they are, he thought.

All three said their goodbyes to Luigi and climbed on board the aircraft. Josh turned the Cessna's nose into the wind and powered the engines. As the plane became airborne, he saw Luigi wave, then Josh did a low-level sweep over him before disappearing into the sky.

* * *

Unbeknown to Josh Emery, his passengers or Luigi Mogliotti on the ground, there were also some interested spectators witnessing the take-off. Tucked away in the bushes and undergrowth a thousand metres from the airstrip were John James McGregor-McWeasely, Senior Sergeant Ken McLoughlin and his partner, Senior Constable Dave Bourke.

McLoughlin whispered to Bourke as both lay flat in the undergrowth eyeing proceedings with binoculars, "I've been on a few stakeouts in my time but by hell, this bastard's got me totally stuffed. The fucking Weasel's about a thousand metres off to our right. He's watching the plane. Did you get its rego?"

Dave Bourke said he did.

"Check that later... be bloody false, bet your balls on it. Then there's this prick delivering his passengers. What do you reckon, two blokes and a sheila?"

"Had trousers on, but yeah, I'd say it was a woman."

"Way the fuck out here? That's bullshit! Pretty strange place to pick up passengers for a sightseeing trip if you ask me."

"Twin-engines, boss. Wherever they're going, you can bet it's going to take more than an hour to get there."

"Yeah, but there was no luggage."

"Unless everything was in those two suitcases."

"Nup... no way. That was the hardware... whatever the bloody hardware might be."

"What's your gut feeling?"

McLoughlin swung his binoculars back to The Weasel. "Don't have one. But if this prick's involved, it could be anything. Now comes the hard part. He's certainly going to follow the joker in the four-wheel-drive, but at a distance. And we've got to follow him—at an even greater distance.

"Talk about a bloody circus! We've come all this way. He's not onto us. If he twigs we're here, it'll be shut the gate. But I'll tell you one thing. He doesn't know when the plane's coming back. If he did, he wouldn't have followed 'em like he has, and he certainly wouldn't be out here now. He's flying blind, Dave. He got a tip about a job this lot are gonna pull, and he's gonna move in on the spoils. But right now, we're more in the bloody dark than he is. We don't know who that mob are in the plane. We don't know who the bloke is in the four-wheel-drive and we don't know The Weasel's involvement. Don't know a hell of a fucking lot, do we? But as sure as hell they don't know he's here. In fact, I'm willing to bet they don't even know he exists."

Bourke listened intently as McLoughlin spoke his thoughts, then, "He's moving, boss."

"Yeah. He's going to follow the bloke in the four-wheel. My guess is he'll go back to Kununurra, keep his head down and keep this bloke in tow. When he makes a move, The Weasel will know the plane's coming back. And we'll need to be there, too."

"Where's that leave us?"

"Sleeping with one eye open. But I want to get a look at the greeter bloke. Might recognise his head."

The two policemen waited for The Weasel to disappear from view then made a dash back to their vehicle they'd hidden and covered with a camouflage net. A short time later they arrived in Kununurra and cautiously drove around. They were doubly aware of The Weasel's vehicle, having followed it all the way from Sydney.

"Sing out if you spot it," McLoughlin warned, "preferably about a hundred metres before I'm on it. That way I can pull over."

As they went slowly past a food store, Luigi Mogliotti was emerging, his gaze fixed to a newspaper. It allowed the two policemen to get a good look at his face.

"Know him?" McLoughlin asked his partner.

Bourke shook his head. "I reckon we should back off a bit. You can bet the bloody Weasel isn't far away."

"Yeah, good point. I'll pull in."

A short time later, Luigi went past their parked vehicle. McLoughlin and Bourke watched where he went and waited. Only moments passed and The Weasel also went past them.

"Jesus Christ, is this cat and mouse or what?"

McLoughlin spotted a vacant cab. "Grab that bloke, Dave. I'll wait here. Follow those bastards."

Bourke was soon in the cab and gone. He returned 20 minutes later.

"The greeter bloke's in a caravan park. The Weasel's parked in off the road about a hundred metres from it."

"So little shit-face is just gonna prop and wait him out?"

"Looks that way."

"Now what?"

"I reckon the greeter will stay put. He might go out for something to eat, but he'll be there for the night."

"So will The Weasel. We'll book in somewhere and get going again at first light."

After three days on the road following The Weasel, rump steaks, cold beer and a hot bath were the orders of the day. They double-checked the location of The Weasel, then turned in early. They were up and ready to go by five-thirty a.m.

"Better check on our little friend," McLoughlin said, as though it was part of their normal routine. He was still there.

When they repeated their routine the following morning, only later, he had gone. And so had the greeter. For several minutes they went into a blind panic, abusing themselves for leaving it so late before getting mobile.

Suddenly Bourke yelled, "Up ahead boss. That's The Weasel's car. The greeter's on the move. Not too long in the one place routine. He's obviously moved to that park over there," he said pointing to another group of cabins. "See if his bus is in there."

McLoughlin drove in around the cabins. It was. "Thank Christ for that! Obviously no movement yet."

* * *

John James had a feeling Luigi would move. Once he had established where he'd be the second night, he went to work.

At his favoured time of ten to four in the morning, John James McGregor-McWeasely drove out to the airstrip where the Cessna had taken off. As dawn began to break he stepped the distance from his earlier hiding place in the trees and bushland to both ends of the landing strip. He then drove to both ends and erected a man-sized target at each. He took out the .50-calibre Barrett and adjusted the Leupold telescopic sight to 1250 metres. There was no wind. The skies were clear and it was too early for haze.

He knew that once he fired the first round of the .50 calibre, the sound of the shot would carry, probably for a couple of kilometres in the stillness of the morning. So he wouldn't have long before there would be one or two curious on-lookers. John James pushed earplugs into his ears, loaded the rifle, then positioned himself flat on the ground behind the stock of the weapon capable of delivering one of mankind's most awesome payloads.

He recalled immediately the reading and the research he'd carried out for firing such a weapon.

Don't pull the trigger. Squeeze it, but only when your breathing is half-way through an exhale. Breathe through the sight. Breathe in, the barrel goes down. Breathe out, the barrel goes up. Bring the sight up to the target. The speed of the sound upon firing, 1121 feet per second. A standard .50-calibre bullet leaves the barrel at 2980 feet per second at a force of 12,756 feet/pound energy. Time taken for the bullet to arrive at the target, approximately one and a half to two seconds. Bullet-drop over 1250 metres, close to eight metres.

He ran through his mind the details of minutes of angle to consider when firing heavy calibres over a long distance and how each minute of angle by distance equated to ten inches in the old measurement. Satisfied he had put his theory into practice, John James put the crosshairs of the Leupold on the man-sized target, adjusted his breathing and squeezed the trigger. The Barrett bucked and rammed hard against his shoulder. He squealed and cursed with excitement and glee at what he'd only ever dreamed such a weapon would be like to fire.

Momentarily, its raw power and energy frightened him and he felt his legs go to jelly. It was the most exhilarating moment of his life. He raised his binoculars and screamed

"*Yeeessss!*" The bullet had been exactly on target. John James was stunned. He loaded another round into the breech and fired again. This time at the second target to the other end of the strip. Again his aim was true. Even wearing ear plugs, the crack from the .50 calibre was deafening. He wanted to stay longer and fire more rounds. But he capped his excitement with logic and told himself to get the hell out of there.

He loaded the weapon back into his vehicle, retrieved his targets and sped back into Kununurra to park about 100 metres from the second place Luigi Mogliotti had booked in to. For four days now he'd watched Luigi. On the morning of the fifth day, Luigi was up early. Pacing.

The Weasel backed off even further. *It's today*, he told himself. *Has to be today.*

Just after eight a.m., Luigi called into a service station and purchased a large quantity of cold drinks and food then headed towards the landing strip. Still with an hour-and-a-half before the plane was due, he pulled in off the road and bided his time. The Weasel, a long way back, watched his quarry through binoculars. He could see Luigi constantly checking his watch. Fortunately for The Weasel, Luigi had chosen to pull off a main road, so there were other occasional vehicles. He knew he needed to get ahead of the Italian to set himself up. So he waited for another vehicle to pass in the same direction he was travelling then slipped in behind. Luigi never suspected a thing.

John James wasted no time in returning to his hiding place after making sure he'd fastidiously camouflaged his vehicle.

* * *

McLoughlin and Bourke, now having lost sight of The Weasel, but believing they knew exactly his destination, did the same. Only they chose to take a different route and stopped at the other end of the landing strip to John James. They, too, hid their vehicle and covered it with a camouflage net. Luigi was still to make his appearance. Bourke and McLoughlin both knew they wouldn't have long to wait to see an end result of sleepless nights, stakeouts and following.

"Mate," McLoughlin said to Bourke, "this little prick's gonna move in as soon as the plane lands. Now I know it's as tempting as shit to grab him, but we can't. We gotta follow that son of a bitch out of here and see where he goes. He's got a hiding a place, man and London to a brick, he'll take whatever's on the plane straight to it.

"That's what I want. I gotta find out where he goes. But how's he going to get it? If he decides to take 'em out, and I can't see him doing that, we can't get involved. Not if we want to nail the little prick in his hideout. When we find that we can hopefully stitch him up with all those unsolveds. The way he bloody disappears it must be some place. I have never known anyone to drop off the map like this joker." McLoughlin checked his watch and looked at the sky. "OK, let's find ourselves a little spot and see what goes on."

"You don't really expect him to take on, what, four people in the plane plus the greeter?"

"Mate, he's got a plan. He wants what they've got. Who knows what he'll do? My guess is he'll wait till they've loaded the four-wheel-drive, and for the plane to take off. He's hardly going to go for a shoot-out from way back here. Christ, it must be over half a mile... more than that. No, he'll follow them and wait his time to make a move."

They were soon nestling their way into an area they felt was secure and would keep them out of sight of The Weasel.

But it was too late. The Weasel had already spotted them. He wriggled his body around until he had the Barrett .50 calibre pointed straight at them.

* * *

As the day for the flight to Portofino became closer, Josh Emery had a great deal of time to think about his passengers. Somehow it had all been too easy. By coincidence, he just 'happened' to walk into The Animal Bar on the day Enrico just 'happened' to be looking for a pilot. And it just 'happened' he would be able to provide for all their needs, with assistance from Spanners Hudson. And it just 'happened' that he was able to find him quickly. It was all so coincidental it began to frighten him.

Three hundred grand plus the plane!... too easy. Too bloody easy! There's no way these pricks are gonna let me walk... no way! He thought of pulling out. *Too late for that. Pull a stunt like that and I'm a dead man.*

Nervousness and fear brought perspiration to his brow. He worked the action of the little Browning .25-calibre blue-metal handgun Spanners had got for him. He loaded and unloaded the five bullets in the magazine to familiarise himself with the weapon.

"Nothing over three feet Josh," he'd told him. "Not if you want to hit what you're aiming at. In today's technological world, a gun like this is not a serious contender. You gotta remember they've been around since about 1910, but it'll be serious enough for what you want it for. Light, reliable, small. If you're on the back foot in close quarters, drop this little mother in your hand and I guarantee you'll win the argument. Strap it to your ankle. The velcro flap will give you quick and easy access."

Josh had never owned a pistol, handgun or revolver before. To the extent he didn't even know into which category the little handgun fell.

Pistol I suppose... what the hell? I sure feel a whole lot happier now I've got it, he said to himself, strapping the weapon's holster to his right ankle.

The holster was also fitted with an extra pocket for a spare magazine. Josh checked and rechecked that. He put a bullet up the spout, homed the magazine and holstered the gun. For several minutes he practiced retrieving and reholstering it. He'd stand to make sure it couldn't be seen to bulge out from beneath his trouser cuffs. It felt funny to walk with it but he consoled himself into thinking it was better to feel funny than be dead.

Josh's passengers settled in well on board the aircraft. It didn't seem they were in the air all that long before he called in his position to Darwin airport. After a quick refuel and toilet stop, the plane was again airborne, enroute to Changi. They were soon up to 31,000 feet in perfect conditions. Josh cast a casual eye over at Gina who was seated next to him in the front.

"So tell me about Portofino?" he asked. "I've never been there, but after this is all over, I want to go back and spend a bit of time there. I'm told it's the playground of the super-rich."

"Someone once said it was as though God so enjoyed the taste of creating the universe he spent a little more time hovering over the Italian west coast. Before moving on, he dug a teaspoon into the coastline around a bit from the top of the leg and said, 'and so the world shall have Portofino'." Gina laughed lightly. "It's sheltered, it's exotic and its beauty is so enthralling, it numbs the brain. And there's all sorts of stories of romance about the place. Famous movie stars walking hand in hand in the moonlight.

"If you're rich and powerful and you have a yacht, then a couple of nights' mooring is a must, especially if you're into impressing the locals and laying out breakfast, lunch or dinner on the quarterdeck. People love to drive out of Genoa through the mountains and back along the Mediterranean seashore. That lets you take in the little fishing villages before arriving at what's regarded as one of the most beautiful places in the world. Houses are multi-coloured and the gorgeous little cove is filled with yachts. Steep, tree-covered hillsides dotted with villas form the backdrop. Lots of little sidewalk cafes to eat and indulge yourself. The tourist brochures say things like," and she broke into a more high-pitched, precise delivery, "an ancient frame in the shade of eucalyptus and olives. A magic atmosphere made precious by the sound of waves splitting on the rocks. It's the nostalgia of an enchanting dream."

Josh laughed. "You remembered all that?"

"I cheated. I saw a description of a place similar to that on the internet," she told him.

Spanners Hudson was on hand to meet the plane in Singapore. Again refuelling was brief. He told Josh he'd arranged for a quick turnaround in Calcutta, but upon arriving in Dubai accommodation had been set up with room service providing Australian or Italian meals.

"All up, if you're on time, six hours," he told Josh. "So eat and sleep quick."

"Enrico's already said he won't leave the plane," Josh said.

Spanners shrugged. "It's up to him. There's a bed there if he wants it. I'll now go direct to Malta and wait for you there." Spanners handed Josh a clipboard. "It's all there. Names and so on to get you through. Might be a bit tricky there, but I reckon you'll be fine."

The remaining hours in the air and stopovers went without a hitch. Spanners Hudson had been true to his word. The accommodation and refuelling stops were a breeze but, by the time the Cessna landed at Malta, the frustrations of cramped conditions and the embarrassment of using the commode had led to bitchy comments and agro, mainly from Enrico. Franco had remained relatively silent throughout the duration of the flight. This was a heist of gigantic proportions and his mind stayed firmly on the job ahead. When Josh called out, "Ten minutes to Malta!" there were audible sighs of relief.

Spanners Hudson was again on hand. "Three dollars US a fucking gallon mate. Doesn't get much blacker than that eh? And ten grand graft. The same blokes will be on again when you come back. I haven't got that sort of dough. What do you want to do?"

"Hang on a minute." Josh went back to the plane. "I was afraid of this. From here to Portofino, this flight will not exist, but it's three dollars a gallon for juice and ten grand graft over and ten grand back."

Enrico was enraged.

"*You fucking sai...*"

"Shut the fuck up, little brother! We're on their territory. What do you want? A goddammed inspection of the plane? How much US have you got?"

"Fifty grand."

"Give me twenty-five."

Enrico took out his wallet and did as his brother ordered. Josh tried not to alter his expression. It was the first time there had ever been any indication of a link between the two men. Franco handed Josh the money.

"Will this get us out of here right now? We can't afford a plane inspection. If we argue they could bung one on, right? I read somewhere they do that shit."

"Yes, it could happen," Josh answered firmly. "I'll try."

Josh handed the money to Spanners. He seemed to be gone for an eternity. But in reality it was only minutes. Suddenly, a tanker pulled in next to the plane. Spanners spoke with Josh.

"I can't get out of here in time to be ahead of you in Sori. I've arranged the car. That's already there. But I'll need to be there for the fuel. I'm gonna have to come with you."

"I'll tell 'em."

Josh quickly explained the situation. Enrico was affronted by the suggestion.

"It's not his fault," Franco interrupted angrily. "You wanna be stuck in fucking Italy without fuel? Don't be an idiot! Tell him to get in, Josh... Gina?"

"No argument from me."

Even as he climbed on board Josh could tell that Spanners' presence would only be condoned, not welcomed. "Gina, can you move back one? Spanners, you sit in the front," he ordered.

Josh was going to introduce him to the passengers, but thought better of it. It seemed in no time at all the Cessna was again climbing into the sky. Josh was particularly uneasy about this leg of the flight. Up until now, everything had been on approved flight paths. Now it was low-level stuff. Just above the waves for about six hours. If they were going to be nabbed by the authorities, this would be the time. But there were no incidents. The coastline appeared and he snuck in undetected to land safely on an airstrip between Sori and Cigana. As pre-arranged by Spanners, a vehicle was parked at the edge of the landing strip. Josh had no sooner cut the engines, when Franco was behind the wheel, backing it up to the plane.

"Six hours," he said to Josh. "OK? When you see us coming, start those bloody engines because we'll need to get the fuck out of here real quick." Moments later the car sped off into the night.

"Any idea what they're up to?" Spanners asked.

Josh shook his head. "Not a bloody clue, but money's never been a problem. That bastard sitting behind me bothers me a bit. That's Enrico. Typical Italian hothead. Gina runs the show and she's bouncing up and down on the other bloke, Franco. Whatever the hell it is they're into it's obviously humongous. Why else would they go to all this trouble?"

"You bring your gun?"

Josh indicated to his ankle.

"OK. It's four hours till the fuel tanker gets here. You want to get a bit of shut-eye? I'll keep an eye on things."

Again, Spanners was true to his word. The fuel tanker arrived as arranged and Spanners paid him off. Josh checked his watch. "How long we got before someone gets nosey?"

"Daylight. But we'll be gone by then, won't we?"

"Out of here in two hours I hope," Josh replied nervously.

* * *

McLoughlin and Bourke were nearly at their wit's end. Literally hundreds of mug-shots of John James McGregor-McWeasely had been distributed in two separate drops and there had not been one reported sighting. Then at three-thirty in the morning, a week before he'd watch Josh Emery take off for Portofino, McLoughlin's phone rang.

"Yeah," he mumbled, trying to wake up.

"Is that someone called Ken?"

"It is."

"You the bloke looking for... ?"

Suddenly wide awake, he blurted, "Bloody oath... who have I got?"

"I drive a cab, and I just dropped a bloke off. I reckon it might have been him. Skinny little bloke. Walks funny..."

"Fantastic. That's him. You remember where?"

"Yeah. Ryde. Twenty-seven Sea Lake Avenue. Block of flats there."

McLoughlin piled out of bed and put the light on. Bourke stirred. "Come on, get up, son, We've found the little motherfucker!"

Suddenly Bourke was wide awake.

"The fucking Weasel. He's in a block of flats in bloody Ryde. Come on, let's go."

Bourke was still buttoning his shirt as McLoughlin sped away from the Motor Inn. At that time of the morning Ryde was only 15 minutes away. Bourke checked the street directory and guided the way. They were soon into Sea Lake Avenue. He slowly cruised past but there was nowhere to stake out.

"I got an idea," chirped Bourke. "Turn around."

McLoughlin did as he was asked.

Bourke pointed. "That joint's for sale. Might even be empty. Good spot. About five doors back on the other side of the road. I reckon it would give us a good view of the flats."

McLoughlin looked at the house, then back at the flats.

"Bloody would, too," he replied, looking at the 'For Sale' sign.

"Who you ringing?" Bourke asked.

"The mobile phone on the billboard."

"Shit, he'll love you. It's four in the bloody morning for Christ sakes!"

"Time he was up," McLoughlin smiled.

It took some minutes for the Senior Sergeant on special assignment to convince the land agent the call wasn't some sort of practical joke. "Yes" the place was empty. "No," he couldn't possibly go to his office for a set of keys at that time of the morning. Moments later, "Of course Sergeant, I'll be there in a few minutes."

"Persuasive bastard aren't you?" Bourke grinned.

"Who do you know would enjoy having the SWAS squad kick your fucking door in at four in the morning?"

The view offered to McLoughlin and Bourke from the front window of the empty house gave them full vision of the block of flats in

Sea Lake Avenue. As one policeman took a nap, the other took over. Their concerns began to mount after they'd been watching and waiting all day and into the night.

Late, around midnight, Bourke noticed a vehicle slowly emerge from the flats' car park. He quickly raised his binoculars. At the entrance to the flats was a street light. John James drove underneath it and stopped to check for traffic before proceeding. It was long enough. Quickly he woke his boss.

"It's him!" he whispered urgently.

McLoughlin sat bolt upright. "Where?"

"He's just left the flats. We couldn't follow if we wanted to. He just snuck out of the car park, stopped under the street light to check for traffic and pissed off. By the time I could've gotten out to the car, I wouldn't have known where he was or which way he went."

"You did good, son. You did bloody good. Definitely him, though?"

Bourke nodded his head. "Definitely him."

"Fantastic!" He reached for his phone and dialled Commissioner Colin Johnson. "Apologies for the hour, sir, it's McLoughlin..."

The Senior Sergeant went on to explain to the Police Commissioner the latest series of events.

"So what do you need?"

"Six unmarked cars around the clock to stake him out. Stay right off him and report to me direct when he moves... anywhere, anytime."

"Done... stay in touch."

Over the few next days various patrols reported in to McLoughlin. The Weasel would drive to a particular suburban street, park for a few hours wait in his car, then return to his flat. But because he parked so far off Luigi's house, it was impossible to determine exactly what he was up to.

McLoughlin resisted the chance to enter his flat when he wasn't there on the off-chance he'd make a mistake and spook his quarry. Suddenly, and out of the blue, The Weasel made his move. A patrol car, staking him out, called it in.

"He went to his usual place. A bit later a four-wheel-drive up the street with four heads in it, pulled out. He followed it. He's still following it. Travelling west."

"Where are you?"

"Heading up the freeway to Katoomba."

"Stay on him. Don't get spotted for Christ sakes. But don't lose him either. We're on our way. We'll put the flashing light on the dash and catch up as quick as we can. I'll ring you in half an hour."

Bourke already had the car engine running. McLoughlin climbed in, Bourke switched on the flashing light then sped off.

"Got everything?" McLoughlin asked.

"You got your ankle back-ups?"

"I have... you check everything... vests, the high powers... ?"

"All done. So where do you reckon he's going?"

"God knows."

Thirty minutes passed and McLoughlin called the patrol car. "We're going through Parramatta. How far ahead are you?"

"Get on the freeway and nudge it to 140 to 150. Give it ten minutes and ring me again. You shouldn't be far away by then. I'll call the highway patrol and tell 'em to back off if they see you coming."

Once on the freeway Bourke dropped the foot and soon the speedo was topping 160. McLoughlin called again and gave his position.

"You're ten minutes behind. Keep it up for another five minutes then cut your flashing light."

White lines on the freeway passed like a picket fence. "That should do it, Dave," he said, turning off the light. He called the patrol again.

"You're coming up behind us I'd say. We're about to head up the mountain. White Falcon XUS-351."

"Gotcha," replied McLoughlin.

"OK. He's up ahead. White falcon. Very plain. Very ordinary. RSB-768. About 500 metres. You need us anymore?"

"You did good. Thank you." Then to Bourke. "You got him, Dave?"

"Think so. Have a look through the glasses. See if you can pick it up. RSB-768."

McLoughlin lifted the binoculars. "Yeah, that's him. OK, shit face, just where are you taking us?"

It was some 400 kilometres north west of Sydney, at Dubbo, before The Weasel stopped for petrol.

"Mate, this joker's not on a Sunday drive. Something tells me this is going to be one helluva long haul." And for the next three days and nights the pursuit continued.

"If he keeps going much further he'll end up in the bloody ocean. What's next?" he asked Bourke, looking at a map.

"Kununurra."

"Surely to Christ that's got to be it."

"But we still don't know what he's up to," Bourke said, frustration creeping into his voice.

"He's obviously following the four-wheel-drive. Now we can't go past him to check that out, so we're stuck. This is the prick we're after. I'm not going to spring him until he gets what he's after and leads us to wherever the hell he hides his arse. Don't be surprised if we have to turn around and follow him all the way back to bloody Sydney. And I'll just bet that's the case."

As the two policemen drove into Kununurra, they stayed well back from The Weasel. It only became obvious to them who he was following when early the next morning The Weasel led them to a deserted airstrip a little to the north of the Durack River.

"Now the game is really on," McLoughlin said to Bourke.

Chapter 16

It was twenty-two minutes past midnight when Franco, Enrico and Gina pulled up outside the Villa belonging to Bruno Formicella. The street was deserted, a far cry from the wining and dining happening far below in the cafes and restaurants at the water's edge. The night was warm. The moon was bright and the skies were clear. A solitary street-light glowed in the distance. After bringing their vehicle to a standstill, Franco cut the motor and the three sat in silence, listening, watching, straining their eyes to see anything that may jeopardise their safety. Franco shot a glance to Gina.

"You sure this is it?" he whispered.

Gina looked at the large and intricately carved white lettering over the front door. It read: White Doves. She allowed herself a slight, knowing smile. "This is it," she assured him.

Suddenly all three were gripped with the enormity of the task at hand. "I don't mind telling you I'm pretty bloody toey about all this, now we're here," Enrico said, his voice quivering slightly.

"I think we all are," Franco added, "You want to call it off?"

Gina's eyes flashed at the two of them.

"I didn't think so," Franco smirked. "OK, let's go."

On the journey into Portofino, Franco turned off one of the roads to allow Enrico time to assemble his thermal lance.

"Jesus, what's *that*?" Gina blurted.

"Our ticket to freedom," Enrico told her.

"What is it, really?"

"Seeing is believing, babe. And when you do, you still won't believe it."

He quickly test-fired it, then shut it down.

"All set," Enrico called. "Let's go melt some steel."

As the three emerged from their vehicle outside the Villa, the stillness of the night spooked them.

"It's so damn quiet, it feels like we're walking into a bloody trap," Franco whispered into Gina's ear.

"Jesus! Don't say that," she flashed back.

Moments later, the three were at the rear of the Villa and shielded by enormous hanging vines. With the tiniest of penlights, Enrico shone it about himself. "Franco, look! It's the bloody fuse box."

"Can you open it?"

"It's already open," he whispered.

"Bullshit!"

"It is... look!"

Franco couldn't believe his eyes either. "Throw the mains," he said.

"What if there's a back-up?"

"Mate, I reckon this bloke is so blasé he wouldn't bother with one."

"Gina?"

"What if all hell breaks loose?"

"Then we're out of here."

Gina shook her head. "I don't think we should."

Franco looked at Enrico and ran his hand across his face. "Shit! Leave it Enrico. Just in case." He put the beam of the little light onto the lock of the rear door. He then ran it round the edges. "Looks pretty clear."

Enrico took a thick steel spike and a massive, short-stopper over the end to cushion the sound of steel on steel. He leaned back and belted the spike with enormous force. Only two hits were required for the lock to shatter and the door to spring open.

The trio was quickly inside. Because of the use of outside reflectors to utilise available light, the villa's interior was dimly lit from the moonlight. Momentarily they stood there, mesmerised by the luxury of their surrounds.

"Cop this joint!" Enrico whispered.

"And this is only the bloody kitchen! You ain't seen nothin' yet," Gina told him. "Come on, we've got a safe to find."

Carefully monitoring every step they took, their hearts nearly beating their brains into submission from pure adrenalin and fear, they found themselves surrounded by the opulence of the sitting-room/reception/lounge area. In the dim light, the trio was overawed by what they could see. Ahead was a smaller room.

"Bruno's office... saw it on the net," she whispered. "I reckon it has to be in here."

The three of them looked around Bruno's sanctuary and at the giant paintings that hung on the walls. Franco walked over and placed a finger under the bottom of the first one to see if it might be hinged. It wasn't, but the second one was. It sprung back to reveal a safe door nearly two metres high and a metre and a half wide.

"Holy shit!" he exclaimed.

Both Enrico and Gina were too stunned to speak.

There was a muffled giggle as one said, "That was too bloody easy."

Enrico regained himself, closed the door to the office, and set up the thermal lance.

"Stand over here Gina, and don't look when he puts that flame on the safe's door," Franco told her.

Enrico covered his eyes with darkened goggles, turned on the gas and lit the end of the lance. There was a roar as the oxygen and welding rods responded to the flame. Enrico worked the valve of the oxygen cylinder until he had the cutting flame he wanted. He plied the heat to the one spot for several seconds, then, like a hot knife through butter, the thermal lance, in a matter of seconds, had the lock of the safe door topple smouldering and molten onto the office floor. Gina's eyes and mouth popped wide open in disbelief. Enrico cut the flame, turned the handle of the safe door and swung it open.

Instead of seeing the interior of a safe, what lay in front of them was a small room. Enrico felt down the side of the wall for a light switch. He found one and turned it on. On the walls of the small room were several priceless works of art, and a very large copy of Picasso's *Still Life With Tulips*, which featured an image of his mistress Marie-Therese Walter. Gina stared at the painting.

"My god!" she gushed, "The original of that has just been sold for fifty million dollars by Christies in New York. I don't believe this guy. Bloody hell, even that would be worth a fortune."

But Enrico wasn't at all captivated in the copy of the 1932 painting. The safe door next to it was what he was more interested in. Apart from the brief diversion, so too was Gina.

She shook her head. "Clever little bastard, isn't he? Two safes!"

Again she and Franco stood aside as Enrico went to work on it with the thermal lance. Moments later it too was being opened as the lock rolled onto the floor in a glowing molten mass. Enrico stepped inside the door and felt for a light. As he switched it on, all three stood aghast at what lay in front of them. The safe was of reasonable size. Probably three metres by three metres, but its shelves were completely empty.

* * *

Gina dropped to her knees in shock. She broke into hysterics, crying, "*No! No! No! My God, no!*"

Enrico burst into uncontrollable rage as Franco dry-retched. Suddenly, Enrico turned his rage onto Gina, lashing out and catching her with a vicious blow to the side of the face. He was screaming at her. Then he turned his rage onto Franco and grabbed him by the throat. Through her haze, Gina could tell her lover was in serious trouble. Enrico had snapped. She screamed at him to let his brother go. He ignored her pleas, So she flew at him, only to be belted in the face again, a blow which sent her sprawling across the floor of the safe. Still with enough presence of mind for survival, she reached into her handbag and pulled out her Remington.

"*Let him go or I'll blow your head off... So help me, I will, Enrico. Let him go!*" she screamed.

Still with his hands around his brother's throat, he glanced over his shoulder. He ignored Gina's threat. Gina could see Enrico's grip tightening. She raised the barrel and fired. The bullet ricocheted off the safe wall and thudded into a shelf. Enrico froze on the spot. He released his brother immediately when he saw Gina lower the barrel and point the gun directly at him.

"Pull yourself together, arsehole!" she screamed, her voice at fever pitch.

"Now what are you gonna do, bitch? Shoot me?"

Gina knew the situation had to be calmed. Immediately she lowered her gun. "Enrico," she tried to say calmly even though her gut was in turmoil, "you're being an idiot. Obviously we're all pissed off about this. Maybe there's another safe."

He started to move towards her and he noticed her gun hand move a fraction. He stopped. "Jesus Christ, Franco! she was going to shoot me. Were you going to shoot me, bitch?"

"You'll never know how close you came."

"Bullshit! You wouldn't have the guts," he sneered.

Gina raised her gun again and pointed it straight at his head. "You had all of three seconds. If I wasn't in love with your brother, you'd be dead already. OK? D-E-D. I'm really sick of your shit, woggo! The two-faced crap you carry on with. Your big mouth. Your bragging. Face it, pally. We both loathe each other's guts. Me more than you if you only knew it. So we carry on like civilised human beings and get on with it or we split now. Your choice, arsehole. But I'll tell you one thing, if we split now, you find your own way home. OK? The plane leaves *without* you. So what's it gonna be?"

Enrico knew he had no options. Normally Franco would spring to his aid. But he'd just destroyed that lifeline. More so at this moment than ever before Enrico knew he was on his own. Franco was still trying to catch his breath and cared little about the future of his brother.

Gina tightened her grip on the little Remington. Enrico saw her knuckles whiten as she brought her other hand up for support.

"Ba... Babe," Franco began.

"Shutup Franco! What's it gonna be, Enrico? Your choice. Three seconds. One. Two. Thr.."

"OK. Jesus Christ! I fucked up, all right? *I fucked up!* Sorry."

Gina made him sweat for a few seconds and lowered her gun. "OK. Now pick up your brother. Let's have a look around the other rooms. I still believe the money's here," she said firmly, relieved that at least for the moment calm was restored. But she didn't uncock her weapon and return it to her handbag. She chose to hang onto it, keeping Enrico always within her view.

As they stepped outside the safe, Enrico glanced at the copy of the Picasso. Quickly he grabbed the lance and lit it. Probably more out of anger at Gina than finding an empty safe.

"Let me totally fuck this guy's day," he sneered, and ran the flame across the painting. As the canvas and oils melted away, all three stood staring in total disbelief. Behind the painting lay another safe door.

"*Yeeesss!*" Gina hissed. "Just how smart is our little bloody Bruno?"

Suddenly Enrico's altercation with Gina was past history as he attacked the safe's door with renewed vigour He plied the flame to the door's lock. Again it was only moments before the lock had toppled to the floor in a smouldering, molten heap. Enrico turned the handle and reefed open the door. He felt inside the wall for the light switch and turned it on.

Before them lay several shelves stacked with bundles and bundles of $1000 bills. Gina uncocked her weapon and placed it back in her handbag. Suddenly all anger and animosities were forgotten. They stood with their chins on their chests, never before having seen such an enormous pile of money. Enrico lunged at it. He grabbed handfuls of it and turned to face his two accomplices.

"Hey, I'm really sorry, you two. Jesus, look at all this! There must be millions here!"

Franco and Gina were momentarily dumbstruck. Gina started to shake uncontrollably. Franco, still trying to recover from nearly being strangled to death by his brother, just wanted to grab it all and get out of there. "Come on! Let's load up and *go!*"

For several minutes all three worked at fever pitch to pack every last bundle. Finally they were done.

"OK," said Franco, "that's it. Out! Come on, let's go! You can't begin to imagine just how many pissed-off, angry people there are going to be over this little lot."

The haul was as Gina expected. Scores of bundles of $1000 notes in US currency. "What do you reckon?" she asked Franco.

He looked at her and touched her face with his hand. "Hey, thank you. I love you, too. Sorry it took such a hell of a moment to say it. But without you, I'd be dead. He would've killed me. I owe you, babe. I owe you big time."

Gina smiled. "Just keep him away from me, all right?"

"I will babe, I will. Promise. I'll sit next to him on the way home. He won't bother you. I didn't know you had a gun."

"Just as well, isn't it?"

Franco raised an eyebrow. "Would you have shot him?"

"If he hadn't let you go, yes. I wouldn't have hesitated."

Franco looked at her. "Somehow, I believe you." Then, "Come on! Let's get the hell out of here!"

Not content with two very large bags jammed tight with cash, Enrico wanted more. He'd found a stash of gold ingots and was jamming as many as he could into his pockets. He became angry when he ran out of the room. So he unzipped one of the bags with the money and crammed a few in around the top.

"Zip it up, man!" Franco said urgently. "Come on! Vamoose!"

Gina went ahead as the trio, as silently as they could, made their way from the villa. She sneaked out the rear and made her way to the front. The night was still dead calm. She made her way to the vehicle, opened the boot and beckoned her two accomplices. Franco and Enrico dumped their haul into the boot and Enrico returned for the thermal lance and the oxygen bottles.

"Can't we leave them?" she whispered to Franco.

"Shit no! They're as good as a fingerprint. We'll dump them later, but not here."

Still with fear and adrenalin racing through their bodies, they sped from the villa with Franco at the wheel. There was laughter inside the car as they celebrated pulling off the impossible. Gina, even more wary of Enrico than before, slowly slid her hand down into her handbag and wrapped her fingers around the Remington.

You never know, she told herself, *you just never bloody know.*

Halfway back to the aeroplane, Franco spotted an old abandoned farmhouse with a well off to its side. He pulled up, turned around and drove over to it. "Dump the cylinders in there," he told Enrico.

"They're bloody expensive, these things," he laughed, listening as they dropped to the depths below.

Two hours into their journey, their headlights picked up the twin-engine Cessna. Franco sped across to the aircraft. Josh already had the doors open. The two Italians emptied their vehicle and Franco drove it to the edge of the strip, then ran back to the plane. Gina was about to board when Franco noticed Spanners sitting in the front.

"Sorry, mate, I promised Gina that one."

"Not a problem," he said, moving to the rear.

The doors closed, Josh turned over the engines and called, "All in?"

"Go! Go! Go!" yelled Franco.

Josh powered the engines and the little plane was soon winging its way at full speed out of Italian airspace. When he became comfortable, flying only metres above the surface of the ocean, he turned to Gina.

"So... how did it go?"

"OK," she shrugged as best she could without tipping off the pilot about what he was carrying for a payload.

Franco heard the exchange. "No questions, Josh, all right?"

Josh could tell it was pointless having anything further to say. But he knew at that moment he'd give half a tank of juice to know what was in those bags in the luggage bay. Flying fast and low he couldn't allow his mind to dwell too much on his cargo. At such low altitude he had to be doubly aware. One false move and the sea would claim them.

* * *

Malta loomed up on the horizon. Josh put the Cessna down and Spanners left to again consult officials. Minutes later he returned. Josh could see the concerned look on his face. "Problems?"

"Big problems!"

"What?" blurted Franco.

"The graft has now doubled."

"Piss off!" said Gina. "What the fuck do they want now?"

"Another twenty grand and four dollars a gallon."

Enrico became enraged. *"That's bloody bullshit, Hudson! How do we know you're not just pocketing the dough and ripping us off?"*

"Have it your way, mister. This is where I get off anyway. If you think you can do it better, be my guest. Nice working with you, Josh. See ya round."

Franco and Gina panicked. They shot their glance to Josh.

"Now what the fuck do we do?"

"I suggest you chase after that man, apologise to him and slip him a couple of grand for his trouble. None of this trip would have been possible without him. And right now, if you don't want the plane to be searched or impounded, you better be real nice to him, because he's our ticket out of here. He's the only one who can get us back onto a legal flightpath to Iraklion. And I'll tell you another thing. If he told you that's what it's going to cost, then you can take that to the bank. It's up to you," he told them calmly.

"Call him back Josh... *call him back!*" yelled Franco.

Josh called to Spanners. He stopped and turned around. He could see Josh calling him back.

Josh quickly told Franco how much was needed. Franco reefed it from his wallet, then thrust it into Josh's hand. "Give him that... let's hope it's enough."

"You give it to him, and make sure you bloody apologise."

Franco climbed from the aircraft and walked towards Spanners. He handed him the money and after a brief exchange returned to the plane.

"How did it go?" Gina asked, urgently.

"Said he'd do what he could, but couldn't promise anything."

Josh smiled inwardly. The bugger was going to make them sweat. He also knew that Spanners saw this as his last opportunity to make a fast buck from a group of people who least of all would want to be questioned about their activities.

Besides, Josh thought, *he bloody well earned it.*

Tensions mounted inside the aircraft as they waited for the fuel tanker to arrive. Spanners was playing this to the very end. It was another ten minutes before fuel was being pumped into the tanks of the Cessna.

Two-and-a-half hours later, the Cessna touched down in Iraklion. The stopover was brief, with just enough time for everyone to stretch their legs. With tanks full, Josh Emery soon had the Cessna in the air and onto a legal flight path at 33,000 feet. As he settled into the journey, he noticed things weren't going quite right. He pulled back on the power levers and adjusted the RPM controls in an attempt to conserve fuel.

Franco heard the engines cut back. "Problems?" he asked.

"Yeah, fairly major, too. The forecast out of Iraklion was for light winds, but right now we've got a bloody doozy. We're full-on into a major headwind and this will kick the shit out of our fuel supply... even the reserves. Sit tight. I'll nurse the engines and get what I can out of them. But I don't think we'll have enough gas. We may have to go down in the desert."

"Oh, Jesus, don't say that. Can we land somewhere else?"

"There is nowhere else. Well, there is, but will your cargo stand a customs check?"

"No fucking way! Shit! What then? Can we ditch stuff and lighten the plane?"

"Open the door at this height and we'll all be sucked out."

"What about if we drop down to a couple of hundred feet?"

"If I do that, the turbines will chew the juice twice as quickly as they are now."

"Well shit, Josh! we can't just sit here and wait to fucking die!"

Gina, in listening to the conversation, was too terrified to speak. Her face was ashen and she was clenching her fists so tightly her fingernails were almost making her palms bleed. Enrico was bellowing from his seat and it took all of Franco's level-headedness to keep his brother under some degree of control.

Josh turned to Franco. "I'm just telling you the situation we're faced with. If I'd known the weather was going to change so dramatically, we wouldn't have taken off. It's no-one's fault. But we gotta lose the headwind. I just can't see how we're going to at this point."

As the flight progressed, Josh became even more concerned about fuel consumption. "We're about half an hour out at the moment," he said.

"How much fuel?" Franco asked.

"Twenty-eight minutes."

"Jesus Christ! Two minutes short," Franco cursed.

"That's if everything is spot-on accurate. The wind is picking up. Another ten minutes and that will mean eighteen minutes to touch down but only with fourteen in the tank, including the reserves."

"Are there emergency ration packs in this thing?" Gina asked.

Josh quickly explained where they were but not to expect a Hilton menu. Enrico was still panicking, bellowing, abusing.

"What are our chances if we ditch?" Franco asked little later, now with panic in his voice.

Josh shook his head. "Not good," he replied. "These things are only light, you know. Bit like an egg. Put one end to end between the palms of your hands and you won't break it. But it takes no effort for you to put your finger through its shell. These planes are like that. End to end as tough as nails. But from the side you could put a fist through the fuselage."

Josh eased back even further on the power levers and made a small adjustment to the RPM controls, keeping his gaze glued to the fuel gauge. "Five minutes from Dubai and on descent," he called to his passengers. "OK... listen to me everyone. According to the fuel gauge, we're out of gas! So right now, we're running on our reputation. Let's hope Cessna has a good one. We can force land while I still have control of the plane or when the engines cut out. The latter is not the best option. Or we can chance it for the next four minutes and try to land. Your choice."

All three looked at each other. Gina spoke up. "You decide, Josh. You've got us this far. It's up to you. None of us know shit about flying."

"I say we chance it. If there's even one degree of error the right way in the gauge, we'll make it. So pull your seat belts in a bit tighter, I'll try and get us onto friendly country."

Perspiration poured from Josh Emery's forehead as he listened intently for the slightest hiccup in the engines. Two minutes to landing. He wiped his brow. He knew that to lose power now would mean certain death. One minute. Wheels down.

"Come on, baby!... Come on, baby!... *Come on... Come on,*" he urged."

Thirty seconds. Twenty. Ten.

"Come on, baby!"

The sweetest sound Josh had ever heard in his life was the wheels kissing the tarmac. The cheering in the cabin was thunderous. Josh wiped his brow again as he brought the Cessna to a standstill. As he did, the engines cut out. He screamed with delight.

"Whoooah... how close was that?"

After declaring Josh to be an outright genius and thanking their lucky stars a thousand times over, all four enjoyed putting their feet back onto mother earth. As none was prepared to leave the plane unattended, each took turns to quickly take care of their personal needs and return to the aircraft.

After refuelling, with tanks now brimming, it wasn't long before Josh again had the Cessna on a recognised flightpath at 33,000 feet. Nervous energy saw Gina chat away endlessly to Josh and, in the hours that followed, she appeared to talk about every movie she and her friends had ever seen. Franco wished she'd shut up as he was trying to sleep, but consoled himself in knowing that at least it was movies she was talking about and not the cargo. The remainder of the flight passed without incident. Just after passing Kupang in West Timor, Josh again spoke to his passengers.

"I told you before we left that we'll need to pull out the smoke and mirrors if we're to get over the Australian coastline undetected. That time has now arrived, so just ignore what I say on the radio, because I'm going to have to drop down under the radar."

He spoke to Control in both Darwin and Kupang and explained that whilst everything was OK, he did have a pressurisation problem and needed to descend to a lower level. Josh told Control he'd damaged a seal on the rear door and the explanation was accepted.

"Home free," he told everyone.

"*Yeeesss!*" exclaimed Gina.

"You bastards gonna tell me now what it was I risked my neck for?"

Franco patted him on the shoulder, "Not a chance, good buddy. Not a snowflake's chance in hell."

Josh laughed. "How long before we're down?" Enrico asked.

"Twenty minutes," Josh told him.

Gina cast a glance over her shoulder at Enrico. "Franco."

He leaned into her.

"Is everything cool?" she whispered.

"Sure, babe."

"Him?" referring to Enrico.

"Not a problem." Then leaning into her ear. "He thinks he's got the shotgun, but I've got it. I slipped it into my bag. Don't worry, if he tries anything, shoot the bastard next time. But he won't."

"Couple of minutes, folks, and we're down," Josh called.

"You reckon Luigi will be there?" Enrico asked.

Franco looked at his watch. "He'll be there," he said reassuringly.

"Coming up, folks... any sign of Luigi?"

Everyone looked out of their windows.

"Told you so," said Franco. "He's there. Down the other end on the right."

"Got him," said the pilot.

"Do a sweep, Josh," said Franco. "I want to take a look around."

Luigi waved as the plane passed low overhead.

"OK?" said Josh. "Looks perfectly all right to me... anyone see anything... any problems?"

Gina and Enrico agreed the coast was clear.

"Take her in, Josh... and let me say on behalf of all of us, thank you. When we leave in a minute you'll probably never see us again. If you do, please don't recognise us. The rest of your money will be left in the luggage bay. It's in American dollars, but I'm sure if you're careful, you won't have a problem with that. The aeroplane is yours to do with what you will."

Josh looked at him. "I trust you. If the money's not there, I'll take off again and land the bastard right on top of your fucking vehicle."

"I reckon you would too." Franco smiled. "We give you our word you won't have to do that."

"Here we go, folks," Josh called. "The Flight of Dreams from Portofino is now landing, ladies and gentlemen. Please remain seated until the aircraft comes to a standstill and the fasten seatbelts lights are turned off."

His passengers seemed to enjoy the light relief. As the Cessna's wheels touched down, Gina again let forth with, "*Yeeees!*" Josh brought the aircraft to a stand-still, spun it round and taxied back to Luigi as he stood waiting by his four-wheel-drive. It was ten minutes after their planned arrival time of ten a.m. The sun was just beginning to have an impact on the day. The skies were clear. There was no wind.

There was an eagle high on the wing.

* * *

McLoughlin's phone rang.

"Is that Signor Mareschallo Ken McLoughlin?" came a polite, but inquiring Italian accent.

"Yes, it is," he grunted abruptly.

"Aah, at last! My kingdom for your phone number. Might I say if my endeavours to find you had dragged on any longer it may well have come to that..."

"Who is this?" McLoughlin demanded, raising his voice.

"My name is Bruno Formicella. I think for the purposes of this phone call it's best if I call you Phillipe."

Chapter 17

As Georgette McKinley stood at the gates of Buckingham Palace, she could have sworn she felt the ghosts of past Kings and Queens pass through her veins. She turned to Bill Murphy.

"This is so awe-inspiring. To stand here in the footprints of history is so overwhelming. We read about it, we see pictures of it... it's on the telly... we see it in the movies, but we don't *really* do we? You've simply got to *stand* here and absorb it if you want to take it all in. The guards, the horses, the uniforms, the ceremony of it all. Oh, *wow*! *This* is London. Thank you for bringing me here," she gushed.

Bill Murphy was a little taken aback at Georgette's enthusiasm, and the fact that the 'old dart' could still affect people in such a way. The two had been absorbing the Palace for what Bill felt was an extended period. Big Ben struck the hour.

"You feel like lunch at the Ritz or do you want to stay a bit longer?"

Without shifting her eyeline she told him she would like to stay another few minutes. Bill Murphy didn't mind. His enjoyment was seeing the pleasure the young woman got from being so close to the pulse of England. He lit a cigarette and backed away to a seat nearby. Georgette didn't even notice he'd moved. She stood at the gates, close to the guard with his bearskin hat and let the grandness of the occasion flow over her. She was totally enthralled. Several minutes had passed when she glanced one way, then the other. Quickly she turned round thinking Bill had moved away. From where he was sitting, he raised an arm and waved to her. Georgette went to him and sat down beside him.

"You're having fun aren't you?" he smiled.

Georgette shook her head and held out her arms. "Do you think we'll see the Queen on the balcony?" She giggled. "Oh, I'm sorry! Here I am rattling on. Lunch! Yes! It's lunch time. Big Ben said so," she giggled again.

As they walked together, taking the long way to 150 Piccadilly, Georgette's mind reflected on how she actually got to be in London with Bill Murphy.

When George Hanks handed Georgette the letter in the newsroom as her working day was coming to an end, she flicked it over to see if there was a return address. There wasn't. She ran a letter opener across the top and withdrew the contents.

> *Dear Miss McKinley,*
>
> *Your presence is required aboard QF1 to London next Saturday morning. Upon arrival at Heathrow airport you will be chauffeur driven by limousine to The Ritz Hotel on Piccadilly. Single room accommodation has been booked in your name for six nights, before boarding QF320 the following Saturday to return to Sydney.*
>
> *Tickets have also been obtained for you to see Agatha Christie's* Mouse Trap. *If you feel you would like to indulge yourself for a few days in a far-off land, which could include activities such as romantic dinners, shopping at Harrods, riding in a horse and carriage through the streets of London plus other wonderful and exotic pastimes like a quick dining and shopping excursion to Paris, please contact Mr Bill Murphy immediately at the number shown at the bottom of this invitation.*

Georgette sat looking at the letter, her jaw wide open.

George Hanks walked over to her. "My god, has someone died? You look like you've seen a ghost."

Georgette's hands dropped to her desk as she shook her head in disbelief at what she'd read. Her face broke into a broad grin. "This," she said, holding up the letter, "is an invitation to go to London for a week, staying at the bloody Ritz of all places."

"Lucky girl!" he exclaimed. "Who from?"

"An anonymous donor," she answered wryly.

"Yeah, pig's arse!" George Hanks said. He was about to enlarge upon his comments when Georgette snapped him up.

"You'll see. Now, excuse me please, I have a phone call to make."

* * *

When Bill Murphy called for Georgette she greeted him at her door dressed in a long, flowing, green, soft-silk gown with full-length sleeves. The neckline, leaving half of each breast exposed, plunged to just above the waist, gathered in full around her hips and joined with a large brooch a little below her navel. The gown flowed evenly to drop half way down the heels of her diamanté stilettos. At the front, the split in the middle rose halfway up her thighs. Since arriving in London, Georgette's feet hadn't touched the ground. Now they rose just that little bit higher.

Bill Murphy was stunned. "Fucking hell, Georgette! I don't think I've ever seen anything more sensational in my life. You could've warned me! How am I supposed to sit opposite you all night with you looking like *that*?"

She giggled. "Sit next to me then."

"And let the rest of bloody London drool all over you? No way! My god! Where did you get it? It's absolutely sensational."

"It's a Versace. When I saw it, I had to have it. So I rang them and they sent me one."

Bill Murphy couldn't take his eyes off Georgette or the dress. "You sure you want to be seen out at the Ritz with a doddery, tired old recluse who can hardly put one step in front of another?"

"Never been more sure of anything in my whole life," she told him, closing the door to her room and handing him her key. "Doesn't have a pocket," she smiled.

Now it was Bill Murphy's turn to walk on air. As they walked through the Ritz to the dining-room, everyone's eyes shot to Georgette.

"You love all this, don't you?" he whispered to her.

"I'm having the time of my life. You?"

"Yeah. It's fun. It really is."

Throughout dinner, the waiters jockeyed for position over who would serve the couple. They, like everyone else, were totally captivated by the glamorous young woman in the flowing, soft, silk gown with the leaf design.

Bill Murphy ordered Dom Perignon then told the waiters to "Surprise us!" with a selection of entrées, main courses and desserts. It turned into a night neither would ever forget. The chefs obviously responded to the request and became very creative in their presentation of the food. Small, bite-sized servings of the very best to offer from the menu. Georgette was constantly asking staff, "What's this one... what's that one?" and so on. Bill Murphy took it all in his stride. He knew the pleasure he was extracting from the moment would never be duplicated if he lived to be a hundred.

Halfway through the second bottle of Dom, Georgette asked Bill, "So, tomorrow?"

"Meet my publisher, have lunch somewhere, then what about the Tower of London, *Mouse Trap* tomorrow night?"

"This is just awesome, Bill Murphy. Simply, simply awesome!"

He smiled, leaned over and clinked her glass. "Here's to a bloody good time, simply on account of why not?"

Leaving the restaurant, she said softly, "At least we don't have far to drive home."

Arriving at her door, he put the key in the lock and stepped back a little from her. "You made a tired old recluse very happy tonight..."

"I wish you wouldn't refer to yourself as that," she said.

He smiled at her. "Babe, you, without a doubt, were the sensation of London tonight. Looking at you suddenly made me realise just how much youth I no longer have."

"You are not an old man."

"I'm more than twice your age."

"What the hell's that got to do with it?"

"My god, Georgette, after this week with you I'll have to take a bloody week off to catch my breath and cool down. I'll ring you at seven and we'll go down for breakfast. God, you'll love that, too. They really go over the top here." He gently touched her cheek with his hand. "Sleep well." Then he was gone.

Bill Murphy didn't tell Felicity Nobleman-Spinks he was coming to London. Much less, he certainly didn't tell her he was bringing Georgette McKinley with him. Along with Georgette he walked into her office unannounced after convincing the receptionist who he was. Felicity was speaking on the phone when suddenly she stopped mid-sentence.

"I... I'll call you back," she stammered, hanging up. She bounced out from behind her desk and threw herself at him. "Oh, my god?" she squealed, "*Bill Murphy!*" throwing her arms around him. "Well *Hello* to you!"

Bill Murphy returned the affectionate greeting then introduced her to Georgette.

"Well hell, Bill!" she exclaimed. "No phone call? My god, I could've been away and I'd have missed you!"

"We'd have found you..."

"So how are you... oh god, this is so exciting..."

Georgette stood idly by as Felicity and Bill chatted. Then, "Can you have lunch with us?"

"Yes, yes, of course, god yes. Now?"

Bill checked his watch. "Why not!"

"So how long are you here?"

"Just the week," he told her.

"Just the *week*? Will we have time to sit down over a few things?"

"Not this time. When I go back home I'll finish the book, then I promise I won't send it to you, I'll *bring* it to you."

Three hours later and after promising to complete *The Corridors of Injustice* post-haste, Bill and Georgette said their good-byes to Felicity and made their way to the Tower of London. Georgette thrilled at seeing the Crown Jewels. She got into deep conversation with a Yeoman about the Ravens and the chopping block used by Henry VIII to dispose of Anne Boleyn.

Georgette returned to Bill. "God, this place is history. Can't you feel it?" she urged.

Their tour of the Tower took longer than expected, mainly because Georgette simply couldn't drag herself away. Again, Bill Murphy didn't mind. This was her week. He just wanted her to have fun.

As time was getting on, they decided to duck into a tiny side-street café and grab a quick bite. It seemed no time at all before they were sitting in a packed theatre and the curtain went up on *The Mouse Trap.* Georgette thrilled at being in the audience.

By the time Bill walked Georgette to her room, both were feeling the effects of jet lag and a hectic schedule. "You're buggered aren't you?" he said to her.

Reluctantly, Georgette nodded her head. "Out on my feet actually. Oh god, Bill, what can I say? Now I've seen *The Mouse Trap.* Thank you. A thousand times over, thank you. No wonder people wait years to see it."

"If I stand here any longer, I'll fall asleep on your shoulder. You ring me in the morning, OK? When you're ready. And believe me, there's no hurry."

"Oh, yes there is!" she said with what eagerness she had left. "It's Harrods tomorrow... *all day*!"

Both enjoyed the late breakfast at the Ritz, but Georgette didn't eat a lot. Bill could tell she was so excited about going to Harrods she couldn't even think straight. He also knew it was pointless trying to get a conversation out of her. Instead he drank his coffee and asked, "Somewhere you'd rather be?"

The young woman's face lit up like a night light. In moments they were on their way to one of the most famous stores in the world.

"So where do you want to start?" he asked, entering the store.

Georgette looked around. "What about right here?"

For a time Bill Murphy thought he was taking a child through Disneyland. He had never heard a grown woman go 'oooh' and 'aaah' so much in all his life. At the end of five hours in Harrods he felt as though he was a pack horse weighed down with so many green carrybags. At every available opportunity he'd have a seat and tell her to carry on while he rested.

Finally, "I'll bet you don't even have a bus fare left on that bloody credit card."

Georgette giggled. "Probably not, but my god, what a way to go?"

"Do you need all this stuff you've bought?"

Again she giggled. "What do you think?"

"Thought so. Have you had enough?"

"For today," she told him.

"Well, you can come back again tomorrow if you like, but, if you do, you'll miss out on Paris."

Georgette didn't hesitate. "Oh, god, no! We have to go to Paris."

Dinner that evening was at the wonderful and charming Park Lane Hotel. "Hungry?" he asked.

"Just for London. *London, glorious London.* But yes, I'm starved."

As they entered the main dining-room, soft lighting and furnishings of olde worlde charm created an atmosphere conducive to the music which flowed from a concert grand piano. Georgette looked around. There was hardly an empty table.

"Popular little spot isn't it?"

"Had to book," he told her as they were showed to their seats.

After ordering, Georgette looked across at Bill. "You're giving me the best time I've ever had in my life... but I don't know why. You don't even know me!"

"Are you having fun?"

"Well, of course..."

"Then seize the moment. Don't worry about tomorrow. If it's there now, grab it now. You see, right now, I'm just getting off on spending time with you. You can waste your life chasing tomorrow. I'm with you today. If I'm still with you tomorrow then, bloody hell Georgette, that's got to be a bonus, too! But I'm not demanding anything from you. I'm not asking anything of you. And one thing I'll never be—and believe this—I'll never be an encumbrance to you."

"Can I ask you a question? Let's say that somewhere, sometime, and totally out of left-field, someone comes into your life and wants a forever. What are you going to tell her?"

Bill Murphy thought for a moment. "I'd tell her she could probably have it... part time."

"So forever to you is three days a week?"

"Forever is now. There are too many unknowns. Sickness, accident, poverty, terminal illness, the eternal triangle, destitution. Forever can go wrong. You've seen it. I've seen it. If it gets to the point where someone comes along and she wants to stay with me and I want to stay with her, hell, that's got to be wonderful. If we get to the end of the day still liking each other, that's forever."

"That's simplistic."

"That's reality."

"That's your reality. What about commitment?"

"If you spend the day with each other, that's commitment."

"That's a cop-out. That special someone might want the Wednesday as well as the Tuesday."

"There's not a living soul on this earth right now who can in all honesty promise the next day to anyone. Look at what terrorism has done to the world. You might die tonight. You can *plan* to spend it together, but you can't promise you will for the reasons I've said."

"So why is your forever only part time?"

"Because of what I do."

"So at the end of the week I may never see you again?"

"I don't think you're a part-time girl," he surmised.

"You don't know that."

"All right, what's 'forever' to you?"

"Love, commitment, trust, you know, all the things that go wrong," she smiled. "I do understand what you're saying, though. But you have to remember, I haven't lived as long as you; I'm still formulating my opinions."

"And they'll change every seven years. You don't realise that till you get older."

"Would you like to meet someone?"

"It's not something I think about," he told her.

"Because of how you feel about things?"

"Pretty well. I mean what right-thinking woman is going to put up with an attitude like mine? Mainstream society has the overwhelming majority view in line with your thinking. I accept that but don't care. You have to work out your priorities, what you want in life."

"Before I spent this time with you I thought I was pretty clear about all that. Now I don't know."

"Why the confusion?"

"Because of how quickly things can change," she replied.

"Don't let me sway you. There's people out there who have been married for 60 years. Their forevers went OK. You have to make up your own mind about what's important to you. Things that were important to me 20 years ago don't mean shit now. But that's just me. Everybody's different. There's no right or wrong on priorities. It's something that's deeply personal."

"But I've never thought about them except for work hard, save your money, buy a house, save your money, save your money and so on."

Bill Murphy looked at Georgette and, for a fleeting moment, he saw a forlorn little child. "Have you ever known a mother's love?" he asked.

Georgette wasn't expecting such a question. Her tears began to well. She shook her head. "Or a father's."

"Whatever could have happened?"

"I lost my entire family in a house fire when I was a child. Then it was foster home after foster home. No-one had anything. So I became determined to make something of myself... no matter what the cost."

Bill Murphy knew exactly what she was referring to. "Are you prepared to go on paying that very high personal price to keep your name up there?"

Georgette knew from the tone of Bill's question that he *knew* the price she paid. She wondered if he felt ashamed of her. "I've just signed a brand new contract for a shit-load. Until two days ago I would have said yes. Now I don't know."

"What do you think about, when you're home, alone in your bed?"

Georgette knew the real answer would be too cold and calculating for Bill Murphy to handle. She went round the edges. "Just to have enough financial security so I don't have to worry about anything."

"My dear, there are always worries, no matter how much money you have. This new contract. Will that give it to you?"

"I don't think it will run its full term. The scoops may no longer be there."

"Yes, you did cream them with the budget didn't you?"

Georgette caught the look Bill Murphy gave her. She wondered if he knew. He couldn't possibly, she told herself.

Georgette didn't comment on the budget, so Bill Murphy decided on a different tack. "If there was a major political story about to break, would you get it first?"

"Not anymore." Georgette wanted to bite her tongue. By uttering those two words, she admitted that her political 'deep throat' had just dried up.

Bill Murphy could see she knew she'd made a blunder and decided to drop the subject. He'd gotten his confession.

Conversation between them fell away, and as a waiter topped up their glasses Georgette said, "I'v a feeling you don't like me very much at the moment?"

"Any regrets?" he asked.

Taking a deep breath she looked at him straight in the eye. "No," she told him firmly. "Not one."

"So when you go back to work, will anything change?"

Georgette sipped from her glass, slowly. She dipped her index finger into the champagne then ran it softly across the top of his hand. "You'll never know how my life has changed in only a few days," she told him.

Bill Murphy wasn't expecting the answer he got, much less the blatant signal this woman wanted more of him. He didn't respond. He wanted to, desperately. But he refused to allow himself to get swept away in a holiday romance that would end when the plane landed and cause him to pine over it for the next six months.

Georgette noted his cool response. She decided to back off. "When we were going up to Port Macquarie to try and grab an interview with you, I was reading through your bio and it said you also used to produce talk-shows on radio. How long for?"

Bill Murphy shrugged his shoulders. "Not a lot, but enough to spark a few questions. Bloody hard work! Sixty, eighty hours a week. I used to coin a phrase, 'Presenters get rich, producers get tired, presenters buy the joint, producers get fired.'"

"Is that how it is?"

"Can be. I did it for a lot of years."

"Tell me about talk-show hosts and what goes on behind the scenes?"

"You gonna visit me in jail?" he told her, in a manner that told Georgette the issue was closed.

Georgette smiled lightly. "Why do you despise women journos?"

He laughed. "Don't get me started on that too," he warned.

"I'm a big girl. I can handle it."

Again he laughed. "I'm not sure that you can. I have a very jaundiced opinion of women journos which many people would find offensive. There used to be a time when it was five years in the bush before you got looked at in the city. Now, it's wham, bam, thank you, ma'am... start Monday. Look at you! Straight into mainstream. How did you get your job?"

Georgette felt her face go crimson.

"Don't answer that," he told her. "As I say, it's a pet topic of mine. Don't get me started."

Georgette glanced around the dining room. Seeing only three tables left with patrons seated at them, she checked her watch. "My god, do you know what time it is?"

Bill Murphy shrugged. "Couldn't care less really. I just asked god to suspend this moment in time so I can sit here with you until forever."

"I don't think god's into part-time," she told him pertly.

Bill smiled. "So... Paris in the morning?"

* * *

The remaining days flew by and before they knew it they were boarding a Qantas jumbo to return to Sydney.

"I have to tell you one thing, Bill Murphy," Georgette said as she settled into her First Class seat. "You're certainly a man of your word. Single rooms. No sleep-walking. No holding hands. No strings eh? Totally no strings."

"Can't guarantee you the same deal next time... if we stretch that far," he replied.

"So when the plane lands, do I see you again?"

"I'll call you," he replied.

But his tone was such that it left enough doubt in Georgette's mind to ask herself, *But will you?*

Chapter 18

Senior Sergeant Ken McLoughlin and Senior Constable Dave Bourke believed their position, tucked away in bushland about a thousand metres from the isolated landing strip out from Kununurra, was safe from prying eyes. They crouched even lower into the undergrowth as the Cessna did a low-level sweep almost over the top of them.

"OK, let's see what happens when this mother lands," McLoughlin said, raising his binoculars.

Dave Bourke had moved to a crouching position near his boss, but still confident he couldn't be seen if there should be anyone about. "Not exactly peak hour in this part of the wo..."

Bourke never finished what he was saying. The Weasel, about a thousand metres off to his right had him square between the cross hairs of his telescopic sight when he squeezed the trigger of the Barrett .50 calibre. Bourke could never have known what hit him. The bullet struck the policeman in the chest and opened him up like an animal in a slaughter house. He folded like a pack of cards, his heart, lungs and other body parts strewn around him.

McLoughlin was splattered with his partner's blood and in the two or three seconds it took for him to realise what had happened, his body was momentarily frozen to the spot in shock. He was quickly brought back to his senses when another shot from the .50 calibre tore through a small tree he was resting his body against. He began screaming as he scrambled to get to Bourke's side. He was physically sick when he saw the damage to his partner's body. When he tried to cradle him, he felt as though he was picking up a small bag of crushed pebbles. His clothes became soaked with Dave Bourke's blood. Blind panic tore through his enraged mind.

Seeing quickly he could do nothing for his partner, he suddenly realised he was also in grave danger. He knew if he moved any great distance, he'd be an easy target. He also knew his attacker was The Weasel. He raised his binoculars.

Perspiration and tears clouded his eyes. He couldn't see anything. He was stunned to think his partner was taken out from such a huge distance. And because of the isolation of the area neither policeman was wearing a bullet-proof vest. He instinctively grabbed for it and put it on. Then he realised the damage caused to his partner's body could not have been caused by a conventional weapon.

No way, he said to himself. *The fucking Weasel's got something military. Has to be. Probably a .50 calibre. Could hardly be anything less. Not from that distance.*

McLoughlin was frantic. He knew if he climbed onto the four-wheel motor bike, he'd be an easy target. His vehicle was a long way away. The Cessna had already landed and was now taxiing back along the runway.

* * *

A thousand metres to McLoughlin's right and twelve hundred metres from the runway, The Weasel was still trying to find McLoughlin in his scope when time ran out. He knew he had to make his move and make it now.

As the Cessna approached Luigi, standing by the side of his vehicle, The Weasel put the Leupold scope right on him. As the aircraft turned away from Luigi, who was standing by the vehicle, causing those on board to momentarily lose sight of him, The Weasel fired. Luigi Mogliotti, his stomach blown to pieces, was dead before his body hit the ground. McLoughlin, however, off to his left, still bothered him.

He'd recognised him as one of the two men. He knew he'd already claimed one of them. Somehow he knew it wasn't McLoughlin. He desperately wanted to seek him out again with the scope, but the main game was about to begin. The small aircraft swung around by Luigi's vehicle and the pilot cut the motors. It was the last thing he'd ever do.

The Weasel fired again. This time the bullet smashed through the glass of the cockpit catching the pilot in the throat, almost decapitating him. The Weasel worked the bolt of the Barrett and fired again.

This time, the projectile tore into the sheila in the front passenger seat. She, too, died instantly. The Weasel could see mass panic in the rear seats of the aircraft. He loaded another magazine into the rifle and fired at random into the rear of the Cessna, not being able to draw a bead on any one person. With his own adrenalin now racing, he lifted his binoculars. He could see no sign of life. As he watched, a rear door was opened and a person dropped onto the ground. It was the guy he recognised as their ringleader, Franco. The Weasel watched for a moment but saw no movement.

He looked across to his left but could see no sign of McLoughlin. He grabbed his Barrett and raced back to his vehicle. He tore off the camouflage cover, dropped his weapon onto the front seat and roared off towards the aircraft. As he approached, a shot rang out, and The Weasel ducked as pellets from a shotgun blast ricocheted off his windscreen. He quickly spotted where the shot was fired from. It was the last desperate act of Franco as he lay torn to pieces from two .50 calibre bullets which partly found their mark. The Weasel spotted him and drove straight towards him, crushing his head under the wheel of his car. He pulled up, quickly checked there'd be no more surprises but was physically stopped in his tracks when he saw the horrific carnage he'd created. Enrico's body had been dismembered. To calm himself he began to scream. He tore open the luggage compartment door of the aircraft and dragged two large bags towards himself. He quickly unzipped one of them and his eyes nearly popped from their sockets.

"The bitch was right!" he yelled. "*The bitch was right!*"

He grabbed wildly at the other bag and pulled open the zip. As he did so, gold ingots spilled onto the floor of the aircraft and the ground. Quickly he snatched them up.

"Jesus Christ, this one's the same. Got to be twenty mill..."

The sound of an approaching vehicle a long way off brought him back to the immediate. He spun round. In the distance he could see a small four-wheel motor bike racing straight towards him. He bolted to his car, dragged out the Barrett and threw himself to the ground with it. He flicked open the tripod and put the small approaching vehicle in the cross hairs, which he figured was about 500 metres away. He worked the bolt, chambered a round and prepared to fire.

"It's that mongrel bloody copper! Farewell, arsehole!" he yelled as he squeezed the trigger. At that precise moment, McLoughlin's motor bike struck a small rise on the ground which catapulted his machine about a third of a metre into the air. The .50 calibre bullet struck the piston head of the bike's engine and smashed it to smithereens. When the bike came to a standstill, McLoughlin had been thrown off and the machine was lying on its side. Dust and smoke were billowing into the air. McLoughlin heard the heavy calibre fire again. This time the seat of the bike was annihilated. He crawled frantically on all-fours to take what cover he could from the gunman. Again the weapon fired. This time the projectile smashing into the bike's gearbox. McLoughlin knew much more of this and he wouldn't survive.

* * *

Back at the plane, The Weasel began to panic. He knew the longer he stayed the greater the chances were of his getting caught. He also knew that while the policeman was alive he would continue to hunt him down. He braced himself for one last shot at McLoughlin. He could make out part of his body hidden behind the remains of the bike. He was about to fire when a bullet ripped into the ground next to him.

* * *

McLoughlin had salvaged the triple two and tried for a shot. He got a lot closer to The Weasel than he expected to, being so far away. The Weasel screamed and cursed, lined up the policeman and fired again. The projectile tore through the front suspension, the petrol tank, headlight and lodged into McLoughlin's bullet proof vest. The impact, even with what it had already passed through, sent him back about 20 centimetres. He knew The Weasel had his range. He also knew if he fired two more shots, he probably wouldn't hear one of them.

* * *

Up at the plane, The Weasel decided to split. He loaded another magazine and fired four shots into the engine and dashboard of the greeter vehicle and quickly slashed its tyres. He then threw the Barrett into his vehicle, opened the boot and loaded the two bags containing the cash.

He was tempted to throw a match into the plane, but chose not to, knowing it would only bring undue attention to the area and limit his chances of escape. He grabbed the hand luggage of the passengers and pilot and did a quick body search. Despite picking up twenty million dollars, he squealed with glee at locating Gina's Remington and the pilot's Browning. He cocked the little .25 calibre and fired several shots into the aircraft's radio. He bolted from the plane, got into his vehicle and roared away.

* * *

McLoughlin, watching from behind the wrecked motor bike, raised his triple two but lowered it again.

Too bloody far, he told himself. *Just too bloody far.*

He turned his body round and slumped against a wheel of the bike. He had never been in a more hopeless position. He knew his only hope of getting any immediate assistance was to get back to his vehicle. He also needed to get to the plane. With much of his clothing soaked with blood, McLoughlin half walked and half ran to the Cessna. Again, the sight of what greeted him had him on all-fours, vomiting profusely. He had never seen such damage caused to human bodies.

What the fuck was this guy using? he cursed.

His question was soon answered. He leaned down and picked up one of the spent cartridges that had obviously been fired at him.

"Jesus Christ!" he uttered in shock and disbelief. ".50 calibre! The bastard's got a .50 calibre. That's Gulf War shit. The bloody snipers used to use them."

Suddenly McLoughlin felt incredibly vulnerable. Christ, he could be lining me up now from half a bloody mile and I'd never know. Quickly he moved to get himself in behind Luigi's four-wheel-drive. It was just as well he did. The instant he moved The Weasel fired again, and the bullet rammed into the fuselage of the aircraft at the precise spot where McLoughlin had been standing. He screamed from the terror of escaping death by a millisecond.

McLoughlin stayed crouched behind the vehicle for several minutes. He looked at the distance from where he was to the aircraft. He wanted to make a dash for the cabin and use the radio. When he felt it was safe to do so, he made a run for it. As soon as he opened the door he saw The Weasel had destroyed it, so he charged back to his safe position. His heart was pounding in his eardrums as he tried to decide what to do. He knew that if The Weasel was still out there he'd pick him off as soon as he showed himself. He also knew he was desperate for help.

He looked around himself. Nothing. Not even the gunfire had provoked curious onlookers. He didn't have his phone either.

Probably wouldn't work out here anyway.

He was desperate to get to his vehicle, but couldn't risk trying to make it across so much open ground. Underneath the Cessna was now a pool of blood. Flies had already begun attacking the bodies of Luigi and Franco. McLoughlin was able to get a quick glance at Luigi but decided he didn't recognise him. Trying to put a make on Franco was impossible because The Weasel had almost crushed his head into the tarmac. His rush to the plane didn't shed any light on the identities of the woman or the pilot. He knew the longer he sat there and did nothing, the better the chances were for The Weasel to escape. He decided The Weasel's desire for self-preservation would be stronger than waiting for him to show himself.

Cautiously McLoughlin began to make his move. He gritted his teeth as he pulled the bodies from the plane and placed them at the edge of the airstrip. He used whatever he could find in an attempt to cover them. He put the greeter's vehicle in neutral and pushed it as far as he could away from the aircraft. Using a drum of fuel in the vehicle, he poured the contents all over it. He stood back and threw a match.

Moments later, Luigi's vehicle was a ball of flames with black smoke pouring into the air.

Jesus, this better work or I'm going to have to try and get to my own bus.

He was beginning to lose hope that the smoke and flames had been noticed by anyone. Finally, he saw a vehicle approaching in the distance.

Chapter 19

It was now three weeks since Bill Murphy had returned home from London. For the first couple of days his routine had been disrupted as he tried to overcome jet lag and generally tidy things up around the place. Lonely was constantly under his feet, almost as though it was some kind of protest in being left to fend for himself for a week in a strange environment. For those initial days he was home, the urge to write had not returned and it began to bother him. He suffered mood swings and he started to blame himself for taking off on a whim. On the morning of the fourth day he was propped in his seat overlooking the ocean when the reality of the situation suddenly dawned on him. He had to admit to himself the problem could be found in two words: Georgette McKinley. He tried to laugh it off by telling himself he was too bloody stupid to see the wood for the trees and the last thing on the mind of a vivacious and beautiful young woman would be a staid old boring conservative who was bordering on the edges of burnout.

As Bill sat looking out over the ocean, a cool breeze running through his four day growth, Lonely appeared to sense that all wasn't well. Instead of chasing seagulls up and down the beach, he sat at his master's feet with his head resting between his master's knees. His eyes were focussed directly onto Bill's face. A gentle hand reached down and stroked his head.

"What's your bloody problem?" he asked.

Lonely's tail wagged in response to being spoken to.

"So what are we gonna do, boy? It's no good getting involved there. Besides, she might have a cat! You want to share your life with a cat?" He laughed. "I'd like to see that! Besides, she's probably forgotten all about me by now anyway."

Bill Murphy slowly made his way back to his house and again sat down at the keyboard. As he did the phone rang.

"Bill? Felicity... have I caught you at a bad time?"

"No, no... g'day luv... how's London? Any problems?"

"I have a few people climbing over me for the book," she replied.

"I'm trying to wrap it up, but I can't get into it right now."

Felicity laughed. "Maybe you better ring her."

"Who?"

"Now Bill! Obviously your mind's elsewhere at the moment. What can I tell them this end? A week... two weeks?"

"I'll walk in your door in four weeks time with it in my hand."

"You're a love. Ring me if there's a problem. But more importantly, I think, you better ring her."

"Goodbye, Felicity."

Bill heard her giggle then hang up.

He sat looking at the phone desperate to speak with Georgette, but he also knew he had chosen the lifestyle he had because he didn't want an involvement. He wanted to be on his own and not be answerable to anyone. He had pined for financial security. He now had it. The more he wanted to pick up the phone, the more he reminded himself of what he'd set out to accomplish.

He lit a cigarette and walked outside. He stood looking out to sea.

Finally, he made a decision.

* * *

Georgette McKinley should've been on top of the world, but her aggressive, win-at-all-costs spark was missing. George Hanks called her into his office.

"What the hell happened in London with you two?"

She looked at him. "Why would you ask me that?"

"Come on, babe, I'm not blind! Where's the Georgette of old? The zip! The zing! The aggressive fuck-you mentality! You in love or just having a bloody downer?"

Georgette was taken aback with such an aggressive line of questioning. "Bloody hell, George, you're a bit tough!"

"It's a tough business. If you're not well, tell me!"

"I'm fine, really! It's been pretty quiet, too. Not a lot happening out there."

"Never stopped you before," he told her matter-of-factly.

"So you want the big one every day?"

"You know what the old man's like."

"The big one's not always there."

"You tell him that."

"So you know about the contract?"

"And the goodwill."

Georgette was floored at her boss's last remark. She had learned early in her career that if she was asked to sign a big contract, always ask for goodwill. Goodwill is a demand stars put on owners as a mark of their goodwill. Georgette had done exactly that with Sylvester Monkhouse. Obviously loaded up with enthusiasm over how his young reporter had performed, he didn't hesitate. When she left the old man's office after signing her new contract she also walked out with a company cheque for fifty thousand dollars.

"Don't tell me he's hanging that over your head?"

"Not in as many words, but he was pretty pissed you weren't here for a week."

Georgette smiled. "He'll live through it," she asserted.

"So you're OK?"

"Never been better," she replied, leaving to return to her desk.

After a week back on the job, Georgette began to see her life in a entirely different perspective. There would be no more John Talbot. And she'd also made up her mind there'd be no more corporate 'games'. Something had happened to her during her week in London, but she didn't know what. The seething, burning, ambitious desire to 'get the story or else' attitude had dissipated. She wondered whether the new contract and the goodwill cheque had quenched her hunger to achieve. She tried to weigh up herself before and after London. Finally, she had to accept the big problem she had was two words: Bill Murphy. She found she had lost interest in chasing down stories, and the mid-week movie she seldom missed had also gone by the way. Instead, she found herself sitting by a telephone that didn't ring.

I don't know why you're stewing over this man, she said to herself. *He told you it was a no-strings-attached week with no mention of a follow-up phone call. Face it, girl, men like that aren't interested in women like me. Besides, he detests women journos. Boy! Does he ever!*

For the next three weeks, Georgette went through the motions of doing her job. She became vague and disinterested. George Hanks again questioned if she was all right and she assured him she was.

"I'm babysitting the bloddy dog again," he said.

"The dog?"

"Yeah, Bill's pissed off to London with his new book, so I've got his dog to look after for the week. Didn't you know?"

"Haven't spoken to him since we got home," she replied glumly.

"Be buggered! Hasn't he phoned you?"

Georgette didn't answer. Instead she shook her head.

George was going to continue the conversation until he saw her eyes fill with tears. He walked over to her desk and moved round behind her, shielding her from other staff. He placed his hand on her shoulder.

"I didn't know that. I'm really sorry. What a prick!"

But Georgette sprang to his defence. "He didn't say he would, you know. It was simply a week away. No strings."

"He's a prick! He could've called you. Wait till I talk to..."

Georgette cut him off. "No... no. You're not to do that. He knows where I am."

"He's back on Sunday morning. British Airways. First flight in, in case you're interested."

Sunday was five days away. She wished George hadn't told her, for she could think of nothing else. All the Saturday night into the Sunday morning, she stayed awake, pacing, sitting or trying to sleep.

She watched the new day begin to emerge on the Sunday and made her decision.

* * *

Senior Sergeant Ken McLoughlin sat with his head in his hands in the office of Victoria's Police Commissioner Jack Rowland. Also present were the Victorian Minister for Police David English, the New South

Wales Police Commissioner Colin Johnson and the New South Wales Minister for Police Andrew Weeks. All five men had returned to Jack Rowland's office after attending the police funeral of Senior Constable Dave Bourke.

McLoughlin had fully briefed Jack Rowland, David English and Colin Johnson on the events leading up to Dave Bourke's death, but Andrew Weeks was still to be informed. Jack Rowland spoke to McLoughlin.

"You want to take Andrew through what happened, Ken, or would you rather I did?"

McLoughlin raised his head and wiped tears from his bloodshot eyes. "No, I can do it," he began. "We'd been trailing the prick..."

McLoughlin stop-started his way through his explanation to the New South Wales Police Minister. As he fought back tears with every word, all four men could feel the anger and determination of the devastated police sergeant.

"So you want to stay with it?" Andrew Weeks asked.

"Oh Christ, don't pull me off it now. I don't even know where to start looking for the bastard, but if it takes me ten years, I'll find him. You fellas going to allow me to do that?"

Jack Rowland cast his gaze amongst the other men present. There were no protests. Rowland then opened a drawer in his desk. "Another phone. Same deal as before. It's programmed with all our numbers. You still got all the other stuff? Cards, ID?"

McLoughlin nodded. Jack Rowland then handed him the keys to a brand new, high-powered, unmarked Ford Falcon sedan. "Armourplate glass and bulletproof panels. The V8's been tweaked so he shouldn't out-run you if it gets to that. Long-range fuel tank. Jesus, Ken!, none of us know what to say to you. There are no words to express our deep and sincere regrets. You're adamant you want to do this thing alone? Christ, we'll give you a partner; just say the word."

McLoughlin shook his head. "No," he said getting out of his seat. "I just need a few days and I'll be back on track. But you blokes have to realise we're not just dealing with a professional thief here. This guy's gone military. All I ask is you do that photo drop again with my phone number.

"I'll call you each week as before, but it could get to the point where I've got him boxed in. If that happens, remember he's now into a .50 calibre. That means anything up to a couple of kilometres away that he can draw a bead. I won't be a hero. I think it's up to you fellas to speak one-on-one with the army and have a couple of SAS blokes on stand-by if need be."

Jack Rowland extended his hand. "Consider it done. I'll do the photos now. Good luck, Ken."

McLoughlin said his farewells to the other men present in the room and left. He went to the police car compound, sought out the new Ford V8, climbed in behind the wheel and drove away.

Sydney, I think. I still believe my best chances of finding the bastard are in Sydney. I can't see him coming back here.

As he drove away from the compound his mind was still in a haze. When he closed his eyes, he could still see his partner being torn to pieces by the heavy-calibre bullet. How he nearly died himself as he tried to squeeze in behind his damaged motor bike for protection. How The Weasel had all but destroyed their vehicle. And the millisecond between life and death when The Weasel took a long-range shot and the bullet thudded into the exact same spot where he'd been standing.

When he squeezed off, I would have had to have moved at that precise moment. Christ! And the cold-blooded way he killed everyone connected with the aircraft. What the hell were they carrying? I won't know the answer to that until I find him... or, more to the point, where he digs himself in. One thing's for sure, he's digging himself in somewhere.

He then recalled his telling Jack Rowland and the other men in his office he would take a few days off. He changed his mind.

No point in that. All I'd do is stew. Best to get on with it.

He drove out of Melbourne and headed towards Sydney.

* * *

Georgette McKinley arrived in South West Rocks a little after four a.m. She had driven up from Sydney on the spur-of-the-moment, not being able to stand the suspense of not knowing any longer. She had decided not to ring. She wanted to stand face to face with Bill Murphy and have him tell her he didn't wish to see her anymore. She quickly located the local newsagency and peered through the window. Bill Murphy had not told her where he lived, so she reverted to the oldest trick in the book. If you want to find out where someone lives, ask the local newsagent. They know everything there is to know about the local scene. She was in luck. He was sitting in his shop rolling the Sunday papers for delivery.

Georgette tapped on the window. A youngish man came to the door. Georgette smiled. "Hell of a time of the day, but I was wondering if you could tell me where Bill Murphy lives?"

The newsagent recognised her from the television. "If anybody else but you was doing the asking I'd say I didn't know. Same as everyone else around here. But you must have a good reason for driving all this way. Here! Take his paper out to him. You'll need to..."

Georgette wrote out the directions to Bill Murphy's place then found an all-night service station. She filled her car with petrol, then ordered a cup of coffee. Before leaving, she purchased a loaf of bread, a dozen eggs, a packet of bacon, a jar of coffee, milk, butter and plum jam. The sun was just beginning to rise when she checked her directions. Ahead, she could see a little house on a small cliff.

That's it, she thought. *Oh well, here goes.*

Slowly she drove in towards it. Lonely heard her coming and ambled out to greet her, his tail wagging furiously. As she brought her vehicle to a standstill, she sat behind the wheel for a moment. A sudden attack of nerves tore through her body. Then her heart began pounding in her brain. Her mouth went dry. Her stomach was in knots.

Bloody hell! she cursed silently. *I'm absolutely scared shitless. Leave! Turn around and leave. Go! Just go!*

But she couldn't follow what her mind was telling her to do. She saw the front door open. A rather groggy Bill Murphy appeared, dressed only in a pair of jeans. Still rubbing the sleep from his eyes, he was straining to see who it was.

"Oh, good god! Georgette!" he exclaimed.

"Hello, Bill. I brought you your paper," she said meekly, expecting him to explode and tell her to leave.

"What the hell are you doing here?" he asked, still trying to wake up.

"You hadn't phoned."

"You haven't phoned me either."

"It's not a girl's place."

Bill Murphy laughed. Georgette didn't know how to gauge his reaction upon seeing her. She felt her knees go to jelly, as if they didn't belong to her. For a few moments, they stood looking at each other. Bill Murphy then walked over to her and held out his hand. As she took it, he dragged her in to himself and kissed her lightly. He felt himself come alive as Georgette thrust her open mouth over his. Holding her head against his chest, he buried his head into the nape of her neck.

"Jesus, I've missed you... you will never know how much."

Tears formed in Georgette's eyes. "When you hadn't phoned, I just had to find you. I needed to stand in front of you and for you to tell me you didn't want to see me anymore."

Holding her at arm's length, he said, "Babe, I was gone the moment I set eyes on you. But come on! I'd be in fairyland if I thought someone like you would be interested in someone like me," he told her, lifting his eyes to watch a vehicle pass by at the end of his driveway. Georgette glanced over her shoulder.

"Visitors?"

"Don't know who that is. Often see him go down there. Don't know where he goes, the road doesn't lead anywhere."

Returning her glance to him, she said, "Would you like some breakfast? I've brought a few things."

Bill Murphy held out an arm. "Just walk on through, you can hardly miss the kitchen. You go and do that and I'll clean myself up a bit."

Bill Murphy stepped into the shower. A minute later, much to his surprise, Georgette was standing outside the shower curtain. Instantly, Bill Murphy grabbed Georgette, hauling her fully clothed under the shower with him. She squealed and cursed and fought to be released. But he just stood there, his arms locked around her, laughing hysterically.

She looked up at him and their mouths found each other. Moments later, they stood naked together. As each explored the other, Georgette threw her arms around his neck, wrapped her legs around his hips and lowered herself onto him. She cried out as he went deeply into her.

"Oh god, yes!" she cried as she tried for even deeper penetration.

Suddenly, neither could get enough of each other. Both felt their bodies explode as they finally exploited the lust that had built up between them. Totally spent, Georgette lowered her legs to stand. Together they stood under the hot steaming water, oblivious to the sounds of the waves crashing onto the beach far below.

Stepping from the shower, each dried the other, and Bill laughed. "I'm not too big on nickers and bras, but I can probably find you a shirt and jeans."

"Why, that would be very nice of you, Mr Murphy," she replied courteously, "seeing it was you who got me into this state."

They didn't bother leaving the house that day.

Chapter 20

Ken McLoughlin decided to base himself in a Parramatta motel in Sydney's western suburbs. Night and day, at various times around the clock, he toured the streets of the city and the suburbs. Since the events at Kununurra, The Weasel had made no attempt to return to his flat in Ryde. Night after night, week after week, McLoughlin continued his relentless pursuit of a man without having the slightest clue as to his whereabouts.

I know he's around the place somewhere. I can feel the bastard. Maybe it's up in the bush a bit, but he's definitely in New South Wales.

Everyday McLoughlin went through the ritual of checking his Glock, his triple two, and the two back-ups on his ankles. He knew when the moment came he'd be damn glad he did. For three months he continued to search. He made his weekly phone call to Jack Rowland. The Victorian Police Commissioner again told him to take as long as he needed, as he now saw The Weasel as public enemy number one.

Casually glancing through a fishing magazine one night, McLoughlin spotted an ad for a sailing regatta at Nambucca Heads, between Port Macquarie and Coffs Harbour. It was only three days away, so he checked the state forecast for the further outlook.

Weather's fine. Might head up there. Could do with a day or two off.

* * *

Bill Murphy rang Georgette every day for the next three weeks with some of their conversations lasting two hours. Over the duration of the calls, each got to learn even the most intimate of details about the other. At one point he was so desperate to see her he hired a helicopter and pilot to fly him to and from Sydney just so they could spend the night together.

As the relationship became more intense, Bill Murphy began to take stock of the situation and to what he was getting himself into. For the first time in three weeks he didn't call Georgette. Sitting by her phone in Sydney, Georgette kept looking at the clock. She waited another hour. Then another. When he hadn't phoned by midnight she picked up the phone and dialled his number. There was no answer. Bill Murphy was sitting at his desk, watching the ringing phone. He knew it would be her, but he didn't know how to tell her he was having second thoughts. He was relieved when the ringing stopped. A few minutes later it rang again. This time he did pick it up.

"Hi, babe."

"God, are you all right? When you hadn't phoned..."

"I'm all right," he cut in.

"Is there something wrong?"

"I'm not sure."

"What do you mean?"

"It's... it's this whole thing, babe. Jesus, it's freaking me out."

"Why, whatever's wrong?"

"There's nothing wrong. I just can't see it lasting, and it frightens the shit out of me."

"So you think I'll walk away?"

He thought about his answer. "I'm thinking I will. I'm not what you want. You're young, vibrant, full of life..."

"So are you."

He laughed. "I used to be."

"So what are you now?"

"Fucked!"

"You're full of it!"

"Georgie... Georgie... wonderful Georgie, I don't think I can do this anymore. You're not what I am. I'm not what you are. All my life I've strived to get to this little hilltop. I just think this mountain's too high for you to climb up... too steep for me to climb down."

"I can't walk away from you, Bill," she said sadly.

"Babe, you're going to have to. It can't always be like this. I have things to do. You have things to do. You can't be stuck up here, cut off from everything; you'd end up hating me. I couldn't live with myself if that happened."

"So what about part-time?"

"No way! You're too special for that. All I can say is that I'm obviously so gone on you I'm prepared to let you go. It tears my guts out having to tell you this, but I'm not a good proposition, Georgette. You wouldn't enjoy being around me all the time."

"So why did you even want to start it off?"

"Hell, I don't know. Young bird. Old man. Might be fun. But it got to be more than that and quite frankly I'm not prepared to stuff your life up. Hook up with me and more than likely I will." Bill could tell Georgette was in tears. "You're young. You're still trying your wings. You'll thank me for this one day. Maybe not now. But one day you will."

Georgette put the phone down and burst loudly into tears.

Bill Murphy did the same. "Sometimes I feel like I just want to cut my tongue out," he said to Lonely.

The next four weeks dragged for Bill Murphy. He lived and breathed every moment for Georgette McKinley. He couldn't sleep. Didn't shave. Only ate scrappy meals. He spent his days sitting in his stone chair overlooking the sea with Lonely at his feet. He tried to justify in his mind the words he spoke to Georgette. He always came back to his original motivation.

This is where I strived to be all my life.

But there was now a hollowed-out emptiness about the place. Georgette had only been there the once but she'd added a vibrancy to the place.

Now you're gone, Bill thought, *it's like someone's hung up a sign reading: Vacancy.*

He also knew he had to shake her off. He wouldn't be able to function until he did.

* * *

Georgette McKinley got a doctor's certificate for a week off. She was so devastated by the breakup, she found her body shut down. She cried all day and into the night and achieved sleep only from total exhaustion. George Hanks knocked on her door. When she let him in, he was visibly shocked by her condition. Gone were the sparkling eyes. They were replaced by swollen up, bloodshot slits. Her hair was unkempt. She wore very little.

"Jesus, are you sick?" he asked.

She didn't answer, instead, turned her back on him and went into her kitchen. "Coffee?"

"Yeah, white and one," he answered, as he followed her. "What is it, babe. Jesus Christ, look at you! What's the problem?"

She turned to face her boss, but instead of words all he got was tears. Buckets of them.

"Has... has someone died?"

She shook her head.

Then it hit him. "Not Bill Murphy?"

At the mere mention of his name, even more tears flowed.

"For god's sakes, babe!" he said softly, wrapping his arms around her. Georgette sobbed hard against his chest. "Obviously, it's all over. Sweetheart, you hardly know the guy. You pregnant and he's dumped you or something? Jesus, I don't believe you could be this upset."

She shook her head. "No, I'm not pregnant. We're... we're just so right for each other, and he's too damn stubborn to see it."

"No, no, no. Listen to me. Bill and I have known each other for probably 30 years. All his life he's dreamed about living on a cliff overlooking the sea. That's been his life's dream. He's a bloody recluse for god's sakes. You don't want to live like that do you?"

"I don't know what I want," she sobbed, "But I do know he's the one I want to wake up next to in the morning."

George Hanks was stunned. "You can't go on like this. What about your job?"

"I'll be all right by Monday. Jesus, George!, can't you see I'm bloody grieving over this. My heart's been broken for Christ sakes."

George Hanks didn't speak. He held the young woman in his arms and stroked her shoulder. "Anything you need?"

Georgette shook her head.

"Go and see him, babe! You gotta take one last shot. Go and see the mongrel. If you want him that bad, fight for him. What do you say? Give it one last roll of the dice?"

Georgette nodded.

"I have to go. You phone me if you need anything, all right? *Anything*"

"I will," she promised.

After George Hanks closed the door behind himself, Georgette began to think about what he told her. She went to her wardrobe and took out *that* dress. She washed her face and hands, took a deep breath, flicked through the pages of the phone book and picked up the phone.

Several calls later she rang her boss.

* * *

Three days later, Bill Murphy was waiting out the front of his house for the helicopter to arrive. George Hanks had called him and asked if could compère a specially convened Heads of Media dinner in Port Macquarie.

"Sorry for the short notice," he'd said, "but the old man was put on the spot by some incoming overseas interests. And they wanted to go up-country a bit, not stay in the city. We'll send a chopper for you. The dinner starts at seven."

The helicopter landed on time and, moments later, it was on its way to Port Macquarie. Upon arrival, a stretch limo was on hand to meet him. "Where is this thing?" he asked the driver.

"The Whalebone Wharf Restaurant I believe, sir."

Bill Murphy smiled. As the limo pulled up outside the restaurant, Bill Murphy looked around. "Are we early? There's no-one here!"

As Bill Murphy climbed from the vehicle, he was greeted by an enthusiastic young waiter. When he walked into the restaurant he noticed the entire dining area had been cleared, with only an elaborately laid out handful of tables in close proximity to one highly decorated with candelabras, a white silk tablecloth and silver service cutlery. There were two chairs. The ceiling was covered in balloons and streamers. The lights were soft and low.

Off to the left was a twelve-foot concert grand piano. A man aged in his mid-thirties was seated at the keyboard. Upon seeing Bill Murphy he began playing *The Prayer.*

Suddenly, he began to think all wasn't coming together as he'd expected. Out of the corner of his eye, he could see the waiter was all about like an excited schoolboy. There'd be a fleeting glimpse of a waitress dashing by. There was no-one to greet him. So he casually made his way across to the highly decorated table.

As the pianist came to the end of *The Prayer,* he followed up with *The Look of Love.* The waiter then casually approached Bill Murphy. "Sir, if you'll just turn around."

Bill Murphy gave the waiter a strange look as he glanced over his shoulder. Standing before him was Georgette McKinley, in *that* dress. Bill Murphy was struck dumb and his eyes filled with tears. "I'm flabbergasted," he managed to say. "Totally and utterly. My god! I don't know what to say."

"You could try 'hello'," she told him.

"I don't think I'm very good at this... um," he mumbled, but the words were getting stuck in his throat.

"I'm trying to climb that mountain," she said, with tears only a moment away.

"God, I miss you. Babe, this is dream stuff! But we can't survive on dreams. There's every day. We have to live every day."

Slowly, tears began to roll from her eyes. "Every hour, every minute, every breath I take, you're in it," she whimpered.

He went to her and held her in his arms. "Georgie, Georgie, Georgie, I don't think we can do this thing. It's not you. It's me."

"Have we got tonight?" she sobbed.

"We've got tonight," he told her. "And look at you! I have never seen a dress I adore more than that and I have never looked at anyone I adore *more* than you," he told her, pulling her in close.

Bill and Georgette stood in each other's arms for the duration of the song... and the next one as well. It was only as the last bars of *The Love Theme* from Romeo and Juliet flowed from the concert grand piano did they take up their seats at the table. Georgette had ordered Dom Perignon and a four-course menu she created herself: freshly shucked oysters in the half shell on ice with lemon and onion in red wine vinegar; roasted duck breast with a salad of pumpkin and watercress, with a parsnip marmalade and macadamia-nut lavish; oven-roasted snapper fillet wrapped in prosciutto with green-olive tapenade and red-capsicum coulis; cherry-ripe icecream gateau with poached strawberries and almond clafoutis with candied apple and sultana with an amaretto anglaise. Bill chose the wine, a 1994 Peter Lehmann Shiraz, winner of six gold medals in the 1996 National Wine Show.

Throughout their time together, there wasn't a lot of conversation. Georgette revelled in the moments of simply being with Bill Murphy. And she enjoyed all the fuss and bother the staff went to. Bill Murphy was totally overawed by the occasion. Songs about love came from the piano and when they sometimes danced together, all the staff stopped what they were doing to watch them. Georgette knew, after spending another five hours with Bill Murphy, there was quite simply nowhere else on earth she wanted to be. Bill Murphy fought with his conscience all evening. He was being pulled every which-way. He knew what his life-long plan had been. He had now achieved it. He also knew that contemplating life without Georgette was more painful than he could bear thinking about.

It was past midnight before they walked from the restaurant to the hotel room Georgette had booked. As they came together as one, the early morning sun was soon waking up their day. The helicopter was still on standby. Firstly to return Bill to his home, then to fly Georgette back to Sydney.

"Come up to the house for the day," he said.

Georgette's eyes lit up. "Oh, I'd love that."

Two hours later, Bill was sitting in his stone chair. Lonely was at his feet and Georgette was sitting on the ground with Bill's jacket across her shoulders, leaning back between his legs. As the waves rolled in on a day of clear skies and bright sunshine, both soaked up the moments of being together. After a while, Georgette moved a little to Bill's side and sat gazing out over the ocean. He noticed a different expression on her face. He thought it peaceful, but distant.

"Where are you?" he asked.

She looked at him, hesitated, then spoke. "About three dreams away," she told him.

"Meaning?"

She paused for a moment and said, "Oh... You. You and Me, and Forever."

Bill Murphy didn't comment. Instead, he rose to his feet and quietly walked down the cliff and onto the beach. Georgette watched him until he became a tiny speck in the distance. As she sat there she began to write some lines, but screwed up the paper, discarded it and returned to the helicopter. It was over an hour later before Bill Murphy returned to where he'd been sitting. First glance told him Georgette had gone. He turned his face to the wind as his eyes filled up. When he sat down in his chair, he saw a screwed up piece of paper lying near his discarded jacket.

Casually he leaned over, picked up the piece of paper and unravelled it. He recognised the writing as Georgette's.

The day that we met, it was only by chance

I felt you were just a lost soul.

But when I looked up and noticed your glance

My forever began to unfold.

But today you say you won't go there again

And a hill can be too high to climb.

But if one dream's too far, then I know that your heart is three dreams away.

I know you said you can't do this anymore

And a hill can be too high to climb.

But your touch is a journey I've not been before and your feelings are where I belong.

Today you say you won't go there again,

And a hill can be too high to climb.

But if one dream's too far, then I know that your heart is three dreams away.

Bill Murphy's heart sank. He folded up the piece of paper and put it in his pocket. Then he leaned into his seat threw his head back and opened up his arms.

"So what the hell am I supposed to do?" he called out. "What the *hell* am I supposed to do?"

The faster he searched his mind for a logical conclusion, the more confused he got. "It can't be," he said out loud. "God knows, it just can't be."

For the next three weeks Bill Murphy suffered the most agonising period of his life. He'd experienced anxieties before a broken marriage, disappointments in jobs, frustrations in waiting on replies from publishers, but this was something totally different. He knew he had to pull himself together. He knew this wasn't what he'd spent his life dreaming about. He knew he had to make a decision. Again. Only this time a *final* decision.

Chapter 21

Ken McLoughlin called the two police ministers and the two Police Commissioners to inform them he'd be taking a couple of days off to drive to Nambucca Heads. He was tempted to unstrap his shoulder holster and his ankle backups. He'd even slipped his shoulder from one of the straps when he changed his mind.

Never bloody know, do you! he thought to himself as he put it back on.

He was driving up the freeway towards Gosford when his thoughts went to Kazumi. He took his phone from his pocket and dialled.

Katie Caplin answered the phone. "Ken, hello. How nice to hear from you." She hesitated before saying, "Are you well? We heard about your partner in the news."

McLoughlin took a deep breath. "We were on a job together..."

"Oh my god... it could have been you then?"

"Katie, I can't talk to you about it now. I will one day when this whole thing's over, OK?"

"So you're still on it?"

"Yes, I'll see it through..."

"But you're not calling to speak to me are you?"

"Now, Katie... !"

"Hold on, I'll get her."

Katie put the phone down and walked outside. She called to Kazumi, who hurried inside the house.

"Hello! Mr Sergeant Ken. Yes?"

McLoughlin giggled. "Kazumi?"

"Oh, Mr Ken... hello."

"I'm driving up the freeway thinking about you. How are you?"

"I good, Mr Ken. You all right good, too?"

McLoughlin chuckled as Kazumi wrestled with the language. "Yes, I'm all right good, too. I thought when I get through with what I'm involved in, I'd call by and pick you up. Maybe go to the beach for a few days... yes?"

"Oh, Mr Ken... a few *days*?"

"Don't you think Katie will give you the time off?"

"Wait. I check." McLoughlin heard her ask Katie in the background if it would be all right to take some leave. She obviously had agreed because Kazumi spoke back into the handset, "Miss Katie. She say all right. But just a couple of days."

"So what do you think? The beach. The city. The country?"

"I think the beach, yes?"

McLoughlin said goodbye and pressed the off-button, thinking about the places he'd like to take her. Suddenly, as if jammed in the rear with a cattle prod, he shot bolt upright in his seat and craned his neck as he drove past a service station.

"*Shit*! it's him. It's fucking him! It's the fucking Weasel! You mother-fuckin' son-of-a-bitch."

McLoughlin quickly checked his mirrors, then brought his car to a standstill in the service lane. He grabbed his binoculars and looked back through the rear window. The first thing he noticed was The Weasel's unusual gait. He was leaving the service station carrying two large paper bags. Then for a brief moment he got a clear view of his face.

Running a bit short on things are you, mongrel?

McLoughlin lowered the binoculars to the number plate of the vehicle he was driving. It was different from before. BJL-998. He wrote it down. But he needed more time. He wanted to take him there and then.

That won't achieve anything. I have to find his hiding-place.

Still watching through the glasses he saw The Weasel move his car to a parking bay, lock it up and walk into the toilets.

He grabbed his phone and pushed the button which would hook him straight up with the New South Wales Police Commissioner.

"Sir, McLoughlin. I'm on him, right now. He's taking a piss. I spotted him at a service station as I was driving past here at Coopernook, about twenty or thirty K's the other side of Taree. Sir, there's a lot of traffic. I need to follow him, but I can't get too close. If he spots me, we're dead in the water."

"What do you need?"

"Where's the chopper?"

"Christ, up your way, I think."

"I need that chopper, sir. Now. I have to get a high-altitude surveillance on this prick. But they'll have to stay well up."

The Commissioner gave him the contact details so McLoughlin could talk direct to the chopper. "Tell them what you want, Ken. If they've got a problem, tell 'em to call me."

McLoughlin had just put his plan in train when The Weasel sped past him. Watching him approach, he slunk down into his seat to avoid any chance of recognition. Quickly he followed, but from a long way back. When he checked his speedo, he saw he was travelling at one hundred and thirty K's. Way over the limit. He reached for his phone again and called Commissioner Johnson. He quickly explained the situation and asked if there were highway patrols in the area to back off and not pull The Weasel over.

"I'm on it, son," the Commissioner told him.

Twenty minutes later, McLoughlin's phone rang.

"Airwing, Sergeant. Right over the top of you I'd reckon."

"OK. Can you go right up? We can't afford for you to get seen on this. Go as high as you can and tell me if you see him."

"Wait on the line." Moments later. "We're at 3200 feet. BJL-998. Is that him?"

"Can you stay on him?"

"We can give you 93 minutes."

"That might just do it. I don't have a bloody clue where he's going, so for Christ sakes don't lose him. I'll hang back a bit. Ring me every couple of minutes, OK?"

The Weasel made good time heading north. Approaching Kempsey, he turned to the right and took the Gladstone road.

"You on him?" McLoughlin called.

"We are."

"How much longer can I have you?"

"Twenty-one minutes... hang on, Sarge, he's slowing down. Back off, Sarge. Jesus Christ. *Back off, Sarge*! Can you pull up?"

McLoughlin slammed on the brakes.

"He's now on a side road leading into the Hat Head National Park. Don't know where he's going because the road doesn't lead anywhere."

McLoughlin was ecstatic. *I think I've got the bastard! I think I've found the fucker's hideout. Woooow!*

"Thanks, guys. That road leads off to the right about half-a-K ahead?"

"Yes, it does. We can stay with you for only another 90 seconds."

"Get me onto that side road."

"Coming up on your right."

"This one now?"

"That's it. Sarge, we gotta go or we're out of gas."

"I love you blokes. Thank you very much."

McLoughlin slowed right down, straining to see any sign of The Weasel's car. As he drove along the dirt road, he noticed a little house sitting on a cliff off to his right with a long driveway leading in to it. A fellow sitting out the front with his dog, waved as he went past. The further he went the more it bothered him that he hadn't spotted The Weasel's car. McLoughlin pulled up. He checked his back-up weapons in his ankle holsters. He double-checked his Glock. He got out of the car and took the triple two from the boot while putting on his bullet-proof vest. He got back in behind the wheel and slowly proceeded along the dirt road. There was still no sign of The Weasel.

Then the fear of god hit him. If I corner this prick and he lines me up with that .50 calibre again, I'll need more than a goddammed vest for protection. He contemplated backing off right then and calling in the SAS. He decided against it. He drove on. As he did so he found himself running out of road. Suddenly, only scrubland was in front of him.

So where the hell did he go?

He backed his vehicle up about fifty metres and got out. The road surface was too hard to pick up any recent tracks. He didn't recall seeing any run-offs as he drove along.

So where the hell is he?

McLoughlin felt the hair stand up on the back of his neck. Instinctively, he moved around the side of the vehicle which he thought would give him the best cover. He leaned in against it, straining his ears for the slightest sound. There was nothing. Slowly he moved forward. He wondered about taking the triple two. He decided against it as he moved away from his car and into the bushland. He suddenly remembered his phone and reached into his pocket and switched it off.

He moved forward, taking one step at a time, being careful where he put his weight. Selecting as much cover as he could, he adopted a semi-crouched position, moving deeper and deeper into the bushland. Constantly checking behind him and on both sides McLoughlin began to perspire profusely. He knew The Weasel was nearby. But was *he* watching *him*?

You son-of-a-bitch, by Christ, I'm close, aren't I? But where's the bloody car?

He was now about 400 metres into thick scrub and bushland. He paused to take a breath and check his surrounds. He took his Glock from its holster and chambered a round. Then added the extra one to the clip. He was about to move off when something alerted him. He didn't know what it was. A breaking twig? A kangaroo darting through the bush? He crouched down, hoping he may hear it again. Seconds later he did. But he still couldn't make out what it was. He felt his heart now begin to pound in his chest.

Is that you, you son-of-a-bitch?

He scanned the area in front of him. He waited. Listening. Watching. Wiping his brow. His nerves were at screaming point. He took deep breaths to try and relax. He knew something was about to break and when it did he needed to be sharp. Focussed.

What McLoughlin heard next frightened the living daylights out of him. He jerked back so suddenly, he cracked his head on a small, overhanging branch. He cursed loudly, but silently.

"*Draw!*" came a scream, not more than 30 metres away from him.

McLoughlin hit the dirt, thinking the command was directed at him. Instantly he heard six shots fired in quick succession.

But they weren't being fired at him. They were going in the opposite direction. Lying prone with his Glock pointing in front of him, he was frantic and totally confused. He scrambled back behind a tree to collect himself, and moments later he heard the command again, "*Draw!*" followed by six shots fired in quick succession.

Jesus, this is bizarre! McLoughlin thought, his heart pounding.

He continued to sink down by the tree. Moments later the same thing again. "*Draw!*" followed by another six shots fired in quick succession.

McLoughlin moved forward on all fours. He was now only metres from The Weasel but heavily screened by thick bush. McLoughlin had him in full view. He wanted to laugh at what he was witnessing. The Weasel was acting out the role of a wild-west hero.

Fucking idiot thinks he's Wyatt Earp, for Christ sakes! What a sick bastard.

"*Draw!*" he yelled, then six shots again rang out.

The Weasel was in full flight. A huge western hat, spurs on his boots and a six-gun holstered to his leg. He'd erected several man-sized targets about 20 paces in front of himself and was acting out a gun fight. Over and over he went through the ritual. Dropping to the ground, the fast draw. Talking to the targets as though they were real people. But every time he fired off six rounds he grouped them all in the chest area.

Jesus, the bastard's good! McLoughlin conceded.

The Weasel was using a Colt .45. McLoughlin had shot one many times and he knew that to group six shots at 20 paces into an area about three times the size of a cigarette packet was no mean feat. The best he'd done was into an area about twice that size. But The Weasel was doing it from the draw and fire position. McLoughlin knew he'd found his quarry's sanctuary. He knew if he waited long enough, he'd be led to his hideout. He strained his neck to see as far as he could without being seen.

Where the hell is his car?

"*Draw!*" came the scream and again six shots followed.

Then all hell broke loose. The Weasel had just reloaded and was about to draw and fire again when McLoughlin moved. He didn't think he'd made a sound. But he had.

The Weasel spun round and fired in the direction of the noise.

McLoughlin dropped down flat, but it was too late.

Chapter 22

When Georgette McKinley boarded the helicopter at Bill Murphy's house she firmly believed that would be the last she'd ever hear of him. She consoled herself in knowing she had given the two of them her best shot. As the weeks dragged by she began to come to terms with a love lost. She was again beginning to take an interest in her work. Not like before, but the old spark was slowly reigniting. One day, however, her entire world was turned on its ear. The station's security guard approached her at her desk and asked her to follow him.

Georgette, puzzled, followed the guard as he left the newsroom and headed for the front desk. When she arrived at reception, there was already a score of people present.

"Have a look at what's just come for you!" the guard said.

"These are for me?"

In front of her was a giant heart-shaped flower arrangement with hundreds of red roses. Amid questions and cat calls from over-awed staff, she reached for the card that was attached. Very timidly she opened it. Immediately she felt herself fill up.

But your smile in my eyes
is burned to my soul,
We were more than just shadows on the wall.
If you were a dream,
I don't dare dream it.
The lingering, the longing,
the moment to moment.
This river's run dry
there's no end to my day.

But is it too late?
Am I too late?
Are we too late?
Ask me again about three dreams away.

She reached for a phone and dialled. "What's a girl supposed to say?"

"You could start with 'hello'," Bill Murphy replied.

"What about the mountain?"

"We'll walk round it."

"Don't do this thing, Bill, if the distance is too far."

"I'll hold onto your hand. I'll never let you go."

"Three days a week or seven?"

"Eight."

"Why now? You didn't want this."

"It's what I've wanted all along, I just didn't know."

"You and me and forever?"

"One's no good without the other."

"How long have I got to think about it?"

"The offer ends at the termination of this phone call."

"I'll be there tomorrow," she told him tearfully. "Whatever forever is, I don't see any point to my life unless you're in it."

"Don't be late," he told her.

Chapter 23

Ken McLoughlin cursed loudly as he felt a .45 slug clip the skin of his right arm. A couple of centimetres further over and his arm would have been completely shattered.

"John James McGregor-McWeasely. Police. Drop your gun and put your hands in the air!" McLoughlin screamed, trying desperately to draw a bead on The Weasel with his Glock.

"Fuck you, arsehole! Come and take me if you think you can!" he screamed back. He followed his verbal barrage with a volley of shots from the colt. Two slammed into the tree McLoughlin was using as cover and a third thudded into the shoulder section of his bullet proof vest. It spun the policeman sideways, but in doing so, gave him a clearer view of The Weasel. McLoughlin was about to fire, when another shot from The Weasel kicked up the dirt in front of him.

McLoughlin knew he didn't have much time. The Weasel was toying with him and he knew it, such was his agility and his total expertise with a firearm.

Although it was only a minor flesh wound to McLoughlin's arm, it bled profusely and he felt a searing pain from his shoulder down. He tried to put it out of his mind as he fought to get The Weasel in his sight. He let go a volley of shots in quick succession, but The Weasel bolted the instant he fired. McLoughlin showed himself for a split second. It was all The Weasel needed. He turned and fanned the trigger. But the chamber was empty. He screamed and cursed loudly.

McLoughlin fired and he saw The Weasel go down. He waited several moments, not knowing if his quarry was foxing. Slowly he crawled over to where he expected The Weasel to be. But he was gone. As he moved a hand, he felt it sink into a wet patch. It was blood. And quite a pool of it. He strained his ears for the slightest sound. Then it came. Off to his right.

Oh, Jesus! Don't tell me he's gonna head for that house back there.

McLoughlin sprang to his feet and charged off through the bushland. His wound concerned him, but the safety of that man he saw and any other people in the house further down concerned him more.

He'd run a short distance then stop, trying to hear the slightest of sounds. It was difficult because the noise of his breathing and his heartbeat were already crashing through his eardrums. When he was convinced The Weasel was still in front of him, he raced forward again. Fear tore through him when he thought of the consequences should The Weasel lay in wait for him. He gambled that he wouldn't. He figured he was now running for his life and would use any means at his disposal to achieve his purpose.

McLoughlin knew only too well the brutality of the man. As he continued his charge forward he looked up ahead and the house he passed on the way down had come into view. But he couldn't see the gunman.

* * *

Georgette McKinley, over the moon with the latest happenings, was wasting no time in getting to Bill Murphy's place. She swung her car off the dirt road into his driveway leading up to the house.

As she approached, she tooted the horn a couple of times and brought her car to a halt. The moment she stepped from her vehicle The Weasel pounced. He shoved her to the ground and jumped in behind the wheel of her car. McLoughlin, seeing what happened, raced from the scrub and screamed for him to stop. The Weasel, seeing the charge towards him, tried to start the engine, but the keys weren't in the ignition.

Georgette still had them in her hand. With McLoughlin rapidly descending upon him he was too panicked to fire. Instead, he bounced out of the vehicle, dragged Georgette to her feet by thrusting his arm around her throat, and put his gun to her head. McLoughlin could see blood seeping from a wound to The Weasel's side.

"Back off, arsehole, or the bitch gets it!"

Bill Murphy, hearing the commotion, peered through a front-room window. He froze, seeing Georgette held hostage with a gun in her face. Stark fear and panic raced through him. He started to charge out the front door when he stopped.

Think, son! Think! It's no good going out there. That's not going to help anyone. Think! he screamed to himself.

He half-walked, half-ran around the room, terror-stricken. He looked out the window again. The gunman was dragging Georgette toward the barn. A police officer was following As he dragged Georgette with him, she was trying to force his arm away from her windpipe in order to breathe. The gunman crashed his gunhand into her face. She screamed loudly.

"Don't fight me, bitch, or you're dead!" he cursed.

The gunman dragged open the barn door with his foot and moved inside, favouring his wounded side, which was visibly bleeding. The police officer was still following. As he stepped inside the barn, Bill Murphy heard the gunman scream, "*OK, arsehole, what's it gonna be, you or the bitch?*"

"Drop it!" the policeman screamed back.

"*Fuck you!*"

Bill Murphy, trying to turn his panic into rational thinking, raced through his house to the back door and ducked across to the barn. Using the outside stairs he climbed into the loft. From there he had a clear view of the events below.

He looked around for something to use as a weapon. There was nothing. Then he remembered the previous owner had left behind an old Lithgow .22 rifle. It was standing in a corner. He went to it and picked it up. As he did, his heart sank. It was very old and very rusted, but still in one piece. It was covered in bird droppings, dust and dirt. He pulled a handkerchief from his pocket and ran it over the breech. There was no elevator in the rear sight and the bolt looked like it was seized up. He withdrew it and pulled back the firing pin. It stayed back.

'*Shit!*'

He looked around for an oil can. Anything that would lubricate. There was nothing. He could hear the yelling and screaming below. Bill was now totally terror-stricken. Suddenly he had to pee, and suddenly he had an idea. He held the bolt under his penis and urinated on it. As he did so, he worked the firing pin back and forth. He couldn't believe how effective it was.

Jesus, that's better than bloody Mobil.

He held the barrel up. A small amount of light was visible.

How bloody clogged up is that? he cursed.

He knew he was running out of time by the threats and counter-threats going on below. Standing next to the old Lithgow, where the previous owner had left it, was a cleaning rod. He cleaned it across his jeans and then worked it through the barrel of the rifle. Satisfied that would be enough, he reached up to where he was sure there was a packet of bullets. There was a packet. But no bullets.

For fuck's sake! he screamed silently.

Now almost blinded by panic, he felt in his pocket and took out a bunch of keys, change, a small pocket knife and a .22 short. It was the bullet he'd carried around for years. Burred, worn down. Even the lead was loose in the casing. It had already been loaded into a rifle but failed to go off, the indent from the firing pin still evident on the rim. Bill Murphy put the tiny round in the breech and inserted the bolt. He peered through a gap in the woodwork. The gunman was no more than six metres from him, his weapon pointed at Georgette's temple.

He pulled back the firing pin and took aim at the gunman's head.

* * *

McLoughlin could tell the situation was reaching its climax.

"Drop your gun, copper, or the bitch gets it! Now!" The Weasel screamed.

McLoughlin was desperate. The Weasel held all the cards and he knew it. He had to buy time. Find an opening. He dropped his gun.

"And the backup you bastards carry. Chuck it out. Now!"

McLoughlin leaned down and withdrew the small handgun from his ankle holster and threw it a short distance away.

"You've been following me for a long time, haven't you, copper? Melbourne, up north. That bastard I took out with the .50 cal. He your partner?"

McLoughlin didn't answer. The Weasel knew from his seething expression that it was. He burst out laughing.

"Certainly fucked his day, eh? And if you hadn't moved when you did, I'd have fucked yours, too. Ah, but all good things come to those who wait. And today's your lucky day. Look at that! All your useless, arsehole training, all your stakeouts and following bullshit and you've been fucked by The Weasel. Ain't that a son-of-a-bitch? Even in the city you couldn't get me. Didn't know I was watching you two pricks all the way back to your car did you? Weak as piss, pig! Weak as bloody piss!"

McLoughlin was desperate to keep him talking. He had to find an opening. "Didn't get up to Queensland at all, did you?" he asked.

Again The Weasel squealed with delight.

"You know about that? Man! Those mother-fuckers were gonna steal my car. Fucked their day, too!"

"What about the two women?"

The Weasel threw his gun arm in the air momentarily before pushing the barrel back into Georgette's face. "Whoooa! Hey, man! You have been busy. Go to hell!" he exulted.

"And all those poor buggers you knocked over in Melbourne?"

"Prove it!" he sneered.

"I will. What was in the plane?"

The Weasel again screeched with laughter. "You don't know, do you? Son-of-a-bitch! *You don't fucking know!* You reckon you know everything else. How come you don't know that? And do you know what, you never will either because..."

The Weasel didn't get to finish the sentence.

* * *

Bill Murphy, standing in the loft, pulled the trigger on the old Lithgow. It fired, but only just. It went off with more of a *ppffftt* than a bang. But the bullet, even though practically powerless, still had enough in it to lodge into the gunman's cheek. It broke the skin and shocked him more than it hurt him. He threw his hand to his face and filled the air with profanity.

But it was all the distraction the police officer needed. He rolled onto his side, pulled his other back-up from his ankle and fired. The bullet took the gunman at the bridge of his nose. He died instantly.

Bill Murphy swung down from the loft and scooped Georgette into his arms. They clung tightly to each other, trembling, crying and touching each other's faces. Both tried to speak, but no words would come.

The police officer moved across to check on the gunman. "Shit!" he cursed. "Now we'll never bloody know, will we?"

Bill Murphy, as white as a ghost and still visibly shaken, looked at him. "What the hell happened here? Who are you?"

Georgette looked at the policeman. "You're the guy from Melbourne, aren't you?" she asked, finding it difficult to speak.

"Yes, I am," he told her, trying to wrap a makeshift tourniquet around his wounded arm.

"You two know each other?" Bill Murphy asked.

Georgette shook her head. "No. He's a cop, Bill. I don't suppose this is the guy you've been after all along is it?"

"Public Enemy Number One."

"This little shit?" Bill Murphy exclaimed.

"This little shit" McLoughlin began, "has pulled more robberies and killed more people than will ever really be known."

"That day when I spoke to you in the city... was he the one you were after?" Georgette asked.

McLoughlin nodded, getting fully to his feet. He held out his hand to Bill Murphy and introduced himself. "Let me say I don't know what the hell it was you fired at that prick, but it saved my life, so thank you. You've certainly got a scoop today if you want one, haven't you?" he threw to Georgette.

"So what now?" Bill Murphy asked McLoughlin.

"If you wouldn't mind running me back to my car, I've a few calls to make. You seen him round here before?" McLoughlin asked.

"Not sure if it was him. But often there'd be a car go down but I'd never see it go back."

"What sort?"

"No. Couldn't say. Just a car."

"Tell me. What's down there?"

Bill Murphy thought for a moment. "Nothing! Just scrub. It's a national park."

McLoughlin looked at the two of them. They were obviously traumatised over all of this. "Is there anything you feel you need? Can I do anything for you?"

It suddenly dawned on Georgette that McLoughlin had been shot. "Oh my god, look at you! Is that a bullet wound?"

"Bit close, eh?" McLoughlin smirked.

"Boy!... Bill, can you get something from the house? Some disinfectant or something. Some bandages?"

"Sure."

As McLoughlin began to take off his bullet proof vest, he felt something fall to the floor. He leaned down and picked it up. It was a .45 slug. McLoughlin held up his vest and poked his finger in an indentation on the shoulder. "That one was a bit too close," he told her.

Suddenly McLoughlin remembered The Weasel's gun. He rolled him over. The weapon was still cocked and still in his hand. He put his thumb between the hammer and the cylinder and pulled the trigger to release it, then eased the hammer down.

"Look at that! A genuine colt .45. How the hell does a creep like that get hold of something like this?"

Then something caught his eye. The Weasel's shirt had been torn away from the bullet wound in his side. McLoughlin, using the barrel of the .45, poked it under the shirt and lifted it up.

What he saw fairly staggered him. He put the colt on the floor and carefully pulled away the rest of the shirt. Strapped to The Weasel's waist was an elaborately fitted-out leather belt with two attached cords leading to the top of his trouser belt. These were attached to two 'finger-sized' key rings.

"What is it... a bloody bomb or something?" she asked.

Georgette started to move to get a closer look.

"Jesus Christ. Don't move, lady!"

"Oh shit, what?"

"This prick's fully loaded. Just sit there. Let me fix this little problem and I'll tell you."

Bill Murphy had returned with a first aid kit he kept in the kitchen.

McLoughlin saw him approach. "Stay with the lady, sir. Don't come any closer," he commanded.

Bill Murphy put the first-aid kit on the floor and put his arms around Georgette. "What is it?" he whispered in her ear.

She shook her head.

McLoughlin was crouched over The Weasel's body with his pocket knife in his hand. Moments later he pulled the belt off of the dead gunman's body and held it up for Bill and Georgette to see.

"Unbelievable!" McLoughlin said, shaking his head. "This is a specially constructed belt containing two pen-guns." He pulled one out and showed them. "Looks just like a normal ballpoint pen. Until you unscrew the back of it. When you do, you'll see it contains a .22 bullet... look at that." He then held the gun up to his eye. "This one's had a bit of use, too. Our friend here had two of them..."

"Is that another one in his pocket?" Georgette asked, pointing to what she thought was an ordinary biro.

McLoughlin looked to where she was indicating. "*Shit!*" he exclaimed. "Certainly looks like it." He carefully withdrew the gun from The Weasel's top pocket. He unscrewed the top and tipped it up. A .22 bullet fell out.

"No end of surprises to this bloke, is there?" He returned to the belt. "He had this thing rigged up so he had a pen-gun in the back of it and one in the front. A cord was attached to each. This reached around to his belt where he had a couple of ring pulls. Anyone grabbing him from behind. Zap. Anyone grabbing him from in front. Zap again. Pretty bloody crude, but by the Jesus, effective as buggery, point blank. There were a couple of shonkos done-in a while back. They were into guns and stuff. The hit was point blank. I reckon when we run the tests on these little buggers, we'll have solved our case."

Georgette McKinley and Bill Murphy found it near impossible to conceive what was going on around them. It was a world they knew nothing of personally and first- hand. Georgette reported on it. And for 30 years Bill Murphy had done the same. But neither of them had ever been this close to it, and it terrified the hell out of them.

Georgette went to the policeman and bandaged the wound.

* * *

"I think you'll be seeing a bit of me for a while. At least until all this gets cleared up," McLoughlin said. He looked at Bill Murphy. "What can I say? You really did save my life."

"Well, you saved mine," Georgette said.

McLoughlin looked hard at Bill Murphy. "You're not that writer bloke, are you?" he asked.

Georgette answered for him. "And a very famous writer bloke, too," she said. "He wanted to be a recluse, but to use the words of a dead man, I just fucked his day."

Ken McLoughlin laughed loudly. Bill Murphy offered a halfway grin.

"Better start writing bloody books, I think," McLoughlin muttered.

He picked up his discarded back-up and replaced it in its ankle holster. He retrieved and holstered his Glock. The .45 colt he held onto after pocketing the pen-guns.

"Can we go?"

"Sure. But don't touch anything. Not even the spurs on his boots. Nothing, all right? The place will be crawling with forensics for the next few days, but there's nothing I can do about that."

Bill turned to Georgette and examined the bruising to her face. "You sure you don't want to see a doctor?" he asked with concern.

She smiled. "Just pour me a brandy and hold me. That's all the treatment I need," she told him, and they walked off together arm in arm toward the house.

* * *

McLoughlin's first thought was to call Kazumi, but he called the Victorian Police Commissioner Jack Rowland instead.

"It's all over. He's dead, sir," he told him.

"Shit!" he exclaimed. "How?"

"It was a hostage situation. I'd been chasing him through scrub. He shot me twice..." McLoughlin explained what had happened to the Commissioner, at length.

"So you dropped the little prick?"

"Yeah, he's gone, sir."

"Thank Christ for that! You stay put there for a day or two. Get to a doctor. Ring me in the morning. I'll grab Johnson and come up. This is great news! Did you find out where he went to ground?"

"It has to be here. Somewhere in the scrub around where I spotted him."

"Well done, Ken! Bloody well done!"

* * *

Within two hours of McLoughlin speaking with Commissioner Jack Rowland, several police cars and the government undertaker had arrived at Bill Murphy's house. Georgette's mobile phone rang. It was George Hanks.

"You've heard?" she asked.

"Not really. Cops. Shoot-out. Dead body. What's the story?"

Georgette quickly explained the situation to her boss. "I'll do a piece to camera, but you can't identify the policeman involved. He's undercover and Bill doesn't want his name mentioned or the location of his house given out."

Bill Murphy was sitting close by Georgette listening to her conversation. So was Ken McLoughlin.

"That's bullshit, babe... put Murphy on. I know exactly what the prick wants. Give it here." He took the phone. "G'day George. Don't even ask!"

"Come on mate, shit! this is huge..."

"I live here because no bugger can find me. You put this on your news and I'll have every bloody ghoul out there stalking the joint."

"Mate. You know how it goes. It's a big story. Gotta do it."

Bill's temper flared. "You put me or this bloody house on your fucking news and I promise you, I'll print your name and address in my next book. By Christ, I will. Then we'll see how you like it."

He handed the phone back to Georgette.

"What's wrong with a stand-up and some high-altitude aerials?" she asked George.

"Come on, babe, the old man will have my balls in a sling. Especially if he knows you're there. Do it for me, will you?"

"George, anything, you know that. But not this. It's too close."

"Well don't bother with a stand-up. That's bullshit. I'll get back to you."

She was about to speak when her phone rang again. She didn't even have time to announce herself.

"Monkhouse, girlie, you get that fucking story on my television station!" he roared.

"I'm sorry, Mr Monkhouse, I can't do that. I'm happy to do a live piece or a stand-up, but I can't identify the policeman or the location where this has taken place," she told him firmly.

"Now you listen to me!" he bellowed. "I don't give a rat's arse about your personal preferences. And I don't give a rat's arse about who or what's involved. Hanks tells me this is huge. I'm telling you to get the story and those involved onto my bloody news bulletin."

Georgette stood her ground. "I can't do that, Mr Monkhouse. I'll do a stand-up or a piece to camera, but I won't identify the people or the location."

"You want to have a think about that?"

"I just did."

"So you won't do it?"

"No sir, I won't."

"Pretty damned expensive refusal on your part!" he told her. "You're not welcome here anymore. Seems to me all you bitches are the same."

Sylvester Monkhouse then abruptly hung up.

As soon as he did, the phone rang again. It was George Hanks. "What are you going to do?" he asked urgently.

"Nothing now," she told him, a degree of shock in her tone. "The old man just fired me."

Bill Murphy and Ken McLoughlin stared at Georgette, too shocked to speak. So was George Hanks. Finally. "He *fired* you?" George exclaimed. "Son-of-a-bitch. So what now?"

"Don't know, George. Don't really care. But *don't* send a crew up here, all right?" She then hung up the phone.

Bill Murphy was still staring at her. "So what now?"

"Who knows?" she shrugged.

"You did that for *me*? You gave up your career for *me*?"

"I gave it up for the third dream," she told him.

* * *

For three days twenty police and emergency service personnel searched the area where The Weasel played cowboy but turned up nothing apart from bucket loads of used .45 bullet shells. Finally Jack Rowland approached McLoughlin.

"Buggered if I know, Ken. Looks like he's taken this one with him. No-one's turned up anything. He obviously dug himself in somewhere else. Wrap it up. Take six weeks off. Use the card. Go where you like. Have a bloody good holiday. Be in my office six weeks Monday. And thank you. You did well."

McLoughlin knocked on Bill Murphy's door. Georgette greeted him and invited him in. "That's about it for me. There'll be the usual inquiries and stuff but I'm out of here. I just wanted to thank you both."

"And you too," she smiled. "That prick was about to blow my head off. You saved my life."

McLoughlin put his arms around both of them. "I'll never forget either of you. For richer, for poorer, for better or worse and forsaking all others... go for it, you two, and I hope you turn out to be the happiest couple in the world. God knows you deserve to be."

"Don't be a stranger," Bill Murphy called after Ken McLoughlin as he walked away.

"Send me a postcard."

"We will... but where?"

He turned round and looked back. "Send it to me care of Kazumi, Katie's Farm, Naracoorte, in South Australia."

Ken McLoughlin was driving back to Sydney when he pulled in off the road. He sat in his car with the engine running, thinking. Suddenly, he wheeled round and drove back to where he had originally located The Weasel. He went to the spot where he lay prone watching The Weasel play games with his colt .45.

It has to be here,' he thought. This prick must have holed up here somewhere. Maybe the searchers didn't go in deep enough.

He walked a long way from where The Weasel was shooting targets and a good deal deeper than searchers had penetrated. He didn't know what he was looking for. Anything. The slightest thread. Footprint. Bullet casing. Drink can. But there was nothing.

He returned to his vehicle and drove into South West Rocks and booked into a motel. The next day, he returned. He backtracked over the same area. He went further afield. Still nothing. He decided to take a breather and sat down on a fallen log by a thick clump of bushes. It was the middle of the afternoon. Then, like a bolt out of the blue, his head spun around, his eyes shot open and his mouth dropped.

What the bloody hell was that?

He checked his watch. It was three p.m. exactly. Ken McLoughlin could've sworn he heard the pips of a time signal, like at the top of the hour on radio stations.

He looked around. Nothing, but he couldn't dismiss the sound of the pips from his mind. He checked his watch. Eight minutes to four. He decided to return to the exact same spot where he was sitting at three p.m. When he did, he watched the second hand move around the dial. If they were the pips, then I should hear them again. At the stroke of four p.m., once more he heard six pips.

This is bullshit! It's just not possible. What am I missing here?

He climbed off the log and pushed his body into the thick bush. He looked around, and if he hadn't have kicked it with his foot, he would have missed it. There was a piece of downpipe inserted into the ground. McLoughlin looked at it and was going to ignore it, but instead decided to shine his torch into it.

He could see something at the bottom, but the light wasn't strong enough. He dropped to bended knee and put his ear to the downpipe. He was jolted backwards by what he heard.

Voices, for Christ sakes. I can hear voices. He put his ear to the pipe again. *There's a radio on down there. A bloody radio!*

He attempted to pull the downpipe up, but it was stuck fast. He stepped outside the thick bushes. Just to his right was a length of cement water pipe covered in debris and bush, about three metres long and a half-metre in diameter. McLoughlin went to the front of it and bent down. He shone his torch into it. It looked empty. On all fours he climbed into it. When he got to the other end, he put his hand on what looked to be nothing but a dirt wall. To his surprise it opened.

As he peered through it he suddenly realised he'd finally found what he'd been looking for. This was The Weasel's hideout. At the entrance to the length of cement piping was a drop of about one-and-a-half metres and a small ladder. A small light was glowing in a corner. McLoughlin climbed onto the ladder and eased himself down.

He found himself standing inside a caravan that had been completely buried beneath the ground. As his eyes became accustomed to the dim light, he saw several other battery-powered lamps. He switched four of them on. Before him was the ultimate hideout. The piece of downpipe he'd kicked was the air vent. Sitting next to it a radio with its aerial run half way up the ventilation pipe. The radio was switched on, but the volume control was turned down.

The pips I heard echoed up the ventilation pipe! I'll be buggered!

The caravan was nearly six metres long. There was a bed at one end, and a massive stack of dry-cell batteries. A tiny electric hotplate. Several casks of spring water and tinned food stacked from the floor to the roof. Plenty of blankets and a full-length curtain about three-quarters of a metre wide on the far wall. McLoughlin moved to pull it aside more from casual curiosity than anything else. This time he got an even bigger shock. The curtain was a doorway which led to an underground shed. McLoughlin grabbed a light and held it up. Other dry-cell lamps were close by so he switched several on. Standing in front of him was The Weasel's car.

No wonder we couldn't find the bastard! The prick buried it.

He wondered where the entrance was but thought he'd get to that later. At the front of the vehicle was a huge box. McLoughlin lifted the lid and held a light over it. Lying on a sheepskin rug was the Barrett .50 calibre and another mobile-phone gun.

Jesus, he even had a spare! he exclaimed to himself.

There were also a number of other weapons including a collection of handguns and umpteen boxes of ammunition. To the left of the box a portable toilet, a big plastic bowl and a deep hole in the ground, the bath. He returned to the caravan and stood looking around. He figured The Weasel could live in here for months. Probably did. So whatever was in the plane has to be in here. Has to be!

There was nothing of consequence under The Weasel's bed. The small cardboard portable wardrobe contained only clothes. Then he lifted up the seats at the table. Two very large black nylon bags were stowed under one seat, and several smaller bags were stowed under the other. McLoughlin dragged them out. When he pulled back the zip of the first black bag, he could see it was stacked with tightly-bound bundles of $1000 bills in US currency. He unzipped the second and immediately several gold ingots fell to the floor. He picked them up and put them on the table.

This one's jam-packed too. Got to be millions. got to be!

"Talk about a pandora's box," he muttered. "Jesus!, I've just found ten of the bastards."

He then proceeded to open the smaller bags. Bundles of cash were plentiful and McLoughlin quickly estimated tens of thousands of dollars. A passport. It showed The Weasel's photograph but a different name. Then a small diary.

McLoughlin seized it. He rested his foot on one of the nylon bags, pulled a light across the table and began to turn the pages.

Christ, it's all here. Names, dates, amounts, victims.

But it was the last entry which rocked McLoughlin. It read: *Bourke. Copper. Kununurra. .50 cal. Fucked his day (arsehole). Bloody near got his mate, too.*

McLoughlin's anger rose. He turned back the pages and there were all the names and dates, even newspaper cuttings showing pictures of the people he'd bashed and robbed.

He closed the diary and sat pondering his situation. Never in his career had he been involved in a case like it. And the effect this one small man had had on so many people's lives was catastrophic. His hands began to shake slightly when he considered how close he came to being a victim himself. He picked up the black nylon bags and tipped out their contents. At the end of counting he'd tallied up exactly $20 million. Plus 47 gold ingots. In the smaller bags, $147,000 in Australian currency.

He sat shaking his head at such a massive amount of cash. What staggered him even more was that no-one in the whole wide world knew he had it. The Weasel was dead. Everyone on the plane was dead. The greeter to the plane was dead. Insurance by now would have paid out the victims of The Weasel's robberies. McLoughlin climbed out of the caravan and returned to his car. He called the Victorian Police Commissioner.

"It's not six weeks yet..."

McLoughlin interrupted him to speak of his discovery.

Jack Rowland was flabbergasted. "He buried a bloody caravan and a shed and lived in them?"

"That's right, sir. And he kept a diary. It's all in there. It'll wipe the slate of your unsolveds. Has to. There's also nearly 150 grand in cash. The .50 calibre's there. Christ, you should see what's there!"

"Any indication of what was on that bloody aeroplane?"

McLoughlin steeled himself to tell the biggest lie of his life. "No sir. Whatever it was, he certainly didn't stash it in the van."

"So we'll never know?"

"No, sir, I guess we won't."

"I'll talk to Johnson and tell him all this. You deserve a bloody medal. Stay by your phone. We'll call you in the morning and work out what to do from here."

McLoughlin headed for Bill Murphy's place. When he arrived at the end of the driveway, he climbed from his car carrying a small bag. He walked to the house, placed it at the front door, then returned to his vehicle. He phoned Bill Murphy.

"I just left you a present at the front door," he told him and hung up. He then called directory assistance and asked to be put through to the Ritz hotel in London. "I'd like a room for two for two weeks in two weeks' time," he told them.

"Indeed, sir. What name?"

"McLoughlin. Ken and Kazumi McLoughlin."

McLoughlin hung up the phone. *Christ, she'd better say yes.*

Such a thought tickled McLoughlin and he found himself laughing out loud. He then dialled Qantas and booked two First Class return air fares.

* * *

Bill Murphy opened his front door and picked up a small black bag. He took it inside, opening the note attached to it as he went.

Hello, you two.
As you prepare to say "I do!"
There are no words
that are special enough
for people like you.
However,
there are six hundred and fifty thousand good reasons for me to say
THANK YOU...

McLoughlin.

* * *

Back in Sydney, McLoughlin felt several gold ingots in his pocket.

Bonus, he grinned as he took a phone number from his wallet. It was an international number. McLoughlin pushed all the digits and put the phone to his ear.

"This is Bruno," came a voice from the other side of the world.

"It's all here, less my fifteen percent, right?"

"Of course."

"You know the place. Six a.m. tomorrow. Two black nylon bags."

"Thank you, you've done well my friend."

Other Titles

Eleven Days by Graham Guy
DoctorZed Publishing
ISBN: 9780987544551 (2nd edition)
Genre: Fiction/Rmance/Epic

Available in print and ebook.

Can one woman's passion be shared between two men?

In the early 1990s Katie McFarlane is a nurse living in suburban Adelaide. For Katie, life is as normal as it gets, but a chance meeting with Paul Redman sends her life into an uncontrollable tailspin. Katie is swept into the fast lane of wealth, happiness and uninhibited emotion. As each glorious day passes, wealthy Paul Redman becomes increasingly determined to weave their futures together as one.

However, tragedy strikes and Katie flees her familiar life in grief and confusion. A near fatal accident sends her on a collision course with Gabe Caplin, a kind, reclusive giant of a man from a suppressed and violent childhood. All he knows is the simple uncomplicated existence of running a farm, but he knows what he wants: he wants desperately to love and to be loved. And he desperately wants Katie McFarlane.

Katie is torn between her love for Paul Redman and her increasing desire for Gabe Caplin. Her world and life is threatened in a final confrontation when vengeful psychopath Scarfe Olsen comes calling - and shooting.

In the tradition of Graham Guy's most popular novels, *Eleven Days* is a sweeping saga of tender love that weaves its way through an explosive adventure.

www.ingramcontent.com/pod-product-compliance
Ingram Content Group UK Ltd.
Pitfield, Milton Keynes, MK11 3LW, UK
UKHW041842190726
13854UKWH00002B/677